OXFORD MONOGRAPHS ON MUSIC

Alessandro Stradella
1639–1682

His Life and Music

CAROLYN GIANTURCO

CLARENDON PRESS · OXFORD
1994

Oxford University Press, Walton Street, Oxford OX2 6DP
Oxford New York Toronto
Delhi Bombay Calcutta Madras Karachi
Kuala Lumpur Singapore Hong Kong Tokyo
Nairobi Dar es Salaam Cape Town
Melbourne Auckland Madrid
and associated companies in
Berlin Ibadan

Oxford is a trade mark of Oxford University Press

Published in the United States
by Oxford University Press Inc., New York

British Library Cataloguing in Publication Data
Data available
ISBN 0–19–816138–7

Library of Congress Cataloging in Publication Data
Gianturco, Carolyn.
Alessandro Stradella (1639–1682): his life and works/
Carolyn Gianturco.
(Oxford monographs on music)
Includes bibliographical references.
1. Stradella, Alessandro, 1639–1682. 2. Composers—
Italy—Biography. I. Series.
ML410.S87G45 1994 780'.92–dc20 [B] 93–23598
ISBN 0–19–816138–7

Set by Hope Services (Abingdon) Ltd.
Printed in Great Britain
on acid-free paper by
Biddles Ltd.
Guildford & King's Lynn

*To the memory of Jack Westrup
and of Fred Sternfeld,
and to Franco Gianturco*

Foreword

IT was Jack Westrup, Heather Professor of Music at Oxford, who suggested I look at Stradella's operas. He was familiar with one of the scores and found it sufficiently attractive to include it in his lectures. This was in 1967 when Stradella's operas were thought to have been composed for Rome, and since I was looking for a research subject in seventeenth-century Roman opera, I took Sir Jack's suggestion. After completing my D.Phil., Fred Sternfeld, also of Oxford, encouraged me to write a book on Stradella. Remo Giazotto's study, *Vita di Alessandro Stradella* (Milan, 1962), hailed as a fund of documents which overturned all previous writings on the composer, was devoted mainly to Stradella's life, and we thought I could incorporate its findings into what would be principally a study of the music.

Owen Jander had added a supplement to his 1962 Harvard Ph.D. dissertation, 'The Works of Alessandro Stradella Related to the Cantata and the Opera', entitled 'A Catalogue of the Manuscripts of Compositions by Alessandro Stradella found in European and American Libraries'; he also later published a thematic catalogue of Stradella's cantatas for one, two, and three voices in *Alessandro Stradella* (*Wellesley Edition Cantata Index Series*, fascs. 4*a*, 4*b*; Wellesley, Mass., 1969). Using these, I set about seeing every copy of every piece of Stradella music. By 1982, when I organized an international conference at the Accademia Chigiana in Siena to commemorate the three-hundredth anniversary of Stradella's death, I had an enormous quantity of notes which corrected and added to the works in Jander's two lists. During the conference I mentioned the difficulty of travelling from one library to another with a huge and heavy briefcase to Eleanor McCrickard. Her comment was that I should use the information and compile a much-needed thematic catalogue of Stradella's music, to which I responded the next day with an invitation for her to join me at the task. It proved to be a wise decision and resulted in a happy and fruitful collaboration. Moreover, the need to identify Stradella's works, determine their genres, forces, and inner structures, and date them—for example—was aided by (and in turn aided) my writing of the book. Our catalogue was published as *Alessandro Stradella (1639–1682): A Thematic Catalogue of his Compositions* (Stuyvesant, NY, 1991).

My graduate work on Stradella's operas had shown that some of the information in Giazotto's book was not accurate, and I therefore decided that before accepting a source I should verify it. I was soon disconcerted. Professor Giazotto assured me his book was accurate, but I could not find most of the documents he reported—such as those recording Stradella's baptism, or related to his parents and siblings, or establishing his contacts with poets and patrons, or dating his works, or tracing his career, or connected with his death. Unfortunately, since I could not simply assume all Giazotto's documents were incorrect and thereby risk overlooking a meaningful piece of information, I spent years in archives and libraries searching for the innumerable sources referred to on his 902 pages. I was finally forced to come to the sad conclusion that Giazotto's book was more fiction than truth. At the end of all these efforts, however, I only knew what documents were *not* related to Stradella. This was clearly not sufficient: I now needed real facts on which to construct a biography. The gathering of these, from scratch, took several further years.

After leaving Oxford I had moved to Italy and in 1971 took up a position at the University of Pisa. After some time I realized that Stradella's father had been a member of an order of Pisan knights. I searched their archives and found he had come from Nepi, a small town near Viterbo. I was still convinced at the time that Giazotto was right about Stradella being a Roman and so put off visiting Nepi. Fortunately for me, this gave Father Roberto Faggioli time to put some order in the Archivio Storico. When I eventually arrived, I was able to find innumerable notarial documents related to the Stradella family; moreover, they proved that the composer was—to everyone's great surprise—a Nepesino.

I also spent some months of each year reading diplomatic correspondence in archives throughout Italy. In this way I came across occasional but crucial comments which shed further light on Stradella's life and music. And my determination to go systematically through all notary documents in Genoa for 1682, the year Stradella died, rewarded me with an inventory of his belongings and a description of their distribution among his heirs.

These are only a few of the trials, tribulations, and joys connected with the researching of this book. Others will no doubt be realized by the reader who is familiar with the problems which inevitably arise when having to deal with seventeenth-century manuscript documents and music, with being able to travel only when free from university responsibilities, with having to work around short library and archive opening hours, with strikes, computer failure, and so on. I should make it clear that I persisted in wanting to do this book (in spite of, or perhaps because of, these and other obstacles) not because I think Stradella is the greatest composer who ever lived, but because I believe in getting the story, any story, right. I felt that Stradella, perhaps more than any other musician, deserved having his real life and his own music known; that after three centuries of being an ever-changing legend and having other composers' works passed off as his, it was 'just' that the truth (as much as we can now know of it, and at least not blatant falsehoods) be written.

The book therefore begins with a biography of Stradella. This offers information on the composer and his family which is almost all new, and besides correcting his dates of birth and death, gives enough details about him to enable us to realize, for the first time, who he was. It traces Stradella's career and personal life in all the cities in which he lived, giving information on patrons and poets as well. The coverage continues even after Stradella's death to trace the fate of his music manuscripts, the formation of important collections of his music, and the spreading of the Stradella legend.

Part II contains a discussion of his music. Stradella contributed to almost every genre of seventeenth-century music, but since he wrote more vocal than instrumental music, this repertoire is considered first and in an order which reflects, in general, his output of vocal genres. Since I am firmly convinced that the form as well as the style of a poetic text more often than not determined these aspects of the music, I have approached each piece from its text, as Stradella would have done, and only after the poetry has been considered do I turn to its musical setting. The next section of the book is devoted to Stradella's instrumental music and his one extant pedagogical manual. The size of the book (already larger than the publisher wanted) and the fact that few monographs on Stradella's contemporaries are available made it necessary for me to limit my considerations to Stradella's own vocal and instrumental music, 308 extant compositions, plus his teaching manual.

Appendix 1 provides a list of the works simply to aid readers, since the Gianturco–McCrickard catalogue will answer more detailed questions on sources. Appendix 2 contains all of Stradella's extant writings. Whereas elsewhere in the book space has been saved by giving only translations of documents and texts, I decided that here it was necessary to include Stradella's own words as well as my translations. The bibliography is mainly of books and articles since a complete list of music editions appears in the Gianturco–McCrickard catalogue.

Stradella was a fine composer whose music, usually extremely interesting and of an identifiable personality, can greatly enrich our repertory of Baroque music. (I and others have thus far been able to edit very few of his works, but this must be our next task.) Whenever Stradella will be played and sung there will be those who will want to know something about the man, about the composer, and about his music. I hope this book will answer their curiosity, and perhaps stimulate further interest in Stradella.

C.G.

Rome,
Winter 1993

Acknowledgements

I WISH to acknowledge my debt and my gratitude to all those who made it possible for me to accomplish my research on Stradella. Foremost among these are the personnel in the 43 libraries holding Stradella music, as well as in the many archives and libraries named in the course of the book, and whose collaboration was necessary in order for me to find information.

Of course, I never should have begun the research had Jack Westrup, enthusiastic over Stradella's score of *La forza dell'amor paterno*, not suggested I examine all his operas for my Oxford D.Phil. Fred Sternfeld thought I should next look at the rest of Stradella's music; he also believed I was capable of writing a book on it. I have benefited from the advice of both these gentlemen and acknowledge the happy fortune which brought me in contact with them. Sir Jack's death in April 1975 deprived me of continuing our friendship, but Fred, until his death in January 1994, had always been a strong supporter of my efforts for Stradella, not at all a short-term involvement since the subject took longer to investigate than either of us expected. I must add here also my gratitude to my husband, Franco, a scientist who believes that in this world there is only science and (luckily for me) whatever research I do: his loving prejudice has made me try to live up to his expectations. In addition, I am extremely grateful that he has not only put up with 'another man' in our lives for so long, but has made it possible for me to pursue him. I hope it is clear from these insufficient words why I chose to dedicate this study to Sir Jack, Fred, and Franco.

There are also those friends—in particular Alberto Basso, Gabriella Biagi-Ravenni, and Giorgio Morelli—who, disinterestedly, kept asking me how the book was going, thus psychologically pushing me on. Perhaps not as disinterested but still friendly were the enquiries of Bruce Phillips of OUP, and I must express my gratitude for his patience and professional advice. In addition, I acknowledge the kindness of those who shared the unpublished results of their own research with me: Peter Allsop, Jonathan Couchman, Victor Crowther, Norbert Dubowy, Sergio Durante, Thomas Griffen, Marinella Laini, Jean Lionnet, Wolfgang Lippmann, Timothy McGee, Arnaldo Morelli, Giorgio Morelli, Licia Sirch, John Suess, Mercedes Viale Ferrero, and Gian Ludovico Masetti Zannini. It was also good that Eleanor McCrickard and I compiled *Alessandro Stradella (1639–1682): A Thematic Catalogue of his Compositions*: working on the book and the catalogue at the same time enabled me to catch errors in both; our catalogue is the basis of Stradella's List of Works in Appendix 1. My translations of Stradella's Writings in Appendix 2 were read by my husband, who also came to my rescue at those moments when seventeenth-century Italian and Latin got too obscure for me. I am also thankful to Fabrizio Guidotti, who made clean copies of the musical examples I hurriedly and messily made in the course of my investigations.

Although whatever omissions or errors of judgement or fact the book contains are mine, I willingly and most gratefully acknowledge those who generously gave their time and professional acumen in an effort to reduce them: Lowell Lindgren and Mercedes Viale Ferrero read Part I on Stradella's life; Stephen Bonta and Alfred Mann read Chapter 12 on his instrumental music; and Eleanor McCrickard and Michael Talbot heroically read and advised me on the entire typescript. I am especially indebted to the editorial staff of OUP for their unbelievably careful attention to detail and sincere concern to help solve the myriad problems arising from a book in English–Italian–Latin.

For permission to reproduce the illustrations, I thank the institutions named in the List of Plates; I also thank the following journals for allowing me to use material from my articles which appeared in them: *Chigiana, Journal of the American Musicological Society, Journal of the Royal Musical Association, Music and Letters, Nuova Rivista Musicale Italiana, Rivista Italiana di Musicologia.*

I should also like to express my gratitude to previous writers on Stradella's life and music, not those who seemed determined to thwart all efforts to approach the real composer, but those who sincerely tried to pave a clear way to our understanding of the man and his music. And naturally I am glad to have had the opportunity of spending these many years uncovering the actual Stradella, a fascinating and lively man, who wrote excellent music of a personal stamp. Had circumstances given him the possibility, he would surely have been surprised by my continual refusal to give up the often discouraging and elusive task; I like to think that he would have been pleased that I did not.

Contents

List of Plates

between pp. 144–145

1. The Stradella Coat of Arms (red lion rampant on a field of yellow crossed with a white band) (Pisa, Archivio di Stato, Ordine di S. Stefano, filza 10, n. inv. 623, n. int. 25).

2. Document dated 20 June 1638 in which the composer's father, Marc'Antonio Stradella, is said to be from Nepi and his uncle from Fivizzano. Marc'Antonio requests here to have his son Giuseppe made a Cavaliere di Santo Stefano (Pisa, Archivio di Stato, Ordine di S. Stefano, filza 27, n. inv. 197, n. int. 79).

3. Fortress of Vignola, where Marc'Antonio Stradella was Vice-Governor and lived with his family in 1642–3 (P. Litta, *Famiglie celebri d'Italia* (Milan, 1819–83), ii. 293; Rome, Biblioteca Vaticana).

4. Palazzo Lante, Rome: (*a*) façade, (*b*) inner courtyard. Alessandro, his mother, and his brother Stefano lived here *c*.1652–60 (Rome, Biblioteca Vaticana).

5. Anonymous caricature of Sebastiano Baldini, poet of several Stradella cantata texts (Rome, Biblioteca Vaticana, Chigi L.V. 153, fo. 18^r).

6. Musical fountain of Mount Parnassus in the Apollo Salon of Villa Aldobrandini, Frascati, Rome. It provided the setting for Stradella's *La Circe* of 1668 (D. Barrière, *Villa Aldobrandini* (n.d. [Rome, 1647]); (Rome, Biblioteca Casanatense).

7. Letter from Alessandro Stradella to Cardinal Flavio Chigi dated 27 Nov. 1670 in which he urgently requests a loan of money: (*a*) beginning of the letter, (*b*) close, with Stradella's signature (Rome, Biblioteca Vaticana, Archivio Chigi, 57, fos. 470^r and 471^v).

8. Church and Convent of SS. Domenico e Sisto. Stradella's motet *Pugna, certamen, militia est vita* was performed here in 1675 when Angelica Lante became a nun (G. B. Falda, *Il terzo libro del Nuovo Teatro delle Chiese di Roma* (Rome, n.d.); (Rome, Biblioteca Casanatense).

9. Queen Christina of Sweden. She devised the scenario for Stradella's *Il Damone* (painting by S. Bourdon; Madrid, Museo del Prado).

10. An autograph page of Stradella's *La forza dell'amor paterno* of 1678 (Turin, Biblioteca Nazionale, Foà 16, fo. 46 *bis*).

11. Expenses for Stradella's burial dated 26 Feb. 1682 (Genoa, Archivio di Stato, Atti notarili, Notaio Gerolamo Camere, scanzio 963, filza 7).

Library and Archive Sigla

A-W:	Austria, Vienna, Stadtbibliothek, Musiksammlung
D-Mbs:	Germany, Munich, Bayerische Staatsbibliothek
GB-Lbl:	Great Britain, London, British Library
I-Bc:	Italy, Bologna, Conservatorio Statale di Musica G. B. Martini
I-Bsp:	Italy, Bologna, Archivio della Basilica di S. Petronio
I-Fas:	Italy, Florence, Archivio di Stato
I-Fm:	Italy, Florence, Biblioteca Marucelliana
I-Gas:	Italy, Genoa, Archivio di Stato
I-Lbs:	Italy, Lucca, Biblioteca Statale
I-MOas:	Italy, Modena, Archivio di Stato, Archivio Segreto Estense
I-MOe:	Italy, Modena, Biblioteca Estense
I-Nc:	Italy, Naples, Conservatorio Statale di Musica S. Pietro a Majella
I-NEast:	Italy, Nepi, Archivio Storico
I-NEd:	Italy, Nepi, Archivio del Duomo
I-PIas:	Italy, Pisa, Archivio di Stato
I-Ras:	Italy, Rome, Archivio di Stato
I-Rasc:	Italy, Rome, Archivio Storico Capitolino
I-Rc:	Italy, Rome, Biblioteca Casanatense
I-Rn:	Italy, Rome, Biblioteca Nazionale
I-Rvat:	Italy, Rome, Città del Vaticano, Biblioteca
I-Rvata:	Italy, Rome, Città del Vaticano, Archivio
I-Tas:	Italy, Turin, Archivio di Stato
I-Tm:	Italy, Turin, Biblioteca Nazionale
I-Vas:	Italy, Venice, Archivio di Stato
I-Vmc:	Italy, Venice, Biblioteca del Museo Civico Correr
I-VTas:	Italy, Viterbo, Archivio di Stato

PART I
The Life (1639–82)

1

Nepi and Bologna

The Stradella Family

In the fifteenth century the Stradella family moved from Borgotaro, a small town in Emilia at the bottom of the Cisa Pass, to Fivizzano in the valley of the River Magra.[1] This attractive mountainous area was the crossroad of profitable commercial routes connecting Emilia, Tuscany, and Liguria, and had often been the scene of disputes between rival factions—the d'Este, Visconti, and Malaspina families, the Guelfs and the Ghibellines; therefore, in order to be assured of some tranquillity, an agreement was reached with the Republic of Florence in 1475 whereby subjugation was exchanged for protection. As a matter of fact, magister Mattheus, the first Fivizzano Stradella and son of 'Ser Johannis Marci di Stradella de Burghe Vallis Tare',[2] was involved in setting forth the contract with the Medici in which it was decided that Fivizzano should become the centre of local Florentine domination: it was here, then, that the 'foreign' Captain resided, that public and private schools were founded, that theatres and academies were encouraged, that artisans such as printers and organ-builders flourished.

In the following period of prosperity, many lower-class youths became mercenaries, while upper-class boys studied to become doctors, lawyers, notaries, scholars, and clergymen. Therefore, it is not surprising to find that in the aristocratic family of Stradella these latter professions predominated. Pellegrino, the son of the above-mentioned medical doctor Matteo, and his wife Alessandra Vugliani, had, for example, the following children: Giovanbattista, a lawyer, 'governor of several cities of the Papal State and . . . of Rieti' and a contributor to changes made in Fivizzano's statute; Matteo, medical doctor for at least thirty years to the Doria

[1] Information concerning the Stradella family of Fivizzano is taken from Patrizia Radicchi, 'La famiglia Stradella e i suoi rapporti con la Toscana', in Carolyn Gianturco and Giancarlo Rostirolla (eds.), *Atti del Convegno di studi 'Alessandro Stradella e il suo tempo', Siena 8–12 settembre 1982, Chigiana*, 39, NS 19 (1988), 17–33. When I realized that Marc'Antonio Stradella, the composer's father, had been a Cavaliere di Santo Stefano of Pisa, I was able to use the order's documents to trace two branches of the family: I then investigated the Nepi branch, and I am grateful to Dr Radicchi for having accepted my invitation to investigate the Fivizzano branch. On a walk through Fivizzano I came upon a street, at the edge of the town leading to the countryside, which still bears the name 'Stradella', probably indicating that family property was once here.

[2] Radicchi, 'La famiglia Stradella', 18, citing Giovanni Sforza, *Saggio d'una bibliografia storica della Lunigiana*, i. 22–3.

Prince of Melfi in the Kingdom of Naples; Caterina, second wife of
Romulo Malaspina; Ciro (or Cividonio), 'imperial and Florentine notary'
who was also involved in local politics; Giannettino, Governor of Melfi;
Fulvio, Chancellor to the Prince of Melfi; and Alessio, who became a
priest.[3]

Ordained in the Augustinian seminary of Genoa around 1530, Alessio
was known for his intelligence and seriousness,[4] although on two occasions
his intellectual curiosity caused him brief encounters with the Inquisition.
Apparently he was a gifted orator, because when Giovanni Angelo de'
Medici was made Pope Pius IV in 1599, Alessio was invited to give the
sermon in Milan; he was also asked to preach at the Council of Trent on
30 May 1562 and before Empress Maria of Austria at the Diet of
Augsburg in 1566, and his *Prediche* were published in 1567.[5] Along with
this more public career, Alessio also taught, first at the Augustinian seminary in Milan, then at San Giacomo in Bologna (site of the present Liceo
musicale). In 1570 and 1575 he was Procuratore Generale of his order,
and during the same years taught theology in Rome where Filippo Neri
was one of his pupils. On 20 July 1575 Alessio was made Bishop of Sutri
and Nepi by the Bolognese Ugo Boncompagni, Pope Gregory XIII, an
honour rarely bestowed on a member of a religious order and therefore a
sign that the Augustinian was held in great esteem.

Alessio's representative took official possession of the cathedral and
bishop's residence in Nepi on 5 August, and he moved there himself on
25 or 26 November.[6] Less than two months later, on 8 January 1576,
Alessio asked the *Comune* of Nepi for financial help in opening a seminary, with a teacher of grammar and music, for eight boys;[7] on 6
November the town made its first contribution, and it continued to do so
until 1580 when Alessio died while on a papal mission to Charles of
Austria.

When he took up residence in Nepi, Alessio encouraged members of
his family to join him.[8] Earlier, Nepi had been under the Orsini family
but now it was part of the Papal State; and its proximity to Rome (45 km.

---

[3] Radicchi, 'La famiglia Stradella', 22–3, whose statements on these members of the family are
based on documents found in the Archivio Parrocchiale of Fivizzano and in I-PIas, Archivio
Stefaniano.

[4] Alessio's biography is to be found in many sources, for example: Giovanni Targioni Tozzetti,
*Relazioni d'alcuni viaggi fatti in diverse parti della Toscana per osservare le produzioni naturali e gli
antichi monumenti di essa*, xi (Bologna, 1777; repr. 1972); Emanuele Gerini, *Memorie storiche di illustri
scrittori e di uomini insigni dell'antica e moderna Lunigiana* (Massa, 1839), 136–7; Achille Neri, 'Scrittori
di Lunigiana', *Giornale storico della Lunigiana*, 1 (1912), 22–30.

[5] A copy of them is in I-Lbs.

[6] I-NEast, Atti notarili, Notaio Pompeo Catelani, prot. D, fos. 24ᵛ–25ᵛ, and Consigli, no. 15, fo. 58ʳ.

[7] I-NEast, Consigli, no. 15, fos. 73ᵛ–74ʳ.

[8] First notice of the presence of the Stradella family in Nepi was given in Carolyn Gianturco,
'Alessandro Stradella: Nuovi documenti biografici', *Nuova rivista musicale italiana*, 3 (1982), 456–66.
As stated there, in 1971 it was decided to separate the documents in Nepi; the civil and notary docu-

to the north-east), especially with a bishop in the family, could prove beneficial to the Stradellas. Moreover, its green and rolling hills were fruitful to cultivate, and offered an abundance of springs of health-restoring mineral water known even to the Romans. Alessio's brothers Giovanbattista, Matteo, and Fulvio therefore came to Nepi;[9] in 1576 Fulvio married a local woman—Lucrezia Tabussi, a widow with three children, Orazio, Artemisia, and Giacomo—became a legal resident of the city, bought property in the area known as 'Conchio', and began to take part in town affairs.[10] On 12 August 1579 their first child, and Alessandro Stradella's father, Marc'Antonio, was baptized, as was their daughter, Costanza, on 26 October 1584.[11] Sometime between the end of 1587 and the beginning of 1588 Fulvio died, and in July Lucrezia married her third husband, Domenico Balada, former secretary to Bishop Alessio Stradella, who now rented property from the Church for his own use.[12] The couple joined their respective families which Domenico Balada on 5 August 1600 would declare to be composed of '14 mouths': his own children, the children of Lucrezia and her first husband Giacomo Ambrosi, plus the child

ments were to be brought to the Archivio di Stato in Viterbo, and those dealing with local history to be kept in the Archivio Storico in Nepi. At present, however, this division is not yet complete, which explains the presence of many *atti notarili* still in Nepi. Further information on some members of the Stradella family was presented by Roberto Fagioli in 'La famiglia Stradella di Nepi', in Carolyn Gianturco (ed.), *Alessandro Stradella e Modena, Atti del Convegno internazionale di studi, Modena, 15–17 dicembre 1983* (Modena, 1985), 17–28. The following section offers documents reported in these articles, together with others which I found more recently.

[9] I-VTas, Atti Notarili, notaio Enea Sansoni, prot. 191, fo. 157^{r-v}; the brothers are named here on 30 Mar. 1577.

[10] Lucrezia was the daughter of Felice and Capitano Giacomo Tabussi of Spoleto (I-NEast, Atti Notarili, Notaio Luca Micinocchi, Prot. H., fos. 33^n–35^v, 25 Jan. 1564). Her marriage to Fulvio is documented in I-NEast, Lista dei Trasunti 1589–1629, Notaio Pietro Salamonio, prot. G. 187, fo. 32^v, 20 July 1576; on her children see I-VTas, Atti notarili, Notaio Fulvio Sansoni, prot. 210, fos. 154^r–161^v, 21 Aug. 1615; and Notaio G. B. Sansoni, prot. 221, fos. 66^r–67^v, 2 July 1625. Documents related to Fulvio's acquisitions of land are in I-VTas, Atti notarili, Notaio Enea Sansoni, prot. 192, fo. 52^{r-v}, 12 Nov. 1578; fos. 57^r–58^r, 15 Dec. 1578; and in I-NEast, Atti notarili, Notaio Luca Mininocchi, prot. H, fos. 408^r–409^v, 24 Mar. 1581, where Fulvio is called a citizen of Nepi and where it states that the property in Conchio was '10 zappe' in area, meaning it took ten days to hoe; affirmation of his participation in the city council is in I-NEast, Consigli, prot. 24, fo. 1^r, 1 Sept. 1581.

[11] I-NEd, Libro dei Battesimi B, fos. 84^r and 113^v. In Gianturco, 'Nuovi documenti biografici', 464 it was stated that the baptismal, marriage, and death records of Nepi were not to be found and therefore were presumed to have been burned by French troops in 1789. Quite by accident, however, Padre Fagioli later came across them in the Cathedral rectory. That these were Fulvio and Lucrezia's only surviving children is clear from a document she signed after his death now in I-VTas, Atti notarili, Notaio Fulvio Sansoni, prot. 201, fo. 31^{r-v}, 29 Mar. 1588.

[12] One assumes Fulvio is dead when Lucrezia conducts business alone on 13 Jan. 1588 (I-VTas, Atti notarili, Notaio Fulvio Sansoni, prot. 200, fos. 162^r–163^r); when Marc'Antonio is given a guardian on 7 Mar. 1588, it is confirmed that Fulvio has died (fos. 175^v–177^r). Other business transactions handled by Lucrezia at this time are noted on 1 July 1588 when she buys property (prot. 201, fo. 7^v), on 14 July 1588 (fo. 10^{r-v}), 7 Sept. 1588 (fos. 38^r–39^v), 22 Sept. 1588 when she sells property (fos. 32^v–33^r), etc. On 16 July 1588 she signed the contract to marry Domenico Balada of Morlupo (fos. 18^v–20^v). In a document of 17 May 1579 in the Archivio della Collegiata in Anguillara (Liber mortuorum et Confirmatorum A, fo. 157^r) Balada says he is secretary to Alessio.

of their daughter whose husband had left her, and the children of Lucrezia and Fulvio Stradella.[13]

Shortly before Lucrezia's marriage, on 10 March 1588 Giannettino Stradella died without issue. He left his property and his membership in the Cavalieri di Santo Stefano to his brother Fulvio, but since Fulvio was dead they passed to Fulvio's son, Marc'Antonio.[14] At the time Marc'Antonio was only eight, but his mother and stepfather protected his inheritance, which was contested by Fivizzano members of the Stradella family whom Giannettino had bypassed when making Fulvio his sole heir.

The Cavalieri di Santo Stefano was a prestigious military seafaring order of knights founded in Pisa in 1561 by Grand Duke Cosimo I. When John Evelyn came to Pisa their church drew his attention. The façade, by Vasari, was of polished marble, he said; moreover, 'It is within full of tables relating to their Order, over which hang divers banners and pennants, with several other Trophes taken by them from the Turks, against whom they are particularly obliged to fight.'[15] The order was also a way for the Medici to keep the restless Tuscan aristocracy occupied: they vied for entrance into the order—no easy task since all four grandparents had to be proven to be aristocrats—declared their fidelity to the Medici in fighting the heathens, and then either went to sea or gave large sums of money to the order. When Giannettino furnished documents which confirmed his nobility, he also gave the Cavalieri a drawing of the Stradella coat of arms: it had a red lion rampant on a field of yellow crossed with a white band. Once knighted, Giannettino opted not to fight (at 50 he felt he was too old), but agreed instead to have the large income from his Fivizzano property given regularly to the order.

In 1591 Lucrezia asked the Grand Duke of Tuscany to allow Marc'Antonio, even though only a boy, to be knighted and to attend an investiture ceremony in Rome. Both requests were granted, and from 1592 Marc'Antonio belonged to the Sacro Militare Ordine Marittimo dei Cavalieri di Santo Stefano.[16] Like his uncle, he opted not to do military service; however, managing the property left to him in far-away Fivizzano, which one assumes continued to be used to pay contributions to the

---

[13] I-NEast, Denuncia del raccolto annuo; Aug.–Sept. 1600.

[14] Fulvio's death is documented in the Libro dei morti, 1566–91, Archivio Parrocchiale of Fivizzano. All information given here on the Stradellas' connections with the Cavalieri di Santo Stefano is taken from records now in I-Pas as reported by Radicchi, 'La famiglia Stradella'.

[15] *The Diary of John Evelyn*, ed. John Bowle (Oxford, 1983), 67. For a history of the order and a list (unfortunately incomplete) of the knights, see the studies by Gino Guarnieri: *I Cavalieri di S. Stefano* (Pisa, 1960); *L'ordine di S. Stefano nei suoi aspetti organizzativi interni sotto il Gran Magistero Mediceo* (Pisa, 1966); and *L'Ordine di S. Stefano nella sua organizzazione interna* (Pisa, 1966).

[16] On 17 Sept. 1592 Lucrezia paid for a knighting ceremony which was certainly for Marc'Antonio (I-NEast, Atti notarili, Copie d'Archivio del Notaio Girolamo Brunetti, unnumbered pages).

order, became problematic, and so in 1611 he sold it for the fine sum of 3,200 scudi, which was reinvested in banks in Rome.[17]

Already in 1601 Marc'Antonio had entered into a business venture with his stepfather, and by September 1603, when barely 25, the legal age of full responsibility, he was acting on his own behalf.[18] Certainly his mother was an excellent example to imitate: for example, it was she who bought a house in the parish of San Pietro in the centre of Nepi, and more property in an area of Conchio known as Il Torrone, which was to be the main source of income for the Stradella family.[19] In 1603, in fact, Marc'Antonio collaborated with his mother, first by paying a business debt for her, and then by guaranteeing her payment for grain bought at Monterosi, a town to the south-east. In 1607 the enterprising young man rented the town mill.[20] On 3 May 1608 he was made a member of the Council General of Nepi; on 3 December of the same year he was selected to become Prior, a position he could assume only on 1 February 1609 because he had been away from Nepi.[21]

It was also in 1609 that Marc'Antonio 'collected' and 'had printed' in Rome Kapsberger's *Libro Primo de Madrigali a Cinque Voci*.[22] Since another Cavaliere di Santo Stefano, Flaminio Flamini, published Kapsberger's first book of *villanelle* in Rome in 1610, it would seem that Marc'Antonio was part of a group of knights who were in touch with music in Rome. It is interesting to speculate that Marc'Antonio's interest in music may have been transmitted both to his younger stepbrother Francesco (son of Domenico Balada and Lucrezia Stradella, born in 1592), who became a Dominican with the name of Fra Giacinto and who, as one of his first activities in 1632 as Vicar of San Tolomeo in Nepi, had an organ built,[23] as well as to his own son, Alessandro.

In 1611, as stated earlier, Marc'Antonio sold his inheritance in Fivizzano and invested the money in Rome; in 1612 he was again Prior

---

[17] Radicchi, 'La famiglia Stradella', 30.

[18] On 17 Feb. 1600 Marc'Antonio (called 'eques Sancti Stephani'), his mother, and stepfather formed a business group (I-VTas, Atti notarili, Notaio Fulvio Sansoni, prot. 203, fos. 88ᵛ–90ᵛ); on 16 Nov. 1601 the boy and Domenico Balada drew up a contract (prot. 204, fo. 13ʳ⁻ᵛ); and then on 3 and 6 Sept. 1603 he acted alone (I-NEast, Atti civili, fo. 362ʳ).

[19] That she owned the house is evident from her will made on 21 Aug. 1615 (I-VTas, Atti notarili, Notaio Fulvio Sansoni, prot. 210, fos. 154ʳ–161ᵛ); the property was bought together with Domenico Balada on 13 Apr. 1591 (I-NEast, Atti notarili, Copia d'Archivio del Notaio Girolamo Brunetti, unnumbered pages).

[20] In a letter of 8 Dec. 1607, he complains about a mill further up the river which damages his (I-NEast, Lettere 1607–21).

[21] I-NEast, Consigli no. 25, fos. 80ʳ, 99ʳ, 112ʳ.

[22] Emil Vogel, *Bibliothek der gedruckten weltlichen Vocalmusik Italiens* (Berlin, 1892), 335.

[23] Nepi, Convento di S. Tolomeo, Archivio, Libro mastro, fo. 195ʳ, and Ricordi, fo. 44ᵛ. Alessandro's apparent affection for the Dominicans could have come from this step-uncle who lived until 1674 (Ricordi, fo. 66).

from September to December;[24] and in 1613 he became part of the city's inner Council of Eight.[25] Obviously he had by this time assumed a position of some importance and autonomy, and so on 28 May 1613 felt ready to marry the noblewoman Laudomia Vaccari of nearby Anguillara.[26] In July 1614 their first child, Maria Agata, was born;[27] they had another daughter, Maria Costanza, but her date of birth is not known; it is probable that their son, who became the Augustinian Fra Francesco, was born in 1618.[28]

During the following years, Marc'Antonio was continually active in local politics as well as in business affairs, such as buying Il Torrone in 1625 from his ageing mother, perhaps when his stepfather died.[29] Around this time his wife must also have died, but he soon married another aristocrat, Vittoria Bartoli, whose family had originally come from Florence but then moved to Viterbo and later to Bagnoreggio. Here in the native city of St Bonaventure, Vittoria's father Simone had been born. He married Isabella of the illustrious Alberii family of Orvieto, which had also contributed a bishop to Sutri and Nepi (the family coat of arms may be seen in the ceiling of the Cathedral of Orvieto, near the Chapel of S. Brizio). Vittoria and her brother Pirro were born in Orvieto, although the Bartoli soon moved to Rome where Simone's mother had come from. Simone Bartoli practised law, and very successfully, judging from the many important positions he held, such as governor of various cities (including Todi) for the Papal State.[30]

It is possible that Marc'Antonio met Bartoli and his daughter in Rome. Once married, he brought his bride not to Nepi but to nearby Gallese, where they lived at least from 1626 to 1632 or 1633, and where he was in the service of Duke Pietro Altemps.[31] By 17 January 1627 he was so

[24] I-NEast, Consigli, no. 25, fo. 247^v.   [25] Ibid., fo. 269^v.

[26] Ibid.; Archivio Collegium Anguillara, Liber matrimoniorum I (1574–1631), fo. 61^v.

[27] Nepi, Archivio Parrocchiale S. Maria, Libro dei battezzati C, fo. 138^r.

[28] This is based on a series of documents which trace his ecclesiastical career. In particular, that in the Archivio della Curia Generalizia Agostiniana in Rome which indicates that he became Prior of San Pietro in Nepi in 1646 (according to Eleanor Simi Bonini, 'Stradella negli archivi di Roma', in Carolyn Gianturco and Giancarlo Rostirolla (eds.), *Atti del Convegno di studi 'Alessandro Stradella e il suo tempo'*, *Siena, 8–12 settembre 1982*, *Chigiana*, 39, NS, 19 (1988), 77), a position which he could have assumed only after having been in the order at least 12 years, which brings one to 1634; and to be an Augustinian priest he would have to have been at least 16, which takes one to 1618.

[29] I-VTas, Atti notarili, Notaio G. B. Sansoni, prot. 221, fo. 63^{r-v}.

[30] When Marc'Antonio's and Vittoria's son, Giuseppe, wanted to become a Cavaliere di Santo Stefano, he too had to prove his nobility and therefore his mother's family history is traced in their records. For the documentation supplied by Vittoria's brother Pirro (since their father was temporarily absent from Rome) see Radicchi, 'La famiglia Stradella', 32.

[31] I am grateful to Wolfgang Lippmann for the information that Marc'Antonio Stradella is named in Altemps payment records of 1626, 1629, 1631, and 1632 (Gallese, Archivio Altemps: Libro mastro 1626–35, fos. 60^r, 63^r, 199^r, and 200^r respectively). Beginning in 1637 one finds instead the name of his nephew, Ippolito. There are several accessible accounts of the Altemps family, such as those in Pompeo Litta, *Famiglie celebri d'Italia*, i (Milan, 1819); Teodoro Ameyden, *Storia delle famiglie romane* (Rome, n.d. [1914?]), i. 40–1; and *DBI*; see also Romolo de Dominicis, 'Nota sulla

much part of the place that he was asked to be godfather at a christening.[32] In March 1627, when his wife was expecting their first child, Marc'Antonio's mother died,[33] and he divided her property with his siblings. From records in Sant'Apollinare in Rome we learn that Vittoria's baby, Giovanni Battista, was baptized there on 23 June 1627 with Duke Pietro Altemps and Caterina Ricciardi (a Florentine and the wife of the papal legate Francesco Nicolini) acting as godparents, and that it died, again in Rome, a few months later on 25 March 1628.[34] While it is always possible that Vittoria went to Rome to be assisted by some relative—as was and still is the Italian habit—it would seem more likely, especially since the Altemps palace was near Sant'Apollinare, that Marc'Antonio either was in Rome on business for the Duke during these months, or was commuting back and forth between Gallese and Rome but preferred to have his wife in lodgings in the larger city. However, even if this were the case, Marc'Antonio did not stay there, because on 9 May 1629, when he gave permission to have a debt paid for him in Nepi, he signed the document in Gallese, in the palace of the Duke. On 22 December of the same year Marc'Antonio's stepsister, Artemisia, drew up her will, and she did so in the Stradella house in Gallese,[35] where she and her son Ippolito apparently also lived, both at Marc'Antonio's expense.

By this time he and Vittoria had had another child, Giuseppe, born in 1628,[36] although it is not known where. On 10 February 1630 she was godmother at a christening in Gallese.[37] Other children followed, beginning in 1633, but now the Stradellas were back in Nepi, a possible sign that Marc'Antonio was no longer in the service of Duke Pietro, or at least not in a position which required his continual presence. In all, Marc'Antonio seems to have been with the Altemps family for at least seven or eight years.

The girl born to the Stradellas on 10 April 1633 was named Maria Angelica, and on 5 March 1635 Alessio Maria was born, but both these children died early.[38] In the same period, Marc'Antonio assisted his

casata Altemps', *Strenna dei Romanisti*, 26 (1965), 126–32. Pietro Altemps first married Cosimo de' Medici's daughter Angelica, and at her death in 1636 Marcantonio Lante's daughter Isabella. A daughter from the first marriage, Maria Christina, married Duke Ippolito Lante, and after Marc'Antonio Stradella's death, Alessandro, his mother, and one brother would live in their palace.

[32] Gallese, Archivio Parrocchiale, Libro dei battezzati II, fo. 20ʳ.

[33] I-VTas, Atti notarili, Notaio Egidio Fedeli, prot. 80, fos. 85ᵛ–89ʳ.

[34] Rome, Archivio del Vicariato, S. Apollinare, Battesimi II, pp. 19 and 130. I am grateful to Giorgio Morelli for this information.

[35] Both documents are in I-NEast, Atti notarili, Copia d'Archivio del Notaio Egidio Fedeli, unnumbered pages.

[36] One learns from records in I-PIas, Archivio Stefaniano that in 1638, when his father wanted him to join the order, Giuseppe was 10 years old: see Radicchi, 'La famiglia Stradella', 31.

[37] Gallese, Archivio Parrocchiale, Libro dei battezzati II, fo 27ᵛ.

[38] I-NEd, Libro dei battezzati D, fos. 3ʳ, 17ʳ. One must assume they died since they never reappear in notary documents, not even those which list Vittoria's children.

daughters by his first marriage to enter a local convent. He supervised the sale of their mother's house in Anguillara (interestingly, the girls named as their legal representative Rodolfo Organtino, Governor of Gallese, which supports the suggestion that the Stradella–Altemps connection was not completely severed) and gave the money as their dowry to enter Santa Maria degli Angeli, the new Franciscan nunnery of Nepi.[39] Maria Agata became Suor Maria Agata Celeste on 20 April 1634, and Maria Costanza took her mother's name to become Suor Maria Laudomia the year after.[40] Notary documents in Nepi record certain events in their cloistered lives: for example, in 1661 Maria Costanza became 'Camerlengo', and in 1682 Maria Agata 'Vicaria'.[41]

Once back in Nepi, Marc'Antonio was again active in local government: from September to December 1634 he was Prior; for the same period of the next year he was in the General Council; from January to April 1636 he was a member of the Council of Eight; and from May to August 1637 he was again Priore. By 1639 he was substituting for Governor Bernardino de Sanctis (who even lived in the Stradella *palazzo* in the centre of the city near San Pietro) whenever he was away.[42] Obviously, at 60, Marc'Antonio Stradella was one of the leading figures of Nepi, an ambitious and capable nobleman who could be given positions of responsibility.

In 1637 Vittoria and Marc'Antonio had had another boy who on 11 February was baptized Stefano; then on 4 April 1639 another Stefano, born the day before, was baptized.[43] Or so it would appear from cathedral records. Actually, however, notary acts of several years later suggest that while the boy born in 1637 was indeed Stefano, the one born in 1639 was Alessandro, the future composer. Even if it entails disturbing the chronology of the present history of the Stradella family, a discrepancy so crucial to the main figure of the account demands immediate clarification.

Given the existence of two baptismal records for a Stefano Stradella, it would seem that the baby Stefano born in 1637 had died, and that, there-

---

[39] I-VTas, Atti notarili, Notaio Egidio Fedeli, prot. 81, fos. 28^{r-v}, 33^r–36^r, 3 Jan. 1633; Notaio G. B. Sansoni, prot. 223, fo. 171^r, 30 Jan. 1633; Notaio Floridi Cesare, prot. 97, fos. 16^r–17^v, 30 June 1633; I-NEast, Atti notarili, copia d'archivio del Notaio Egidio Fedeli, unnumbered pages, 28 Feb. 1633. Their step-aunt, Virginia Bartoli, Vittoria's sister, was a nun in the same convent (I-VTas, Atti notarili, Notaio Cesare Floridi, prot. 97, fos. 34^r–36^r, 9 May 1634).

[40] I-VTas, Atti notarili, Notaio Cesare Floridi, prot. 97, fos. 32^{r-v}, 109^r–111^r.

[41] I-NEast, Atti notarili, copia d'archivio del Notaio Domenico Fedeli, unnumbered pages, 13 Apr. 1661; I-VTas, Atti notarili, Notaio Nicola Petroni, prot. 166, fo. 23^r, 2 Oct. 1682. Maria Agata also sang in the special monastery choir (Notaio Stefano Ponti, instrumenta, prot. 169, fo. 811^r, 28 Mar. 1693) and one wonders if she, too, was introduced to music by Marc'Antonio.

[42] I-NEast, Consigli, prot. 27, fo. 267^r; prot. 28, fos. 1^v, 8^r, 63^r; Atti notarili, copia d'archivio del Notaio Egidio Fedeli, unnumbered pages, where he is named Vice-Governor on 11 Feb., 23 Aug., 7, 24, and 30 Sept. 1639.

[43] I-NEd, Libro dei Battezzati D, fo. 33^r for the first Stefano and fo. 48^r for the second.

fore, the next Stradella male child of 1639 was given the same name. It is true that this was a typical custom in Italy; however, it should be noted that it was never a custom in Marc'Antonio's family: the names of their dead children Giovanni Battista and Alessio Maria were never used again for other male babies. Of course, the parents could have behaved differently in this one instance. Other factors, legal ones, argue more convincingly that the child of 1639 could not have been Stefano.

It was stated earlier that only a male who had reached 25 years of age was able to sign alone a document drawn up by a notary: till 14 he was considered a minor; at 21, although of age, he still needed someone older to second his signature. In other words, he was fully mature legally, and therefore could act alone, only when he was 25. This was seen in the case of Marc'Antonio himself, and numerous other *atti notarili* now in Nepi and Viterbo confirm that this law was always applied, not surprisingly, since the notary's very function was to ascertain that legality was maintained in any recorded act. It follows, then, that whenever Stefano or Alessandro were to transact business alone, they had to be at least 25. On 20 January 1663 Stefano sold his part of the inheritance from his parents to his older brother Giuseppe, and he signed the notary act alone.[44] Had he been the 'second' Stefano Stradella, the one born on 3 April 1639, he would have been only 24 years old, and therefore not able to conduct business alone. In short, the Stradella child born on 3 April 1639 could not have been Stefano. The only possible Stefano Stradella is the one baptized on 11 February 1637, which means that he was the Stefano who was 25 on 20 January 1663 and able to sell his inheritance alone. It only remains to decide who the 1639 child was.

On 20 September 1664 Alessandro Stradella now sold his share of his parents' inheritance, also to Giuseppe.[45] Since he signed the *atto notarile* alone, he had to be at least 25 years old at the time. If he had been born on 3 April 1639, Alessandro would have been, in fact, 25 years of age on 20 September 1664. It is suggested that the priest who kept a record of all the babies he baptized in Nepi simply made a mistake, and in 1639 wrote the name of the Stradella child he had baptized the previous time, in 1637. The following lines which he quickly entered into the cathedral register in Nepi were obviously written after the ceremony, when he was alone, and when no one was around to correct him.

Anno Dm̄i 1639 die 4. mensis Aprilis. Ego Lucas Sansonius Archip̄r et Parochus Cathed.lis Eccles. Nep.na baptizavi infantem die 3. d. mensis natum ex. Ill.i D. Marco Antonio q. D. Fulvii Stradella de Nepe et ex D. Victoria de Bartolis da Urbeveteri coniugibus Parochia suprad.a Eccles., cui impositum est nomen

[44] I-VTas, Atti notarili, Notaio Nicola Petroni, prot. 165, fos. 180^r–181^r.
[45] Ibid., fos. 278^v–279^r.

Stephanus. Patrini fuerunt R.dus D. Franciscus Lilius Can.cus d.ae Eccles. et D. Lucretia q. D. Curtij de Pettis de Caprarola.[46]

The wording of such entries varies from one to another, and even the presentation of the facts set forth follows no strict order, suggesting that while the priest meant to keep a record of the souls he baptized, he was not a stickler for detail. Comparing just the two 'Stefano' entries, in one he gave the date of birth, in the other he did not; in one he gave the paternal grandfather's name, in the other he did not; in one he gave the maternal grandfather's name, in the other he did not; in one Marc'Antonio is titled 'knight', in the other he is not; in one the Stradellas are correctly said to live in the parish of San Pietro, in the other they are mistakenly said to live in that of Santa Maria, the Cathedral. For our purpose, it is also important to notice that no witness ever signed the register, which means that an occasional mistake could easily have been made by the priest, which no one would ever have corrected.

A double check on this reasonable supposition is offered by two other notary documents from Nepi. In November 1650 and in August 1651 both Stefano and Alessandro were said to be minors,[47] that is, not over 14: if Stefano were born in February 1637 and Alessandro in April 1639, in 1650 they would have been respectively 13 and 11, and then 14 and 12 the next year. When Alessandro sold his inheritance in 1664, in order for him to have been 25 he had to have been born either in 1639 or earlier; but these two other documents rule out any possibility of him having been born before 1639 since, if he had been, he would not still have been a minor in 1650 and 1651. In short, Alessandro Stradella could have been born only in 1639, and since 3 April 1639 is when we know a Stradella male child came into the world in Nepi, it must be his date of birth.

To return to affairs in Nepi, in September 1639 Marc'Antonio and others began to discuss the construction of a three-kilometre aqueduct,[48] a difficult project which had to be abandoned because of the terrible War of Castro which was to involve most of Italy for the next several years.[49] Since those who lived in the area between Castro and Rome were in the midst of the continual battles between the directly involved Barberini and Farnese families, it comes as no surprise that Marc'Antonio decided to

---

[46] The wording of the first 'Stefano' baptismal record is as follows: 'Anno D$\overline{\text{mi}}$ 1637 die 11 mensis februarii. Ego Lucas Sansonius Archip$\overline{\text{r}}$ et Parochus Eccles. Nepesinae, baptizavi infantem ex Ill. Equite Marco Antonio Stradella de Nepe et ex D. Victoria filia D. Simonis de Bartolis de Urbeveteri coniugibus parochiae S. Petri, cui impositum est nomen Stephanus, Matrina fuit D. Hieronima Hortentia Pisana.'

[47] I-NEast, Atti notarili, Notaio Cesare Floridi, prot. E, fos. 92^v–93^v, and Notaio Egidio Fedeli, prot. 84, fo. 9^{r-v}.

[48] I-NEast, Consigli, no. 28, fo. 204^r.

[49] A good account of the War of Castro is given by Ludwig von Pastor, *Storia dei Papi*, xiii. (Rome, 1943), 881–94.

remove his family from the area. Perhaps as a Cavaliere di Santo Stefano who had sworn fidelity to the Medici he felt particularly vulnerable living in the Papal State where, if he openly opposed the Church, at the very least his property would have been taken away. Wisely, Marc'Antonio took up the position of Vice-Governor of Vignola, 20 km. to the southeast of Modena.[50]

In 1577 the *marchesato* of Vignola, in the Duchy of Modena, had been given to Jacopo Boncompagni, the natural son of Pope Gregory XIII, and it remained in his family. Since their principal properties were elsewhere, the Boncompagni rarely came to Vignola, but instead had a representative who lived in the fortress and took care of all local civil and criminal affairs. Although it was the Boncompagni Pope Gregory XIII who had made Alessio Stradella a bishop, it is hardly likely that the Stradellas would have been able to enjoy other benefits through such a contact, certainly not after 67 years. It would have been Marc'Antonio's father-in-law instead who, concerned for his daughter and her family, put them in touch with Ugo Boncompagni, the present Marquis of Vignola, Duke of Sora, and Marquis of Riano, since he was a judiciary official for Boncompagni in this last district.[51] The Stradella family must have left Nepi as soon as war broke out, since on 9 March 1642 the investiture of the eldest son, Giuseppe, as a Cavaliere di Santo Stefano was held in Vignola.[52]

From various documents which bear his signature,[53] one sees that Marc'Antonio, although he had to ready Vignola for battle, was at first concerned mainly with the routine administration of the territory under his control. Occasionally he was in contact with the Duke of Modena on military questions, such as on 9 August 1642 when he sent him 500 soldiers or on 23 September when he reported that he had given supplies to the passing Florentine army; but he also made him the odd gift, such as seven pairs of live partridges sent on 15 November which he hoped the duke would enjoy.[54]

In a letter of 23 July 1642 Marc'Antonio asked Cardinal d'Este to intercede for his son by his first marriage, Francesco, with Padre Fra Ippolito Monti, Head of the Augustinian Order, so that the young seminarian might be sent from Acquapendente to study at the University of Bologna, and not to Rome or Perugia where Nepesini usually went.[55] One can

---

[50] On Vignola see Arsenio Crespellani, *Memorie Storiche Vignolesi* (Modena, 1872), 107 ff.

[51] According to various documents now in the Archivio Storico Comunale of Vignola.

[52] Radicchi, 'La famiglia Stradella', 32.

[53] These are now in the Archivio Storico Comunale of Vignola. See two such documents in *Alessandro Stradella e Modena: Musica, Documenti, Immagini. Catalogo della Mostra* (Modena, 1983), nos. 1–2.

[54] I-MOas, Cancelleria Ducale, Particolari, busta 1035.

[55] The letter is given in full in Heinz Hess, *Die Opern Alessandro Stradella's* (Leipzig, 1906), 2–3, and is in I-MOas, Carteggi di Regolari, busta 115; another letter (undated) by Marc'Antonio on the same subject is in the same file: for both letters see *Alessandro Stradella e Modena*, nos. 8–9.

perhaps add that Marc'Antonio wanted his son near him not only for reasons of filial affection but also because he expected that Acquapendente
would be besieged by the Farnese—which it was, and disastrously so, the
following October[56]—whereas Bologna, a major stronghold of the Church,
was relatively safe (in fact, in September Odoardo Farnese arrived at the
city gates but did not enter); moreover any trip to Rome or Perugia would
have been extremely dangerous in those years of war.

The various advances and retreats of the several belligerent factions
gradually moved closer to Vignola, and papal troops eventually took
Spilamberto 7 km. to the north-east of Marc'Antonio's fort from where
they began their attacks on Vignola. As he reported afterwards, on 12
June 1643 Marc'Antonio surrendered under the conditions by which
Spilamberto had been taken: no resistance was to be made to the enemy
and in return the papal soldiers were to respect the lives and property of
the Vignolesi.[57] One could say Marc'Antonio was 'afraid', as did the Duke
of Modena;[58] or that he simply felt that the line of least resistance was the
wisest for the people in his charge. However, it is also possible that
Marc'Antonio was simply following the orders of Ugo Boncompagni who,
although he wanted his Vice-Marquis to keep on good terms with
Modena, did not want him to oppose the papal troops too much; this
would have jeopardized Boncompagni property in Rome and Bologna, had
the Church felt the marquis were an enemy.[59]

Whatever the reasons, the papal troops were allowed to enter Vignola;
but they did not keep to their part of the bargain and began to take food,
order people out of their homes, and tax them. Marc'Antonio protested
repeatedly but when he saw he could do nothing to stop them, he fled to
another Boncompagni fort in nearby Monfestino from where the Duke of
Modena, who said he no longer trusted him, sent him home, probably in
July 1643. One assumes that not only his son Giuseppe, but also his wife
and the other boys, Stefano and Alessandro, were with Marc'Antonio during these difficult years in Vignola and Monfestino, which means that
Alessandro's first games at ages 2 to 4 were played in the midst of
soldiers.

By September the family was back in Nepi,[60] and on 7 August 1644
Marc'Antonio bought a house in Via del Foro in the Piazza del Duomo.[61]

---

[56] On Acquapendente and the War of Castro see Nazareno Costantini, *Memorie storiche di Acquapendente* (Rome, 1903), 128–34.

[57] Crespellani, *Memorie*, 110–11.

[58] Letter dated 16 July 1643 in Crespellani, *Memorie*, 113–14.

[59] Ugo Boncompagni repeats his fears on 2 Aug. 1643 in his reply to the above letter to the Duke of Modena now in I-MOe, Autografoteca Campori: Boncompagni, Ugo (Generale).

[60] I-VTas, Atti notarili, Notaio Biagio Floridi, prot. 89, fos. 192^r–194^v.

[61] I-VTas, Atti notarili, Notaio Gerolamo Sansoni, prot. 218, fo. 290^r.

Since in various later documents he is said to be briefly in Rome,[62] it seems that once the Peace of Castro had been signed on 31 March, he resumed whatever business had taken him to the city before going to Vignola, either returning to Altemps or perhaps continuing his employ with Boncompagni. On 26 February 1646 he rented out a barn in Nepi; on 26 March he himself rented a barn from the bishop in the cathedral square near his home, which he then bought on 24 January 1647, and sold back on 29 October so that it could be demolished to improve the look of the piazza. Marc'Antonio also returned to local politics and from January to April 1648 he was Prior. In July he sold the house in the parish of San Pietro, although through a representative since he was again in Rome. By September he was back in Nepi and involved in a court case, his last activity for which there is any record.[63] Marc'Antonio Stradella died at the age of 69 in autumn or winter 1648.

He must have left his family sufficiently well off since on 16 November 1650 his wife bought land near the lake of Monterosi (the village which was one of the first bones of contention in the War of Castro) on which there was a house and vineyard. A few days later, on 29 November, she carried out another business transaction and here she is said to be the 'tutrice e curatrice pro tempore' of her sons Stefano and Alessandro, who are minors, and of Giuseppe, a Cavaliere, who is of 'maggiore età': as said earlier, they were respectively 13, 11, and 22 years of age. The following year, on 31 August, Vittoria took out a loan, and once again she is said to be 'tutrice e curatrice dei figli Giuseppe, Stefano e Alessandro'; and when she paid back a loan on 29 November the family situation is said to be the same.[64]

Alessandro Stradella's Early Years

Although no documents reveal what education Alessandro Stradella received, one can speculate on the possibilities. From the ages of 2 to 4 he was probably in the fortresses of Vignola and Monfestino. Either there or back in Nepi, his father could have taught him to read and write and

---

[62] For example, a letter from Marc'Antonio is dated Rome, 3 Jan. 1645 (I-NEast, Atti notarili, Notaio Egidio Fedeli, prot. D, fo. 187^r).

[63] For 1646 the relevant documents are in I-NEast, Atti civili 1646, fo. 32^r, and Atti notarili, Notaio Egidio Fedeli, prot. D, fo. 186^r; for 1647, I-NEast, Atti notarili, copia d'archivio del Notaio Egidio Fedeli, unnumbered pages, and Notaio Egidio Fedeli, prot. D, fo. 294^r; for 1648, I-NEast, Consigli, no. 29, fo. 213^r; I-VTas, Atti notarili, Notaio Gerolamo Sansoni, prot. 215, vol. ii, fo. 43^{r-v}, and Marc'Antonio's letter inserted there after fo. 50; as well as I-VTas, Nepi—Registro di Atti Civili, prot. 160, fos. 15^v, 22^v, 23^v, 35^v.

[64] The relevant documents for 1650 are I-NEast, Atti notarili, Notaio Cesare Floridi, prot. E (copy made by Domenico Fedeli, 3 Jan. 1667, unnumbered pages) and fos. 92^r–93^v; and for 1651, I-VTas, Atti notarili, Notaio Egidio Fedeli, prot. 84, fo. 9^{r-v}, and I-NEast, Atti notarili, Notaio Cesare Floridi, prot. E.

perhaps have interested him in music, but Marc'Antonio then died when the boy was only 9. It is not known if Vittoria would have been able to instruct her son: she may have been intelligent in business but still not know how to read and write. However, in Nepi at the time, apart from those who could have taught him either at the public school founded in 1544 or at the church school of the Augustinians (San Pietro) or Dominicans (San Tolomeo), there were two other relatives quite capable of tutoring Alessandro.

First there was his stepbrother Padre Fra Francesco, an Augustinian priest who had gone away to study for a university degree but who was back in Nepi in 1646: it is possible that, at age 7, Alessandro began to have lessons with him, or perhaps only from age 9 when his father died. Until 1650–1 Padre Fra Francesco remained in Nepi and therefore until age 12 Alessandro's education could have been entrusted to him. During all of these same years Alessandro's step-uncle, the Dominican Padre Giacinto Balada, was also in Nepi and he, too, could have instructed the boy. While it is not known if Padre Francesco was a musician, Padre Giacinto's long struggle to have an organ put in the Church of San Tolomeo would suggest that he was more than a little interested in music. Perhaps Fra Francesco taught Alessandro general subjects and Padre Giacinto gave him music lessons.[65]

It is quite possible, however, that Alessandro was sent to study in Bologna. This is suggested by the fact that later documents connect him with Bologna, albeit in a confused way: in 1659 he is said to be Bolognese, but in 1660 the same records say he is from Nepi; in documents from 1682, Nepi as well as Bologna are mentioned.[66] Therefore, one might deduce that, although born in Nepi, he lived a sufficient number of years in Bologna to have been considered Bolognese (as was Corelli, who was born in Fusignano). Various suppositions about when Alessandro was in Bologna may be put forth. It is possible that he did not return to Nepi with the Stradella family in 1643 but went instead to Bologna; or else he went to Bologna after his father's death in 1648; or he went to Bologna at some time between 1643 and 1648. While there was no reason for him to have been in Nepi in 1650 and 1651 when his mother declared he was still under her charge (which he was legally), when she moved to the Lante palace in Rome in 1652 he might have come with her; certainly he was there in 1653. In short, Alessandro Stradella was in Bologna, if at all, at most from ages 4 to 14 (1643 to 1653), and quite possibly only from ages 7 or 9 to 13 (1646 or 1648 to 1652).

Whenever he went to Bologna, most likely his Augustinian stepbrother

---

[65] Francesco Stradella's ecclesiastical career is traced by Simi Bonini, 'Stradella negli archivi di Roma', 77–8.

[66] The relevant documents will be discussed in the sections devoted to these years.

would have wanted him to be in his order's seminary of San Giacomo (where Alessio had taught), while his step-uncle would have preferred San Domenico. One realizes from his ability to express himself clearly in excellent written Italian and from his knowledge of Latin[67] that Alessandro had received a good academic education; and the high quality of his compositions in all vocal and instrumental genres attests to his having had professional training in music as well. Certainly San Domenico could have tutored him in both areas: it was famous for its intellectual and academic contributions made throughout the ages; and a regular *cappella musicale*, founded by its Confraternita del Rosario at the beginning of the century, performed in concert each Saturday and on all feasts of the Virgin Mary. During Alessandro's years in Bologna, the Maestro di Cappella at San Domenico, the confraternity's first, was Francesco Milani (1624–52).

But if not at San Domenico or San Giacomo, Alessandro could easily have studied music at some other church or convent, perhaps with Lucio Barbieri, organist at San Petronio; Alberto Bertelli, who preceded Cazzati as Maestro di Cappella there, and before him the above-mentioned Milani; Bartolomeo Montalbano, Maestro di Cappella at San Francesco; or Giacomo d'Alessandria, Maestro di Cappella at S. Maria dei Servi. Stradella's *sonate da chiesa* indicate that he would have had lessons as well with one of several renowned teachers of string instruments, such as Ercole Gaibara, Giovanni Benvenuti, or Leonardo Brugnoli, who would attract Corelli to Bologna a few years later.

---

[67] See App. 2 for Stradella's extant writings in Italian and Latin.

2

Rome

In the years immediately after her husband's death, Vittoria Bartoli Stradella continued to live in Nepi, as the notarial documents cited above testify. However, for reasons which are not known but which could simply be a mother's desire to offer greater opportunities to her children, she then became part of the household of Duke Ippolito Lante.[1] As stated earlier, Marc'Antonio had been in the service of Pietro Altemps, Duke of Gallese. When the duke's first wife Angelica de' Medici died, he married Isabella Lante della Rovere. Therefore, Vittoria's connection to the Lantes could have come through her rapport with the Altemps family.

The Lantes were related, however, not just to the Altemps family, but to most of Italy's nobility—to Cardinal Boncompagni of Bologna, to the Grand Duke of Tuscany, the Dukes of Modena and of Parma, to the Princess of Rossano, Duke Caffarelli, Marchese Marino of Genoa—to name only a few.[2] It should be noted that many of these would become patrons of Alessandro Stradella. The Lante palace where Vittoria lived had been designed by Sansovino. It is situated in Piazza de' Caprettari (where the baths of Agrippa once were), diagonally across from S. Eustachio. In church records of 1652 one reads that 'Vittoria matrona vedova' is a member of the Lante household and in 1658 she is listed among 'the women of the duchess', dignified and fitting employment for a widowed aristocrat.

On 23 December 1653, a relative in Nepi, Tommaso Petroni, asked that an inventory be made of what was in the carpenter's workshop under the Stradella house, saying that it belonged to Giuseppe.[3] The document confirms what Giuseppe was to declare in 1677: that Vittoria sold her part of Marc'Antonio's inheritance to her eldest son and that he remained in Nepi.[4] For their part, according to records of S. Eustachio for 1653, both Stefano and Alessandro had moved to Rome with their mother, where

---

[1] Rome, Archivio del Vicariato, Liber Status Animarum Ab Anno 1625 usq. ad Annum 1662, Parochiae S. Eustachij, as reported by Simi Bonini, 'Addenda' to 'Stradella negli archivi di Roma'.

[2] An account of the Lante (also Lanti) family may be had from their archives presently housed in I-Ras, Archivio Lante–Della Rovere, buste 290 and 455–6. In the latter file several notices refer to members of a Bartoli family, perhaps Vittoria's family. On the Lantes also see Ameyden, *Famiglie romane*, ii. 2–4.

[3] I-VTas, Notaio Nicola Petroni, prot. 164, fo. 22^r.

[4] I-NEast, Notaio Cesare Floridi, prot. E, fos. 83^r–86^r.

they became 'pages' of the Lante household. They remained as such until 1656. No mention of the Stradellas is found in 1657, but they could have left the city as many did to escape the plague. In 1658 the names of Alessandro and his mother reappear, and in 1659 both brothers are listed together with their supposed cities of origin: 'D. Stephanus Stradella de Nepi' and 'D. Alexander Stradella Bononiensis'. The error is corrected in 1660 when Alessandro is now said to be from Nepi ('Alexander Stradella Nepesinus'). The Lante family left Rome for Sabbioneta in 1661–2 and none of their household is mentioned in S. Eustachio records: we do not know if the Stradellas went with the Lantes or elsewhere. Unfortunately, no records concerning S. Eustachio exist for the years 1663–88, and therefore Alessandro Stradella's further dependence on the Lante family cannot at present be documented.

What and with whom the 14–year-old adolescent studied in Rome is not known. The most famous musician of the period in Rome was Giacomo Carissimi (1605–74), teacher at the Collegio Germanico and Maestro di Cappella at the college church of Sant'Apollinare (near the Altemps palace) from 1629. Another musical authority at the time was Orazio Benevoli (1605–72), Maestro di Cappella of the Cappella Giulia at San Pietro from 1646. It has been affirmed that Stradella studied with one of Benevoli's pupils, Ercole Bernabei (1622–87),[5] who became organist at San Luigi dei Francesi in 1653, the year Stradella arrived in Rome. He remained in this position until 1665 when he became Maestro di Cappella at San Giovanni in Laterano; in 1667 he returned to San Luigi dei Francesi until 1672 when he took Benevoli's position at San Pietro; two years later he left Rome. However, no contemporary evidence documents a pupil–teacher relationship between Stradella and Bernabei or anyone else. It is, of course, very tantalizing to find notices such as the following at San Luigi dei Francesi: for the feast of San Luigi on 26 August 1663 a 'Bolognese Viola' played; and for the same feast in 1665 'Sr. Alessandro della Chiesa Nova' was organist.[6]

On 20 September 1664, having reached legal maturity, Stradella was back in Nepi to sell his share of inheritance to his older brother Giuseppe.

[5] Francesco Veracini (1690–1768) says this in the second part of his treatise, *Trionfo della pratica musicale*, Op. 3, in the section entitled 'Cronichetta ovvero Memorie musicale'. The manuscript was discovered by Arnaldo Bonaventura in the Conservatorio statale di musica L. Cherubini and described by him under the signature A. R. Naldo in 'Un trattato inedito e ignoto di Veracini', *Rivista musicale italiana*, 42 (1938), 617–35. Part of the treatise is quoted in Gino Roncaglia, 'Le composizioni strumentali di Alessandro Stradella esistenti presso la R. Biblioteca Estense di Modena', *Rivista musicale italiana*, 44 (1940), 82; this same portion, translated into English, appears in Edward Allam, 'Alessandro Stradella', *Proceedings of the Royal Musical Association*, 80 (1953–4), 32–4.

[6] Jean Lionnet, *La musique à Saint-Louis des Français de Rome au XVIIIᵉ siècle, Note d'archivio*, NS 4, supplement (1986), 124, 128 respectively. The notices from 1667 referring to a soprano by the name of Alessandro probably do not refer to Stradella because by this time his voice would have broken.

As clearly stated by the notary, he was entitled to a third of the family property, having to divide it with his two brothers Stefano and Giuseppe. This was, then, a third of the Stradella house in the Via del Foro in the Cathedral square, of their land in Torrone, and of their house and arbour on the lake of Monterosi. It must have all been valued at 1,500 scudi since Stefano and Alessandro each received 500 scudi when they sold their shares to Giuseppe. This was certainly not very much if one remembers that their father had sold the property he inherited in Fivizzano for 3,200 scudi but, as well-paid Roman church singers received only 1 or 2 scudi for some special performance,[7] Alessandro would have been able to survive for a while on the sum.

Who besides the Lantes might have been able to help him between 1664 and 1667 when his presence is next recorded in Rome? One knows that Stradella had relatives living in the city. For example, there was Fra Antonio Stradella of Nepi, a Franciscan who in 1663 was said to be a master of music. Unfortunately, when walking down the street in summer 1666 a sword was drawn on him when he asked a man for leave to pass, and he died several months later from his wounds. Perhaps his brother, Domenico, then assisted Alessandro.[8] Fra Cirillo Stradella (1643–1720), an organist, was in the Carmelite monastery of S. Maria in Traspontina in 1677 but he may have arrived earlier.[9] Alessandro's maternal uncle, Pirro Bartoli, was also in the city. In addition, there were the Altemps and Boncompagni families upon which he could have called. In short, Alessandro should not have found himself alone or without a door to knock upon, and his subsequent career shows that, in fact, he enjoyed excellent contacts.

For example, on 11 February 1667 he was invited to compose an oratorio for the coming Lenten season. Ash Wednesday fell on 23 February and beginning with the second following Friday and for five consecutive weeks a member of the prestigious Arciconfraternita del Santissimo Crocifisso, the society of aristocrats which sponsored the oratory of the church of San Marcello, paid for a Latin oratorio to be performed.

---

[7] According to Lelio Colista's expenditure records when he was in the employ of Cardinal Flavio Chigi, this is what his singers earned for Vespers on 8 Sept. each year, the Nativity of the Blessed Virgin: see Jean Lionnet, 'Les Activités musicales de Flavio Chigi, Cardinal neveu d'Alexandre VII', *Studi musicali*, 9 (1980), esp. 297–301.

[8] One learns that Fra Antonio Stradella of Nepi was a musician from documents gathered by Stefano Rinaldi and published by Raffaele Casimiri in 'Musicisti dell'Ordine Francescano dei Minori Conventuali dei sec. XVI–XVII', *Note d'archivio*, 16 (1939), 240. I am assuming that he is the same Antonio Francesco Stradella, 'Cappellano vul. in pectore', son of Francesco and brother of Domenico, whom I came across in Roman trial proceedings of 1667 (I-Ras, Tribunale Criminale del Governatore, Processi 1667, busta 603). A 3-voice motet (SSA, bc), *Eia angeli veloces*, by Fra Antonio is in I-Bc: BB364; since it is dated 1669, I would doubt it is an autograph as the catalogue states.

[9] According to documents in I-Ras, Carmelitani calzati in S. Maria in Traspontina, busta 118, fos. 222^v–232^r. I am grateful to Arnaldo Morelli for this information.

Stradella's sponsor is not known but his music, composed to words by Padre Giovanni Lotti, was heard on 11 March.[10] That Stradella should even have been considered for the series, during which works by Carlo Caprioli and Lelio Colista would also be performed, is confirmation that he was known to the right people; Carissimi, a regular contributor to the Crocifisso services, could also have recommended a pupil.

Fabio Chigi, Pope Alexander VIII, died on 22 May, and on 20 June Giulio Rospigliosi was elected Pope Clement IX. He made Monsignor Altemps his *Cameriere segreto*,[11] but Stradella may not have been able to take advantage of the connection since, on 17 September 1667, it is stated that he has arranged a marriage and, because of it, has had to escape to a religious institution and may even have to leave Rome. The information comes to us from Abate Settimio Olgiati[12] in one of his many letters to the Venetian noble, Polo Michiel.[13] It is obvious from the correspondence

---

[10] I-Rvata, Archivio SS. Crocifisso in S. Marcello, viii: Congregazioni e Decreti 1665–74. Giovanni Lotti (Pomarance, now in the province of Pisa, 1604–Rome, 1686) studied in Bologna and then went to Naples and Rome, where he became a priest at the Basilica of Santa Maria Maggiore, and was connected with Cardinal Antonio Barberini; during the last 20 years of his life he was tutor to the Colonna children. From 1641 to 1644 he was Reader in Logic at the University of Rome. Much of his poetry celebrated political, ecclesiastical, and matrimonial occasions; he also wrote texts for cantatas and oratorios. Lotti became a member of the Academies of the 'Umoristi' and of the 'Disinvolti'. He was buried in Santa Maria Maggiore. Two years after Lotti's death, in fulfilment of his will, his nephew published his poetry as *Poesie latine e toscane*. For more information, see Elisabetta Duranti, 'Giovanni Lotti (1604–1686): Biografia, trascrizione ed analisi del codice barberiniano Latino 4220, catalogo delle sue poesie per musica' (*laurea* thesis, University of Pisa, 1985–6), and Steven Plank, 'Of Sinners and Suns: Some Cantatas for the Roman Oratory', *Music and Letters*, 66 (1985), 344–53, as well as the several pages of Lotti's texts for music in I-Rvat, Inventario dei Codici Barberiniani musicali, 113–31.

[11] I-Rvat, Avvisi, Barb. lat. 6369.

[12] I-Vmc, Mss. Provenienze Diverse (hereafter PD), C. 1057, no. 197. Not much is known about Olgiati or his family. There is an undated printed plot summary by Settimio in I-Rc, Vol. Misc. 1137/18: *Argomento e scenario del Chivano re di Bungo convertito da S. Francesco Xaverio dell'Indie dramma* (title-page); 'Da recitarsi nel salone del Collegio Romano, per la distributione de' premij . . . Fatto stendere dal Sig. Settimio Olgiati' (fo. 2). Agostino Olgiati also had a part in this play of 81 roles. Settimio may have been related to Marquis Giovanni Battista Olgiati, who had dealings with Taddeo Barberini in 1631 (I-Rvat, Barb. lat. 10042, fo. 8ʳ), as well as to Giuseppe Olgiati, Bishop of Parma from 1694 (several letters of his are in I-MOe, Autografoteca Campori), and who was present at a supper and musical entertainment offered by Duke Sforza to the Rospigliosi in Aug. 1668 (I-Rc MS 5006, 'Memorie diverse' by Don Giuseppe Contini, 'Sacerdote Romano'); one finds notice also of the brothers Marc'Antonio, Ascanio, and Ottavio Olgiati as well as a Bernardo Olgiati (this last in Naples) at the beginning of the seventeenth century (I-MOe, Autografoteca Camori, letters of Marc'Antonio Olgiati). According to Ameyden, *Famiglie romane*, ii. 115–16, the Olgiati family chapel in Rome was in Santa Prassede.

[13] A member of one of Venice's most notable families. According to G. A. Cappellari Vivaro, 'Il Campidoglio Veneto' (I-Vas, Codd. Soranzo, 31) and M. Barbaro and A. Tasca, 'Arbori de' patritii veneti' (I-Vas, Miscellanea Codici, I, St. Veneta, 18)—for which sources I am grateful to Marinella Laini—Polo Michiel was born on 19 May 1640 to Marc'Antonio (of the Santa Sofia branch of the family) and Marina Dandolo. In a letter of 26 May 1665 he is called 'Governor of the Provinces of Dalmatia' (I-Vmc, PD C. 1065, no. 465 from Gianetto di Giusti to P. Michiel), and therefore he was probably the same Polo Michiel who fought against the Turks soon after 9 Dec. 1679 (I-Fas, Mediceo del Principato, 3040, *avviso* dated Venice, 9 Dec. 1679; my thanks to Timothy McGee for this source); it is also known that in 1684 he left as a volunteer in the combat against the same enemy

that the abate encouraged Michiel's patronage of Stradella and that, by September 1667, Stradella was already well known to Michiel. It was to be a contact, really a friendship, which would be to Stradella's advantage both personally and musically all his life.

As far as the notice of Stradella having arranged a wedding is concerned, it was of course the usual way people married, certainly those of the upper class. Since important financial and political ties were made through marriage, all members of a family would be involved in trying to set up the most profitable relationship for any unattached man or woman. If necessary, nuns would be released from convents and cardinals (if they had not become priests) relieved of duties in order to marry. There were problems only when someone who would suffer from the match objected. Therefore, the fact that Stradella had arranged a marriage or had profited financially from it was not in itself unusual. What is to be noted, instead, is that he chose to get involved in a controversial alliance. One wonders where Stradella escaped, whether to the Augustinians, the Dominicans (as he was to do some years later in Turin when he again found himself in difficulty), or perhaps to whichever institution Abate Olgiati was connected with. No matter which *chiesa* offered him immunity, it would suggest he was on good terms with its clergy.

If Stradella actually left Rome, it could not have been for too long (which meant that his unfortunate affair had quietened down rather quickly) since, by the beginning of 1668, he had composed the prologue *O di Cocito oscure deità* to the comic opera *Il Girello*. The opera, full of satire and a pointed criticism of absolutism, was the result of a collaboration between Jacopo Melani (music) and Filippo Acciaiuoli (text).[14] *Il Girello* was Acciaiuoli's début in the city and to be certain of success he had

in Dalmatia. The following year he was made General of the Cavalry; however, on 24 Sept. 1686 he died from serious wounds in Zara at the age of 46. His passion for music is revealed by his correspondence with Olgiati (extant from 30 Sept. 1663 in I-Vmc, PD C. 1054, no. 516) and with composers, singers, and impresarios (also in I-Vmc, PD). Polo Michiel was probably related to Francesco Michiel who was ambassador to Louis XIV from 1670 to 1674 and later to the court of Vienna (see Francesca Antonibon, *Le relazioni a stampa di ambasciatori veneti, Collana di bibliografie minori,* i (Padua, 1939), 58, 72). Another relative might have been Pietro Michiel, who published collections of poetry in 1632, 1634, 1640, 1641, and 1642. This Venetian married a noblewoman from Ferrara, Apollonia; and together with G. F. Loredano was among the founders of the Accademia degli Incogniti (see Lucio Felici (ed.), *Poesia italiana del Seicento* (Milan, 1978), 217–18 for one of his poems). Polo Michiel had a daughter named Marina (I-Vmc, PD C. 1066, nos. 230, 249, 517); love-letters from Cecilia Contarini (I-Vmc, PD C. 1058 and 1059) could be either to Polo or to his brother Girolamo. Polo's letters to Cardinal Flavio Chigi (I-Rvat, Archivio Chigi, 34, fos. 270ʳ, 272ʳ, 274ʳ) show extreme cordiality bordering on obsequiousness.

[14] See Robert L. Weaver, '*Il Girello*, a 17th-Century Burlesque Opera', *Memorie e contributi alla musica dal medioevo all'età moderna offerti a F. Ghisi nel settantesimo compleanno (1901–1971)* (Bologna, 1971), ii. 141–63. On Acciaiuoli, see Giovan Mario Crescimbeni, *Notizie istoriche degli Arcadi morti* (Rome, 1720), i. 357–61; Elena Tamburini, 'Filippo Acciaioli: Un "avventuriere" e il teatro', in A. Ottai (ed.), *Teatro Oriente/Occidente* (Rome, 1986), 449–76; and Curzio Ugurgieri Della Berardenga, *Gli Acciaioli di Firenze nella luce dei loro tempi (1160–1834)* (Florence, 1962).

asked Giovan Filippo Apolloni to edit it for him. Apolloni also wrote the text for Stradella's prologue.[15] Although this comic opera was said to be rather vulgar at times,[16] it was a huge success. Moreover, since it was one of the most frequently performed operas of the seventeenth century, Stradella's prologue was thereby heard everywhere from Naples to Milan.

The next known collaboration between Apolloni and Stradella was *La Circe*, written to honour the arrival in Rome of Leopoldo de' Medici, who had been made a cardinal. On Monday, 12 March 1668 Leopoldo rode into the city through the Porta del Popolo greeted by the Roman nobility in some 100 carriages each drawn by six horses. The Barberini lodged him, and the Chigi fed and entertained him.[17] He was accompanied everywhere by his ten pages in splendid livery and by his coachmen outfitted in black velvet with silk trim to match his carriage. *La Circe* had been commissioned by Olimpia Aldobrandini Pamphili, the Princess of Rossano, and on 10 May Ferdinando Raggi, the Genoese agent in Rome, wrote home that it was to be 'a *pastorale* for three voices';[18] the simple and delightful serenata was performed in the Apollo salon of the Villa Belvedere, Wednesday, 16 May 1668.[19]

In these years Stradella lived in Via Giulia, a street which runs parallel to the River Tiber from Palazzo Farnese to the church of S. Giovanni dei Fiorentini. In the seventeenth century it was one of the most elegant residential streets, housing nobles and cardinals—many of whom were Tuscans—and ambassadors. Unfortunately, no parish records exist for the period, and therefore the exact building in which Stradella lived cannot be determined. In the 1668 household accounts of the Chigi family one reads that they had paid 10 lire 'to a man who took a gift to Signor Stradella, musician-composer who lives in Via Giulia, at the order of His Most Eminent Master for *Ferragosto*', that is for 15 August, the Feast of the Assumption.[20] One assumes the payment was for music, but at present no

---

[15] Giovan Filippo Apolloni (Arezzo *c*.1620–Rome 1688) fought as a mercenary but then turned to writing. He was in touch with Tuscan writers of Salvator Rosa's circle in Florence and Pisa (*c*.1640–50) where he met Cesti, with whom he collaborated in Austria and Italy. From 1660 to 1667 he was at the court of Cardinal Voluminio Bandinelli (d. 1667) in Rome, then with Sigismondo Chigi (till 1678), and next with Flavio Chigi. Apolloni wrote texts for Cesti (19 thus far identified) and Stradella (16), as well as for Abbatini, Agostini, Caprioli, Carissimi, Colista, Atto Melani, Bernardo Pasquini, and Alessandro Scarlatti. For more information see Giorgio Morelli, 'L'Apolloni librettista di Cesti, Stradella e Pasquini', in Carolyn Gianturco and Giancarlo Rostirolla (eds.), *Atti del Convegno di Studi 'Alessandro Stradella e il suo tempo', Siena, 8–12 settembre 1982, Chigiana*, 39, NS 19 (1988), 211–64.

[16] Alessandro Ademollo, *I teatri di Roma nel secolo decimosettimo* (Rome, 1888; repr. 1969), 99.

[17] It is possible that Leopoldo heard *Il Girello*: see I-Rvata, Avvisi di Roma, no. 134 dated 18 Feb. 1668.   [18] Cited by Ademollo, *I teatri di Roma*, 101.

[19] Complete documentation for the performance is given in the section dealing with the music of *La Circe*.

[20] I-Rvat, Archivio Chigi, 690, Spese diverse, 6 Aug. 1668 (David Merrell Bridges, 'The Social Setting of "Musica da Camera" in Rome: 1667–1700' (Ph.D. diss., George Peabody College for Teachers, 1976), 32–3, incorrectly gives the archival source number as 689).

work can be associated with it. However, the notice establishes that the powerful and munificent Chigi family were among Stradella's patrons.

It was at this time that Christina of Sweden[21] was beginning to urge one of her favourite poets and dramatists, Giulio Rospigliosi, Pope Clement IX, to allow operas to be put on for a paying public at the Teatro Tordinona, an enterprise in which Stradella would be involved. In the mean time, on 4 December 1668, Flavio Orsini, Duke of Bracciano, put on a comedy for the Venetian ambassador and other nobles which had originally been done in 1666 at the French ambassador's home.[22] Since the duke is named as the poet of Stradella's prologue *Reggetemi, non posso più*, and since the character Costanza in dialogue with Costume speaks in favour of the French, it could be that the prologue was sung before the comedy, perhaps even in 1666.[23]

When Clement IX died in December 1669, Rome was immediately filled with cardinals who began politicking for 4 months and 20 days to elect a new pope.[24] Of their choice, Clement X, Emilio Altieri, the Venetian ambassador Antonio Grimani said that he was 'an angel of sentiment, of humble heart, charitable, sincere, kindly'.[25] While this may have been so, he was already over 80 and not really up to solving problems. The person who made the Pope's life easier and who actually ruled in his stead was his Secretary of State, Cardinal Paluzzo Paluzzi, whose brother Gaspare Altieri was to be a patron of Stradella's.[26]

Autumn 1670 found the composer in financial difficulty. As he explained in a letter to Cardinal Flavio Chigi,[27] he was in debt for 7,000 scudi; he had managed to put together 5,000 scudi but still needed to raise 2,000 by the following Saturday, which was in two days. He explained that his plight, which could cost him his 'belongings, reputation, and perhaps also freedom', had come about because he was without a protector. In fact, for two years he had been free-lancing, and although he

---

[21] See John Bergsagel, 'Christina', *The New Grove*.

[22] An *avviso* cited by Ademollo, *I teatri di Roma*, 103.

[23] A possible occasion for the first presentation of the comedy may have been the celebration of the return from France of Cardinal Orsini in June 1666. He had left Rome in Oct. 1665 and came back laden with precious gifts from Louis XIV.

[24] A wealth of information on the conclave is to be had from Leopoldo de' Medici's letters to his brother in I-Fas, Mediceo del Principato, 3995.

[25] Niccolò Barozzi and Guglielmo Berchet (eds.), *Le relazioni della Corte di Roma lette al Senato dagli Ambasciatori Veneti nel secolo decimosettimo* (Venice, 1879), ii. 356.

[26] According to the same source (p. 383), the Pope had given all the Altieri money to his cousin, Laura Caterina Altieri, and in 1669 she married Gaspare Paluzzi-Albertoni, who then took the name of Altieri, as did his sisters Lodovica and Tarquinia and his brother Cardinal Paluzzo Paluzzi. Gaspare, Prince of Oriolo and Viano, Duke of Monterano, was made a *Generalissimo* of the Church and given command of Castel Sant'Angelo, and his despotic and money-seeking brother became Secretary of State to Clement X, all to the family's benefit.

[27] I-Rvat, Archivio Chigi, 57, fos. 470^r–471^v, letter dated 27 Nov. 1670. I am most grateful to Giorgio Morelli for this source. For a transcription and translation of the letter, see App. 2a, no. 1.

had had work from both Rome and elsewhere (we know of his music for Venice), payment had not been prompt. Offering Cardinal Chigi 'my own person, my blood, and my strength', and pledging to repay him in six months at great interest and under any conditions Chigi would stipulate, Stradella pleaded for a loan of the required sum. He was concerned that his request be kept secret and asked the cardinal to write him just 'yes' or 'no' on a sealed slip of paper and have it delivered by Apolloni, the Chigi family poet and Stradella's collaborator.

The debt seems huge (it will be remembered that he received only 500 scudi for his inheritance), and even if the aristocracy were loath to pay as he suggests, it encourages the doubt that Stradella may not have handled his money wisely. He was certainly often desperately in need of funds when in Rome:[28] this had been the case in 1667 when he had arranged a marriage; and in 1677 he would be accused of spending an old woman's money and then trying to marry her off. His affirmation about now being 'unattached' implies that up until 1668 he has had, instead, a fixed position, and it is to our loss that he does not mention to which church or noble he has been connected. One is also curious about his offer of using his 'strength' for Chigi and wonders whether he had ever been employed as a court guard or spy. It is not known if Flavio Chigi helped Stradella out of his difficulty, but obviously someone did because there is no succeeding suggestion that he was stripped of his possessions or imprisoned. What is more, towards the end of the year he was involved with Rome's first public opera theatre (Acciaiuoli was impresario), the Teatro Tordinona, an activity which should have brought him financial relief.[29]

The theatre opened on Thursday, 8 January 1671 with Nicolò Minato's and Francesco Cavalli's Venetian success of 1664, *Lo Scipione Affricano*, originally dedicated to Lorenzo Colonna but now 'Alla Sacra Real Maestà della Regina di Svetia' and it was followed on 24 January 1671 by another Venetian success by Cavalli, *Il novello Giasone*, this one on a libretto by Giacinto Andrea Cicognini and previously performed in 1649 and 1666. Acciaiuoli, who had initially been worried because the theatre was not full, was pleased enough to organize another series of operas the next year.

The year 1671 also saw preparations for the wedding that joined the Colonna and Cesarini families:[30] on 7 February 1671 Filippo Colonna,

---

[28] It could have been this huge debt which prompted him to ask for 300 scudi when invited to compose an opera in 1671; the sum was refused him and the commission given to someone else (reported in a letter from Giovanni Lucatelli dated Rome, 26 Nov. 1672; my thanks to Licia Sirch for this information, though she refused to tell me the present whereabouts of the letter).

[29] Unless stated otherwise, all information on the Tordinona is taken from Alberto Cametti, *Il teatro di Tordinona poi di Apollo* (Tivoli, 1938). See also Ademollo, *I teatri di Roma*, 123–9; Owen Jander, 'The Prologues and Intermezzos of Alessandro Stradella', *Analecta Musicologica*, 7 (1969), 93 ff. and Ch. 7 below.

[30] On the following marriages and the families involved, see the accounts in I-Rvat, Avvisi, Barb. lat. 6373.

Prince of Sonnino married Cleria Cesarini in Santa Caterina da Siena in great style. That evening the prince offered guests a lavish meal and a 'comedia' which was more than likely the spoken play *Il Biante* to which Stradella contributed a fantastical prologue, three intermezzos, and other incidental vocal music. To celebrate the wedding contracted in winter 1671 between Anna Pamphili, daughter of the Princess of Rossano, and Giovanni Andrea of the prestigious Genoese Doria family, Stradella composed a cantata entitled *Lamento del Tebro e due ninfe per lo sposalizio della SS: D'Anna Pamfilia Aldobrandini e S: Prencipe Doria* (which begins 'L'avviso al Tebro giunto').

In August Polo Michiel was in Rome[31] and it is quite reasonable to assume that he met Stradella personally on this occasion, if not before. The second Tordinona Carnival season opened with *La Dori ovvero la Schiava fedele*. The libretto was by Apolloni and had been set by Cesti in 1657 for Innsbruck and presented numerous times thereafter. The opera was dedicated in Rome to 'principe Gaspare Altieri, Generalissimo di S. Chiesa', and Stradella composed a new prologue for it, *Dormi, Titone*, and perhaps several other pieces; it is probable that the new text was also by Apolloni. Although *La Dori* was scheduled to open on 7 January 1672, a performance was held on 31 December 1671 so that the Princes of Vendôme, in the company of the Pope, could see it before their departure for Paris. The audience commented afterwards that the opera, one of the most popular and most performed in the seventeenth century, had been a bit dull in the Tordinona version because Acciaiuoli had kept down expenses;[32] but he cut the less successful scenes and had new ones added, and the formal opening went somewhat better.

On 12 February Stradella's music was heard again, this time a prologue and intermezzo for the season's last opera, *Il Tito*. The libretto was by Nicolò Beregan and the opera had been composed by Cesti for Venice in 1666. Dedicated originally to the Colonnas, it was revived in Rome at Maria Colonna's request and was now dedicated to her.[33]

At the end of Carnival 1672 Filippo Acciaiuoli had to admit that opera was too expensive a business for him and the Tordinona contract was given to Marcello De Rosis for 1,400 scudi, a transaction which was to exclude Stradella from further productions. In truth his loss was not too terrible, since the theatre was forced to close for the Holy Year of 1675 and then was not allowed to reopen for 16 years due to papal conservatism. In all Stradella had contributed to two of the four first seasons of public opera in Rome.

---

[31] I-Vmc, PD C. 1058, no. 419.   [32] I-Fas, Avvisi, Mediceo del Principato, 3394, 2 Jan. 1672.
[33] Cametti, *Tordinona* does not know the names of the performers, but the following sonnet written by Sebastiano Baldini in 1672 gives us at least one singer: 'Elena Passarelli che nel Dramma Il Tito rappresenta il personaggio di Martio' (cited by Giorgio Morelli, 'Sebastiano Baldini (1615–1685)', *Strenna dei Romanisti*, 39 (1978), 266).

In 1673 Maria Beatrice, sister to Duke Francesco d'Este of Modena, married the Duke of York, James Stuart (later James II of England). Throughout the year details of the contract were closely followed by her mother, Laura Martinozzi, and the Protector of England, Cardinal Barberini.[34] It might have seemed opportune to the ever more impoverished Orsinis[35] to honour the future Duchess and her husband, especially since they were related to the English crown, and therefore it could have been during the negotiations that Lelio Orsini, Prince of Vicovaro and brother of Flavio, Duke of Bracciano, wrote his oratorio about Edith, the medieval English Queen and holy woman (*Santa Editta, vergine e monaca*), which Stradella set to music.[36]

Stradella's oratorio *Santa Pelagia* may have been performed in the same year, on 8 October, the saint's feast-day. On the title-page of the only extant score and in the same hand as the copyist is the abbreviation 'Br.ta' which could well refer to Brigitta, Sweden's greatest female saint, whose feast falls on the same day. In 1673 the Holy Saviour order of nuns which she founded celebrated Brigitta's three-hundredth anniversary and perhaps Christina, their chief benefactress, in addition to honouring Brigitta had Stradella compose an oratorio based on the penitent and widely venerated Pelagia as well.[37]

August 1674 saw the performance of a work by Stradella on a text by Sebastiano Baldini.[38] On the poet's copy one reads: *Il duello. Serenata fatta dal Prencipe D. Gaspare Altieri alla Regina di Svetia l'agosto 1674.*[39] *Il duello*, more familiarly known by its opening text *Vola, vola in altri petti*,

---

[34] The marriage is discussed in several *avvisi* of I-Rvat, Barb. lat. 6376.

[35] On their continual sale of property, see their papers now in I-Ras, Archivio Lante–Della Rovere, buste 300–1.

[36] Don Lelio Orsini proposed to Livia Cesarini (a nun who, instead of Cleria, got the family money) and many *avvisi* are devoted to the affair (see I-Rvat, Barb. lat. 6374 and 6376, and Alessandro Ademollo, *Il matrimonio di Suor Maria Pulcheria al secolo Livia Cesarini* (Rome, 1883; repr. 1967), but she rejected the *c*.40–year-old nobleman.

[37] I am grateful to Victor Crowther for this hypothesis. See Ch. 3. n. 30 for yet another possible date of composition.

[38] Abate Sebastiano Baldini (1615–85) had been secretary to various cardinals (Francesco Rapaccioli, Antonio Barberini, Flavio Chigi), as well as to the University of Rome, and later would also serve Gasparo de Haro y Guzman, Viceroy of Naples. His enormous correspondence, sent out from his villa in Via S. Pietro in Montorio (I-Rvat, Chigi L.VI.190, fo. 248ʳ), reveals him to have written without effort and most readily in a humorous vein. This is equally true of Baldini's works for music. Almost all of Rome's composers made use of his poetry (L. Rossi, Carissimi, Savioni, Caprioli, Cesti, Alessandro Melani, Pasqualini, Marazzoli, and Laurenzani have thus far been identified), as well as the Venetian Barbara Strozzi and the Emilian Giovanni Bononcini. For his part, the poet complained in verse that lovers asked him too often for *canzoni* which they then gave to composers: 'one wants it for Stradella, [another] for Bernardo [Pasquini], and [another] for Pier Simone [Agostini]', 'three without equal who know how to write only beautiful music' (I-Rvat, Chigi L.VI.190, fos. 318ʳ–320ᵛ). For more detail see Morelli, 'Baldini'.

[39] I-Rvat, Ottoboni lat. 2478, III, fos. 398ʳ–403ʳ. I am extremely grateful to Giorgio Morelli for having allowed me to see the catalogue he is preparing on Baldini which enabled me to identify the poet as the author of Stradella's text.

has the honour of being the earliest datable composition presently known employing concerto grosso instrumentation. From September to December 1674 Polo Michiel was again in Rome,[40] which allowed Stradella to renew his personal acquaintance with the Venetian. The composer may well have returned briefly to Nepi at this time, too, as his Dominican step-uncle, Padre Giacinto Balada, died on 3 October.[41]

The 30,000 visitors coming and going to Rome in 1675[42] were perhaps more than usual since it was a Holy Year. To encourage piety there was, as Ademollo puts it, 'complete silence from theatres'.[43] In spite of the ban, though, Stradella had enough music to compose. Of the children which resulted from Ippolito Lante's marriage, both daughters entered Roman nunneries. In 1666 Lavinia joined the Sette Dolori convent recently opened by Isabella Farnese, although in 1676 she came out and married Filippo Marino of Genoa[44] (whose relative Goffredo was to acquaint the Duke of Modena with Stradella's music). The other daughter, Angelica, entered the convent of SS. Domenico e Sisto, without doubt the most aristocratic of all Rome's convents: for example in 1646 Suor Anna Margharita Altemps had been part of the same Dominican order, and all of Lorenzo Onofrio Colonna's sisters were currently there. Before Angelica took final vows, various notary acts had to be signed. The young girl had to renounce her rights to any family property in favour of her father, otherwise it would all have gone to the order;[45] and although the Dominicans were a cloistered and strict order, the noble ladies were allowed to have servants, called *converse*, and Ippolito thoughtfully gave a dowry to SS. Domenico e Sisto not only for his daughter but also for her *conversa*, Anna Zanini.[46] While Angelica may have done her period of probation in the convent when still a little girl, the religious rule forbade her taking the veil before 16 years of age.[47] It was only on Monday, 28 January 1675 that the housekeeper of SS. Domenico e Sisto noted that no meat had been bought for that day since Angelica Lante, now called Suor Maria Christina, 'gave a party for her investiture'.[48]

It must have been for this solemn ceremony that Stradella composed his motet *Pugna, certamen* (*Dialogo nel monacato della Sig.ra Angelica Lanti [sic] chiamata S. Maria Christina nella religione*) scored for a concerto

---

[40] Gleaned from correspondence in I-Vmc, PD C. 1060, nos. 664 and 667.

[41] Nepi, San Tolomeo, Archivio conventuale, Sezione domenicani, Ricordi, fo. 66[r–v].

[42] A census in Ademollo, *I teatri di Roma*, 231 is said to be from a report by Antonio Barbaro, Venetian ambassador to Rome.

[43] Ademollo, *I teatri di Roma*, 141.   [44] I-Ras, Archivio Lante–Della Rovere, buste 455–6.

[45] Ibid., busta 290.   [46] Ibid., busta 659.

[47] For this and other rules and regulations of Dominican nuns, see Antonio Cloche, *Regola, e costituzioni delle Suore di S. Domenico* (Rome, 1709).

[48] Although the archives of SS. Domenico e Sisto presently in I-Rvata have not as yet been catalogued, I was kindly allowed to go through them. The notice on Angelica Lante is in the 'Libro dello Spenditore' for 1675.

grosso ensemble. The order's convent was situated on Monte Magnanapoli (it is now the Angelicum, the international study house for male Dominicans) near the Quirinale, the Pope's residence; it was connected by a gallery to their church—in which it is presumed Stradella's piece was performed—a single-nave structure with three chapels on either side. The nuns were in choir-stalls behind a grille above the main door, whereas family members and friends would have sat in the nave. The motet was not performed by the nuns, but whether the musicians were hired by Ippolito Lante or whether the music was the gift of someone else, perhaps the nun's uncle Duke Pietro Altemps, is not known.[49]

Another Stradella concerto grosso work was performed only a few months later. It was his oratorio *San Giovanni Battista* commissioned by the Venerabile Compagnia della Pietà della Natione Fiorentina.[50] This society of Florentine gentlemen living in Rome used the church of San Giovanni dei Fiorentini for their liturgical services, but the series of oratorios they organized to celebrate the Holy Year was put on at the church oratory. They had commissioned fourteen works from some of Rome's major composers and had them performed from January to April. Stradella's was the eleventh of the series and was heard on 31 March, the Sunday before Palm Sunday. Although Apolloni wrote three of the fourteen oratorios (all of them for Antonio Masini), the libretto for *San Giovanni Battista* was written by Abate Ansaldo Ansaldi, an eminent Florentine.[51] The poet's choice of subject is not surprising, since John the

[49] The only music the order itself seems ever to have paid for was on the feast of Saint Dominic, when the nuns also uncovered 'la superbissima volta dipinta a chiaro oscuro' (I-Rvat, Barb. lat. 6380, *avviso* of 10 Aug. 1675), a madonna believed to have been painted miraculously.

[50] The following account is based on documents in Raffaele Casimiri, 'Oratorii del Masini, Bernabei, Melani, Di Pio, Pasquini e Stradella, in Roma nell'Anno Santo 1675', *Note d'archivio per la storia musicale*, 13 (1936), 157–69.

[51] Payment records state that the libretto was by 'Abbate Ansaldi' and it has usually been assumed (as recently as Giancarlo Rostirolla, 'La musica nelle istituzioni religiose romane al tempo di Stradella', in Carolyn Gianturco and Giancarlo Rostirolla (eds.), *Atti del Convegno di studi 'Alessandro Stradella e il suo tempo', Siena, 8–12 settembre 1982, Chigiana*, 39, NS 19 (1988), 588) that this refers to Gherardo (or Girardo) Ansaldi, a Sicilian from Catania (1654–92) who became a Franciscan priest and was at the College of San Bonaventura in Rome. However, a more likely author is Ansaldo Ansaldi. Born in Florence in 1651 to a noble family (several members were Cavalieri di Santo Stefano), Ansaldi first studied under the Jesuits in Florence and then at the University of Pisa. He went to Rome to continue his studies at law, and had an illustrious career: he became Canon at the Basilica of Santa Maria Maggiore, a member of the Apostolic Signatura (the supreme tribunal of the Church which had jurisdiction to act in the name of the Pope), Consultant to the Congregation of Rites, Examiner of Bishops, Auditor to Pope Innocent XII, and Auditor and Deacon to the Holy Rote. He was also esteemed for his writing and was a member of the Accademia Fiorentina and of Arcadia. Ansaldi died in 1719 and was buried in San Giovanni dei Fiorentini, an event which proves his connection to the patrons of Stradella's oratorio. (For more detail on Ansaldi, see I-Ras, Misc. Famiglie, Arch. della Superintendenza, Sigillari romani, busta 182–1–1; E. Boxich, 'Ansaldo Ansaldi', in Emilio De Tipaldo (ed.), *Biografia degli Italiani illustri nelle scienze, lettere ed arti del secolo XVIII, e de' contemporanei*, i (Venice, 1834), 479–82; and Giammaria Mazzucchelli, *Scrittori d'Italia* (Brescia, 1753–63), I. ii. 810–12.)

Baptist is the patron of Florence and was the saint most venerated by the society. Their having chosen Stradella to set Ansaldi's libretto is a sign of their special regard for him, and perhaps recognition of his family's connections with Florence and the Cavalieri di Santo Stefano.

Payment records for the oratorio series name among others Carlo Ambrogio [Lonati], the hunchback singer, violinist, and composer who had arrived in Rome in 1668, served Christina both as singer and leader of the orchestra (which gave him the unofficial title ever after of 'the queen's hunchback'), and who would leave in 1677 when Stradella did.[52] The '*Il Bolognese*' mentioned in the accounts is most probably Arcangelo Corelli. According to Pitoni,[53] Stradella considered *San Giovanni Battista* his best work to date, and to judge from the several extant copies and librettos, the oratorio was appreciated and performed until well into the next century.

In the same year as *San Giovanni Battista* Stradella received an honorary appointment, that of an 'extra servant' to the Pope.[54] He received the symbolic payment of a ration of bread and of *ciambelle* (a type of cake in the form of a circle), two rations of sweet biscuits, a goblet of wine, half a litre of oil, half a goblet of vinegar, a broom, and some sticks of wood to burn. However, the real 'payment' was the appointment itself, a papal recognition of his qualities.

The new year 1676 had barely begun when Christina offered an *Accademia in musica* at her palace, at which the invited cardinals and princes judged the best composition presented there to date.[55] No composer or poet is named but Stradella's *Il Damone*, with a text by Sebastiano Baldini based on Christina's own scenario, would be a likely candidate. On 13 January 1676 Abate Settimio Olgiati wrote to Polo Michiel in Venice that a private opera was being rehearsed in Rome, and that the Colonna children were going to dance in the intermezzo.[56] From another source one learns that the work was *La prosperità d'Elio Seiano*, that it opened at the Colonna palace on 21 January, and that it was sung 'very well' by several cavalieri. Moreover, the Colonna children's inter-

---

[52] Lonati sang the hunchback-violinist role of Vafrindo in Pasquini's *L'amor per vendetta* at the Tordinona in 1673, and may have been the hunchback Ireno in Aureli's *Eliogabalo* the same year, as well as the dwarf Lupino in Sartorio's *Massenzio* the following season; he also sang the comic role of Lesbo in Cavalli's *Scipione Affricano* in Naples. Lonati was principal violinist at San Luigi de' Francesi in 1673–4. (I thank Norbert Dubowy for the information regarding Lonati.)

[53] Giuseppe Ottavio Pitoni, 'Alessandro Stradella', in *Notitia de' contrapuntisti e compositori di musica* [compiled *c*.1695–*c*.1730], ed. Cesarino Ruini (Florence, 1988), 324. For the exact wording, see the last section of Ch. 5 below.

[54] I-Rvat, Ruoli, fo. 4ᵛ, no. 167 of 1675 and fo. 5ᵛ, no. 169 of 1676 as reported by Rostirolla, 'Istituzioni religiose', 586. A photo of the page for 1675 is inserted in Rostirolla before p. 687.

[55] I-Rvat, Barb. lat. 6381, *avviso* of 4 Jan. 1676.

[56] I-Vmc, PD C. 1063, letter no. 362 dated 12 Jan. 1676.

mezzo was 'very gallant'.[57] An opera with this same title had been written by Nicolò Minato and composed by Antonio Sartorio for Venice in 1667 and redone at the Tordinona in 1672, and it was most likely this work which Colonna presented at his palace. The prologue, however, was by Filippo Acciaiuoli[58] and one is inclined to believe that Stradella's prologue *Lasciai di Cipro il soglio* is this very one. Perhaps he even set some of the numbers of the opera itself, as is implied in Olgiati's letter in May to Michiel where he says that, together with other pieces, he will send 'also some from Seiano newly done by Stradella'.[59] The opera was apparently well received and was given several times, certainly on 21, 25, and 31 January and apparently every day in February.[60] One is tempted to assign Stradella's cantata *Son principe, son re*, subtitled by its poet Apolloni *Il Seiano*, to this same period.[61]

Another occasion which most likely involved Stradella was the *comedia in musica* put on in June at Oriolo to celebrate the second marriage of the old Duke of Anticoli, Egidio Colonna, this time with the Pope's niece Anna Vittoria Altieri. They had obtained 'the best musicians of Rome' as well as 'la Pia' for the 'most superb comedy'.[62] This was probably Stradella's serenata *Ecco Amore ch'altero risplende* which alludes to both families.

In July 1676 Emilio Altieri, Clement X, died and once again there was much politicking over the election of a new pope.[63] In this same month and through to the end of August Stradella was busy composing for Polo Michiel. He had apparently been asked to write first a piece of instrumental music and then another composition which might have been either instrumental or vocal because Olgiati simply communicated that according to Stradella 'one never composes for eight, but it would be better to do so for four with the parts doubled'.[64] On 8 August Abate Olgiati wrote to Michiel that Stradella was busy composing and that he, Olgiati, would pay the copyist (Stradella's hand was not very neat), and this procedure

---

[57] I-Rvat, Barb. lat. 6381, *avviso* of 25 Jan. 1676.

[58] Ibid.

[59] I-Vmc, PD C. 1063, letter no. 83, dated [?] May 1676.

[60] Deduced from the following *avvisi*: I-Rvat, Barb. lat. 6381, 25 Jan. and 15 Feb. 1676; I-Fas, Mediceo del Principato, 3942, 1 Feb. 1676; and I-Vmc, PD C. 1063, letter no. 295, 26 Jan. 1676.

[61] See Morelli, 'Apolloni'. The literary source for the cantata is in I-MOe, Autografoteca Campori, fos. 33ᵛ–35ᵛ.

[62] I-Rvat, Barb. lat. 6381, *avvisi* of 6, 13, and 20 June 1676. The surname of the singer Pia eludes us. The marriage itself took place on 14 June (I-Rc MS 5006, 'Memorie diverse' by Don Giuseppe Contini, 'Sacerdote Romano'). Jander in his Stradella *WECIS* catalogue states that this work was for Anna Colonna's marriage, but she wedded Don Taddeo Barberini in 1629; the only other Anna Colonna was Lorenzo Onofrio's daughter, who became a nun. On the marriage between Anna Altieri and Egidio Colonna and other Altieri marriages, see Pastor, *Papi*, xiv/1, 636–9.

[63] I-Rvat, Barb. lat. 6382, several *avvisi* from after Altieri's death on 20 July 1676.

[64] I-Vmc, PD C. 1063, no. 146 dated July 1676 (no day is given).

may explain why so few of his autograph scores are extant.[65] On the 15th the report is more or less the same,[66] and on the 21st Olgiati says that Stradella has not yet completed Michiel's 'sonata'.[67] But·as soon as this letter was sent off, Stradella arrived with the music: he advised Michiel that the effect of his work depended on having the instruments play well together.[68] From these few indications one realizes that the piece in question was indeed a sonata, and that it was probably for several instruments since in order to do it well there was need to rehearse the music, something Stradella would not have specifically requested if only one or two strings and continuo were involved.

Olgiati makes another interesting comment in his first letter of 21 August to Polo Michiel: he says that Stradella has given himself over completely to composing and that he also teaches 'for money'. The query which immediately comes to mind is: what else has Stradella been doing up to now if not composing? Has he been singing, too, or playing—perhaps harpsichord, lute, or some bowed instrument? Leaving off these other activities could explain why he now needed to supplement his income by teaching. Even if these questions cannot be answered, at least two things are apparent: by 1676 Stradella felt that he could devote himself entirely to composing, an indication that his success and patrons were such that economically and artistically he could do so; and the financial difficulties he had complained of to Flavio Chigi in November 1670 had abated.

To thank him for his several pieces of music (which by the way were not paid for), Olgiati suggested that Michiel send Stradella a lace collar and cuffs; he had to repeat his request to Michiel various times before the items were finally sent in October.[69] By that time Benedetto Odescalchi had been elected Pope Innocent XI and until his death in 1689 the Romans lived in irritable opposition to this 'maniac reformer',[70] who was convinced that all theatre, musical and otherwise, was evil. In such an austere climate the most affected were the Roman musicians and, in fact, many began to look elsewhere for employment. Taking advantage of his connection with Polo Michiel, Stradella wrote to him on behalf of one

[65] PD C. 1063, no. 133. On Stradella's habitual use of a copyist, see his letter of 24 May 1681 to Flavio Orsini (I-Rasc, Arch. Orsini, I. 279, no. 487; no. 23 in App. 2*a*). He also had a copyist for *San Giovanni Battista*, but this may have been simply for parts.

[66] PD C. 1063, no. 139.

[67] PD C. 1063, no. 152.

[68] PD C. 1063, no. 151, dated only Aug. 1676 but probably also written on the 21st, after the letter just cited.

[69] Ibid., as well as no. 184 of 2 Sept., no. 72 of 19 Sept., no. 409 of 3 Oct.; Stradella thanked Michiel in a letter of 20 Oct. 1676, no. 350 (see no. 3 in App. 2*a*). The payment in goods and not currency was typical of the period, and confirms Stradella's need either of money or of a patron who would keep him fed, clothed, and housed.

[70] Ademollo, *I teatri di Roma*, 143.

such singer, Caterina Saminiati, recommending her as being superior on all counts.[71]

In spite of performing this kindness, Stradella's mind was actually elsewhere and his worries made him, too, consider leaving Rome. He wrote to Michiel that not only was he delighted to serve him but he would be prepared to do so 'in persona'; he stated the reason for his wanting to leave rather vaguely: 'a certain misfortune having happened to me here in Rome, which does not permit me to live here at the moment'.[72] Actually he had once again arranged a marriage and had got into trouble over it. Contemporary accounts may not be correct in all details as none is from a person directly involved; however, generally speaking, they seem plausible.[73]

For this controversial wedding Stradella had an accomplice, Giovanni Battista Vulpio, a well-known contralto castrato.[74] Stradella and Vulpio could have met either through shared patrons or through the Tordinona where both were employed in 1671. It is not clear if Vulpio was a partner from the very beginning of the affair, because only Stradella is mentioned in the one account which says he contrived to get 10,000 scudi from a woman 'of low birth, not respectable, . . . also ugly and old'. However another report says he and Stradella together arranged to have her marry a relative of Cardinal Cibo, someone who had an annual income of 7,000 scudi. Apparently they entertained him with 'canti e suoni', got the 'empty-headed' fellow drunk, and then called for the priest who performed the marriage, all of this with the aim of helping the woman who was now living in 'miserable poverty'. Her identity is not known, nor is that of her intended husband, except that he was a Cibo and had built his palace opposite that of Contestabile Colonna.

However, Cardinal Alderano Cibo was a man of great importance—the Pope had made him his Secretary of State at the end of September—and

---

[71] I-Vmc, PD C. 1063, no. 389 dated 10 Oct. 1676 (no. 2 in App. 2*a*).

[72] PD C. 1063, no. 350 dated 20 Oct. 1676 (no. 3 in App. 2*a*).

[73] These are two *avvisi* (of which Thomas Griffen kindly informed me) sent from Rome to Munich (now in D-Mbs, Cod. Ital. 192, fos. 419ʳ and 659ʳ), dated 17 Oct. 1676 and 30 Oct. 1677 respectively (the second of these, with the same date, is also to be found in I-Rvat, Barb. lat. 6384), and a letter from Lorenzo Valleroy (about whom nothing is known) to Polo Michiel dated Rome, 13 Feb. 1677 (I-Vmc, PD C. 1064, no. 141).

[74] On Vulpio as a singer, see Lionnet, 'Flavio Chigi'; and Cametti, *Tordinona*, i. 12, ii. 324, 327; and on Vulpio as composer see GB-Lbl, Harley 1265 which contains his arias *Voglio amarti, sì mio ben* and *Nel mirarvi pupille vezzose*, as well as the cantata *Chi credete che sia*, all indicated as his. Thomas D. Culley, *Jesuits and Music*, i: *A Study of the Musicians connected with the German College in Rome during the 17th Century and of their Activities in Northern Europe* (Rome, 1970), 240 n. 265 says that Vulpio, a Papal singer, wrote from Turin on 20 Sept. 1663 regarding the permission he had to serve the Princess of Savoy, and it could be that he spoke well of his employment there and thus encouraged Stradella to think of establishing himself later on at the northern court. He and Vulpio remained friends to the end of Stradella's life (see Stradella's letter to Flavio Orsini, no. 23 in App. 2*a*).

was not to be trifled with.[75] He immediately had the woman put in a nunnery, 'one of the most vile' Rome had to offer, and it was expected she
would stay there for the rest of her life. Next the marriage was annulled,
which meant that the whole point of the scheme was thwarted.
Apparently Cardinal Cibo also wanted both Vulpio and Stradella imprisoned, in fact one account says Vulpio was even tried and found guilty,
although there is no record of the case, nor was the singer ever absent
from his duties at the Papal Chapel. Stradella was said to have avoided
being directly reprimanded by taking refuge in a convent. The same
source says that he and Vulpio were on very friendly terms with the
French ambassador and that this further infuriated Cibo, who feared they
would be given political asylum and thus be beyond his reach. On 23
January when Settimio Olgiati again wrote to Polo Michiel, the situation
must still have been tense as Stradella was still with the 'frati', although
seemingly able to go out since the abate expected him the next day.[76]

Stradella was certainly foolish to have thought he could arrange such a
marriage for a member of the esteemed and powerful Cibo family without
there being negative consequences, and certainly he was morally in the
wrong. But as had happened in the 1667 affair, people continued even
now to befriend him and to request his music, which is perhaps the clearest proof that, while his behaviour was a source of exasperation to his
friends and acquaintances, they somehow excused it as part of an extravagant personality which had little to do with the composer's creative
ability.[77]

[75] According to Enrico Stumpo, 'Alderano Cibo', *Dizionario biografico degli Italiani*, after a few
years the Pope no longer took Cibo into his confidence because of his blatant nepotism and determined accumulation of wealth. He and Stradella were both obviously not above behaving in a mercenary manner, but Cibo could not contain himself when family money might be channelled elsewhere,
or when some operation was organized without his approval.

[76] I-Vmc, PD C. 1064, no. 70. As the term 'frati' simply means members of a religious order, it is
not possible even to suggest where Stradella took refuge.

[77] For example, Olgiati wrote to Michiel that he was certain the Venetian would want every courtesy shown the composer (ibid.). According to Lorenzo Valleroy in letters to Michiel dated Rome, 2
Jan. and 13 Feb. 1677 (I-Vmc, PD C. 1065, unnumbered, and C. 1064, no. 141 respectively),
Stradella—in spite of his present ticklish situation—had written to the Venetian asking that 'Nina', a
singer or actress, be hired by the Teatro San Luca (no such letter has come to light), and Valleroy
was glad that Michiel ignored the request. He felt Stradella was not reliable in matters outside his
profession, a judgement one would have to agree with.

3

Venice and Turin

In spite of Stradella's friends, the Cibo wrath was not to be calmed and he was forced to leave Rome. Of course it was not a bad time to do so professionally because of the Papal restraints on music; however colleagues such as Bernardo Pasquini, Alessandro Melani, and Corelli remained and weathered the Odescalchi storm to their advantage, and Stradella could have done the same had he behaved differently. As it was, at the beginning of February 1677 he went to Venice where he was welcomed by Polo Michiel. Exactly what Stradella did there is not known. In *avvisi* accounts of his recent escapade he is called a *virtuoso* and a *musico*, terms generally referring to a singer but which could also have meant an instrumentalist. Had he wanted to compose, there were churches and noblemen who could have used him. It was also Carnival and four public theatres presented operas. For example the new Teatro S. Angelo opened with Domenico Freschi's *Helena rapita da Paride* and one wonders if Stradella's prologue *Dal luminoso impero*, wherein the mythical Leda refers to her daughter Helen of Troy, could have been composed for this production, and if so whether or not it was used. At SS. Giovanni e Paolo, the Grimani theatre, managed by relatives of Polo Michiel, Apolloni's libretto *Alcasta* was revised by Matteo Noris and under the title *Astiage* set to music by Giovanni Bonaventura Viviani;[1] it is always possible that Stradella rehearsed the singers or played in the orchestra as he would do later in Genoa.[2]

One also knows that his Roman patrons Contestabile Colonna and Don Gaspare Altieri were in the city from January to March for Carnival, and they could have asked Stradella for music for their private parties.[3] This was true as well of Polo Michiel, or his brother Girolamo whom Stradella also knew.[4] As a matter of fact, in later correspondence Stradella called

---

[1] The opera was dedicated to Alvise Contarini, but this was probably not the nobleman of the same name with whom Stradella would soon be in difficulty.

[2] He may have accompanied singers at rehearsals on the lute (he owned three when he died), a common theatrical practice (see Lorenzo Bianconi and Thomas Walker, 'Production, Consumption and Political Function of Seventeenth-Century Italian Opera', *Early Music History*, 4 (1984), 219).

[3] On this and other information about Carnival 1677 in Venice, see the following *avvisi*: I-Rvat, Barb. lat. 6383, dated 2, 16, and 30 Jan., 13, 20 Feb.; I-MOas, Cancelleria Ducale, Avvisi dall'Estero, Venezia, vol. 113, dated 30 Jan., 6, 13 Feb., and vol. 118, dated 19, 27 Feb., 6 Mar. (where the year is sometimes written as 1676 although actually 1677).

[4] Girolamo Michiel was born on 1 Aug. 1644. Together with his brother, Polo, he went to fight the

himself a 'servant' of Girolamo and said that the Venetian was his 'principal patron', surely an exaggeration but implying that he composed for him as well as for his brother.[5]

In the same letter, Stradella asked for Girolamo's intercession with Polo in order to obtain letters of recommendation from him;[6] Girolamo had already sent him a letter he could use and Polo sent one soon after.[7] Further proof of Polo's help in Stradella's awkward situation is found in a letter Olgiati wrote to Venice on 6 March 1677 in which he says that Stradella is thankful for the many 'favours' and 'good advice' that Michiel offered him.[8]

On 1 May Marcello Severoli wrote to Michiel in response to his request to do something for Stradella. He affirmed that he was obligated to the composer and considered him a friend. Monsignor Severoli was Deacon of the ecclesiastical court and an extremely cultivated gentleman. His library was exceptional, his home a gathering-place for the intelligentsia of letters and science.[9] That he should consider Stradella a friend, as expressed here and in an earlier letter to Michiel of 6 February 1677 (after the problems with Cardinal Cibo), reinforces the conclusion that the composer had qualities which were appreciated in spite of his behaviour.[10]

In June Olgiati wrote to Polo Michiel the first of several letters about an opera by the Florentine poet Gianfrancesco Saliti that Stradella was supposed to compose, and which it was hoped Michiel would have put on at the Teatro SS. Giovanni e Paolo, possibly in Carnival 1678.[11] We are unable to say whether he composed the intermezzo *Chi mi conoscerà?* for Cavalli's *Lo Scipione Affricano*, performed during the same season but which in the end had changes and additions by Viviani. At some time

Turks in 1684. His successful career as an officer ended when he was wounded while leading a large convoy. He died on 10 Sept. 1695 at the age of 51. (See I-Vas, Miscellanea Codici, III, Codd. Soranzo, 31: G. A. Cappellari Vivaro, 'Il Campidoglio Veneto'; and Miscellanea Codici, I, St. Veneta, 18: M. Barbaro and A. Tasca, 'Arbori de' patritii veneti'.

[5] I-Vmc, PD C. 1065, no. 429, 4 Sept. 1677, a letter from Stradella to Girolamo Michiel (no. 6 in App. 2*a*).

[6] Mercedes Viale Ferrero, 'Alessandro Stradella a Torino (1677): Nuovi documenti', in G. Ioli (ed.), *Atti del Convegno nazionale 'Da Carlo Emanuele I a Vittore Amadeo II', San Salvatore Monferrato, 20–21–22 settembre 1985* (San Salvatore Monferrato, 1987), 179 erroneously says the letter was written to Polo Michiel.

[7] See Stradella's letter to Polo Michiel dated 11 Sept. 1677 (I-Vmc, PD C. 1044, no. 288; no. 7 in App. 2*a*).

[8] I-Vmc, PD C. 1064, no. 333.

[9] Giovan Mario Crescimbeni, *Comentarij intorno alla storia della volgar poesia*, i (Rome, 1702), '*Introduzione*' (pages unnumbered) and *Notizie istoriche degli arcadi morti*, ii (Rome, 1720), 186–8.

[10] I-Vmc, PD C. 1602, no. 52, dated 6 Feb. 1677, and C. 1064, no. 31, dated 1 May 1677. On 29 May Giovanni Battista Caffarelli sent Polo Michiel a box containing music (C. 1064, no. 227), requesting that he give it to Stradella.

[11] On Saliti see Giulio Negri, *Storia degli scrittori Fiorentini* (Ferrara, 1722), 255; and on his libretto for Stradella, see Olgiati's letters in I-Vmc, PD C. 1064: no. 201 of 30 June; no. 192 of 17 July; no. 278, undated but probably Aug.; no. 265 of 27(?) Aug.; and no. 299 of 25 Sept.; and no. 190, Saliti's own letter of 17 July where he admits some of his arias were rewritten by Abate Ranieri.

during his stay in Venice—roughly January to June 1677—Stradella would have composed the cantata *Il mar gira ne' fiumi*: here the poet (Stradella?) laments being in Venice far from his Roman beloved and makes a play on the word 'polo', saying that it is the attraction of this 'pole' which keeps him there.

From letters of a later date we know Stradella was quite settled in the city and had his tools for making music with him. For instance he spoke of having 'istromenti'[12] (perhaps the three lutes which were in his possession at the time of his death)[13] and 'libri', such as a leather-bound volume of arias and the 'sonetto' *Apre l'uomo infelice*.[14] As far as his acquaintances are concerned, in addition to Polo and Girolamo Michiel, he also knew 'Signora Maria Felice';[15] in fact, since Girolamo Michiel was later to send the music she had to Stradella, she could have been a noblewoman (perhaps even Girolamo's wife) who sang or had others sing the pieces. Girolamo would tell Stradella to send a letter about the shipment to 'Signore Iacomo Poleni' who lived in the area of the church of San Vitale.[16] Stradella's oft-mentioned contacts with the man could suggest that Stradella also lived at San Vitale, in Poleni's house or in the neighbourhood, during his months in Venice: this would have been near the Grand Canal opposite S. Maria della Carità, the present Galleria dell'Accademia. Another name which comes up in Stradella's correspondence is that of Signor Felice Pietogalli on the Rio S. Felice,[17] a street which comes in from the Canal Grande at the Palazzo Fontana not far from the Ca' d'Oro.

Any list of singers and instrumentalists Stradella could have known in Venice, even a very select one, would be exceedingly long; however, perhaps one name should be mentioned. On 13 February 1677 Lorenzo Valleroy wrote to Polo Michiel and told him to be careful of Stradella and not let him know of their correspondence about 'Nina'.[18] As Nina can be a diminutive of Antonia, it could be that the famous Roman singer Antonia Coresi was being discussed for Venetian roles now that women

[12] His letter to Polo Michiel dated Turin, 4 Sept. 1677 (I-Vmc, PD C. 1064, no. 429; no. 6 in App. 2a).

[13] These were given to his brother Stefano's daughters in 1686; see 'Stradella's Instruments and Early Collections of His Music', in Ch. 5 below.

[14] Books in general are mentioned in his letter from Turin of 4 Sept. 1677 (I-Vmc, PD C. 1064, no. 429; no. 6 in App. 2a), and specific musical works are named in his letter to Michiel dated Genoa, 30 Apr. 1678 (PD C. 1065, no. 218; no. 11 in App. 2a).

[15] She is named in Stradella's letters from Turin of 4 Sept. 1677 (I-Vmc, PD C. 1064, no. 429; no. 6 in App. 2a) and 30 Apr. 1678 (PD C. 1065, no. 218; no. 11 in App. 2a).

[16] He is named in letters from Turin of 4 Sept. 1677 (I-Vmc, PD C. 1064, no. 429; no. 6 in App. 2a) and 26 Nov. 1677 (PD C. 1065, no. 364; no. 8 in App. 2a). Stradella had another letter delivered to Poleni by Polo Michiel in Nov.–Dec. 1677 (see Stradella's letters from Turin dated 26 Nov. and 16 Dec. 1677 in PD C. 1064, nos. 364 and 317 respectively; nos. 8 and 9 in App. 2a).

[17] Letter dated Genoa, 8 Jan. 1678 (I-Vmc, PD C. 1065, no. 348; no. 10 in App. 2a).

[18] I-Vmc, PD C. 1064, no. 141. In some unclear way, Marcello Severoli was also involved.

could no longer perform on stage in the Papal State. Stradella would have known her as she and her husband, Nicola, had sung at the Tordinona and had been in the employ of Contestabile Colonna and Queen Christina; she would also sing in a Stradella opera in Genoa. But even if 'Nina' were indeed Antonia Coresi, the necessity for intrigue is not clear.

Another woman, however, was certainly in Stradella's life in Venice, and this was Agnese (or Agnesa, as Stradella always called her) Van Uffele,[19] the mistress of Alvise Contarini, a member of one of Venice's wealthiest and most powerful families.[20] It would have been easy for Stradella to have met the nobleman through the Michiel brothers[21] because politics and business affairs would naturally have brought these aristocrats of the uppermost rung of the Venetian social ladder (and all related to the Grimanis) in contact. Alvise Contarini asked the composer to teach his mistress music. Although versions of how it all happened are conflicting, the short of the matter is that, in June of the same year, Stradella and Agnese Van Uffele left Venice together, much to the displeasure of Contarini.

The Venetian first said he was upset because they had stolen 10,000 ducats from him, but this accusation was denied since he was talking about jewels of little value which he had given his mistress as gifts. From later developments, from Stradella's own behaviour, from Abate Olgiati's referring to the musician as being 'without brains' and as one who fell in love easily, one can conclude that Stradella had simply run off with

---

[19] Various sources for the Stradella–Van Uffele affair have been known and published for some time, the most fruitful being: documents in French archives in Paolino Richard, 'Stradella et les Contarini Episode des mœurs vénitiennes au XVIIᵉ siècle', *Le Ménestrel*, 32, no. 52 (26 Nov. 1865), 409–11; 33, no. 1 (3 Dec. 1865), 9–10; no. 2 (10 Dec. 1865), 1–3; no. 3 (17 Dec. 1865), 17–18; no. 4 (24 Dec. 1865), 25–26; no. 5 (31 Dec. 1865), 33–4; letters from Schalk, the Bavarian representative in Turin, in Alfred Einstein, 'Ein Bericht über den Turiner Mordanfall auf Alessandro Stradella', *Festschrift zum 50. Geburtstag Adolf Sandberger* (Munich, 1918), 135–7; the report of the Savoy minister De L'Escheraine in Andrea Della Corte, 'La forza d'amor paterno di Alessandro Stradella', *Musica d'oggi*, 13 (1931), 395–6; letters of Matteo del Teglia, Florentine ambassador to Venice, in Giuseppe Baccini, 'Il Maestro Stradella', *Giornale di erudizione*, 3 (1890–1), 277–9. However, neither singly nor together do these sources tell the whole story (for example, the name of the young woman is not mentioned in any of them).

[20] Among their members the Contarini had more than one 'Alvise' (the Venetian form of Luigi or Aluigi, as Stradella always called him in his letters): Emmanuele Antonio Cicogna, *Delle inscrizioni veneziane* (Venice, 1824–53), lists 16 Alvise Contarini; and in I-Vas, Miscellanea, Codici, I, St. Veneta, 18: M. Barbaro and A. Tasca, 'Arbori de' patritii veneti', there are 4. One Alvise was ambassador to the principal courts of Europe and Constantinople in the first half of the century, and another was Doge in 1676. But perhaps Stradella's Alvise was the one born on 19 May 1636, who married Bianca Mocenigo in 1679, had three children (the first, Piero, born in 1682), and who seems to have been a *procuratore* or legal administrator (a letter in I-Rvat, Barb. lat. 6449, dated 6 Aug. 1672, is from Pietro Mocenigo (a relative of Bianca's?) to 'Sig.r Cav.re Procuratore Alvise Contarini'). Or perhaps he was the Alvise born on 23 Oct. 1662 to Lazzaro Contarini and Elizabetta Tiepolo, who took charge of a castle in Verona in 1681, wrote poetry (manuscripts are dated 1681 and 1687) and an unpublished history of Venice in 1687, and died on 17 Aug. 1690 (Cicogna, *Delle inscrizioni veneziane*, iii. 316–17 and v. 674–5).

[21] Cecilia Contarini had written one of them love letters in 1671–2 (I-Vmc, PD C. 1058, 1059).

Contarini's mistress and the Venetian meant to have such impertinent behaviour punished. Although probably not the whole truth, it is interesting, and revealing, to read Stradella's own account of the affair in a letter he wrote to Polo Michiel on 21 August 1677[22] and to realize that, in spite of his compromising position, he was brash enough to ask Michiel to provide him with character references.[23] The surprising thing is that Michiel did, which is yet another confirmation that, with all his defects, Stradella was liked personally and appreciated professionally.

Stradella's choice of the Savoyard court as his refuge was not strange. Duke Carlo Emanuele II had died in 1675, and in 1677 the usual two years of mourning were up and theatrical entertainments were resumed.[24] As his widow, Maria Giovanna, would need musicians for her rather depleted cappella, instrumentalists and singers had been arriving in Turin during the past year in the hope of being hired. Generally this was done after performing for Maria Giovanna at court: if she approved a salary would be offered (generally a low one), which could be accepted or not; if she did not approve, only a single monetary gift was given. One such new arrival was the soprano castrato Marchetto Godia, a singer whom Stradella knew from Rome:[25] it is very possible that he had written to Stradella in Venice, encouraging him to join him and try his fortune there, too. Another arrival from Rome was Count d'Alibert, unemployed since the closing of the Tordinona. His frequent correspondence with Carlo Emanuele II had earlier led him to hope for the position of manager of the Turin court theatre, the only one the city had to offer, but the death of the duke frustrated his plan. Now, however, two Savoy diplomats in Rome, Orazio Provana and Paolo Negri, recommended him highly to Turin and after some objections were removed d'Alibert was asked to produce the court entertainment of 5 December at which Christmas gifts were distributed, the *Zapato*. When he arrived in Turin, Stradella was

---

[22] I-Vmc, PD C. 1064, no. 263; no. 4 in App. 2*a*.

[23] A letter by Agnese Van Uffele to Polo Michiel, asking him to comply with the request of 'Signor Alessandro' and send the needed letters, is in I-Vmc, PD C. 1054, no. 269. It seems to be dated 'Turino, li [blank space] agosto 1661', an error—since there is no evidence to suggest that Stradella and Agnese knew one another in 1661, that Stradella knew Michiel in 1661, or that Stradella would have urgently required letters in that year—and one not easily explained, except by suggesting that the ill-educated girl simply forgot to add the horizontal crossing of the final number '1' to make it a '7'.

[24] Information on the general state of musical affairs in Turin (including facts about D'Alibert and Godia) is taken from Mercedes Viale Ferrero, 'Alessandro Stradella a Torino', in Carolyn Gianturco and Giancarlo Rostirolla (eds.), *Atti del Convegno di Studi 'Alessandro Stradella e il suo tempo', Siena, 8–12 settembre 1982*, Chigiana, 39, NS 19 (1988), 35–68; she published the same material in 'Stradella a Torino (1677)'.

[25] In fact he had been in Turin since Dec. 1676, had been hired with an excellent salary of 2,812 lire a year, and even had his rent in Via Bellezia (which no longer exists, but which was between the present Via S. Chiara and Via S. Domenico) paid by the court.

already there: perhaps d'Alibert had suggested the composer join him; certainly he expected to have Stradella's collaboration on the *Zapato*.

Less than a month later (between 23 and 29 July), though, Alvise Contarini arrived in Turin and all Stradella's plans for a career in the employ of Maria Giovanna were to be shattered.[26] Contarini travelled in the company of Fabio Gradenigo, a friend from Vicenza, and three or four others. Once in Turin he sought out the two fugitives, but Agnese Van Uffele had taken refuge in the convent of S. Maria Maddalena (founded in 1633 for 'lost sheep'; although it no longer exists, it was situated on what is today the crossing between Via XX Settembre and Via Arcivescovado), and Stradella in that of San Domenico (still in Via S. Domenico). Although Contarini paid his respects to Maria Giovanna, she wrote afterwards that he did not speak to her of the affair;[27] instead it was to Archbishop Michele Beggiamo that he insisted that the girl either marry Stradella or take the veil. At this point, the end of July, Contarini left and pressure began to be applied on the composer to marry Agnese. Although he could not visit her, Stradella was allowed to send her necessities and music; at the beginning of August he sent her a cantata which was actually a letter, but the *badessa* discovered the trick. Not only the story but the music itself made its way to Polo Michiel through his 'informer' Recaldini,[28] a Venetian merchant who traded with Turin and was therefore in a position to know what was going on. He was also in the employ of Alvise Contarini and, hence, the same information made its way to the rejected lover as well.

According to Recaldini, Agnese expected money owed her from Contarini. She was also anxious to leave the convent and get married. Stradella, once Contarini left, was allowed to go about freely, but evidently Maria Giovanna did not want to be associated with someone who could strain her relations with Venice. She wrote, for example, that on the occasion of 'une grande devotion' at the church of San Domenico (in which convent Stradella had run for refuge) she had wanted to attend the *Salut*, but upon hearing that Stradella had composed some motets for the service, decided not to go because of his treatment of the girl, the intrigue, and the embarrassment. This 'great devotion' could have been

---

[26] Many important details on the following developments are found in a series of letters from Recaldini, a Venetian merchant in Turin, to Polo Michiel beginning on 23 July 1677 (I-Vmc, PD C. 1064, no. 280).

[27] Other pertinent details are from a draft of an exceedingly long letter explaining the whole Stradella affair written by Maria Giovanna to the Marquis of San Maurizio, Chabo (now in I-Tas, Sezione Corte, Registro lettere Corte, vol. 51, 1677, 'Stradella'); Viale Ferrero, 'Stradella a Torino', has the whole text on pp. 61–8.

[28] I-Vmc, PD C. 1064, no. 189, dated 6 Aug. 1677; unfortunately the music is no longer with the letter.

the feast either of St Dominic, celebrated on 4 August, or of the Assumption of the Blessed Virgin Mary, celebrated on 15 August.[29]

On 20 August Recaldini wrote to Michiel that Stradella went about trying to change local opinion of him but that Maria Giovanna still thought him 'of little moral worth'.[30] There was also a rumour that Contarini would pay the girl something, and he wrote four letters urging the Archbishop to get her to marry Stradella.[31] The next day was when Stradella asked Michiel for letters of recommendation to the court.[32] On 24 August Stradella wrote to Michiel again repeating the request for help, and saying he was enclosing a letter (now lost but no doubt in the same tone) from Agnese.[33] He says he is on good terms with some 'ladies', a worrying comment in his circumstances; he also asks Michiel to put in a good word for him with Alvise Contarini, a sign that he is feeling the pinch of the Venetian's attitude and perhaps regretting his foolish behaviour.

Towards the end of August, Olgiati again wrote to Michiel about the Saliti libretto Stradella was to set to music.[34] He informs him that, as the work is to be presented in Venice, 'new, short, and amusing arias' have been written to suit local taste; he has also asked Stradella to send on the score. When Stradella wrote to Michiel on 11 September[35] pledging to compose whatever music his patron wanted, it would seem he was responding to a specific request, perhaps to do the opera. Amazingly, in view of the scandal involving Michiel's friends, the Venetian continued to ask music of Stradella; furthermore, he sent him a letter of recommendation to one Marquis Parella.

Throughout, one is at a loss how to evaluate the affair: Stradella's running off with a woman 'belonging' to a Contarini was, of course, stupid; however, since she was only a mistress and not a proper fiancée, perhaps acquaintances of both parties felt that Contarini was over-reacting. Quite tellingly, Stradella never lost a friend or patron (except Contarini) over the matter.

---

[29] The order of the *Salut* (or *Salve*, from *Salve Regina*) service is given in Viale Ferrero, 'Stradella a Torino', 44 n. 32. Of Stradella's extant works, three are suitable Marian motets: *Dixit angelis suis iratus Deus* (for which he wrote the words himself), *In tribulationibus, in angustiis*, and *Sistite sidera, coeli motus otiamini*.

[30] I-Vmc, PD C. 1064, no. 261. His statement there that Stradella was beginning to make his musical talents known probably refers to the service at S. Domenico; however it is also possible that Stradella composed his oratorio *Santa Pelagia* for Turin, since the city boasted an order of Augustinian nuns dedicated to her, a supposition further supported by the scoring of 2 violins, viola, and continuo, typical of Turinese music and not found in any other of his works.

[31] Communicated privately to me by Mercedes Viale Ferrero.

[32] The same day Olgiati wrote to Michiel saying that he, too, had had an explanatory letter from Stradella who was trying to hide what he had done from his friends by telling 'many lies'. Disillusioned or not, Olgiati asked Michiel to send him all other news of the composer (I-Vmc, PD C. 1064, no. 276).

[33] I-Vmc, PD C. 1064, no. 262; no. 5 in App. 2*a*.   [34] PD C. 1064, no. 265.

[35] PD C. 1064, no. 288; no. 7 in App. 2*a*.

During the rest of September Stradella continued to gain favour in Turin. On the 3rd Recaldini wrote to Polo Michiel of a rumour that finally Maria Giovanna wanted to hear Stradella, although from the remark it is not clear whether it is as a performer or composer.[36] On the 4th Olgiati let Michiel know that the Stradella affair had reached Rome.[37] The version recounted there was more or less what the composer himself wrote. Olgiati wondered (rather naïvely, as a good friend) whether Stradella might not be innocent after all. On the same day Stradella wrote to Girolamo Michiel[38] letting him know he had received the Venetian's two previous letters (of 22 and 28 August), further proof that he was never out of the Michiels' good graces. The Turinesi are saying Stradella is a 'gran virtuoso' according to Recaldini, but as Maria Giovanna has not heard him, Stradella must have performed (perhaps as a singer or a lutenist) elsewhere, in a church or in some aristocrat's salon.[39] On 25 September Olgiati wrote to Michiel about Saliti's 'opera teatrale', saying Stradella had now agreed to give it to someone in Turin (probably Recaldini) who would forward it to Michiel, and he could see and hear it for himself and decide whether to sponsor its production in Carnival. (Unfortunately, Olgiati never gives the title or subject of the opera.)[40]

On 8 October Recaldini continued to keep Michiel informed.[41] Apparently Stradella finally agreed to marry Agnese Van Uffele; once wedded, Contarini would send on the girl's belongings, as well as writing a letter to Monsieur Grémonville in which he would pardon Stradella and recommend him to Maria Giovanna. Agnese's comment was that Contarini had always promised to be generous to her if she ever married. With the prospect of receiving 500 lire from him, she and Stradella were having meals together in great 'allegria'. However, all of these festivities came to an abrupt halt as an *avviso* from Turin to Rome related with the following lines:

Sunday evening [10 October] Alessandro Stradella, *Musico Romano*, was assaulted by two outsiders [*forestieri*], and they dealt him several knife wounds, leaving him on the ground for dead, and being brought into the *Palazzo* of S. Giovanni, orders were immediately given by Madama Reale [Maria Giovanna] to bring him to the rooms he has in the Convent of San Domenico, and therefore a rigorous search is being made to find the emissaries.[42]

[36] PD C. 1064, no. 260.   [37] PD C. 1064, no. 310.

[38] PD C. 1064, no. 429; no. 6 in App. 2a.

[39] PD C. 1064, no. 306. During the same month, Goffredo Marino was in Turin (Armando Fabio Ivaldi, 'Teatro e società genovese al tempo di Alessandro Stradella', in Carolyn Gianturco and Giancarlo Rostirolla (eds.), *Atti del Convegno di studi 'Alessandro Stradella e il suo tempo'*, Siena, 8–12 settembre 1982, Chigiana, 39, NS 19 (1988), 460), and since he later sent Stradella's music to Francesco II d'Este, he may have become acquainted with the composer and his music during this trip.

[40] PD C. 1064, no. 299.   [41] PD C. 1064, no. 106.

[42] I-Rvat, Avvisi, Barb. lat. 6383 dated Turin, 15 Oct. 1677. This source confirms where Stradella lived.

From Maria Giovanna one learns further details, some contrasting and probably more correct.[43] On the particular Sunday Stradella was at the Convent of S. Maria Maddalena, where, having been given certain guarantees by Contarini and the girl's father, he had signed a contract to marry Agnese with her father as witness. When Signor Van Uffele tarried, Stradella left on his own. He walked away from the convent in the direction of the Church of San Carlo where, having arrived at its side door, he was attacked from behind by two thugs. According to Maria Giovanna he was not knifed but given a powerful blow on the head, and two more as he lay on the ground, after which he was left for dead. The henchmen then escaped to the palace of the French ambassador, the Marquis de Villars, where they presented him with a letter from the French ambassador to Venice, Abbé d'Estrades, and were given asylum.[44]

Holding him responsible at least in part, Maria Giovanna put Van Uffele père in the citadel and began diplomatic proceedings intended to show her outrage at the affront by 'foreign' powers in her territory; she objected particularly to the French offer of asylum to those whom she considered her prisoners. Naturally such an international episode was transmitted immediately by the various court representatives.[45] On 12 October de Villars wrote to Arnault de Pomponne, Minister of Foreign Affairs, in Paris with his version in which he affirmed Contarini to have sent the *bravi*.[46] Strangely, Stradella is unnamed and said to be simply one of Contarini's house musicians. Probably true, however, is the statement that Contarini had asked de Villars specifically not to let Stradella escape by way of Pignerol, known to be the easiest route into French territory. Thereafter de Villars claims he was simply a victim of circumstance in this unfortunate episode. On 16 October Johann Bartholomäus Schalck, the Bavarian representative at Turin, reported the affair to Munich specifying that the attack had been made between 5 and 6 p.m., that it was generally known that the mandate had come from Contarini, and that Maria Giovanna was going to write to Louis XIV about the disreputable behaviour of his ambassadors.

From now on, in fact, Stradella as a 'person' disappears from the enormous ensuing correspondence which involved relations between France

---

[43] The draft of her letter in I-Tas, Sezione corte, Registro lettere corte, vol. 51, 1677.

[44] The letter (pub. in Richard, 'Stradella et les Contarini', 32, no. 52 (26 Nov. 1865), 411) makes it clear that the thugs had been in Turin at least since the beginning of September, awaiting their chance. Moreover, d'Estrades affirms that their job was just to 'maltraiter' Stradella in Piazza San Carlo. The French Embassy presently houses the Whist-Accademia Filarmonica.

[45] Another telling of the story may be read in an *avviso* dated Venice, 30 Oct. 1677 in I-Fas, Mediceo del Principato, 3039; a summary appears in the *avviso* sent from Munich to Rome, 30 Oct. 1677 in D-Mbs, Cod. Ital. 192, fo. 659ʳ.

[46] Richard, 'Stradella et les Contarini', 32, no. 52 (26 Nov. 1865), 409–10. It is in this letter that de Villars says Contarini had come to Turin earlier with 41 men in his entourage, a number oft-repeated in accounts of the affair but highly unlikely for business of such small consequence.

and Savoy and, instead, the Stradella 'affair' takes over and, in fact, is used to resolve another ticklish situation between the two courts.[47] Sometime prior to the present problem a Turin state official had been stopped at the border near Avanchy by the French who claimed he was in their territory, in contradiction to Marquis Chabo's affirmation that he was in Savoy. The same minister hoped that now, by exaggerating Turin's offence at the French ambassador's behaviour, he could obtain the official's release—which in fact he did, but only at the price of Maria Giovanna losing face, since the Marquis de Villars, his wife, and son left Turin for Pignerol hiding the two *sicari* in their carriage, a ruse carried out in daytime and in full view of her guards.[48] She soon seems to have regained her composure, however, and de Villars was allowed to return, but Maria Giovanna's anger was not abated and she contrived to have him replaced, if only by another figure in the scandal, Abbé d'Estrades.[49]

On 13 November the Florentine representative in Venice wrote to his court that Contarini had managed to get permission from the Consiglio di Dieci to go around Venice with armed men:[50] he obviously felt he was in danger of retaliation for his act. He had no reason to fear Stradella, however, who was concerned mainly to quieten things down as quickly as possible. In fact, by 5 November Stradella was back to normal. According to Recaldini[51] he was staying with Marchetto Godia, and through the intercession of a friend from Rome, Cardinal d'Estrées (brother to the French ambassador to Rome), had even returned to court. Another one who gave a hand in smoothing things out was Abate Vincenzo Grimani, Contarini's relative who was often in Turin for political or theatrical reasons and whose presence, therefore, was not thought exceptional although his role now was rather particular. It was due to him, for example, that Signor Van Uffele and someone called Bernardini obviously also involved were released from prison.

Since the Grimani were theatre people,[52] he was also quite interested in preparations for the *Zapato* for which Stradella had been asked to compose music. Understandably, though, this was not to be. As Stradella

---

[47] See Richard, 'Stradella et les Contarini', 33, no. 2 (10 Dec. 1865), 1–3 for a letter from Louis XIV to the Marquis de Villars in which his careful diplomacy reveals him wanting to stay on good terms with Maria Giovanna (he would soon send Cardinal d'Estrées to her asking permission to march French troops through Savoy in his war against Milan) and yet not wanting to condemn too strongly his minister's aid to a member of the powerful Contarini family.

[48] Pertinent to the bargaining between the two courts and the attackers' escape are the letters between San Maurizio, San Tommaso, and Maria Giovanna in I-Tas, Sezione corte, Lettere ministri Francia, mazzo 105: no. 257, 23 Oct.; no. 266, 6 Nov.; no. 297, 18 Dec.; ibid., Registro lettere corte, vol. 51, (1677), Maria Giovanna's drafts dated 13, 14, 28 Oct., and 6 Nov. 1677.

[49] I-Tas, Lettere ministri Francia, mazzo 105, no. 297, 18 Dec. 1677. See also I-Rvat, Barb. lat. 6383, *avviso* dated 5 Nov. 1677.

[50] I-Fas, Mediceo del Principato, 3039.   [51] I-Vmc, PD C. 1064, no. 343.

[52] Their new opera theatre, S. Giovanni Crisostomo, was soon to open with *Vespasiano* by Pallavicino which d'Alibert would see and try unsuccessfully to put on in Turin.

wrote on 26 November to Polo Michiel, due to his 'mishaps'—a rather mild way of defining an international affair which had almost cost him his life—Giovanni Carisio's music would be heard instead.[53] When he wrote to Michiel again on 16 December, he said it had had Italian, French, and Spanish scenes (probably Lalouette's was the French music heard) and that Maria Giovanna had enjoyed it.[54]

Stradella also announced that he was off to Genoa for Carnival, invited there by some *cavalieri*. Given the situation, things had been resolved rather satisfactorily in Turin. He was well, he felt that Contarini would now leave him alone,[55] and he knew Maria Giovanna and the Princess (probably Ludovica, sister to Carlo Emanuele II) were receptive to him. True, his fine opportunity of serving the court had been lost (although perhaps at least his *Se del pianeta ardente* had been heard as a prologue to the *Zapato*),[56] but he now had another attractive offer on the horizon and was anxious to be off, asking again for his belongings which had been left behind in Venice.[57]

It should be noted that in these two news-filled letters of 26 November and 16 December Stradella made no mention of Agnese Van Uffele, nor was he ever to mention her again. Had it really been a one-sided affair, as he implied from the beginning? Had it only been safety and money which encouraged him to agree to the marriage? Together with these unresolved doubts are also one's questions about the girl herself. It would seem she was an *amante* and something of a musician, but this is all we know of Agnese; she may even have decided to stay on in S. Maria Maddalena as one of their 'lost sheep', a fate impossible to verify given the loss of the convent's records.

[53] I-Vmc, PD C. 1064, no. 364; no. 8 in App. 2a. In Feb. 1678 Carisio was made court composer of Turin, quite likely a position originally indended for Stradella.

[54] PD C. 1064, no. 317; no. 9 in App. 2a.

[55] Unfortunately Stradella does not explain what has transpired between him and Contarini to resolve their differences.

[56] Suggested by Viale Ferrero, 'Stradella a Torino', 52–4, who believes, moreover, that the text for this work as well as for his *Sciogliete in dolci nodi*, which also praises Maria Giovanna, could have been by Bernardino Bianco (or Bianchi), Secretary of Ceremonies to the Savoy court.

[57] Together with his letter of request dated 26 Nov. to Michiel (I-Vmc, PD C. 1064, no. 364; no. 8 in App. 2a), he included one to Iacomo Poleni in San Vitale.

4

Genoa

The Citty [of Genoa] is built in the hollow, or boosome of a Mountaine, whose ascent is very steepe, high and rocky; so as from the Lanterne, and Mole, to the hill it represents the Shape of a Theater; the Streets and buildings so ranged one above the other; as our seates are in Playhouses: but by reason of their incomparable materials, beauty and structure: never was any artificial sceane more beautifull to the eye of the beholder; nor is any place certainely in the World, so full for the bignesse of well designed and stately Palaces.[1]

In 1668, some 20 years after John Evelyn wrote these words, Count Galeazzo Gualdo Priorato offered his own equally enthusiastic description of Genoa and added that:

Every sort of great armada is able to fit into this port, and for maximum security from hostile attempts at the feet of the very beautiful buildings which adorn it all around, there is a strong well-guarded wall, equipped with a quantity of artillery.[2]

Later writers remarked on Genoa's particular republican form of government:

In Genoa the nobility is the state; state and nobility are nothing but two aspects of the same thing; moreover the history of the nobility of Genoa is the real history of the Republic of Genoa . . .[3]

Although he did not mention the unusual setting of the city, its beauties, or its government when he wrote to Polo Michiel on 8 January 1678, Stradella was sufficiently settled in Genoa by that date to be able to discuss his own situation.[4] He had arrived the week before 'safe and sound' and, while various nobles offered to house him, he had chosen to stay with Franco Lercaro. After boasting that he was much fêted by all the ladies and knights, he went on to report the opera news which he knew Michiel was always ready to hear. He also said that he had taken charge of the orchestra (which could mean either at the harpsichord or as leader of the violins) and given some help to the female singers, asked to do so, in fact, by two of the first ladies of the city. Three of the women singers

[1] Evelyn, *Diary*, ed. Bowle, 65.

[2] Galeazzo Gualdo Priorato, *Relazione della città di Genova, e suo dominio* (Cologne, 1668), 1–2.

[3] Girolamo F. De Ferrari, 'Storia della nobiltà di Genoa', *Giornale araldico genealogico, diplomatico*, 25 (1897), 25.

[4] I-Vmc, PD C. 1065, no. 348; no. 10 in App. 2*a*.

(although not necessarily those who needed help) were 'Centoventi', 'la Riminese', and 'Antonia', with Centoventi the most applauded.[5]

The theatre which housed opera was the Teatro Falcone, opened some years before by the Durazzo family on the site of an inn, the Hostaria Falconis. At present the theatre was managed by a group of nobles—Giuseppe Maria Garibaldi, Giovanni Niccolò Spinola, Domenico Doria, and Giovanni Carlo Imperiale Lercaro (the latter perhaps financed by Stradella's host)—who were renting it from the Adorno family for nine years with the obligation, imposed by the government, to give one evening's profits to the poor each season.[6]

It is not known exactly how Stradella had come to know his host Franco Maria Imperiale Lercaro, although as an honorary 'gentleman' of the Vatican since 1677, Lercaro would often have been in Rome and in contact with the musician's patrons. As a matter of fact, there were various Roman connections for Stradella to rely upon in Genoa. Foremost among these were the two Pamphili sisters, Anna Teresa (b. 1652), married to Giovanni Andrea Doria (for whose wedding celebrations Stradella had composed a serenata), and Flaminia, Princess of Venafro (b. 1651), soon to be married to Nicolò Pallavicino, Prince of Civitella.[7] This young man was a nephew of Cardinal Pallavicino whose niece, Maria, married Giovanni Battista Rospigliosi (Duke of Zagarola and nephew of Pope Clement IX). Lavinia Lante, daughter of Ippolito, was also in Genoa, married to Filippo Marino (a relative of Goffredo Marino, who would later send a score of Stradella's to Francesco II of Modena). While he renewed Roman acquaintances, Stradella was himself being remembered in the city of the Pope.[8] Settimio Olgiati continued to mention him in his letters to Michiel in connection with the Saliti opera;[9] unfortunately, on 1 April Olgiati had to confess that the 'already composed' Stradella score had not yet arrived,[10] and therefore Saliti had been obliged to begin another libretto.

By 30 April Stradella had decided to stay on in Genoa and he wrote to

---

[5] More information on these and other singers in Genoa will be given further on.

[6] For information on the Teatro Falcone see: Luigi T. Belgrano, 'Delle feste e dei giuochi dei Genovesi', *Archivio storico italiano*, 3rd ser., 15 (1871), 442; Claudio Bertieri, 'Genoa', *Enciclopedia dello Spettacolo*, v (Florence and Rome, 1958), col. 1041; Armando Fabio Ivaldi, 'Gli Adorno e l'hostaria–teatro del Falcone di Genova (1600–1680)', *Rivista italiana di musicologia*, 15 (1980), 87–152, and 'Teatro'.

[7] Dates of birth are from Ignazio Adami, *I secoli delle principesse di bellezza impareggiabile o vero i periodi delle influenze celesti* (Amsterdam, 1692), where it is also said that the sisters were incomparably beautiful, especially Flaminia.

[8] I-Fas, Mediceo del Principato, 3658, *avviso* of 9 Feb. 1678 mentions a performance of *Il Girello* with Acciaiuoli's marionettes for the Princess of Sonnino, and it may have had Stradella's prologue.

[9] I-Vmc, PD C. 1065, no. 385 of 25 Feb. and no. 400 of 12 Mar. A letter from Saliti to Michiel about the opera, undated but written in Mar. 1678, is no. 282 in the same file.

[10] PD C. 1065, no. 377.

Polo Michiel, giving his reasons for doing so.[11] After having received various proofs of his talents, a group of nobles had drawn up a contract in which they agreed to pay him 100 Spanish doubloons a year just so he would stay in Genoa; they would also provide him with a house, food, and a servant. Moreover, he was not obliged to do anything in return. Understandably, he accepted such a flattering and economically attractive arrangement from these Genoese, who one suspects were the management of the Teatro Falcone. He also had six noble ladies as pupils, and was well paid by them. Moreover, there were opportunities for him to do both chamber and church music in Genoa, and the coming season of the Teatro Falcone had been put into his hands (indicating that he had met with more favour than Lonati).

As a matter of fact, now that he was acting as impresario, he had already begun to think of the programme and wanted to do Sartorio's *Seleuco*, but he needed to know from Michiel if it had been a success in Venice and what sort of voices were required. He also asked Michiel to have his brother Girolamo send him some music he had left in Venice. He added that Prince and Princess Doria were extremely kind to him and showered him with favours and gifts, confirmation that both his Roman and Venetian–Turinese scandals had been forgiven if not forgotten.[12]

On 11 June Stradella again wrote to Michiel, this time thanking him for his request for music which the composer is happy to provide.[13] He will send on some of his own *canzoni* but isn't sure about works by others (as Michiel desired) except Lonati, the reason being that Genoa did not itself produce great composers and there were no other outsiders. If Michiel can wait, he will write to friends in Rome for their canzonas. However, he would like to know whether they are to be 'ariettas, or chamber cantatas' and whether they are to be 'long, bizarre, or even sad', and for what sort of voice and range. As far as the sonatas Michiel wants are concerned, he needs to know whether they are to be 'sonatas for harpsichord, organ, lute, harp, violins in two or three parts, or string concerti grossi'. At the end of these attempts at clarifying Michiel's desires, Stradella again asked that Girolamo send him his music.

On 18 June the composer sent three of his canzonas, each one different and of different length.[14] He repeated that he would ask Lonati for some-

---

[11] PD C. 1065, no. 218; no. 11 in App. 2*a*.

[12] In a letter Princess Anna Pamphili Doria wrote to Cardinal Flavio Chigi, dated Genoa, 29 Apr. 1679 (I-Rvat, Archivio Chigi, 22, fo. 629[r–v]), one reads: 'the Muses stay little in this city, neither are there academies; hence, I desire that Your Excellency favour me with an operetta, or rather accademia by Sig. Apolloni along the lines of the enclosed note [missing] to set to music'. It is very possible that whatever poetic text was sent her, she had it set by Stradella. Her evaluation of the lack of culture in Genoa corroborates Stradella's description (see his letter in I-Vmc, PD C. 1065, no. 260; no. 12 in App.2*a*).

[13] Ibid.

[14] I-Vmc, PD C. 1065, no. 260 *bis*; no. 13 in App. 2*a*.

thing, too, but at the moment his friend was in Milan. In any event he would send more of his own music the following week, and would keep doing so until Michiel would let him know he had enough, a remark obviously intended to show his respect and gratitude to the nobleman. Stradella kept his word, and on 2 July he wrote again[15] saying that he was glad that the first three *canzoni* had arrived and that he expected that five others had come in the mean time. He awaited more specific details before continuing to compose.

On 10 November 1678 Stradella's opera *La forza dell'amor paterno* was presented at the Teatro Falcone.[16] Stradella himself wrote the dedication in the libretto to Teresa Raggi Saoli on the occasion of the marriage of her son.[17] The composer says that he is 'without any attachment of servitude' to her but nevertheless seeks 'the beneficence' of her 'rays' (a play on *raggi*). The lines addressed 'To the Reader' are by someone else, who praised the composer in the following terms: 'Let it suffice to say that the concert of such perfect melody is the effort of an Alessandro, that is Signor Stradella, well known without contradiction as the first Apollo of music.'[18] On 1 January 1679 the second of Stradella's operas opened. *Le gare dell'amor eroico* was dedicated by Stradella to Bianca Maria Spinola, apparently the patroness of his opera, on the occasion of her marriage into the Fieschi family.[19] Also in January Don Gaspare Altieri arrived in Genoa, probably wanting to hear Stradella's opera.[20]

Then on 27 January Stradella wrote to Michiel with all sorts of news of the theatre.[21] First, though, he explained that he had been very busy because of the operas and other music (presumably Christmas sacred music), and had not been well around the holidays and so had had to slow down. He then went on to recount his successes. Not only had *La forza* been put on 15 times but, after the first act, sonnets praising him were thrown down from the boxes (Stradella included two for Michiel to see but they are now lost) and his patron-*cavalieri* had given several of them to him publicly on a solid gold tray, which he says is worth more than what he will be paid for the entire season. *Le gare*, too, had been a great success; in fact at times it had been impossible to continue the performance due to 'the noise of the applause'. His work was not over, either, because on either Monday or Tuesday, 30 or 31 January, another of his

---

[15] PD C. 1065, no. 143; no. 14 in App. 2*a*.

[16] PD C. 1066, no. 577, Stradella's letter of 27 Jan. 1679; no. 15 in App. 2*a*.

[17] It was not unusual for an opera in the Genoese public theatre to celebrate a private occasion. For Stradella's dedication, see no. 1 in App. 2*b*.

[18] What is probably Burney's copy of the libretto is now in GB-Lbl.

[19] See the libretto in I-Nc, Rari, 10.1.4(2). For Stradella's dedication see no. 2 in App. 2*b*.

[20] I-Fas, Mediceo del Principato, 2839, *avviso* of 6 Jan. 1679. On 21 Jan. Olgiati wrote to Michiel asking for the 'operas' and 'arias', and one is curious to know if he means those by Stradella: see I-Vmc, PD C. 1066, no. 576.

[21] I-Vmc, PD C. 1066, no. 577; no. 15 in App. 2*a*.

operas would be presented at the Falcone. *Il Trespolo tutore*, he explains, 'is a comic opera but most beautiful', noting that 'here they delight in comic things'.

Therefore, because of his three new operas, his pupils (now including 'cavalieri' as well as 'dame'), church music, and other duties, he has been very busy. Unfortunately, Stradella does not name his pupils, nor does he indicate what 'feste di chiese' occupied him or in which churches; moreover, his other 'duties' also remain vague. However, he does give Michiel a great deal of specific information about singers at the Teatro Falcone, thus offering us some insight into the composer's way of judging opera performers.

Before closing Stradella again mentioned the kindness of Prince and Princess Doria who 'shower him with kindnesses'. A sign of approval from abroad was Girolamo Pignani's inclusion of three of Stradella's vocal compositions in *Scielta di canzonette italiane de più autori* published by Godbid and Playford: *Care labbra che d'amore* and two pieces from *Il Biante*, 'Non sa mai Amor ferir' and 'So ben che mi saettano'. From another point of view, the year 1679 was unfavourable. Filippo Casoni in his account of Genoa says that, in fact, there was a terrible epidemic which took many people's lives, both rich and poor, and especially the young.[22] Stradella, too, was ill with fever, as he wrote to Michiel on 25 March,[23] and although the fever had left him, he continued to feel unwell occasionally.[24]

However, by his letter of 2 May[25] he had resumed activity and was able to send more music to Venice ('ariette' is written in the margin of his letter). After other comments on music, he goes on to say that 22 Dutch ships had arrived full of grain and spices and that many Genoese had left for Messina with goods which they hoped to sell in exchange for silk. Strange as these remarks are for him, it could be that being impresario of a theatre had made him aware that only men who were well off financially could sponsor music.

Only a few days later, on 12 May, Stradella wrote to Michiel[26] to say that he will send the requested motet. He would have sent it already had Michiel told him the range of the singer who was to perform it. He also promises that it will be a new and exclusive work. In the mean time he begs his patron to request something more important than this 'bagatella'. Unfortunately, on 2 June Stradella had to write that he had not composed

[22] I-Rn, Fondo Vittorio Emanuele, 899, 'Annali di Genova del secolo decimo settimo descritti da Filippo Casoni e riformati da Gio. Benedetti Gritta gentiluomini genovesi anno MDCC. Genova', p. 809.
[23] I-Vmc, PD C. 1066, no. 205; no. 16 in App. 2a.
[24] PD C. 1066, no. 201, letter dated 2 June 1679; no. 19 in App. 2a.
[25] PD C. 1066, no. 252; no. 17 in App. 2a.   [26] PD C. 1066, no. 207; no. 18 in App. 2a.

anything because he had not been well;[27] but on 10 June, even though he was still unwell, he managed to send off the (unfortunately unidentified) piece.[28] At the end of his letter Stradella asks Michiel for other requests which must have been forthcoming since on 26 June he sent Michiel five more compositions of various sorts[29] and says he will send a sonata in the next mail. He will also get Lonati to send some music. On 3 August Isabella Casa Sagia (?) wrote to Polo Michiel from Mantua asking if he could have the enclosed motet text set by some good composer: she wanted to have it performed by a soprano in Santa Redegonda in Milan.[30] It is always possible that Michiel also asked Stradella to fulfil requests such as these which came from his aristocratic friends.

Given later developments, it would be worth while to describe the social environment in which Stradella lived. During his stay in Genoa there were three doges—Giannettino Odone, Agostino Spinola, and Luca Maria Ivrea (Francesco Lercaro would be elected the year after the composer's death)—and they were all, together with the Senate, concerned with the morality of the city. For example, Genoa's nobility gambled a great deal and at such high stakes that they often ruined their families,[31] and therefore the government tried to control them. From time to time state rules of behaviour were also published. One such *prammatica* dated 25 October 1680, which was to be in effect until the end of 1683, discussed clothing in great detail.[32] Dressmakers had to have their designs approved and afterwards were not to make any changes. Going about the city, women were to be dressed in black and could have no more than three servants, whose dress was also stipulated. In like fashion, dress for men and their servants and the furnishing of carriages was decreed. Jewellery was to be simple and wigs were not to be ostentatious. (The hairdresser known as 'il Romano' was often brought to task for inventing new and extravagant styles.)[33] To ensure the enforcement of the *prammatica*, various fines and punishments including imprisonment had been devised.

The state exacted such strict behaviour from the nobility in order to keep the very poor lower class free from envy and discontent. In short, modesty was necessary for political reasons. What is surprising, though, is that many Genoese joined the state in shaking a finger at wrongdoers and wrote anonymous letters informing the government of the misbehaviour of others. At the same time their efforts did not stop crime, as Evelyn noted:

Indeed this beautiful city is more stained with such horrid acts of revenge and murders, than any one place in Europe, or haply the world, where there is a

---

[27] PD C. 1066, no. 201; no. 19 in App. 2*a*.
[28] PD C. 1066, no. 190; no. 20 in App. 2*a*.
[29] PD C. 1066, no. 251; no. 21 in App. 2*a*.
[30] PD C. 1066, no. 517.
[31] Various unnumbered documents in I-Gas, Archivio segreto, Minor Consiglio.
[32] I-Fas, Mediceo del Principato, 1604.
[33] On the hairdresser, see also n. 54 below and the related passage in the text.

political government, which makes it unsafe to strangers. It is made a galley matter to carry a knife whose point is not broken off.[34]

It was in this climate of public puritanism and private crime that Stradella lived quite contentedly. A partial explanation for this may be found in the following lines by Gualdo Priorato which describe the exquisite surroundings in which Stradella's secular music would have been performed, and which suggest that the composer himself would most likely have had a comfortable life in Genoa:

> There is no lack in all these palaces of majestic doors, considerable entrances, magnificent staircases, loggias, very ample salons, rooms, well-distributed back rooms, gardens full of flowers, and of fruits, of fountains, of statues, and of other lovely adornments. The furnishings then are so precious that they seem dwellings of princes rather than of private individuals. There is no lack of very fine tapestries, excellent paintings, unusual pretty objects, and other things suitable to the grandness and magnificence.
>
> Not to mention the silver which is incredible for its quantity as there are not nobles or merchants even of lower classes who do not eat on silver plates, and in short this metal is so common that even the lowest people have some silver in their homes.[35]

As far as Stradella's sacred music was concerned, there were innumerable places for it to have been heard to judge from Gualdo Priorato again, who wrote that there were in Genoa 'many churches, monasteries, convents, oratories, hospitals, and pious places'.[36]

Two works he composed in 1680 were cantatas, the moralistic *Alle selve, agli studi, all'armi* to words by Benedetto Pamphili,[37] brother of Stradella's oft-mentioned friend Princess Anna Doria; and the sacred cantata *Esule dalle sfere* on a text by Pompeo Figari, an *abate* from Genoa who had lived many years in Rome and who would be a founder of the Arcadian Academy.[38] Stradella may have made contact with both poets in Rome. Also in 1680 one of his four-movement sinfonias (actually the two-movement sinfonia to *Esule dalle sfere* plus two other movements) was published by Marino Silvani in his anthology of Bolognese music (another reinforcement of Stradella's possible connection with the city) entitled *Scielta delle suonate a due violini, con il basso continuo per l'organo, raccolte da diversi eccellenti autori*.

Relations with an unexpected centre of music were initiated by the Genoese nobleman Goffredo Marino. On 23 February 1681 he wrote to Francesco II of Modena telling him that he would soon give the duke's *virtuoso* Marcantonio Orrigoni the score of *Trespolo* so that he could bring

---

[34] Evelyn, *Diary*, ed. Bowle, 65.   [35] Gualdo Priorato, *Genova*, 12.   [36] p. 29.

[37] Literary sources of his oratorio *Il figliol prodigo* are in I-Rn, Fondo Gesuitico, 240 and 1481.

[38] According to Crescimbeni, Arcadia's first historian: see Anna Maria Giorgetti Vichi, *Gli Arcadi dal 1690 al 1800: Onomasticon* (Rome, 1977).

it to Modena and let the duke admire 'the merits of the most eminent authors of the words and of the music, who were Signor Ricciardi of Florence and Signor Alessandro Stradella'. Marino assured the duke that the opera was completely original and different from the usual style to be heard in Italian theatres; moreover, it was new and had not already been presented elsewhere. He ended with the hope that it would soon be possible for him to accompany the composer to the Estense court.[39] Although Stradella's prologue *O di Cocito oscure deità* to Jacopo Melani's *Il Girello* had been heard in Modena in 1675, no mention of it was made either in Marino's letter or in the answer to it which came from the court. Dated 8 March, it states simply that Orrigoni had delivered the score, that inquiries were being made as to the possibility of putting on the opera in the public theatre, and that consideration was being given to Marino's suggestion to have Stradella come to Modena.[40] In the end *Il Trespolo tutore* was not performed in Modena until after the composer's death, in 1686. However, while Genoa in this period offered 'maximum quiet, and nothing worth attending',[41] Stradella received a commission from Modena to do an oratorio.

In 1663 Laura Martinozzi d'Este, regent for her son Francesco, nominated Giovanni Battista Giardini as court chancellor, a position he retained when the young ruler assumed power in 1674. Francesco was religious and his interest in music was directed especially to oratorios. In fact, in the 20 years before his death in 1694, about 90 oratorios were performed in Modena, and many of the librettos were written by Giardini.[42]

---

[39] I-MOas, Archivio segreto estense, Carteggio e documenti di Particolari, busta 654. It should be noted that Stradella called the good copy of his score by the term 'original', an expression common for the period. After the opening salutation, Marino's letter reads: 'Marco Antonio Orrigoni who, coming to Genoa, has brought me the most precious honour of your commands, on his return will bring you the most humble expression of my sentiments proportionate to that great respect which I nourish for your most glorious person. A small sign of this will be the score of *Trespolo*, which will be presented to you in my name, with the assurance that this small tribute will be received in the measure of your great generosity, not in that of my small merit to manifest myself the most respectful servant of such a great prince. I have dared so much knowing well how your noble personality is many-faceted and a protector of virtue, and particularly since this composition is not known, entirely new, and different from the usual style of the theatres of Italy, and admirable for the most eminent merits of the composers of the words and of the music, who were Signor Ricciardi of Florence, and Signor Alessandro Stradella; the latter of these will always give me the honour of bringing him there to serve you when you might like to see the noble effect that this kind of entertainment has on stage, since he has some specific dependence on me. I affirm on this page the most humble respect with which I venerate with the most lively of hearts such a high and such a grandiose person, and not being able to do more for the moment, I bow deeply before you.'

[40] Ibid.

[41] I-Fas, Mediceo del Principato, 2859, *avviso* of 29 Mar. 1681. One supposes this comment refers also to Carlo Pallavicino's *Il Nerone* (text by G. C. Corradi) given at the Teatro Falcone in Jan. 1681; the opera was dedicated to Anna Pamphili Doria.

[42] See Victor Crowther, 'Alessandro Stradella and the Oratorio Tradition in Modena', in Carolyn Gianturco (ed.), *Alessandro Stradella e Modena, Atti del Convegno internazionale di studi, Modena, 15–17 dicembre 1983* (Modena, 1985), 51–64, and *The Oratorio in Modena* (Oxford, 1992), 192–200.

Stradella was, therefore, asked to set the secretary's *La Susanna* for the Oratory of San Carlo. Whether the composer went to Modena for rehearsals and the performance in April 1681 is not known, although it would not be surprising to learn that he had.[43] That the performance was a success can be deduced from the following sources. First there is the copy of a letter from someone who heard rehearsals of *La Susanna* in Giardini's home and who wrote that he was 'ecstatic about the sinfonias, the variety of the arias, the exquisiteness of the recitative, and about the diversity and originality of the themes, and the rarity of the basso continuo';[44] and second are the librettos which show that *La Susanna* was repeated in Modena in 1687, and again in 1692.

Another commission for Stradella in 1681 arrived from Rome, from Flavio Orsini, who wanted Stradella to set his opera libretto *Moro per amore*.[45] On 24 May the composer wrote to Orsini sending him the finished score.[46] Stradella admits he has not been quick with his task but it was because he wanted to do a careful job, although—as the duke knows—he can hurry when necessary. Interestingly, Stradella suggests that the score be copied in Rome because there are no good amanuenses in Genoa, only some musicians who do copying; and a priest 'who wrote well has in fact recently left'. He thinks that the notes are clear and, even if the words are written in not too good a hand, the score is quite legible. Stradella has checked the copy several times so there should not be any errors. He adds that he wrote the music in sections and that he has no

---

[43] However, since the same copyists of *Trespolo* were involved, one knows that the score was prepared in Genoa.

[44] I-MOas, Archivio segreto estense, Carteggio e documenti di particoli, busta 504.

[45] Flavio Orsini married in 1641 at the age of 21. His bride was Ippolita Ludovisi, a 40–year-old widow who died in 1674. He then married another widow, the Frenchwoman Marianna de la Trémouille, in 1675. Although the Orsini had been one of the wealthiest families in Rome, they were beset with economic difficulties and were forced to sell three of their castles to the Chigi in 1671, and all of the Duchy of Bracciano to Livio Odescalchi in 1698. Flavio was considered a scholar, one interested in music, oratory, and mathematics; he had an important collection of ancient stone inscriptions. He was a member of Arcadia under the name Clearco Simbolio. He also wrote ten opera librettos, although when and where they were performed is not known. One of these is *Doriclea* and one wonders if Orsini is therefore the author of the Stradella opera of the same name found by Mario Tiberti in Rieti (see his article 'Un importante riuvenimento musicale, la *Doriclea*, opera di Alessandro Stradella', *Musica d'oggi*, 20 (1938), 85–8) but which he gave to someone he refuses to name. Orsini also wrote the text of *La dama di spirito geloso e la guerriera costante*, a prose comedy which, at the end of Act I, introduces an *opera in musica*. (On Orsini, see Prosperio Mandosi, *Biblioteca Romana, seu Romanorum Scriptorum Centuriae* (Rome, 1682), 108–9; Crescimbeni, *Notizie istoriche*, iii. (Rome, 1721), 172–4; and Carolyn Gianturco, 'Flavio Orsini', in Stanley Sadie (ed.), *The New Grove Dictionary of Opera* (London, 1992).)

[46] I-Rasc, Archivio Orsini, I. 279, no. 487; no. 23 in App. 2*a*. The opera is unnamed in the letter, but from Orsini's manuscript preface to *Moro per Amore* (I-Fas, Miscellanea Medicea, 506, discussed in my 'Sources for Stradella's *Moro per amore*', in *Memorie e contributi alla musica dal medioevo all'età moderna offerta a F. Ghisi nel settantesimo compleanno (1901–1971)* (Bologna, 1971), ii. 129–40), and from the printed libretto (I-Lbs), it is known that the opera was a collaboration between Orsini and Stradella.

other 'original' but the one he is sending Orsini, comments which tell us something about his method of composing and his habit of employing copyists and destroying his own pages. The practical musician comes to the fore when Stradella insists that Orsini have a 'bella copia' made so that singers and instrumentalists can perform the opera straight off without difficulty, and so that Orsini can enjoy the music on first hearing. Again because this is the only copy he has, he would like it back and asks Orsini to give it to Giovanni Battista Vulpio (his singer friend from Rome and confederate in marriage-arranging), who will bring it to Genoa. In spite of all these considerations and arrangements, Orsini never managed to have *Moro per amore* performed in a public theatre.

Stradella's letter also gives news of his other activities. He is busy writing 'a cloak-and-dagger operetta' for six characters which is to be done 'in a villa and on the sea' the following summer. Singers have already been contacted and Stradella says the work will be accompanied by other 'cose ben fatte' (perhaps meaning special sets, costumes, effects, and dances), not just his 'weak' music. Unfortunately, he does not name the production, but since the sponsors of the opera were Duke Spinola of San Pietro, Duke Doria, Signor Goffredo Marino, Signor Francesco Maria Spinola, and Don Francesco Serra, some considerations as to where the entertainment was to be performed can be put forth.

Although the Spinola villa (built in the second half of the sixteenth century and sufficiently noteworthy for Rubens to include it in his *Palazzi di Genova*[47] and Gauthier in his *Les Plus beaux édifices de la ville de Gênes*)[48] was in one of the summer residential areas just outside the city at Sampierdarena, it was not on the sea. The Villa Doria, on the other hand, with its gardens and woods extending from the hills down to the sea at Fasolo, could easily have been the site of an entertainment such as Stradella described.[49] The property was an enormous one which, coincidentally, had been acquired by Andrea Doria, the sixteenth-century Prince of Melfi in whose service some of Stradella's relatives had been.

The last bit of news the composer included in his letter to Flavio Orsini was that he was doing 'un barcheggio', a boating entertainment, for two local *sposi* (Carlo Spinola and Paola Brignole) the following week. The weather must have been inclement, however, because the festivities actually took place some days later, on 19 June.[50] The wedding itself took place on 6 July in Santa Maria Maddalena,[51] the parish church of Strada Nuova.

[47] Antwerp, 1622.   [48] Paris, 1818–32, ii. 10–13.
[49] On these and other buildings in Genoa and its environs see the series *Guide di Genova*.
[50] See 'Secular Cantatas with Instrumental Accompaniment' in Ch. 6 below for all contemporary reports on the performance of *Il barcheggio* as well as a discussion of the music.
[51] Angelo Catelani, *Delle opere di Alessandro Stradella esistenti nell'Archivio Musicale della R. Biblioteca Palatina di Modena* (Modena, 1866), 37.

This was the street where the most important aristocrats (including Franco Lercaro) lived. The Spinola family had built four *palazzi* in the Strada Nuova in the sixteenth century (all noted by Rubens in his *Palazzi di Genova*), while Ridolfo and Giovanni Francesco Brignole began theirs in 1671. The Dorias, too, had their magnificent cinquecento palace in the same street, a princely mansion three times the width of the other buildings.[52] Therefore, it is certain that Stradella, not only because he had stayed with Lercaro but also because of his musical and theatrical connections with the other nobles, was often in Strada Nuova. It is also more than likely that these same families often requested sacred music of him for their church of Santa Maria Maddalena, but whether the Spinola–Brignole marriage was one of these occasions is not known.

Before leaving the couple it would be worth mentioning them in connection with the strict rules of behaviour the republic tried to inforce: on 6 June Carlo had been reprimanded for having his carriage too richly decorated, and in September Paola would be cautioned against wearing her diamond watch.[53] In this same vein is an anonymous letter of 9 June sent to the governing council which mentions Stradella.[54] In irate tones, the writer complains that women were too ostentatious and that their husbands gave too much money 'to the Roman to touch their faces under the pretence of fixing their hair; at Stradella and the Gobbo, I mean Carlo Ambrosio [Lonati], they throw money so that these brazen scoundrels can stay in Genoa'. The letter ends by saying that something had to be done or problems would arise and he would suggest expelling these three from the city.

The author of these lines is a harsh critic of contemporary society. He is opposed to women being glamorous and, what is more, suspicious of their dealings with men outside the family: he is even concerned when the hairdresser, 'il Romano', touches their faces. He is against all expenditures for things he believes valueless, for example money paid to Stradella and Lonati supposedly for their compositions or music lessons. He would presumably have seen their lessons to ladies as immoral encounters simply because of the proximity of the sexes.

Many Genoese sent anonymous letters to the government complaining about the loose morals of the nobility and those connected with them, and they would have considered the comportment mentioned above reprehensible. That Stradella was rash and impetuous has already been seen, and it

---

[52] Strada Nuova is now called Via Garibaldi: the Spinola palaces are at nos. 2, 5, 6, 8/10; the Brignole at no. 18, presently the city art museum; and the Doria at no. 9, since 1848 the town hall. Rubens showed designs of all these buildings, except the Brignole which was built after he visited the city.

[53] I-Gas, Archivio segreto, Minor Consiglio.

[54] Cited by Marcello Staglieno in 'Aneddoti sopra diversi artisti del secolo xvii', *Giornale Ligustico*, 1 (1874), 381.

is always possible that he and Lonati, an old friend from Rome, enjoyed certain pastimes together, pastimes which gave cause for complaint and scandal. But that their behaviour was such as to warrant their banishment from the city seems an exaggeration, especially when it is coupled with that of an apparently harmless hairdresser.

That such opinions did not affect Stradella's rapport with the nobility is clear from a letter sent from Genoa on 23 August by Giovanni Battista Busseti to Francesco II d'Este. He says that the composer has not been absent from the city for some time (which implies he had been away in the past, perhaps even to Modena for the performance of *La Susanna*) except for occasional trips to villas in the surrounding area.[55] One thinks immediately of the Spinola and Doria villas mentioned above; other nobles also gave alfresco entertainments which could have had music, such as that held by Goffredo Marino by the sea on 16 August, Feast of San Rocco, which offered fireworks as well.[56]

On several evenings in September great festivities were held by the Doria and Spinola families to celebrate Benedetto Pamphili's nomination to the position of cardinal,[57] a celebration which surely required Stradella's music. On 16 October the opera season began (apparently without Stradella's involvement) and since the music was good, the audience was large.[58] Beginning on 2 December a whole series of anonymous letters were sent to the government about the wounding of Pier Francesco Guano the day before.[59] He had had to have 12 stitches on his face, and people said Giorgio Spinola and Goffredo Marino were responsible although they were never actually charged. Instead, several months later, the Minor Consiglio condemned Silvestro Grimaldi and Costantino Pinello for the crime. The letters said that Guano had talked too loudly and sarcastically especially about having seen nude noblewomen, and that was why he had been attacked.

Notice of an even more serious crime was sent from Genoa to Florence on 28 February 1682:

Wednesday evening [25 February] at two at night [about 7 p.m.] while he was going home accompanied by his servant who had a cape in his hand, the musician Stradella was stabbed three times, and died immediately without being able to say a word, and the servant whom he had ahead [of him] observed nothing until he saw him fall flat on his face, and thus he died, and it is not yet known who did it.[60]

[55] I-MOas, Cancelleria ducale, Carteggio ambasciatori, Genova, busta 13.

[56] I-MOas, Cancelleria ducale, Avvisi dall'Estero, Genova, busta 63, letter dated 21 Aug. 1681.

[57] Ibid., letter dated 6 Sept. 1681.

[58] Ibid., letter of 22 Oct. 1681. One learns more from Stradella's letter to Polo Michiel dated 21 Dec. (I-Vmc, PD C. 1067, no. 359; no. 24 in App. 2a).

[59] I-Gas, Archivio segreto, Minor Consiglio.   [60] I-Fas, Mediceo del Principato, 1604.

On the same day a shorter *avviso* was sent to Modena which read simply: 'Wednesday evening the famous *musico* Stradella was killed'.[61] The criminal records (which will be discussed below) state that the murder had taken place in Piazza Banchi.

The following bill shows what expenses were incurred for Stradella's burial:

1682 on 26 February expense to
bury the dead Signor Alessandro Stradella.

given to the movers to carry him home in the seat [stretcher] and clean him	lire	8.13.4
given to a guard to watch over him	"	1
for a casket [in which] to put the said body	"	7
given to six movers to carry him to the burial	"	13
given for the [burial] cloth and the casket	"	8
paid to the grave-digger for the burial slab	"	1.10
for sewing him and keeping vigil	"	6
for bells and burial	"	15.4
for carrying things home	"	2
for wax to the candle-maker	"	55.11.8
for n.24 masses for the said [person]	"	14.8
paid to the official for his documents	"	7.12
	lire	139.19[62]

On 26 February, at the age of 42, Stradella was buried in Santa Maria delle Vigne, one of Genoa's loveliest and most aristocratic churches.[63]

The treatment given Stradella after his death was that of a respected gentleman. That he should have been wrapped in a cloth and put into a coffin was already a sign of distinction. Even though he died without the sacraments (as is obvious from the Florence *avviso* but is also stated in the church records), Stradella was buried in church, not something a blatant criminal would have enjoyed. Moreover, bells were rung for him, an enormous number of candles lighted (to judge from their cost), he was given the honour of a guard, and prayers were said for him throughout the

---

[61] I-MOas, Cancelleria ducale, Avvisi dall'Estero, Venezia, vol. 118.

[62] I-Gas, Atti notarili, Notaio Gerolamo Camere, scanzia 963, filza 7. The first notice I gave of this important file which contained the slip of expenses was in 'La famiglia Stradella: Nuovi documenti biografici', *Nuova rivista musicale italiana*, 3 (1982), 456–66. The bill continues and shows how many of each currency denomination were used to pay it: '1682 on 26 February | received fifty lire [in] money   lire 50 | plus six silver scudi   lire 45.12 | plus thirty-six lire   lire 36 | plus silver scudi   lire 7.12 | [total:] lire 139.4.'

[63] On the building, see the *Guide di Genova*. The document recording Stradella's burial there (carried out soon after death, as was and still is the custom in Italy) was found by Padre Luigi Alfonso, archivist of the church, in its Libro dei defunti 1569–1708, fo. 141ᵛ. The notice, exactly the same as in the volume *Diversorum primus* where events were first recorded, reads as follows: 'die 25 februarii 1682. D. Alexander Stradella q. [followed by a space since his father's name was apparently not known] Musicus Romanus gladio confossus obijt sine sacramentis et die 26 dicti in nostra sepultus est ecclesia.'

night as well as in 24 masses. In addition, the church selected for his repose was an elegant one frequented by Genoa's nobility. All of these facts lead one to conclude that Alessandro Stradella had been esteemed by his patrons and contemporaries, and that his death was lamented by them.

The identity of his killers was what occupied the Senate and Minor Consiglio soon after the event; in fact they opened the case on 3 March.[64] The evidence which was taken into consideration, since none other was forthcoming, was provided by *biglietti di calice*, that is, notes slipped in anonymously during voting by council members reluctant to speak publicly, and by anonymous letters from the people. Among the several notes of both types which are to be found together with the records of the investigation, one reads the following: 'The death of Stradella was executed by orders of the four Lomellino brothers, sons of the dead Nicolo Maria, and for this reason they are not seen.' '. . . as happened now in the death of the *musico* Alessandro Stradella deeply felt by his lady students, and if he had paid attention to the admonitions he had received in Turin he would not have had such an accident which might have been caused by his wanting to raise his sight to the sun. Therefore whoever rises too high is bound to fall.' 'It is public and well known that the other assassination, that of Stradella, was committed by Bacciollo Lomellino and his brothers, excluding Giuseppe who was informed after it happened.' 'It is said that the death of Alessandro Stradella, famous as a master of the musical art, was caused by three or four sharp knife-wounds by Gio. Battista and his brothers of the Lomellino family, [sons] of the deceased Nicolo Maria. The consideration of such an atrocious and terrible act, so vile and atrociously executed, encourages the greatest suspicion, the inner conviction that it happened at the moment when he wrongly fell in love with their sister.' Someone even wrote that Goffredo Marino had seen, 'shortly before the said death in the same place, the said Magnifico Giovanni Battista [Lomellino] with some people'.

Avvisi of the period also refer to the Lomellino family as being responsible for the crime, and say that Stradella had been killed because (putting it in musical terms) 'in order to touch too high he had played in the bass'. They report that, as a consequence of Stradella's death, three other first-rate musicians were made to leave Genoa, including Lonati 'so that he would not run the same miserable course as Stradella'.[65] One *avviso* from

[64] Unless stated otherwise, the information presented here on the investigations relevant to Stradella's murder are taken from I-Gas, Criminali, no. 121. First notice of this file was given by Remo Giazotto in *La musica a Genova* (Genoa, 1951) and *Vita di Alessandro Stradella* (2 vols.; Milan, 1962), where unfortunately he sometimes made errors in transcribing the documents, sometimes omitted important words or phrases, or sometimes simply did not understand the meaning or relevance of a document.

[65] See I-MOas, Cancelleria ducale, Avvisi dall'Estero, Venezia, vol. 118, dated 7 Mar.; and ibid., dated 3 Mar.—not 7 Mar. as stated by Hess, *Die Opern*, 10—(for the first *avviso* citation) where it is

Genoa gives another, quite plausible reason for the dispute between the Lomellino brothers and Stradella: an actress. Apparently, she had become pregnant (supposedly by Abate Granvella, who then abandoned her) and Giovanni Battista Lomellino took her under his wing. He became jealous when he realized the lady preferred Stradella, and, together with his brothers, organized the assassination.[66]

As no others were named as guilty, on 5 March the Senate ordered Giovanni Battista (known as Bacciollo or Baccio) and Domenico Lomellino to be put in prison. On 17 March the brothers asked if they could be moved from the prison tower to the criminal gaol; and on 8 April it was voted to let them go free after they paid two thousand silver scudi. It must be noted, though, that they were never formally charged with Stradella's murder and that actually there was never enough proof to do so.

The accusations made in anonymous letters that Stradella was having an affair with their sister, and that this is what made them order his death,[67] do not sound unreasonable given the composer's past. At the same time, if this is true, it is a bit surprising to learn that Maria Caterina Lomellino's husband, Giuseppe Maria Garibaldi (one of the managers of the Teatro Falcone), took care of distributing the composer's possessions to his heirs, and not only kept Stradella's music for himself but tried later on to enlarge his personal collection of it, behaviour one would think too generous and full of respect for a nobleman towards a musician who had cuckolded him.[68]

Unfortunately, at the moment no certain explanation for Stradella's death can be put forth, except perhaps the censorious attitude of many of the Genoese of the period which could have seen evil in his rapport with women pupils, or envy of either a professional or personal nature (such as jealousy over an actress). Since three other musicians were banished from the city as a consequence of his death, one has to believe that they were all having affairs with noblewomen or else, and this would be a more reasonable supposition, that local puritanism and suspicion endangered the lives of artists who would of course have been nonconformists.

said that Stradella had taught music and how to play instruments to several ladies, and that he and Lonati were frequently called upon by ladies to entertain them, both certainly cause for curiosity if not scandal in Genoa. The identity of the two other musicians asked to leave the city is not known. See also I-Fas, Mediceo del Principato, 1604, *avvisi* dated 7 Mar. (from which the second *avviso* citation was taken) and 14 Mar.

[66] I-MOas, Cancelleria ducale, Avvisi dall'Estero, Genoa, 7 Mar. 1682, reported in Della Corte, '*La forza d'amor paterno*', 396.

[67] In the anonymous notes Guano's case is often mentioned together with Stradella's, and in one it is said that Guano was attacked by a 'monferrino', someone from Monferrato (then under Savoy and today part of Piedmont): the wording could mean that it was suspected that both he and Stradella were wounded by the same man.

[68] His wife's name appears on the libretto for *Helvio Pertinace* by Piccioli, an opera dedicated to her in Jan. 1677 at the Teatro Falcone (according to Ivaldi, 'Teatro', 450).

5

After 1682

Stradella's Estate

Stradella had no wife, no children, and left no will, and therefore his other relatives were notified immediately of his death and notary documents attest to the division of his belongings among them.[1] As is known, Stradella had had two brothers, Giuseppe and Stefano, and a stepbrother (from the same father but a different mother), Francesco. The first two were dead by the date of his murder, and therefore their heirs— Giuseppe's son Marc'Antonio, and Stefano's daughters Vittoria Agata and Maria—took their shares. Francesco had renounced all right to any inheritance when he became an Augustinian, but he participated in the division of property because Marc'Antonio, on 2 March in Rome, had named him as his proxy (an office Francesco officially accepted on 2 April), perhaps because he could not travel from his home in Nepi to Genoa but more probably because the priest had a university degree and was therefore quite able to handle the transaction for him. Since young girls were not allowed to act for themselves, nor were women unless authorization had been given, Stefano's daughters' share was dealt with by their mother, Caterina de Acerbis of Novellaria, their legal 'tutrice e curatrice'. Since the family lived in Mantua, Caterina named the Genoese count, Giovanni Paolo della Chiesa, as her proxy on 10 April.[2]

On 27 May the proxies and notary met in Giuseppe Maria Garibaldi's house near Piccapietra where, after the funeral expenses which had been paid were deducted from the liquid cash, Stradella's belongings were inventoried, their value estimated, and, as it was decided to consider the heirs according to family branch and not number ('in stirpe et non in capita'), they were divided in two groups for which lists were made. Since

[1] All documents related to Stradella's property and heirs are to be found in I-Gas, Atti notarili, Notaio Gerolamo Camere, scanzia 963, filza 7.

[2] It is interesting to note that in Marc'Antonio's *procura* Alessandro Stradella is called a 'Nepesinus' by his close relatives, whereas the Genoese notary says he is a 'Civitate Bononie', thus continuing the confusion about his origin. In Caterina's notary act, Stefano is said to be a 'Romano', probably because he lived some years in Rome before moving on to Mantua. Research in files for the years 1641–1700 in the State Archives of Mantua unfortunately resulted in no documents relating either to Stefano Stradella or to his wife and children.

later notary acts were drawn up in Garibaldi's house near Luccoli, one is inclined to believe that, for the present task of examining Stradella's possessions, they were in the building where the composer had lived. That this was owned by Garibaldi is not surprising, since it is assumed that Garibaldi was one of the Genoese nobles who supported Stradella and provided him with a house.

Of the two lists, the proxies chose the first for Stefano's daughters, and the second for Marc'Antonio.[3]

List 1 of the effects of the deceased Alessandro Stradella of the deceased Marc'Antonio to be given to the Misses Vittoria Agata, and Maria, daughters of the deceased Stefano Stradella, heirs for half [of the estate] of the deceased Alessandro Stradella of the deceased Marc'Antonio.

one pair of trestles with its table
one small stool
two mattresses with pillow
one woollen blanket
one hemp sheet
three used linen shirts
one wool and linen suit with its shirt threaded with gold
one woollen cape
one suit and cape of tufted material
one pair of red breeches
two parchment collars
two pairs of parchment cuffs
three pairs of silk cuffs
two berets
one silk necktie with a kerchief
silk kerchiefs, two
two ordinary kerchiefs with veiling
four ribbons with gold
twelve bows of ribbon, various colours
one large velvet beret decorated with gold
one pair of silk stockings
one pair of old gloves
one gold box or rather tobacco box decorated with diamonds
one coconut tobacco box with silver rim
one wooden box with a [decorative] ring of gold
one painted box with a large silver clasp

[3] The following dictionaries have been useful in understanding particular and antiquated expressions for the belongings which were passed on: Giovanni Casaccia, *Vocabolario genovese–italiano* (Genoa, 1851), Angelo Paganini, *Vocabolario domestico genovese–italiano* (Genoa, 1857), Gaetano Frisoni, *Dizionario moderno genovese–italiano* (Genoa, 1910), Carlo Battisti and Giovanni Alessio, *Dizionario etimologico italiano* (Florence, 1950); comparison was also made with what the notaries of Marc'Antonio Stradella and of the daughters of Stefano later said they received (see the next section, 'Stradella's Instruments and Early Collections of his Music'). I am also grateful to Mercedes Viale Ferrero for her help in elucidating certain terms.

one small box of fine [gold or silver] metalwork
one silver medal
one false stone decorated with silver
one small rosary with [a] silver medal
currency: 51 lire and 17 soldi in present currency

List 2 of the effects of the deceased Alessandro Stradella of the deceased
  Marc'Antonio to go to Mr Marc'Antonio Stradella, son of the deceased
  Giuseppe, nephew of the said deceased Alessandro.

one pair of trestles with its table
one mattress with pillow
one woollen blanket
one hemp sheet
one dressing-gown
one black silk suit with cape
another one of black silk without cape, old
one coloured suit decorated with parchment with its ribbons
two linen shirts
one hat, and one collar
two neckties, one of parchment, and the other of silk
two parchment collars with two pairs of cuffs
six kerchiefs
two white berets
one [piece of] veiling
one belt or undershirt [decorated or embroidered] with gold
six ribbons or rather bows
one St Dominic devotional scapular
one pair of silver candlesticks with their snuffers
one silver tray
one silver fruit bowl
four silver tobacco boxes
one book decorated with silver
one silver spoon, and one silver case
three sticks [toothpicks?] of silver
one bunch of silver harpsichord strings
one coconut tobacco box decorated with silver
one painted box with its silver case
one silver reliquary
two silver clasps with false stones
one medal with a silver clasp
one rosary with [a] gold medal
another with [a] silver medal
one small box with four small gold buttons
two belts with two silver clasps with false stones
currency: 51 lire and 17 soldi

The object of most value, the gold tobacco box decorated with diamonds which was estimated at 600 lire, went to the girls; but the greater number of items plus other single important possessions—such as the 220-lira silver candlesticks, the 80-lira silver fruit bowl, and the 126-lira silver saucer or tray—went to Marc'Antonio, which would have balanced the inheritances. In any event, the two lists—evidence that Stradella was relatively well off and well away from his desperate situation of debt noted in 1670—could not have been a complete inventory of Stradella's belongings: first, because no ordinary items of dress are mentioned (no underclothes, no shoes, no objects of toiletry, etc.); and second, because no musical instruments, scores, books of any sort (except one with a silver clasp) are said to exist. It would appear that only the better of his non-musical possessions were to be divided, many of these clearly being expensive gifts he must have received from noble patrons. Later events indicate that Garibaldi and Padre Stradella must have made a secret agreement to exclude, at the very least, the composer's music and instruments from the inventory, and therefore from being shared with Stefano's daughters, and the two men probably privately divided many more belongings among themselves.

While these dealings were going on, events in Genoa proceeded normally: on 21 November Franco Maria Imperiale Lercaro wrote to Florence saying that a group of *cavalieri* wanted to put on a 'capa e spada' opera and were considering as librettists either Francesco Redi or Villifranchi, whose *Trespolo* with music by Stradella had already been enjoyed.[4] Stradella was also remembered in a collection of sonatas which Carlo Mannelli published in 1682. It was dedicated to Cardinal Pamphili and contained 14 works, each bearing as its title the name of a composer active in Rome: Stradella's homage is the last in the volume.

Stradella's Instruments and Early Collections of his Music

The next notice dealing directly with Stradella is from 19 August, and it is one which confirms that his music was (illegally?) not inventoried. On this date a letter was sent from Modena to Padre Francesco Stradella[5] informing him that his request, made in the name of his nephew, for 600 doubloons in exchange for 'musical compositions' by Alessandro Stradella was considered 'exorbitant', and suggesting that, instead, he simply offer the works as a gift to Duke Francesco II and accept the sum he would receive. The outcome of the correspondence is not known, although it is most likely that the Stradella manuscripts now in the Biblioteca Estense

---

[4] I-Fas, Mediceo del Principato, 2859.

[5] I-MOas, Cancelleria ducale, Carteggi di regolari, busta 115. The letter was first published by Hess, *Die Opern*, 2 (albeit with the usual mistakes in reading occasional Italian letters which characterize his transcriptions; the catalogue number he gives has since been changed).

catalogued Mus. F. came into the library through the composer himself as well as shortly after his death through his stepbrother's offer. It is curious that Padre Stradella was in touch with Modena even before Marc'Antonio had actually received his share of the inheritance: obviously, the nephew had no use for his uncle's compositions.

On 11 January 1683 Marc'Antonio legally accepted his inheritance from his uncle, Padre Francesco. Included with the notary act signed in Nepi is the list of what he received (List 2 above), which was said to have been obtained by the priest 'from the hands of Giuseppe Garibaldi'.[6] Naturally there is no mention of the music or other possible belongings he got privately from the nobleman. On 13 March Giovanni Battista Busseti, who had informed Duke Francesco II in summer 1681 of Stradella's activities, wrote again from Genoa saying that he had shipped a box of 'libri di musica' given to him by Goffredo Marino, which by 10 April he had heard had arrived safely.[7] Although one knows nothing of the contents of the box, one is inclined to be suspicious of any information regarding music in the hands of those once associated with Stradella in Genoa.

Equally disturbing is the letter Busseti wrote to the Este court on 29 May informing them that he had received a harpsichord for the duke from Marino,[8] especially since, although no instrument was said to be in the composer's home, List 2 of his possessions itemizes silver harpsichord strings, something one is rather unlikely to have unless one also has an instrument. Once again, though, no definite answer is forthcoming as to whether the instrument sent by Marino to Modena was actually Stradella's.

Proof that all of Stradella's belongings were not inventoried comes from further documents. For some inexplicable reason, Caterina Stradella did not receive her daughters' inheritance as quickly as did Marc'Antonio. In fact as late as 11 August 1685 she named Garibaldi as her proxy, asking him to give what was due her family to two other proxies she sent to Genoa, and on the next day a notary in Novellaria (Caterina's native town) authenticated that Della Chiesa, her first proxy in Genoa, had accepted it.[9] What or who then made Caterina become dubious about the two lists is not known, but she certainly was not content with what was given to her daughters. She obviously complained soon after since by 8 May 1686 both parties had come to an agreement whereby Caterina, in

---

[6] I-VTas, Notaio Angelo Fantauzzi, prot. 68, fos. 135ʳ–136ᵛ, 138ʳ⁻ᵛ. Actually several small items of clothing, the belts and clasps with fake stones, and the more important painted box in its silver case, were not received, or at least not declared by Marc'Antonio to have been received. A last notice about Marc'Antonio was kindly brought to my attention by Gian Ludovico Masetti Zannini. It regards a request of 1699 to have his 7-year-old daughter, Portia, study in a convent in Civita Castellana (I-Rvata, S. Congregazioni Vescovi e Regolari, Posizione Monache, 23 Jan. 1699).

[7] Both in I-MOas, Cancelleria ducale, Ambasciatori, Genoa, busta 13.   [8] Ibid.

[9] I-Gas, Atti notarili, Notaio Gerolamo Camere, scanzio 963, filza 7.

the name of her daughters, would give back to Garibaldi the hemp sheet, and receive from him 'three lutes with their cases [were the girls lutenists?], three wigs, and a trunk' (said to be 'outside the list') as well as 'a pair of parchment cuffs' (also 'not described in the above-mentioned list').[10] Whether the trunk contained music is unfortunately not known; but the fact that Stradella had not one but three lutes (if not more) would suggest that he was a performer on the instrument and entertained his patrons in this capacity. It would also shed some light on his occasionally calling for a lute in his compositions in a period when it was generally not named specifically.

Further developments regarding Stradella's music occurred on 30 January 1688 when the Modena court organist, Domenico Bratti, wrote from Genoa that Giuseppe Maria Garibaldi, in possession 'of some of the most unknown chamber compositions by Stradella', would like to let the duke copy these in exchange for works which the Genoese did not have.[11] Bratti goes on to mention a certain 'Domenico who I introduced to Your Serene Highness' who has 'the originals' of some Stradella compositions, which would probably have been (as one has learned from the composer himself) not his autographs but good first copies made under his supervision.[12]

While the identity of this Domenico has not been ascertained, since Bratti calls him familiarly by his first name only, he would not have been one of the noblemen with whom Stradella had been in contact; more than likely he was a singer or some other musician who had performed the works he had in his possession, or perhaps he had been a copyist for the composer; he may even have been a person with whom Padre Francesco Stradella had left some or all of his brother's music to sell. In February of 1700 Giuseppe Maria Garibaldi died leaving everything to his son and wife,[13] but his will does not clarify whether among his possessions there was any music. As a matter of fact, what happened to Garibaldi's collection of Stradella music is somewhat of a mystery, as shall be seen by tracing yet another collection of the composer's works.

The Venetian bibliophile Jacopo Soranzo (1686–1761) was the son of Contarina Contarini and in 1718 married Elena Contarini. It is possible that it was through them that he came into possession of Stradella music

[10] I-Gas, Atti notarili, Notaio Gerolamo Camere, scanzio 963, filza 7.

[11] The letter is in I-MOas, Archivio per materie, musica e musicisti, busta 5.

[12] In I-MOas, Archivio per materia, Serie musica, busta 3, 'Copisti di musica', one finds payments for the copying of Stradella's music in 1688. For a history of Stradella's music in Modena, see Alessandra Chiarelli, 'La collezione estense di musica stradelliana: Per un'indagine sulla sua formazione', in Carolyn Gianturco (ed.), *Alessandro Stradella e Modena, Atti del Convegno internazionale di studi, Modena, 15–17 dicembre 1983* (Modena, 1985), 116–24.

[13] Ivaldi, 'Teatro', 563–4. Garibaldi named his wife's brother Domenico Lomellino, who had been one of those accused of Stradella's murder, among those who should see that his will was carried out.

owned by the Contarini and Michiel families (the latter also related to the Contarini). When Soranzo died his heirs divided his library: one part was bought eventually by Abate Matteo Luigi Canonici (1727–1805), many volumes of which went on to enrich the Bodleian Library of Oxford. Other volumes once owned by Canonici and by heirs of Soranzo, including those containing music (some in autograph) by Stradella, were bought *c.*1778–80 by Count Giacomo Durazzo (1717–94) (the same Genoese ambassador to Vienna whose connection with Gluck is known to historians of opera) while he was Viennese ambassador to Venice. After the count's death his library passed from one generation of heirs to another until 1895 when it was divided and eventually went, in part, to the Salesian College of S. Carlo in Borgo S. Martino (Monferrato) and, in part, to Marquis Giuseppe Maria Durazzo. The volumes of music were purchased from them both in 1927 and 1930 respectively by two families wishing to honour their dead sons, and were then donated to the Biblioteca Nazionale of Turin as the Mauro Foà and Renzo Giordano collections.[14]

It has been supposed that whatever Stradella music Garibaldi had also found its way to the Soranzo–Durazzo–Turin collection. If this were so then one should find the same music both in Turin (Garibaldi's scores) and Modena catalogued as Mus. G. (copies the Este duke had made from Garibaldi's scores). However, this is not the case.[15] Music in Garibaldi's possession which he let the duke copy was apparently dispersed at his death. It should be noted, though, that many volumes now in Turin offer the same music catalogued as Mus. F. in Modena—those works it is supposed entered the duke's library through Stradella's stepbrother—and it may be that the composer often had two copies (occasionally one an autograph) of his music. Garibaldi and Padre Francesco Stradella could have divided them: the priest's volumes went to Modena and Garibaldi's found their way to the Soranzo–Durazzo–Turin collection.[16]

The important Stradella autographs and other manuscripts now in the Venice Biblioteca Marciana were most likely left in the city by the composer or sent to Polo and Girolamo Michiel. It is also likely that the

[14] On the history of these collections, see Gabriella Gentili Verona, 'Le collezioni Foà e Giordano della Biblioteca Nazionale di Torino', *Accademie e biblioteche d'Italia*, 32/6 (1964), 405–30, and Alberto Basso's 'Introduzione' to Isabella Data Fragalà and Annarita Colturato (compilers), *Biblioteca Nazionale Università di Torino, La raccolta Mauro Foà—La raccolta Renzo Giordano* (Cataloghi di fondi musicali italiani, 7; Rome, 1987), pp. ix–lxxxvi. Jander's decision in *WECIS*, fasc. 4*a*, 45–9 to associate Carlo Ambrogio Lonati with a peculiar, unsteady hand which appears in this collection in contemporary copies of Stradella's music is difficult to accept. Jander believed that a hunchback would have had such a 'shaky' calligraphy; however, this does not take into consideration that Lonati was an esteemed violinist and, as such, could not have trembled continuously (as the copyist did) either when bowing (if the copyist were right-handed) or when stopping the strings (if he were left-handed).

[15] Only one violin sonata is common to both collections: Gianturco-McCrickard, *Stradella Catalogue* 7.1–10, in Foà 11 and Mus. G. 210.

[16] Not through Polo Michiel, however, since he died before Garibaldi in 1686.

dukes of Modena were responsible for the Stradella pieces in Vienna since Francesco V d'Este brought there what he considered his family's private collection; after being kept at the Hofburg, in 1908–28 it was transferred to the Österreichische Nationalbibliothek.

As is known, Handel was in Rome probably from 1706 to 1709 where he performed for Cardinal Pietro Ottoboni, in whose salon Stradella's music was sung by Andrea Adami; moreover Corelli, who had played in Stradella's *San Giovanni Battista*, was Ottoboni's *maestro di musica*; and a poet of Stradella's, Benedetto Pamphili, was also a patron and poet for Handel. All of these contacts, plus the themes Handel took from Stradella's *Qual prodigio* and utilized in his *Israel in Egypt*, and the Stradella scores now in the British Library which once belonged to Handel, make it clear that Handel knew and owned some of Stradella's music.[17]

In his will, Charles Burney wrote that in his collection 'there are many curious scarce and excellent compositions for voices such as the [blank] works of Carissimi, Stradella, Colonna, Steffani, Clari', a statement which was repeated in the 1844 announcement for the auction of the music.[18] Contained there was *San Giovanni Battista* as well as several volumes of 'Italian cantate' which probably also included Stradella music. Richard Goodson, both father and son, and Dean Henry Aldrich were instrumental in getting Stradella's works for Christ Church, Oxford at the end of the seventeenth and beginning of the eighteenth century. The Fitzwilliam Museum, Cambridge houses a great many Stradella manuscripts, among which are volumes once owned by Cardinal Ottoboni and Andrea Adami, which were collected over the years by Richard, Viscount Fitzwilliam. And many of Stradella's works now in the Paris Bibliothèque Nationale were brought there from Italy by Napoleon as spoils of war. In short, the seventeenth and eighteenth centuries saw the preserving of Stradella's music throughout Europe and the formation of the most important collections of it.[19]

---

[17] See Ebenezer Prout, 'Handel's Obligations to Stradella', *Monthly Musical Record*, 1 (1871), 154–6; John South Shedlock, 'Handel's Borrowings', *Musical Times*, 42 (1901), 451, 526, 596, and Sedley Taylor, *The Indebtedness of Handel to Works by Other Composers: A Presentation of Evidence* (Cambridge, 1906).

[18] For a facsimile edition of the latter see Alec Hyatt King, *Auction Catalogues of Music*, ii: *Charles Burney, Catalogue of the Valuable Collection of Music, London, 1844* (Amsterdam, 1973).

[19] For information on the present whereabouts of all of Stradella's music see Gianturco–McCrickard, *Stradella Catalogue*. Jander (*WECIS*, fasc. 4a, pp. 3–5, 25–69) discusses scribes, watermarks, and bindings of Stradella's sources in detail and includes illustrations of each. I have also long studied them. However, it is usually not possible to draw sufficient conclusions from the physical aspects of the manuscripts in order to date their composition or establish the city of origin. The reasons for this are several: because Stradella composed for patrons in several cities and sent his music from one place to another throughout his career; because there is only occasionally an autograph of a work; and because copies of his music were made both during his life and soon after it.

Posthumous Performances of Stradella's Music

These same centuries also witnessed the continued performance of his music. In November 1683, just under two years after his death, the Compagnia di S. Caterina of Florence had an oratorio Stradella had written about St Catherine performed.[20] This would seem to be the first oratorio ever given by the Compagnia, and as they continued to do an oratorio about Saint Catherine each year until 1693 it could be that it was always Stradella's. At present no composition on this saint by him has come to light, although the anonymous *Oratorio di Santa Caterina* in the Biblioteca Vaticana (Barb. lat. 4209) might be his.[21] Stradella's *San Giovanni Battista* was also appreciated in Florence, and was performed by the Congregazione di S. Filippo Neri there in 1693 and again in 1695.[22]

The Oratory of San Carlo in Modena favoured Stradella's oratorios and had the following works performed: *La Santa Editta* (1684), *Santa Pelagia, San Giovanni Battista* (both in 1688), *La Susanna* and *Santa Editta* again (both in 1692). *La Susanna* was also given in Bologna in 1690. The year 1686 saw the presentation in Modena of Stradella's comic opera now entitled *Il Trespolo tutore balordo*.[23] The existence of parts copied in Modena for several of his motets would suggest that these, too, were performed at the court.

In the 1690s, according to Crescimbeni, Andrea Adami was singing Stradella's cantatas in Rome at Cardinal Pietro Ottoboni's gatherings; and in 1692 the cardinal paid to have nine of his chamber works copied in the home of Giovanni Battista Vulpio, which suggests they were Stradella arias or cantatas owned by the singer.[24] A few years later, in 1712, Stradella's cantata *Pria di punir, crudele* was published in the anthology *Armonia di Pindo, Cantate da camera a voce sola di diversi eccellenti autori* by Francesco Vignone in Milan. Stradella remained popular in England, too, in the eighteenth century, to judge from the many copies especially of

---

[20] I-Fas, Fondo Compagnia di S. Caterina, 254, fo. 89^v, according to Paolo Guasconi, 'L'Oratorio musicale a Firenze dalle origini al 1785' (*laurea* thesis, University of Florence, 1978–9), xxxii–xxxiii, and John Walter Hill, 'Oratory Music in Florence, iii: The Confraternities from 1655 to 1785', *Acta Musicologica*, 53 (1986), 137. Guasconi reads the date of the account as 23 Nov., whereas Hill reads 28 Nov.

[21] According to Howard E. Smither, *A History of the Oratorio*, i: *The Oratorio in the Baroque Era: Italy, Vienna, Paris* (Chapel Hill, NC, 1977) (where the oratorio is discussed in detail on pp. 191–4), p. 191, it has been ascribed to both Luigi Rossi and Marco Marazzoli; Smither favours Marazzoli's authorship. The poet is supposedly Lelio Orsini. For more information, see Ch. 8 below.

[22] Copies of the librettos are in I-Fm.

[23] Copies of the relevant librettos are in I-MOe. *Il Trespolo balordo* presented in Bologna in 1682 was not Stradella's comedy.

[24] These were *Chi non sa che la costanza, Riderete in verità, Non è al certo vanità, Mentre in un dolce, Ti lascierò, Crudi ferri, Ecco il petto, Sotto vedovo cielo, Dove aggiri mia vita*: see Hans Joachim Marx, 'Die Musik am Hofe Pietro Kardinal Ottobonis', *Analecta musicologica*, 5 (1968), item 37a, pp. 132–3.

his madrigals and cantatas made there at this time. The Academy of Ancient Music, for example, performed two of his madrigals at the Crown Tavern in 1726.[25] However, this was the last real interest in performing his compositions for purely musical, and not also historical, motives.

Biography and Legend

As performances on the Continent waned, though, Stradella's life began to attract biographers, unfortunately not always the most accurate ones. As early as 1715 Pierre Bourdelot gave a long account of him in his *Histoire de la musique et de ses effets*, calling him there 'le plus excellent Musicien de toute l'Italie, environ l'an 1670'.[26] Although most of the cities Stradella is known to have lived in—Rome, Venice, Turin, Genoa—are listed, what happened in them and when is all incorrect, actually a most fantastic tale of excitement and love. What is more, and worse, Bourdelot's version became the basis for most succeeding biographies of Stradella in the eighteenth and nineteenth centuries, including those by Burney, Hawkins, Larousse, Fétis, and Ambros. More or less contemporary with Bourdelot were two Italian biographies of Stradella, one by Francesco Maria Veracini which was different but equally incorrect,[27] and the other by Giuseppe Ottavio Pitoni, which although incomplete was accurate as far as it went. In Pitoni's manuscript entitled 'Notizia de' Contrapuntisti e de' Compositori di Musica' one reads the following:

Alessandro Stradella. Chamber [music] composer of eminent art, and of great spirit, who with always fervent style gave life to harmonic compositions and presented in the theatres of Italy the great liveliness of his artful talent; [he] quite pleased the Roman princes, and [was] esteemed in all of Italy. [He] lived at length in Rome from where he was forced to leave because of women, and having arrived in Genoa did many theatrical compositions; but persecuted by adverse fortune he had an unfortunate encounter for the same reason again in that city of Genoa, whereby he was unhappily mortally stabbed. This was [a] man as great in composing as in handling the keys with velocity and marvellous art. It is not possible to know the precise number of works, [they] being copious; this however I can say, that from his mouth the same Alessandro confessed that the best work composed by him was the oratorio of San Giovanni Battista; moreover this virtuoso had a great name and was respected [as a composer] of rather unique duets, and for proceeding surprisingly with much art and counterpoint, and liveliness of spirit in which his compositions always abounded.[28]

[25] GB-Lbl, Add. 1732, the society's Minute Book.

[26] Pierre Bourdelot and Pierre Bonnet, *Histoire de la musique et de ses effets* (Paris, 1715); Stradella is discussed on pp. 59–65 and the citation here is from p. 65.

[27] See Bonaventura's description of Veracini's manuscript treatise *Il Trionfo della pratica musicale* in 'Un trattato inedito'. Veracini's claim that Stradella studied with Ercole Bernabei could have arisen from confusion with Agostino Steffani, whose initials are the same and who did study with Bernabei.

[28] I-Rvat, Capella Giulia, I. 1, pp. 699–700, and in Pitoni's *Notitia*, ed. Ruini, 324.

A successful musical ruse concerns the vocal piece known variously as *Pietà, Signore*; *Aria da chiesa*; *Agnus Dei*; among other titles. This was a work which Fétis claimed he had discovered and which he said was by Stradella. He had it performed for the French Music Society in Paris at the Salle Ventadour on 24 March 1833, and it was so appreciated then and afterwards that it has enjoyed great popularity ever since. For example, its many editions fill a page and a half of *The Catalogue of Printed Music in the British Library to 1980* (London, 1986). It is an example of pure nineteenth-century romanticism, perhaps even one composed by Fétis himself. That the French musicologists were not able to discern the hoax proves not only how unfamiliar they were with Stradella's music, but how little baroque music in general they knew.[29] Another work passed off as Stradella's was the aria 'O del mio dolce ardor' from Gluck's *Elena e Paride* (1770; Paride's aria from Act I, scene 1): it was less popular but still published several times beginning in 1852, sometimes with the sacred text 'O salutaris'.

The year 1841 saw the beginning of a correspondence which was to have direct bearing on research into Stradella's life. It was then that the Modenese composer Angelo Catelani sent his opera *Carattaco* to Giacomo Rossini in Paris and asked his evaluation of it. Catelani continued to send his compositions (and local foods) to Rossini from time to time, and thus their friendship was established.[30]

Since he was also librarian of the Estense collection of music in Modena, Catelani became interested in Stradella. In 1861 he published a first list of the Stradella music manuscripts in his charge, and pieced together what biographical information he could from facts gleaned from them; he also undertook archival research in Modena and elsewhere in order to ascertain something about the composer's life and music, and published these findings in 1865.[31]

Thinking that the archives of Paris might offer information on the composer, Catelani wrote to Rossini for help. Rossini's answer reveals how little was known about Stradella at the time:

In my infancy one spoke of Stradella, the castrated, as an incomparable singer; in my adolescence one spoke of vocal miracles by one uncastrated Stradella; finally, in my maturity I am assured that Stradella is an encyclopaedic composer of music

---

[29] On the history of this piece, see Richard, 'Stradella et les Contarini', 33, no. 15 (11 Mar. 1866), 113–15, and Guido Salvetti, 'La verità di una falsificazione', in Carolyn Gianturco and Giancarlo Rostirolla (eds.), *Atti del Convegno di studi 'Alessandro Stradella e il suo tempo', Siena, 8–12 settembre 1982, Chigiana*, 39, NS 19 (1988), 201–10.

[30] See Rossini's side of the correspondence in *Lettere inedite e rare di G. Rossini*, ed. Giuseppe Mazzatinti (Imola, 1892), 76 ff.

[31] Angelo Catelani, 'Dell'archivio musicale della biblioteca palatina di Modena, e particolarmente di Alessandro Stradella', *Effemeride della pubblica istruzione*, 2, no. 24 (4 Mar. 1861), 404–5, and *Delle opere* (1865/6) respectively.

of great value. . . . . [The French] declare that only one Stradella existed, the author *of the only thing which exists in France, 'Pietà, Signore'!*[32]

Rossini then made inquiries and put Catelani in touch with Paolino Richard. Encouraged by Catelani, and manifesting a similar spirit of honest attention to detail and respect for the past, Richard undertook research in Paris: in 1865–6 he published archival documents which shed light on Stradella's stay in Turin.[33] Rossini read both their results with great interest and was pleased when Catelani published his 1865 article separately in 1866 and dedicated it to him. Rossini hoped Catelani would fulfil his ambition to publish some of Stradella's music (the maestro was especially interested in Stradella's use of trumpet and trombone in *Il barcheggio*), but Catelani died soon after. Not until 1906 were other relevant documents uncovered in Modena due to the research of Heinz Hess.[34] In spite of all these meritorious investigations, however, Stradella's life was still largely a mystery.

Then Remo Giazotto's book *La musica a Genova* and his two-volume *Vita di Alessandro Stradella* were published in 1951 and 1962 respectively,[35] and from their affirmations, seemingly documented, they were understandably hailed as finally providing a complete and accurate biography of the composer. In fact, for several years Giazotto's work was accepted as truth and used as the basis for encyclopaedia articles and subsequent research by others. It has turned out, however, that many of the documents which Giazotto cites cannot be found, whereas others which contradict them have since come to light; in addition, many documents in his books which do exist (usually having been discovered by someone else) are either mistranscribed, misquoted, or misunderstood.

For one reason or another, then, the name of Alessandro Stradella has been kept alive since the seventeenth century. Sometimes this was due to the collecting of his music[36] or the performing of it; at other times it was the false tale of a colourful character which attracted attention. This latter 'Stradella legend' was circulated through an enormous quantity of literature. In addition to being the subject of novels, a play, and a poem, the 'fictitious' Stradella was also the main character of a surprisingly large number of operas: Louis Niedermeyer, *Stradella* (1837); Friedrich von Flotow, *Alessandro Stradella* (1844); Franz Doppler, *Alessandro Stradella*

---

[32] Rossini, *Lettere inedite*, letter of 5 July 1865, p. 178.

[33] Richard, 'Stradella et les Contarini'.   [34] Hess, *Die Opern*.

[35] The first was printed in Genoa, the second in Milan.

[36] A brief history of catalogues of Stradella's music may be read in Gianturco–McCrickard, *Stradella Catalogue*. Both Basso's 'Introduzione' to Data Fragalà and Colurato, *Biblioteca di Torino* and David Allen, 'The "Lost" Stradella Manuscripts and their Relationship to the Estense Holdings of his Music in Modena', in Carolyn Gianturco (ed.), *Alessandro Stradella e Modena, Atti del Convegno internazionale di studi, Modena, 15–17 dicembre 1983* (Modena, 1985), 125–35, suggest that probably almost all of Stradella's music has come down to us.

(1845); Adolph Schimon, *Alessandro Stradella* (1846); Giuseppe Sinico, *Alessandro Stradella* (1863); Virginio Marchi, *Il cantore di Venezia* (1867).[37] It may have been the fascination with a murdered composer, stimulated by these operas, which encouraged the unusually late, nine-teenth-century publication of several of Stradella's compositions. For example, in 1845 Sir Henry Bishop (composer of the nostalgic 'Home, Sweet Home') published 'Se nel ben sempre incostante' (an aria from the opera *Le gare dell'amor eroico*), affirming that it had already been 'sung by Signor [Giovanni Matteo] Mario at the Concerts of Ancient Music' which Bishop himself conducted. In 1864, as part of *Gemme d'antichità*, the can-tata *Sopra un'eccelsa torre* was dedicated to the famous baritone, Manuel Garcia; and sections of the cantata *Già languiva la notte* were dedicated to Pauline Viardot-Garcia.[38]

As will be seen, Stradella's music justifies being studied and performed; and now that the facts have been put forth, one can also claim that its creator, the 'real' Stradella, is as interesting a figure as was his legend.

---

[37] For a list of the spurious Stradella literature see the introduction to Owen Jander, 'Alessandro Stradella and his Minor Dramatic Works' (Ph.D. diss., Harvard University, 1962), and Eleanor F. McCrickard, 'Stradella Never Dies: The Composer as Hero in Literature and Song', *Yearbook of Interdisciplinary Studies in the Fine Arts*, 2 (1990), 209–33.

[38] For all editions of Stradella's music, see Gianturco–McCrickard, *Stradella Catalogue*.

PART II
The Music

6

Cantatas

Although Stradella composed in all of the usual Italian seventeenth-century genres, his greatest output was in the area of secular vocal music, a result no doubt of location and opportunity. He never held, nor does it seem he was offered or wanted, a church position, which would have augmented both his instrumental production and his sacred vocal music. At the same time, all secular vocal music did not receive Stradella's attention equally. Contemporary composers located in Venice normally devoted themselves to the theatre, but those working in the rest of Italy had fewer such opportunities. Moreover, his contributions to Roman opera were limited, at first because the Tordinona offered only works already staged elsewhere, and then because the Pope forced all public theatres to close; the time he later spent in Venice and Turin was too short to allow him to write operas. Only when Stradella was in Genoa was this feasible, and he then pursued an operatic career with seeming ease and success. Even so, his *drammi in musica* are very few in comparison with the rest of his vocal secular music. Instead, Stradella's largest contribution was to the cantata.

The Italian cantata in Stradella's lifetime was not fixed in either its poetic or musical structure. Once a patron had made his wishes, preferences, and resources known, the poet decided what his subject was to be and how many verses he would write; the composer then collaborated by deciding how best to employ the patron's instrumental and vocal forces in setting the text. Neither subject, length, forms, nor forces defined the genre. Rather, other criteria established whether a poetic–musical composition was a cantata, criteria which were well known and adhered to by both poets and composers without discussion.[1]

One whose comments can be taken as authoritative is Giovan Mario Crescimbeni, the first secretary of the Arcadian Academy and therefore qualified to comment on the poetry of his time. In 1702 he wrote that in the seicento 'they introduced certain other kinds of poetry for music, which today are generally called cantatas, which are composed of verses and shorter verses [unstructured lines of eleven and seven syllables

---

[1] See Carolyn Gianturco, 'The Italian Seventeenth-Century Cantata: A Textual Approach', in John Caldwell, Edward Olleson, and Susan Wollenberg (eds.), *The Well Enchanting Skill: Music, Poetry, and Drama in the Culture of the Renaissance. Essays in Honour of F. W. Sternfeld* (Oxford, 1990), 41–51, and *The Italian Cantata in the Seventeenth Century* (16 vols.; New York, 1985–7).

(known as *versi sciolti*)] rhymed without rule, with arias therein [rhymed poetry in formally organized strophes], sometimes for one voice, sometimes for more; and they made and make them also mixed of dramatic and narrative [elements]'.[2] By this time the Italian cantata was so well known and well established that it was clear even in Paris what the genre entailed, as Sébastien de Brossard made evident when he wrote of the cantata that 'It is a large piece, where the words are in Italian, varied with *Recitatives, Ariettas,* and different tempos'.[3] All writers differentiated between true dramas (operas and oratorios) and the cantata, a poetic genre containing only some elements of drama.[4] Its usual construction was through description, explanation, and discussion.

Secular Cantatas for Solo Voice with Continuo

The overwhelming majority of Stradella's secular cantatas with basso continuo are for solo voice, 125 in all.[5] The style of the text in all of them is generally that of Marino, one of Italy's greatest poets, whose skilful use of rhetoric, combined with a rich vocabulary and an intimate knowledge of classical literature and history, resulted in verses that were calculated to appeal objectively to the intellect although professing to deal passionately with emotions. Perhaps what one notices first in Stradella's solo cantatas is the language, which is generally bold, direct, and impassioned. Moreover, its aim is to simulate more anger or desperation than a situation would reasonably call for, such as in *L'avete fatta a me!* where the beloved is accused with the lines: 'Intanto crudele, | ingrata, infedele, | vantatevi, gloriatevi | d'aver tradito e non saper perché.' (Meanwhile cruel, | ungrateful, unfaithful, | pride yourself, praise yourself | for having betrayed and not knowing why.)

Even more impassioned are the following verses from *Già languiva la notte* for Medea, who has just wished for the death of the unfaithful Giasone: 'Ah no, fermate, o numi! | Lasciate pur in vita | lo spergiuro, l'ingrato, | l'infedel adorato, | ché s'egli è la mia vita, egl'è il mio core: | viver già non poss'io s'egli sen more.' (Ah no, stop, O Gods! | Let live | the perjurer, the ungrateful one, | the unfaithful adored one, | since, if he is my life, he is my heart: | I am not able to live if he dies.)

Contrasts in rapid succession are also employed frequently in the poetry. They encourage a manneristic feeling of instability or discontent,

---

[2] *Comentarij*, (Rome), i. 240.

[3] *Dictionaire de musique* (Paris, 1703; repr. Amsterdam, 1964).

[4] For example, see Giuseppe Gaetano Salvadori, *Poetica toscana* (Naples, 1691), where 'Drami [*sic*] in Musica' (ch. 7) and 'Oratori o Dialoghi o Drametti' [*sic*] (ch. 10) are treated separately from cantatas (ch. 8).

[5] See App. 1 for a list of the cantatas and their forces; see also Gianturco–McCrickard, *Stradella Catalogue.*

as in *Forsennato pensier, che far poss'io,* where 'torments', 'desire', 'cruel whirlwind', 'joys', 'pleasures', 'tears', follow quickly one upon the other: 'Fra le Sirti de' tormenti | del desio spinge le vele | e con turbine crudele | le mie gioie e i miei contenti | chiude ognor nel pianto mio. | Forsennato pensier, che far poss'io?' (Between the shifting sand of torments | of desire he pushes the sails | and with cruel whirlwind | my joys and my pleasures | he always ends in my tears. | Insane thought, what can I do?)

Lines from *Disperata rimembranza* alternate 'sad eyes' with 'beautiful beloved eyes, and 'joy' with 'tears': 'Ahi, quanto, oh cielo, ahi, quanto | quest'occhi addolorati | divide, oh Dio, da quei bei lumi amati, | cagion pria di mia gioia, ora di pianto!' (Ah, how much, O Heaven, ah, how much | divides these sad eyes, | O God, from those beautiful beloved lights, | reason before of my joy, now of tears.)

Imagery, too, plays an enormous role in creating a desired atmosphere, such as in the opening lines of *Quando stanco dal corso* which call upon mythological figures to describe the quietness of the passing of day and oncoming night: 'Quando stanco dal corso in grembo a Teti | in traccia del riposo | Febo s'asconde e già la notte oscura, | emula al giorno, in nere bende accolta | passeggia in ciel, allor ch'il tutto tace' (When tired from the race in Thetis' lap | in search of repose | Phoebus hides and already the night darkens, | rivals day, wrapped in black cloths | walks in heaven, until all is silent); or the following pastoral verses which, in contrast, describe the delicate flurry of activity occurring at the break of day: 'Già languiva la notte | e i zeffiretti alati | con aliti odorati | scorreano a ravvivar sui campi i fiori; | già i pargoletti albori | sorgean dal Gange a colorir le sponde; | e già tremole l'onde | attendeano inquiete | goder fra molli argenti | dell'adorato sol i rai nascenti' (The night already languished | and the little winged zephyrs | with sweet-smelling breaths | ran to revive the flowers in the fields; | already the cherub dawns | had risen from the Ganges to colour the banks; | and already the trembling waves | awaited impatient | to enjoy among silver springs | the nascent rays of the adored sun.)

Cantata poetry abounds, too, in oft-repeated images, such as the above-mentioned 'lights' equated with 'eyes'; or fire normally associated with the ardour of love, such as 'the flame of love' (in *Quando stanco dal corso*), 'in amorous burning flame' (in *Il più misero amante*), 'in the loving furnace' (in *Io non vuò più star così*), 'A mountain, | the volcano Etna | burning with a thousand flames' (in *Un Mongibello ardente*). In even greater abundance are the images of water, an element which in all its various manifestations was dear to the baroque spirit, chosen to illustrate the fluctuations of passion and life's troubles and rescue from them. One finds, for example, that almost every other *verso sciolto* in *O mio cor, quanto t'inganni* contains either 'sea' or 'wave'; words such as 'ocean', 'shipwreck', 'port', 'storm', 'wave', 'anchor', 'gulf', permeate *Forsennato pensier, che far poss'io*. A rich traditional imagery is also used for that source of much trouble and delight, Love. He is called variously 'the son of Venus' (in *L'anima incenerita* and *Già languiva la notte*), 'the blindfolded God' (in *Che più speri, mio cor*), 'Wicked Love, tyrannical archer' (in *Empio Amor, tiranno arciero*), and so forth.

In Stradella's solo secular cantatas with continuo accompaniment, there is often a narrator. In many cantatas he sets the scene: for example, in *A' pie' d'annoso pino* he describes the lover who is in tears at the base of a pine tree encircled by tall, dark cypresses, after which the protagonist grieves aloud; in *Dove il Tebro famoso* the narrator describes Silvio sitting by the River Tiber and lets him release his anger against Amor; and in *Fuor della Stigia sponda* the scene for Orfeo's rescue and subsequent loss of Euridice is set by the narrator. In some solo cantatas there is more than one protagonist, such as *Da mille pene e mille* where both Eurillo and his beloved are introduced. Regardless of the number of characters, the narrator may reappear during the course of a cantata if description is needed. Occasionally, however, the narrator does not set the scene but appears only at the end of a cantata to sum it up, as in *Vincesti, o ciel*, which opens directly with the lover accusing Rosina of killing him by her lack of response. *Non mi curo di fedeltà* offers yet another scheme: it is the lover who begins, and the narrator enters afterwards to introduce Lilla.

In more or less equal number to the cantatas with a narrator are those without one. These are conducted solely by the protagonist. This is the case, for example, with *Quando mai vi stancherete*, which is an outpouring of a lover's grief over Filli, and with *Quando sembra che nuoti*, where the protagonist is desperate because love is again at war inside him. A special type of cantata continues a tradition first seen in Monteverdi, that of the letter scene: *Figli del mio cordoglio* (entirely in direct speech) is a love-letter from Fileno to Filli, and *Il più misero amante* (which by contrast has a narrator) is one from Eurillo to his beloved.

In all these categories, the lover as well as his beloved may either be anonymous or named. In the latter event, and following traditional Renaissance poetic practice, characters are generally taken from mythology. Filli appears most often, but Clori (or Cloride) is also rather frequently employed, as is Eurillo; one also occasionally finds Fileno, Cinzia, Lidia, Lilla, and Eurilla. Rare appearances are made as well by Erminda, Laura, Silvio, Teti, Arianna (to Teseo), Orfeo, Euridice, Lorindo, Lidio, Alindo, Dorillo, Rosina, Dori, Licori, and Medea (about Giasone).

The protagonists of several cantatas are, instead, historical characters. Some of these also deal with love, such as Mark Antony's passion for Cleopatra which is portrayed in *Già le spade nemiche;* in *Ecco chi già nell'Asia* Helen of Troy, now that Paris is dead, blames Amor for having made her betray her husband. Still other cantatas are more dramatic accounts based on non-amorous facts of history. For example, in *A difender le mura dell'antica Sionne* the King of Nicea swears revenge for the death of Lesbino; in *Figli, amici, Agrippina*, Julius Caesar exhorts his family to revenge his death; both *Se Nerone lo vuole* and *Se Nerone mi vuol morto* deal with Seneca's suicide; and in *Sopra un'eccelsa torre* Nero watches as Rome burns.

Besides plots dealing with love in exaggerated and mythological terms, and those which present stronger emotions based on historical reality, there are a few humorous cantatas for solo voice with continuo. In excited language, the protagonist of *Si salvi chi può* urges everyone to save himself: the world is falling, and Bacchus' poison and Mars' fury have infected everyone; it isn't certain if the world will survive! *Un editto l'altro dì in Parnaso* deals with the offering of a reward by the muses for 'lots of verses' lost by a poet. The lover in *Voi volete il mio cor* will reciprocate his lady's affections only if she agrees not to give him any trouble. In contrast with these more comic cantatas are the equally exceptional ones which end tragically: for example, Seneca commits suicide in *Se Nerone lo vuole*; Eurillo dies of lovesickness in *Con un cor tutto pianti*; and Mark Antony expires of his battle wounds in *Già le spade nemiche*.

As was normal for the period, the main character of most of Stradella's solo cantatas with continuo accompaniment is a man, such as the lover in *L'avete fatta a me!* and in *Il più tenero affetto*. There are also examples of cantatas which imply a woman protagonist, such as Medea who laments her betrayal by Giasone in *Già languiva la notte*; Lidia who, in *Io non vuò più star così*, does not want love if it is not constant; and the anonymous scorned woman of *Sprezzata mi credei, ma non tradita*. There are, of course, those works which leave a character's gender unspecified: it is not clear who is asking troublesome thoughts to disappear in *Noiosi pensieri*, or who reprimands the heart for believing in love in *O mio cor, quanto t'inganni*.

While none of these texts has been proven to have been written by Stradella,[6] those that name specific places which are not mythological or associated with a historical subject do encourage biographical interpretations. *Dalle sponde del Tebro*, *Aure, voi che spirate di Partenope*, and *Dove il Tebro famoso* all take place by the River Tiber; *Il più tenero affetto* mentions both the Tiber and Arbia rivers; and *Eccomi accinto* and *Che vuoi più da me, Fortuna?* also refer to Rome. It is not obvious where the protagonist of *Vaganti pensieri* is at the moment, but she wants to go to the Adriatic Sea; whereas in *Il mar gira ne' fiumi* the lover wants to go from

---

[6] One possibility could be *Se t'ama, Filli, o cor*, where the protagonist makes a comparison between the 'musico' who rescued Euridice and himself, also a 'musico'.

the Adriatic to Rome. However, even in such cases one must be cautious: for example, the text of *Solcava incauto legno* was probably written by Apolloni before he came in contact with Stradella, and therefore its mention of the Arno River cannot be said to prove a connection between the composer and Tuscany.

As far as poetic structure is concerned, it is possible for any sort of cantata (with or without a narrator, and on any subject) to have a refrain. Occasionally called an *intercalare* but also known as a *ritornello*, the refrain was one or more lines which the poet brought back in such a way that the repetition made sense in the text. In *Chi ben ama un sol giorno*, for example, the opening text returns twice in the course of the piece to repeat the complaint that he who loves, even for a single day, will always be a lover. Other cantatas repeat internal lines, such as *Con un cor tutto pianti* which has Eurillo say at three different times that it is sad that no one understands him ('Ma la cosa è penar'). A refrain can be text intended to be set either as recitative or as an aria, as the above examples show.

The poet alternated *versi sciolti* and closed poetic forms as he chose. For example, *Se Nerone lo vuole* and *Il più tenero affetto* are long texts almost all in recitative, whereas *Bella bocca, taci, taci* and *Eppur sempre a' miei desiri* are composed almost exclusively of closed forms. A straightforward and simple alternation may be seen in *Ben è vile quel core* which consists of reciting text followed by just one closed form. Most cantatas, however, have greater alternation of the two types of text: *Forsennato pensier, che far poss'io*, for example, is structured as recitative–aria–recitative–aria; also beginning with reciting text is *Già languiva la notte*, which augments the alternation to r–a–r–a–r–a–r–a. Alternating structures may also begin with a closed form, as does *A che vale il sospirar*, which follows the pattern a–r–a–r; a longer example of this type is *Noiosi pensieri*, which is a–r–a–r–a–r. As will have been noted, the cantata could end in either kind of text.

The length of a section of reciting text was also not fixed. While lines of seven and eleven syllables alternated freely, it was usual for the section to end with a hendecasyllabic line. The same freedom of length is true of the closed forms as well, although individual strophes are generally either of four lines ('Disperata rimembranza' in the cantata of the same title), six lines ('Chi desia di salde tempre' in *Sopra un'eccelsa torre*), or eight lines ('Oh Dio, che farò?' in *Il più tenero affetto*). Rhyme-schemes in the closed forms are also traditional (abba, etc.; abab, etc.; and aba bcb, etc. are the most popular). Their structures were varied and Stradella's cantatas exhibit closed forms of one strophe ('Fra le Sirti de' tormenti' in *Forsennato pensier, che far poss'io*), three strophes ('Si creda piuttosto' in *Ch'io non ami, oh, questo no!*), and four strophes ('Cielo, oh Dio, cielo, che tardi?' in *Già languiva la notte*); but most closed poetic forms have two strophes.

These may be alike in number of lines, length of line, and rhyme-scheme: in short, a repeated structure. Examples of this arrangement are numerous in Stradella's cantatas (and include 'Su, su sparite, pensieri' in *Aure, voi che spirate di Partenope*; 'E' sì bello il foco mio' in *Ch'io nasconda il mio foco*; 'Chi non sa che la costanza' in the cantata with the same title). However, poets often wrote two strophes of unlike structure. 'Chi d'amor le salde tempre' in *Quando stanco dal corso in grembo a Teti* has two strophes of four lines each; the lines are all eight syllables long, but the rhyme-schemes are different: strophe I is abba, whereas strophe II is cdec. The two strophes of 'Sì, ch'io temo e non disamo' in the cantata of the same name are even more unlike: the first has nine lines, but the second only eight; the first is composed wholly of 8-syllable lines, but the second has also one 4-syllable line; the rhyme-scheme of the first strophe is abbaaccdd, but in the second strophe it is ababccdd.

Of Stradella's 125 extant solo cantatas with basso continuo accompaniment, 109 are for soprano. Only 7 cantatas are for bass, 5 for alto, 2 for tenor, and 1 each for mezzo-soprano and baritone. One assumes that each composition was written with known performers in mind, and therefore that certain aspects of style may be understood as conforming to their abilities. At the same time, several features of the cantatas are so recurrent that they may be considered normal compositional procedures for Stradella. These concern mainly questions of form, although some aspects of style are also involved.

The dominating factor in all of Stradella's vocal music, but especially in his cantatas, is his response to poetic text. On the largest scale, he normally set freely structured text as recitative, and closed forms as arias. Deviations from this procedure occur only in rare cases, such as *Il più tenero affetto* which begins with an extremely long section of reciting text, 59 lines in all; this is followed by a closed form of 16 lines; the work concludes with another long section of reciting text, this time 46 lines long. To balance the large proportion of recitative which would have resulted had he complied with the poet's scheme, Stradella set the first five lines of reciting text instead as an aria. In all such cases, however, he exercised great discrimination when deciding to overrule the poetic structure.

As was stated earlier, the poet most often ended sections of *versi sciolti* with a hendecasyllabic line; often he wrote the same length of line during a long section of reciting text, or perhaps alone after a closed form, but wherever he employed it, it was to conclude a section or idea. The placement of these hendecasyllabic lines, therefore, constituted an element of poetic structure. Stradella frequently indicated their different and peculiar 'weighty' nature by changing style at these moments. First of all, contrary to normal recitative practice, which states words only once, he repeated the text: for example, 'Che degno è di perdono un cor pentito' in

Genuflesso a tue piante is repeated twice; 'Tu non sorgi mai più se un dì tramonti' in *In quel sol che in grembo al Tago* is repeated three times; 'Perché sol per penar nasce un amante' in *Costanza, mio core* is repeated four times. Stradella also composed a more melodic, aria-like line for the voice than was usual in recitative, and he quickened the rhythm of the continuo. Such sections of recitative text set to aria-style music (NB not aria *form*), also known as *ariosi*, were generally in ternary rhythm.[7] The arioso is habitually well organized, often sequentially, as in the case of 'Che i confini del riso occupa il pianto' (*Amor, io son contento*) where the technique is shared by voice and continuo through imitation (Ex. 1); furthermore, it is always in the spirit of the text, as is the cry which calls for the attention of lovers at the beginning of *Udite, amanti, un prodigio novello* (Ex. 2).

Ex. 1.

Many of Stradella's solo cantatas with continuo accompaniment, again because they follow poetic structure, are refrain-cantatas. Specifically, the line of recitative 'Datti pace, Fileno, e torna in te' appears with the same music three times in the course of *Presso un rivo ch'avea*; the opening closed form (four verses), text and music, of *L'avete fatta a me!* returns at the end of the cantata; the text and music of the opening aria of *Chi ben ama un sol giorno* returns five times in the course of the work, so often that it makes an overall rondo structure; and so forth. Occasionally, a refrain creates an ABA aria form, as with the opening lines of *Ch'io non ami*, *Noiosi pensieri*, *Si salvi chi può*, and *Piangete, occhi, piangete*. There are only rare instances where Stradella decided not to set a textual refrain

---

[7] Kathleen Ann Chaikin, 'The Solo Soprano Cantatas of Alessandro Stradella' (Ph.D. diss., Stanford University, 1975), mistakes ariosos for short arias, even though she correctly states that the sections are based on only one line of text (123 ff.). Therefore, her discussion of the arioso proper is also incorrect (105–6): for example, she erroneously says ariosos are only in 4/4 metre.

Ex. 2.

to the same music: one example is the line 'Nascon le gioie ad arricchirmi il petto' in *Vaganti pensieri*, which appears twice, both times set as an arioso, but to different music; another case is that of the opening line of *Sprezzata mi credei, ma non tradita*, which is heard three times in the course of the cantata but each time with different music.

The structure of poetic closed forms is also usually mirrored by Stradella, the simplest forms being those of one strophe which he set to continuous music, such as 'Se m'alletta dolce calma' in *Sono in dubbio d'amar* and 'Or lampo vivace di volto sereno' in *Chi dà fede alla speranza*. Repeated poetic structures were set as strophic musical settings. Examples of this very frequent form are the already-mentioned 'Oh Dio, che farò' in *Il più tenero affetto*, as well as 'Scuotami pur la sorte' in *Ben è vile quel core*. When two strophes of poetry exhibit differences, Stradella provided a matching AB form: this is the case with 'Chi d'amor le salde tempre' in *Quando stanco dal corso in grembo a Teti* and 'Sì, ch'io temo e non disamo' in the cantata of the same name. A more extended example of his repeating or changing music in accordance with the poetry is 'Cielo, oh Dio, cielo, che tardi?' from *Già languiva la notte:* four strophes of poetry follow one upon another exhibiting an AABB form, and Stradella set them correspondingly.

Only a few structures were decided upon by Stradella for purely musical reasons. For example, a rare example of a repeated poetic structure not being treated strophically by Stradella is 'Ogni lingua sempre infeconda' in *Bella bocca, taci, taci,* where he obviously did not want more repetitions in a work which already had a refrain aria. There are also the ABA arias which are the result of the composer's decision to repeat text and music: two examples are the opening aria of *Amor, io son contento* and 'Mai più vi rivedrò' in *Il più misero amante*. However, where no independent literary source exists—and this is usually the case—Stradella's contribution to the ternary or da capo aria form (that is, his decision and not the poet's to have a refrain) cannot be adequately ascertained.

On the other hand, the ABB' aria form was a choice which was solely his. A few examples will suffice to illustrate this. The poetic closed form 'Se ne' flutti dell'orgoglio' in *Forsennato pensier, che far poss'io* contains only one 6-line strophe: Stradella set the first four lines as an A section; he then set the last two lines differently and repeated the section in a different key to produce the design BB'. 'Chi desia di salde tempre' in *Sopra un'eccelsa torre* has a similar poetic structure, and Stradella set it, too, in an ABB' musical form. *Chi non sa che la bellezza* is a 2-strophe aria where, even though the strophes are poetically equivalent, Stradella decided to set them differently (AB). However, they have the same internal structure and consist of four lines of text: Stradella set the first two strophes as one section (A), and the other two to different music, which he then repeated in another key (BB'). In these cases, it would seem that Stradella reorganized the text—in sections and with repetitions—in order to allow for musical contrast, repetition, and modulation.

In questions of musical style, Stradella was also guided by the dictates of the poetry. First and foremost is his careful attention to grammatical phrases, to word accent, and to the rise and fall which a line would require for its correct declamation. His approach is the same whether he is writing a recitative or an aria. The opening of *Sono in dubbio d'amar* is typical (Ex. 3): musical phrases are shaped according to the poetic phrases with cadences and held notes used to outline verbal ideas; the syllable 'dub-' is always given its due stress; the adjacent vowels of '-no in' are properly melted together; 'I am in doubt' is repeated and each time pitched higher to insist upon the protagonist's confusion; when the source of doubt, 'd'amar', is finally stated, it is given a fioritura for emphasis.

The beginning of *Già languiva la notte* illustrates still further characteristics of Stradella's manner of responding to the text. The first line, which describes the quiet disappearance of the night, is set syllabically in somewhat sustained values, while the continuo remains absolutely immobile; but as soon as the 'little winged zephyrs' are mentioned, the vocal and continuo rhythm picks up; and when they are said to blow on the flowers in the fields, fiorituras are employed to illustrate the continual movement. Here attention is paid not only to poetic phrases and text declamation, but to the meanings of individual words (musical imagery) and to the general atmosphere.

Because they aimed at declaiming the text, Stradella's cantatas offer the voice music which is predominantly syllabic, stepwise or with small skips, and in ever-changing rhythmic patterns which follow the rhythms of the words. Whenever this approach is altered, it is perhaps either because he felt another style would interpret the text better or because he had a par-

Ex. 3.

ticular singer's abilities in mind. An especially florid treatment of the voice is to be found, for example, in all the cantatas in a manuscript which belonged to the singer Andrea Adami.[8] Whether they were composed specifically for Adami or not is unknown, but they were certainly conceived for an especially gifted singer.[9] However, as fiorituras occur only on important words and on stressed syllables, the text remains comprehensible. In this example and in general in his vocal music, Stradella made certain that the text would be understood also by beginning with a

[8] These are published in facsimile in Carolyn Gianturco, *The Italian Cantata in the Seventeenth Century*, ix: *Cantatas by Alessandro Stradella* (New York, 1987). The individual titles are: *Presso un rivo ch'avea*; *O mio cor, quanto t'inganni*; *Forsennato pensier, che far poss'io*; *Noiosi pensieri*; *L'avete fatta a me!*; *Se Nerone lo vuole*; *Disperata rimembranza*; *Il più tenero affetto*; *Quando stanco dal corso in grembo a Teti*; *Il più misero amante*.

[9] Even the instrumental bass requires a first-rate performer.

fairly syllabic setting and reserving more complex treatment for successive repetitions of a text.

Another aspect of Stradella's solo secular cantatas is the instrumental bass. Often virtuoso instrumentalists would have been employed: for example, see the bass part of 'Chi provò sdegnoso il fato adirato' in *Tante perle non versa l'Aurora* which is in almost continuous sixteenth-notes (Ex. 4), as is that of the opening section of 'Voi del cielo, dorate fiammelle' in *Arrest'il pie' fugace*. Such writing implies the use of a melody instrument—a violoncello, perhaps a member of the lute family, or harp—and alone, without a keyboard, so that it can move easily and in clear rapport (often imitative) with the voice. This latter feature is certainly the intent of the instrumental part of 'Qual farfalla ambiziosa' in *Ecco chi già nell'Asia,* which is so high at times that it enters the vocal range.

Ex. 4.

Still other bass parts, because they offer occasional realizations, suggest instead the use of chordal continuo instruments, as in the opening of *Empio Amor, tiranno arciero* (aria) and *Stanco dalla speranza* (recitative). A unique situation in these cantatas is the aria 'Una larva è la speranza' in *M'è venuto a fastidio lo sperare.* Here, two instrumental bass parts are given in one of the sections: one part is only in the bass clef and is in quarter-notes; the other begins with sixteenth-notes in the bass clef but then rises to the treble clef, at which point the bass clef has slower values against the rapid treble passage (Ex. 5). It could well be that the simpler part was intended for a sustaining bowed string instrument, whereas a harpsichord or lute, for example, was meant to play the music extended over two clefs.

Ex. 5.

The instrumental bass part may also be organized in ostinato fashion. 'Dal più barbaro dolore' in *Voi siete sventurate* is an example of a classic ostinato, the descending tetrachord outlined chromatically. It moves to three different tonal levels during the course of the cantata, but the voice never participates in the pattern.[10] In opposition to this rather rigid use of

[10] Chaikin, 'Solo Soprano Cantatas', gives the title of this aria as 'Non si creda al penar', but this is a phrase of text which precedes the closed form by several measures. Curiously, in the related musical example on p. 184, she puts the double bar correctly after this text and before 'Dal più barbaro dolore'.

an ostinato is the opening aria of *Son gradito, e pur m'affanno* (same title). Here a sixteenth-note figure appears in almost every measure, and usually twice. The figure itself is part of a longer phrase of music, but since it is often stated alone, the whole phrase does not dominate the piece as much as the single figure. In the second section of the aria, the voice takes up the figure, albeit in conjunction with others, in long (four-measure) fiorituras. Other solo cantatas which make use of an ostinato of one type or another are *Non più piaghe al mio cor, Dove l'ali spiegate, Da mille pene e mille,* and *Arrest'il pie' fugace.*

In all the cantatas where the instrumental bass requires an especially fine performer for its execution or where it has been composed with particular attention, it is obvious that Stradella was striving for a texture as contrapuntal as such reduced forces would allow. To those already cited, one may add numerous other cantata arias which insist upon the importance and equality of both the vocal and instrumental lines: 'Non temerà quest'alma stabile' in *Che vuoi più da me, Fortuna?*, where there are running eighth-notes in both voice and instrumental parts; 'Solca il mar da rie tempeste' (same title) for similar treatment; 'Vaganti pensieri' (also the title of the work), where the same material is utilized by both parts; 'Ah, che pro' con finti vezzi' in *Tradito, mio core*, which also exhibits interplay between voice and instrument; etc.

In addition, Stradella's music is tonal, and the solo cantatas present features associated with this language. Works always begin and end in the same key, for example. Closed forms are sometimes all in the main key of a cantata (as *A che vale il sospirar*, where all arias are in D minor, and *A quel candido foglio*, where all are in C minor), and sometimes in related keys (as in *Bella bocca*, whose arias are in G minor, the overall key of the work, and B flat major). Closed forms will normally modulate internally at least once, usually to the relative major, dominant, or subdominant when in a minor key, and to the dominant or subdominant if in a major key. There are, however, many examples of arias which modulate even more (such as 'Così m'atterra del fato vile' in *Vincesti, o ciel*, which departs from the basic key of E minor to modulate to the relative major, the minor dominant, and the minor subdominant keys).

Although it is possible to have modulation during the course of a recitative, an aria usually continues in the same key in which the preceding recitative has ended. In this way, the recitative serves as an introduction to an aria, and leads into it in accordance with the poetic relationship between recitative and aria. On the other hand, it is common for recitative following an aria not to be in the same key, but to begin directly in another key, normally a third away, either higher or lower. Once again, the music thus follows the text by allowing a new climate (other facts, changed or differently stated attitudes) to be sensed in the recitative.

Different sections of a recitative may also be in different keys if some dramatic situation is mentioned. On the whole, recitatives begin with sustained harmony (long-held notes in the continuo) which becomes more mobile as the section proceeds; this is once again in accordance with the text, which also generally begins quietly to set the scene and then goes on to add more details and events.

Mention should be made, too, of unusual or atypical procedures which are found in some of these cantatas. For example, 'Ire implacabili' in *A difender le mura dell'antica Sionne* features the rare time signature of 12/16. 'La fortuna è un sogno' in *Troppo oppressa dal sonno nel suo letto*, because of its insistent placement of syllables on rhythmically unstressed notes which are then tied over to stressed notes, offers a quasi-French rhythmic pattern in the vocal line, a rarity for Stradella. Another unusual rhythmic device is found in 'Tranquilli e lucidi' in *Vaghe calme, io non vi credo*: here the voice occasionally has a pattern of three notes against two in the bass.

Not rare but still striking are the arpeggiated motifs written for the voice in some cantatas. Examples may be found in the opening of *Costanza, mio core*, in various moments of *Dopo incessante corso di lagrimoso umore*, and also in *Udite, amanti, udite, Troppo oppressa dal sonno nel suo letto*, and *Solca il mar da rie tempeste*. Not surprisingly, such phrases are presented in connection with strong verbal images, such as constancy or battle. To represent sadness, Stradella resorted to an interesting use of chromaticism in 'Deh, ferma [also 'frena'] il pianto' from *Già le spade nemiche* (Ex. 6), and in the continuo of 'Quando mai vi stancherete' (same title); to illustrate the same emotion, both the voice and continuo employ a tritone motif in 'Che più speri, mio cor' (same title).

Ex. 6.

While most of Stradella's cantatas are to be found in one or two sources, some are extant in several manuscripts. There are those for which we have, for example, six copies, such as *Aure, voi che spirate di Partenope, Figli del mio cordoglio*, and *Piangete, occhi, piangete;* or seven copies, such as *Già languiva la notte*; or eight copies, such as *Ombre, voi che celate dell'Etra i rai*, and *Quando mai vi stancherete*. But if the number of extant copies of a cantata is any indication of its popularity, then the eighteen manuscripts containing *Sopra un'eccelsa torre* attest to its having been an outstanding success. Certainly, Giovan Filippo Apolloni's text is a masterly recapturing of a terrible historical tragedy—the burning of Rome—coupled with the depiction of Nero's warped, cruel personality. However, Stradella's music is equally expressive as he describes Claudio Nerone's crimes and his wild laughter while Rome is enveloped in flames. This dramatic soliloquy for bass voice is generally syllabic as the scene is set and as Nerone cries out to his city to burn; but for the recurring phrases of 'Claudio rida' (Claudio laughs) which are heard throughout the cantata, Stradella employs sixteenth-note fiorituras, which not only adequately portray the ruler's laughter, but which seem appropriately arrogant, if not unbalanced, in the otherwise sober setting. *Sopra un'eccelsa torre* is not the only masterpiece among Stradella's solo cantatas, but it is definitely one of them.[11]

Secular Cantatas for Two and Three Voices with Continuo

Stradella's extant secular cantatas with continuo accompaniment for two voices are only ten, and those for three voices as few as four. The vocal combinations in the two-voice works are several: two sopranos, soprano and alto, soprano and baritone, and soprano and bass. The three-voice cantatas are all for two sopranos and bass except one which is set for alto, tenor, and bass.

The texts of the two- and three-voice cantatas do not exhibit the variety of themes of the solo ones, but instead deal exclusively with love, albeit in various forms. Once again pastoral mythological characters are present: Lidia seeking love in *Che speranza aver si può* (a 3); Clori lamenting the absence of Lindoro in *Con mesto ciglio e dolorosi accenti* (a 2); someone (perhaps Silvio) bemoaning his love for Filli in *Fra quest'ombre* (a 2); etc. Occasionally, real places are mentioned, such as Rome in one textual version of *Che speranza aver si può* (a 3), and Genoa in another. While no characters from classical history appear in these works, *L'avviso al Tebro giunto* (a 3) does mention real people since it is a lament by two nymphs and the River Tiber over the loss to Rome of the young aristocrat Anna Pamphili Aldobrandini, who is to marry Giovanni Andrea Doria of Genoa.

Occasionally the text in these multi-voice cantatas need not have been set for more than one singer (for example, the words of *In grembo all'oblio sommerger l'ardore* (a 2) and *Lilla mia, su queste sponde* (a 3) make it clear that only one character is present) and one suspects that this typical seventeenth- and eighteenth-century treatment is a carry-over from the

---

[11] Edward J. Dent discussed *Sopra un'eccelsa torre* in 'Italian Chamber Cantatas', *Musical Antiquary*, 2 (1911), 185–6. A facsimile of the cantata is in Gianturco, *Cantatas by Stradella*, no. 11.

madrigal. On the whole, however, the texts of Stradella's two- and three-voice cantatas imply an equivalent number of roles: one is the already cited (a 3) *L'avviso al Tebro giunto* for two nymphs and the personified River Tiber; another is *Che speranza aver si può* (a 3), where Lidia is without love and the two poor pilgrims without everything else; Filli and her lover are both present in *Fra quest'ombre* (a 2); and she and Silvio are the protagonists of *Son pur dolci le ferite* (a 2).

Generally in the multi-character cantatas, a short scene is presented. For example, the man of *A dispetto della sorte* (a 2) is terribly unsure of his beloved and jealous of her, and the woman, although resenting his attitude, tries to defend herself. A less complicated situation is offered in *Chi dirà che nel veleno* (a 2), where the woman does not realize at first that she is loved. *Quel tuo petto di diamante* (a 2) presents an argument between two lovers, due to her refusal of his attentions.

Two of these two-voice cantatas are humorous pieces. In *Io rimango stordito solo in veder* both characters are unhappy and agree that there are no rules in love: while one will love a bat, another desires a cuckoo; while some want a lion, others a pig; and so forth. The scene of *Fra quest'ombre* is a hot night in Rome's Piazza di Spagna. A woman has come out to get a breath of air and happens upon a lover lamenting in song the absence of Filli. The cantata ends without the two protagonists ever conversing together: the lover goes off to die and the woman to bed! Another singular text among the multi-character cantatas is *Con mesto ciglio e dolorosi accenti* (a 2), which has a scene for Clori and an echo in the typical and popular manner found more commonly in seventeenth-century opera.

As in the solo cantatas, a narrator may be employed in the two- and three-voice cantatas, such as in *Con mesto ciglio* (a 2) and *L'avviso al Tebro giunto* (a 3); but generally the works proceed in only direct speech. The use of closed- and open-structured text is also varied as it was in the solo cantatas: *A dispetto della sorte* (a 2) has rather regular alternation between the two, whereas *Piangete, occhi dolenti, piangete* (a 2) is almost entirely in closed forms. Here, too, Stradella follows the poets' indications by setting the open-structured text as recitative and the closed forms as closed musical forms. In both two-voice and three-voice cantatas there are poetic closed forms written for only one character, to be translated into arias by Stradella: *Fra quest'ombre* (a 2), *Chi dirà che nel veleno* (a 2), and *Che speranza aver si può* (a 3) offer such examples. However, closed forms for two people (musically duets) are to be found only in the two-voice cantatas; in those for three voices there are, instead, closed forms for three people (musically trios). Naturally, within a duet or trio Stradella may employ voices singly or in combination.

The structure of the closed musical forms also normally mirrors textual organization. There are, for example, non-repeating or continuous forms (such as the opening duet of *In grembo all'oblio* (a 2)), strophic forms (as in the trio 'E perché da noi lontano' from *L'avviso al Tebro giunto* (a 3)) and binary forms (as in the duet 'Il gel di gelosia' from *Chi dirà che nel veleno* (a 2)); ABA' forms (such as the opening aria of *Fra quest'ombre io cerco il mio sole* (a 2)) may also be instances of the music following the text. ABB' forms, instead, result—as was seen in the solo cantatas—from a musical structure being imposed on the text (as in the duet 'Lusinghiero un ciglio nero' from *Baldanzosa una bellezza* (a 2)). The opening duet from this same cantata shows that, whatever the form, Stradella worked as his creativity suggested, repeating text as often as needed in order to develop internal sections: the single line of poetry 'sfida i cori a guerreggiar', in fact, goes on for 48 measures of music.

Again, as in the solo cantatas, there may be a poetic refrain in the cantata which Stradella set similarly. In the two-voice work *Io rimango stordito*, it is a section of the duet 'In amor non si dà regola' which returns; and the opening duet of *Piangete, occhi dolenti, piangete* (a 2) also receives refrain treatment. One also finds important hendecasyllabic lines of text put into arioso relief by Stradella, such as the solo line 'Nuovo tributo accresca il pianto mio' in *Con mesto ciglio e dolorosi accenti* (a 2), and the two-voice line 'Gela il sen, arde il cor, l'alma tormenta' in *In grembo all'oblio* (a 2).

Notwithstanding his general tendency to provide lines which allow singers to pronounce the poetry in an intelligible fashion, it cannot be said that Stradella's two- and three-voice cantatas are simple syllabic settings which offer nothing for the virtuoso. As proof to the contrary one may cite *A dispetto della sorte* (a 2), which requires both the soprano and baritone to execute difficult fiorituras, as well as the trio 'Ma già sento ch'il nume Imeneo' from *L'avviso al Tebro giunto* (a 3), which tosses such phrases from one voice to the other; even recitative in *Io rimango stordito* (a 2) has occasional florid phrases. Actually, since the general texture in Stradella's multi-voiced cantatas is imitative, all the music requires expert musicians for its execution. This may be applied to the continuo player(s) as well, and not only in sections based on an ostinato, such as the aria 'Scendete pur dall'etra' from *A dispetto della sorte* (a 2) and the opening aria of *Che speranza aver si può* (a 3).

While the three-voice cantatas have come down to us in only one copy each, some of the two-voice works exist in several manuscripts. For example, there are four extant copies of *In grembo all'oblio* and seven copies of *Piangete, occhi dolenti, piangete*. However, the 23 copies of *Chi dirà che nel veleno* (plus the nine excerpts from it found separately) attest to its having enjoyed great popularity, particularly in England. The simple sentiment of love tortured by jealousy could not have been what attracted performers to the cantata; rather, its warm reception must be attributed to the music:

imitative, full of characteristic motifs, with a tightly knit and yet varied structure, in C minor but with frequent internal modulations. The voices are given attractive music to sing (with expressive passages such as is found at the opening of its closing duet 'Il gel di gelosia') and the continuo is not slavishly tied to the bass. In short, *Chi dirà che nel veleno* is a mature composition, pleasurable both to perform and to hear performed.

Secular Cantatas with Instrumental Accompaniment

Stradella's secular cantatas with instrumental accompaniment are often called serenatas.[12] Crescimbeni said that such works were offered in the evening to a larger or more public audience,[13] and that he heard many performed with great magnificence before ambassadors and princes. On such occasions, for reasons both of volume as well as of festivity, the accompaniment would have been augmented to include instruments other than those for the basso continuo.

The texts generally once again discussed love, although a particular guest or occasion could have dictated that another subject be treated. When a longer piece was desired for the evening, it was possible for the poet to conceive the serenata in two parts, and during the interval refreshments would have been served.[14] Of Stradella's twenty-two serenatas, seven celebrate specific occasions. The two entirely different versions of *La Circe* were intended to honour Leopoldo de' Medici when he became a cardinal (December 1667). *Vola, vola in altri petti* was commissioned by Prince Gaspare Altieri as an entertainment for Queen Christina of Sweden (August 1674). *Ecco Amore ch'altero risplende* celebrated the wedding of Anna Altieri to Egidio Colonna (14 June 1676). *Sciogliete in dolci nodi* and *Se del pianeta ardente i luminosi raggi* were in praise of Maria Giovanna of Turin (July–December 1677). *Il barcheggio* lauded the marriage of Paola Brignole and Carlo Spinola in Genoa (June 1681). From these works alone one sees that Stradella composed serenatas throughout his career; they also confirm that the genre was not connected with just one centre in Italy, but—like the chamber cantata—was popular everywhere.

[12] Seven of Stradella's secular cantatas with instrumental accompaniment are preserved in his own hand. One of these, *Infinite son le pene*, is described on the score as a 'Cantata . . . fatta per Serenata'; six others are specifically called serenatas; one is termed simply a cantata. The range of subjects, length, and musical forces is wide, but all conform to the general description of 'cantata'. What they have in common beyond this is simply an instrumental ensemble in addition to the continuo.

[13] Giovan Mario Crescimbeni, *L'istoria della volgar poesia*, 3rd edn. (Venice, 1730–1), i. 300. Also see Julianne Baird, 'The Vocal Serenata of the 17th and 18th Centuries' (MA thesis, Rochester University, 1976), and Michael Talbot, 'Vivaldi's Serenatas: Long Cantatas or Short Operas', in Lorenzo Bianconi and Giovanni Morelli (eds.), *Antonio Vivaldi: Teatro musicale. Cultura e Società* (Florence, 1982), i. 67–96, esp. 67–79.

[14] For example, I-Rn, Fondo Gesuitico, 240, a Roman collection of 36 serenatas with mainly anonymous texts, concurs with this definition.

Stradella's undated serenatas were probably composed in Rome and, therefore, before January 1677. Several works may be assigned to this period because the poets were in Rome: *Arsi già d'una fiamma* and *Solitudine amata della pace* by Giovan Filippo Apolloni; *Il Damone* (in two versions), *Lo schiavo liberato*, and *Vola, vola in altri petti*, by Sebastiano Baldini; and *L'accademia d'Amore* by Giampietro Monesio. Since a manuscript of *Per tua vaga beltade* bears the coat of arms of the Roman Orsini family, it is probably also a Roman composition. *Lasciate ch'io respiri* and *Chi resiste al dio bendato*, found in a manuscript that contains cantatas with words by Flavio Orsini and music by composers associated with Rome, were most likely also destined for that city. In *Qui dove fa soggiorno il più bel sol* Rome's seven hills are mentioned; and in the autograph copy of *Or ch'alla dea notturna* the original line 'Fasto altero, superbo decoro' would associate it with the Altieri pope, Clement X (1670–6). In conclusion, only very few of Stradella's serenatas are not datable: they are *Furie del nero Tartaro*, *Infinite son le pene*, *Misero amante a che mi vale*, and *Qual prodigio è ch'io miri?*

The instrumental accompaniment of almost all of Stradella's serenatas is composed of either two violin parts plus continuo or a concertino–concerto grosso ensemble. Only the two serenatas written for Turin exhibit an entirely different accompaniment—one violin and two viola parts plus continuo. The vocal scoring ranges from one soprano (2 works) or one bass (1 work), to two sopranos (3) or one soprano and one tenor or soprano (1) or one soprano and bass (2) or one mezzo-soprano and one tenor (1); three sopranos (1) or two sopranos and one bass (4) or soprano–alto–bass (2) or soprano–tenor–bass (1); a quartet of soprano–alto–tenor–bass (2) or of two sopranos–mezzo-soprano–bass (1); a quintet of two sopranos–alto–tenor–bass (2); a septet of four sopranos–alto–tenor–bass (1). Texts written for several singers were more complex than those for only one or two characters; and Stradella reserved the larger concerto grosso ensemble as an accompaniment for these works.

The two texts he composed for Turin—*Sciogliete in dolci nodi* and *Se del pianeta ardente*—are possibly the most banal and ordinary Stradella ever set: they are simply a continuous litany of praises to Maria Giovanna. She is named specifically in *Sciogliete in dolci nodi*, where the poet (probably the Turinese Bernardino Bianco or Bianchi) assures us that Venice ('the lion') will be conquered by Turin ('the bull') to the benefit of France ('the golden lilies'), and that Europe will then have peace. In *Se del pianeta ardente* the poet realizes that his humble song cannot reach the 'royal sovereign, heavenly ruler, superior mortal, queen'. *Sciogliete in dolci nodi* is also quite simple in structure, with recitative leading into an aria for each of the two sopranos and closing with a duet. Although *Se del pianeta ardente* contains only one (strophic) aria for the soprano soloist ('Sovrana reale'), the work concludes in a manner worth noting. After the aria there is recitative which ends with a hendecasyllabic line of text. Here the poet affirms that to Maria Giovanna's sceptre he will 'consecrate [his] songs, heart, voice, and plectrum'. It is a culminating line which Stradella, as was his habit in such cases, set as an arioso recitative. However, he used the instrumental ensemble to accompany the line, thus creating an accompanied arioso or, as one may more properly term it, an accompanied recitative.

Several of Stradella's serenatas discuss the usual subject of cantatas—love and its miseries—but in uncommonly excellent poetry. This is certainly true of *Arsi già d'una fiamma*, Apolloni's passionate outcry. Stradella understood well the importance of the opening text directed to Cupid, 'I once burned from a flame, and now I burn from two; thus, blind tyrant, these are my losses and your victories', and set it as accompanied recitative (Ex. 7). Another interesting aspect of the cantata is its employment of two echoes. The texture in the arias and closing trio (an alternative to an aria provided by Stradella in case the main soloist and two echoes wish to have an ensemble) is imitative throughout, both for voices and instruments.

Similar to those texts for multi-voice cantatas with continuo accompaniment which could have been scored for just one voice is *Qui dove fa soggiorno il più bel sol.* Here the poetry expands on the luminosity of the beloved, and although it is divided between two singers, it need not have been. In *Infinite son le pene*, by contrast, there are three real roles: two lovers who lament the torments of Love and a third person who refuses to love. In both cantatas, arias, duets and, in the case of *Infinite son le pene*, trios, alternate in pleasing variety. As in Stradella's operas which also employ an orchestra of two violin parts and continuo, there are often instrumental ritornellos connected to the closed forms (which are accompanied instead by just basso continuo). *Infinite son le pene*, in addition, opens with a well-developed two-movement sinfonia.

Or ch'alla dea notturna is another serenata which uses its instrumental ensemble mainly for ritornellos. Of its six arias and three duets, only one aria, 'Cortesia, gentilezza e decoro', is accompanied by the two violins as well as continuo, and even here the instruments play only between vocal phrases. At the same time, the contrapuntal instrumental writing is always interesting whether in ritornellos or the opening two-movement sinfonia. The text, written so that all five arias are strophic, presents an unhappy lover who asks for help in his torments; he is told that the only assurance he can be given is that the tempests of love will continue.

In *Lasciate ch'io respiri, ombre gradite* Tirsi and Licori accuse one another of infidelity, but then reaffirm their love. Here also, although two

Ex. 7.

[continues as *recitativo secco*]

violins and continuo accompany the arias 'Pensavo adesso a te' (for Tirsi) and 'Che pretendi arcier volante' (for Licori), the instruments offer mainly ritornellos; in 'Che pretendi' they play ritornellos in addition to accompanying the voice, a most uncommon practice for Stradella. Another unusual feature of the serenata is the binary form in both movements of the opening sinfonia.

Characters are named in yet other amorous cantatas: Dorillo and Lilla in *Per tua vaga beltade,* and Fido Amante and Infido Amante in *Misero amante.* In the first work, Dorillo tries to win Lilla's affection but she wants her liberty and so resists, telling him that it was all the fault of Amor's arrows; in the second piece, the Unfaithful Lover also hopes to keep his freedom, whereas the Faithful Lover desires the servitude of constant love. In contrast with *Qui dove fa soggiorno il bel sole, Infinite son le pene,* and *Or ch'alla dea notturna,* where the closed forms were accompanied mainly by continuo only, the several arias and duets of *Per tua vaga beltade* and *Misero amante* are almost all accompanied throughout by two violins as well, and the richness of the contrapuntal texture of instruments and voices in these works is most striking. *Solitudine amata della pace* and *Furie del nero Tartaro* also employ the instrumental ensemble to accompany closed forms, but they are much shorter works: *Furie del nero Tartaro* has just three arias for the bass soloist, and *Solitudine amata della pace* an aria each for the mezzo-soprano and tenor plus a duet for them.

Whether closed forms are accompanied by basso continuo only, by other instruments but only between vocal phrases, or by the ensemble in a continuous manner is not indicative of the date of a composition, not even to identify it simply as 'early' or 'late', since Stradella used all these accompaniments throughout his career. Typically serenatas begin with a sinfonia, but this is also not related to one particular period.

The three remaining serenatas accompanied by two violins and continuo present problems difficult to resolve. The two versions of *La Circe* are both for three characters, Circe or the Ombra di Circe (soprano),[15] Zeffiro (soprano), and Algido (bass), and both contain six arias; but whereas *Se desio curioso il cor v'ingombra* (1.4–11) has one duet and one trio, *Bei ruscelli cristallini* (1.4–10) has no duet but five trios,[16] one of which is heard three times. In fact this work begins with a trio, while *Se desio curioso il cor v'ingombra* starts with a two-movement sinfonia.[17]

[15] In 'O de' regi alto germoglio' the character is named simply Circe, although in the course of the text she is referred to as the Shade of Circe; in 'Bei ruscelli cristallini' she is named properly Ombra di Circe.

[16] The numbers here and elsewhere refer to the Gianturco–McCrickard *Stradella Catalogue.*

[17] The thematic material of the second movement of this sinfonia presents similarities with that in the fourth movement of Stradella's Sonata di Viole (Gianturco–McCrickard, *Stradella Catalogue,* 7.4–2), and the third movement of the opening sinfonia to *Qual prodigio è ch'io miri?*

It is not at all clear why the poet Apolloni and Stradella wrote two cantatas regarding Apollo's daughter, Circe, especially since both are explicit in their intent to pay homage to Leopoldo de' Medici when he became cardinal[18] (he was notified on 13 December 1667 but was personally 'raised to the purple' by the Pope in Rome only on 15 March 1668). Since in both works Circe has come to visit the tomb of the son she bore to Ulysses, Telegonus, the founder of the ancient city of Tusculum, the site of the serenatas is the hills of Frascati to the south-east of Rome. Moreover, the character Algido bears the name of a river in Frascati. While nothing has come to light about a specific performance of *Bei ruscelli cristallini*, many pertinent details are known concerning *Se desio curioso il cor v'ingombra*.

As Leopoldo explained in a letter to his brother the Grand Duke dated 19 May 1668,[19] he had accepted an invitation from the Princess of Rossano, Olimpia Aldobrandini Pamphili, to visit her at her villa in Frascati and set out from Rome rather early on the previous Wednesday, 16 May; about four miles from the villa, the princess's two sons, Giovanni Battista and Benedetto Pamphili, came out to meet him, and they continued the trip with him in his carriage. From Marquis Francesco Riccardi, who accompanied Leopoldo, one learns that several other cardinals came out from Rome too, such as Borromeo, Gualtieri, Imperiali, and Acquaviva.[20] Besides remarking on the beauties of the villa's 'most delicious garden', Riccardi wrote that the guests were served a marvellous meal, and it is possible that a drawing by Sevin is of the lavishly bedecked table since it is decorated with the Medici coat of arms surmounted by a cardinal's hat.[21] The drawing shows the salon decorated with frescos painted by Domenichino depicting the adventures of Apollo—exactly where Leopoldo told his brother the festivities took place; moreover, the elaborate centrepiece depicts Mount Parnassus with Apollo and the Muses.

Riccardi wrote that after eating, a much applauded 'Dramma Musicale' was heard which, together with the nymphs and the fountains of Frascati, solemnized the new cardinal's arrival. Leopoldo added that the setting for

---

[18] Some of the following background information is taken from Gabriella Biagi-Ravenni, 'Le due *Circe* dello Stradella ovvero notizie circa l'esecuzione di una *Circe* di Alessandro Stradella, in Carolyn Gianturco (ed.), *Alessandro Stradella e Modena, Atti del Convegno internazionale di studi, Modena, 15–17 dicembre 1983* (Modena, 1985), 31–43. I am grateful to her for having accepted my invitation to research this subject for the Modena meeting.

[19] I-Fas, Mediceo del Principato, 5508, as reported in Biagi-Ravenni, 'Le due *Circe*', 41 n. 8.

[20] A letter from Riccardi to the Grand Duke dated 19 May 1668 in I-Fas, Mediceo del Principato, 3939. An *avviso* bearing the same date (I-Rvat, Barb. lat. 6369) affirms that there were 28 people: cardinals, princes, gentlemen, and ladies of the nobility. On the villa itself, see Cesare d'Onofrio, *La Villa Aldobrandini di Frascati* (Rome, 1963), esp. pp. 130, 131, 139, and the lengthy caption to fig. 93.

[21] An illustration of the table is in Per Bjurström, *Feast and Theatre in Queen Christina's Rome* (Stockholm, 1966), 62, but it is not stated for which occasion the table served.

the entertainment was a fountain, and engravings by Barrière and Falda of the Apollo room of the Villa Aldobrandini show a fountain representing Mount Parnassus with Apollo and the Muses[22]—the very subject of the table centrepiece. A wonderful feature of the wooden sculpture as designed by Giovanni Guglielmi and executed by Giovanni Anguilla and Giacomo Sarrazin is that it is mobile: when the fountain is activated each figure pretends to play a musical instrument; in fact actual music was heard as the water ran. Leopoldo explained that a piece of scenery representing woods was added to either side of the fountain, and it was from behind this setting that the three characters emerged one by one as the serenata progressed. According to Ferdinando Raggi, the Genoese agent in Rome, the performers were the Princess of Rossano's 'virtuosa', who sang well (Circe, soprano), Giuseppe Vecchi (Zeffiro, soprano), and Francesco Verdoni (Algido, bass).[23] From the manuscript of Apolloni's text[24] one learns that Circe was dressed as a queen, complete with crown, sceptre, and a rich cape; Leopoldo suggests that all three were in costume. The new cardinal continued that 'these began to discuss among themselves, each one trying most to honour my coming since the festivity was for me'.

The cantata begins with Circe explaining that she has come to the tomb of her son, Telegono; but a bright light surprises and disturbs her and she calls on Algido to explain it. He tells her it is due to the presence of a Medici. After Circe has an 'echo' conversation with Zeffiro, he also comes out from behind Mount Parnassus. He then names Leopoldo specifically, saying that no praises are sufficient for him. The three decide to pay tribute to Leopoldo, but are undecided as to what gifts would be worthy of him. They resolve the problem in the following manner: Algido transforms the waters of Tusculum into a crystal vase handed to Leopoldo by a page, Zeffiro has a little winged zephyr give him beautiful silk flowers to represent those of the fields, and a shade from Elysium presents him with a finely decorated box filled with perfume, fans, and gloves from Circe.[25] At the end of the serenata, called 'una pastorale' by Raggi, Apolloni requested that Apollo and the Muses on Mount Parnassus play their instruments to accompany the withdrawal of the characters behind the set.

Although *Se desio curioso il cor v'ingombra* made use of scenery and costumes and even required a certain amount of movement when gifts were presented to the new cardinal, it cannot be considered an opera. A seicento opera was quite another sort of poetic genre: to list the most obvious differences, it would have had three acts, the scene would have

---

[22] Barrière's engraving is reproduced here as Pl. 6; that by G. B. Falda is included in his volume *Le fontane delle ville di Frascati*, pt. 2 (Rome, n.d. but *c*.1670), as no. 7.

[23] Ademollo, *I teatri di Roma*, 101.   [24] I-Rvat, Chigi L.VI.193, fos. 4ʳ–10ᵛ.

[25] The gifts are named by both Leopoldo and Apolloni. They differ only in the description of the flowers, which Leopoldo said were dried; however, he may have meant simply that they were false.

changed during the course of the work, a greater number of characters would have been involved and these would have entered and exited with frequency, the plot would have made a real attempt at drama. Neither this nor the other *Circe* can be considered a one-act opera, either, as this genre did not exist in the period; nor should the inappropriate and anachronistic term 'operetta' be applied to them (as it was by a former librarian at the Biblioteca Estense, who wrote the word on the scores in question). One is dealing here simply with cantatas for a specific occasion which required the surroundings and the dress of the performers to suit its importance.

Bei ruscelli cristallini offers the same story as *Se desio curioso il cor v'ingombra* but through completely different text and music. The style of both is simple, which is surprising in *Se desio curioso il cor v'ingombra* since the singers are known to have been excellent. The scoring of SSB voices accompanied by two violins and basso continuo is also the same in both scores. Princess Rossano is known to have had a harpsichord, small organ, archlute, and chitarrino at Frascati,[26] and therefore they could have been employed in the continuo of *Se desio curioso*. In *Bei ruscelli cristallini* most of the vocal pieces are accompanied by basso continuo only with instrumental ritornellos following them, whereas there is more direct accompaniment by the ensemble in *Se desio curioso il cor v'ingombra*. The trios in both versions are in Stradella's usual polyphonic imitative style. Interestingly, Circe's long opening recitative in *Se desio curioso il cor v'ingombra* is interspersed with short phrases by the instruments, not exactly in the manner of an accompanied recitative but obviously related to it; and her aria 'O degl'eterni elisi' is a *cavata* aria, that is, an aria 'carved out' of recitative text of 7- and 11-syllable lines.[27] One curious difference between the two cantatas is their key: *Bei ruscelli cristallini* is in C major and *Se desio curioso il cor v'ingombra* in B flat major.

Why there are two different scores of *La Circe*, both on the same basic plot, cannot be ascertained. Given that the same number of singers was required and similar music written for them, it was certainly not because of a change of cast. Neither was the occasion for the festivity nor its location modified. It has been suggested that the poetry of *Bei ruscelli cristallini* was not as fine as Apolloni was capable of,[28] and that he may have been asked to improve it. It also may be that the poet and composer were asked to create something which offered less ensemble vocal music.

---

[26] Claudio Annibaldi, 'L'Archivio musicale Doria Pamphili: Saggio sulla cultura aristocratica a Roma fra 16° e 18° secolo', *Studi musicali*, 11 (1982), 295.

[27] See Colin Timms, 'The Cavata at the Time of Vivaldi', in Antonio Fanna and Giovanni Morelli (eds.), *Nuovi Studi Vivaldi* (Florence, 1988), 451–77, for various interpretations of the term.

[28] Biagi-Ravenni, 'Le due *Circe*', 38–9.

Another 'occasional' cantata is *Ecco Amore ch'altero risplende*. It was composed to celebrate the wedding of Anna Altieri and Egidio Colonna which took place on 14 June 1676. As she was the Pope's niece and he came from one of the most important Roman families, the marriage was of great social, financial, and political importance even though it was perhaps not the most love-inspired since the groom was said to be quite old. Festivities—including 'comedie in musica', fireworks, and fountains of wine—were offered at the Colonna castle in nearby Oriolo, and the best musicians of Rome were engaged to take part in them.[29] It is quite possible that Stradella's *Ecco Amore ch'altero risplende* was heard at this time.

The simple text, filled with allusions to the two families ('columns' for Colonna, 'stars' for Altieri), is a brief discussion about whether Time or Love reigns supreme; the conclusion is that Anna Altieri is Amor's greatest victory and that her children will adorn Rome as its heroes. The final lines praise the Altieri Pope: 'where Clement/Clemency reigns, Love triumphs'. Each of the three soloists (SAB) has two arias; the bass and alto join together in a duet which is heard three times at the beginning of the cantata, and all three sing two different trios, one which is repeated during the course of the work and another which serves to conclude the composition. *Ecco Amore ch'altero risplende* is a rather long work but beautifully organized. In order to avoid tediousness, Stradella often varied music which might normally have been simply repeated: for example, the second strophe of the alto aria 'Di legiti mi diletti dispensier' is not exactly the same as the first; the ritornello connected with the trio 'Ecco Amore ch'altero risplende' offers material which is only vaguely related to it; the three consecutive arias for soprano, alto, and bass—'Lascia omai regio Imeneo', 'Dio fecondo affretta omai', 'In due guancie offre ai tuoi crini'—even though they are all binary in form, have 3/2 metre followed by 3/8, and are in F major, are three different pieces, in a sense variations.

Ecco Amore ch'altero risplende is continually interesting, lively, and varied. It is also very much for fine professional musicians: for example, the opening duet is a lovely and lilting composition where the bass and alto must perform exacting fiorituras together; the trio 'Sono il Tempo' is especially demanding when the text talks of 'arms' in the battle between the two champions, Time and Love; and the aria 'Veglio è il Tempo, Amore infante' pushes ahead unremittingly, affording the bass hardly a pause in his running eighth- and sixteenth-notes.

The seven remaining Stradella secular cantatas to be discussed are accompanied by concertino–concerto grosso ensembles. An instrumental force of

---

[29] I-Rvat, Barb. lat. 6381, *avvisi* of 6, 13, and 20 June 1676.

two violin parts added to the continuo was often indicative that the occasion which prompted the composition of the cantata was an important one. It only stands to reason that a further augmentation of the accompanying ensemble would have meant that something even more special was desired, perhaps because the occasion or guest to be honoured merited such treatment, perhaps because the performance was to be held in larger surroundings for a greater public, or perhaps simply because more money was available. It might be worth while to discuss first the compositions which not only have concertino–concerto grosso instrumentation, but which fall into yet another category of cantata, that of the *accademia*.

The term comes from Academus, a Greek mythological character associated with the grove where Plato taught; later on it was the name of a school on Cicero's estate in Tusculum. The same idea of learning through discussion was present in the Accademia Platonica which Marsilio Ficino founded in Florence in 1470 and in the hundreds of other academies which then sprouted up all over Italy.[30] In Stradella's time, Rome boasted several academies, and his poets were members of one or more of them: for example, Giovan Filippo Apolloni, Sebastiano Baldini, Francesco Maria Sereni, and Benedetto Pamphili were members of the Accademia degli Umoristi.

While most *accademie* were literary or scientific societies, some met mainly for musical reasons. Whatever its principal interest, however, an academy could always organize a musical entertainment. This would have been a cantata, similar in dimension and forces to the serenata but which had as its theme a debate, a *cantata per un'accademia* or simply an *accademia*. The subjects discussed were the most varied, such as: 'whether the world gets better or worse'; 'which wounds more, the tongue or the sword'; 'whether it is worse to speak badly about others or to praise oneself'.[31] Like serenatas, accademias were often written to honour some important person or a particular event. Not surprisingly, however, one of the most popular topics was love, and Stradella's accademias are all on this very subject.

In one of them this is evident both in the title, *L'accademia d'Amore*, and opening text, 'Amanti, olà!', a call to lovers to give ear to the following debate in the Land of Love. Amore, as prince of the learned accademia, presides over the ensuing discussion (called a 'litteral battaglia') between Bellezza (Beauty) and Cortesia (Courtesy) about which of them is more necessary in love. According to Bellezza, love results when one is attracted to beauty; she justifies this by reminding her audience that even the name 'Cupido' means 'one who desires'. She concludes her argumen-

---

[30] Percy M. Young, 'Academy', *New Grove*.

[31] See Owen Jander, 'The Cantata in Accademia: Music for the Accademia de' Dissonanti and their Duke, Francesco II d'Este, *Rivista italiana di musicologia*, 10 (1975), 519–44.

tation with a list of lovers who responded to beauty, such as Orlando to Angelica, Tembano to Iole, Amore himself to Psyche. One of the academicians immediately agrees with her. Now it is Cortesia's turn, and she insists that more than vain beauty it is she who is of importance to love, that while the affection produced by beauty is quickly spent, love which is born of courtesy (meaning kindness and noble behaviour) never dies. She, too, names lovers who were attracted because of her quality, and ends: 'It is only Courtesy which binds loving hearts in slavery to love through obligatory chains.' The debate is summed up by Amore, who says that while it is Beauty who gives birth to love, it is Courtesy who keeps it alive. In short, both win the discussion. At this point *L'accademia d'Amore* could have ended; however, this is only the first half of it.

In the second part, as is usual after a debate, other academicians (Primo Accademico and Secondo Accademico) enter into the discussion, and in a manner which would have been especially appropriate for a literary audience. Amore now calls upon erudite Rigore (Rigour), who states his opinion that every beautiful woman is bereft of pity, and he does so in that most classical and 'rigorous' of poetic forms, a sonnet of fourteen traditional hendecasyllabic lines ('Chiedi il riso agli Eracliti piangenti'). Next, Capriccio (Caprice) expresses the 'capricious' idea that a modern lover is no longer attracted to dark eyes but to white ones, and he does so in a less formal genre, the canzona ('Nere luci, il vostro sole')—in this case two strophes of six lines, each made up of four octosyllabic verses and two concluding hendecasyllabic verses. Now Disinganno (Truth) decides to speak out and warn lovers that Amore's arrows are poisonous and the resulting wounds painful. He does so in one of the newest and most free of poetic genres, one devised by Chiabrera especially to be set to music, the scherzo, or as it is termed here a 'scherzo musicale', ten lines of nine or ten syllables each where, moreover, all but one are foreshortened or *tronchi* ('Si guardi dai dadi d'Amor'): a real display of technique and thus delightful, as a scherzo should be.[32] Amore, however, is annoyed that Disinganno has dared to come to his academy and speak so rudely about him, and to stop any further 'new excesses of poetic competition', he decides to end the meeting. He does so with yet another poetic genre, a madrigal ('Dotto maestro è Amore') of five heptasyllabic and two hendecasyllabic lines ending with the dictum, 'He who is not a lover cannot be a good poet.'

Giampietro Monesio, the author of *L'accademia d'Amore*, wrote an accademia within an accademia. He represented a meeting of an accademia, during which there was a debate or accademia about whether Beauty

---

[32] One notes Stradella's close adherence to the text in these three arias: Rigore's sonnet is set as recitative, Capriccio's canzone as a strophic aria, and Disinganno's scherzo as one of the major arias of the cantata, exhibiting great inventiveness for both voice and instruments.

or Courtesy prompts love, followed by comments on the subject offered by the academicians. What is more, they give their opinions in poetry just as members of a real literary academy would have done (or at least would have attempted to do).[33]

Stradella's setting of *L'accademia d'Amore* is for two sopranos (Bellezza and Cortesia, who doubles as Capriccio), alto (Amore), tenor (Secondo Accademico, who doubles as Rigore), and bass (Primo Accademico, who doubles as Disinganno). All five voices are called upon to sing florid, difficult music. This is true whether the accompaniment is by continuo alone (as is the case of Bellezza's aria 'Non sempre dispiega l'alato garzone' which is filled with long phrases of fiorituras) or whether it employs additional instruments. The singers must have been among Rome's best, another reason to believe that Stradella's accademia had been commissioned for a prestigious occasion.

Perhaps even more fascinating than the brilliant vocal lines is Stradella's handling of the instruments in the accademia, and the enormous variety of texture he achieves by varying the scoring. The instruments are a concertino (indicated as such) of two violins and continuo, and a concerto grosso (also so called) of one violin, two violas (mezzosoprano and contralto clefs), and continuo (no instruments are named). Some arias are accompanied by the continuo only, such as the example already given and Amore's aria 'Di rai biancheggianti al vago'. The next largest group employed is the concerto grosso alone, which does ritornellos to vocal pieces such as Bellezza's aria, 'La beltade persuade co' suoi rai' (the second strophe of which, 'Quell'affetto ch'in un petto', is transposed and sung by Amore), as well as the sinfonias which open Part I (two movements) and Part II (one movement). Only slightly increased is the accompaniment of Amore's aria 'Dal libro d'Amor', where the voice has its own continuo in addition to the concerto grosso ensemble. Of equivalent size is the instrumentation of the ritornello following the duet (accompanied by continuo alone) for Bellezza and Cortesia, 'D'Amore all'invito', which is for concerto grosso, now increased to five parts by having the two violins of the concertino play together on an additional line. Cortesia's aria 'Quel violento affetto' (indicated as 'Aria concertata con concerto piccolo e grosso') is accompanied by the concertino together

[33] It was more than likely that copies of the text were distributed to the audience. Confirmation of such practice is found in a payment which Flavio Chigi made in July 1659 'for the copying of another serenata . . . and for some copies of the words of the said serenata', reported by Lionnet in 'Flavio Chigi', 298. Since an anonymous cantata (I-Rvat, Chigi Q.V.72) also offers a discussion between Bellezza and Cortesia which, although different in its plot, presents several similarities of text, it could be that Monesio was the poet of the Vatican score as well, or that he and the anonymous author both used some other unknown model for their works. For a comparison of the two works, see Agostino Ziino, 'Osservazioni sulla struttura de *L'accademia d'Amore* di Alessandro Stradella', *Chigiana*, 26–7 (1969–70), 137–69.

with the concerto grosso, and in Disinganno's aria 'Si guardi dai dardi d'Amor' the voice has its own continuo, and the concerto grosso is divided into two groups, called 'Primo Choro' and 'Secondo Choro'.[34]

These six different types of accompaniment enormously enrich the variety of the *accademia*. As will be seen, such manipulation was Stradella's usual approach when working with a concertino–concerto grosso ensemble. One is at first surprised at the continual change of instrumentation, especially since operas of the period, including Stradella's, did not do so; but opera relied on the surprises inherent in its plot, and in the different scenes, entrances and exits, as well as machines for its variety. Instead it was through instrumentation that Stradella created the change and variety which the cantata, because of its very nature, did not provide, not even visually.

Variety also dominates the individual treatments of the forces. Cortesia's aria 'Quel violento affetto', accompanied by concertino and concerto grosso, is a good example of this. Here the larger ensemble is always a homophonic unit alternating with a contrapuntal concertino. There is no structural reason why one or the other plays, nor is the voice tied to a particular group. The voice is similarly independent in Disinganno's 'Si guardi dai dardi d'Amor'. The two concerto grosso 'choruses' behave generally as two ensembles, frequently alternating or joining together; but at one point only the first violin of each group plays while the other instruments rest, introducing yet another internal change in texture and sonority. The music for the two ensembles is generally homophonic, but counterpoint is also employed. As was stated earlier, the voice has its own supporting continuo and, as is usual for Stradella in such cases, these two lines provide a foundation which is decorated, as it were, by the other instrumental forces.

The propulsive rhythm and fast tempos of *L'accademia d'Amore* would have required competent instrumentalists. This is equally true of the continuo since its ostinato lines (as in the Secondo Accademico's aria 'Sembianza ch'è bella') or quasi-ostinato lines move with great regularity and insistence. One nicety of the score is the opening of the two-movement sinfonia to Part I. Here the strings of the concerto grosso are divided into three groups, and requested to enter one group at a time. A natural crescendo was thereby achieved, exactly what Stradella wanted, since he says on the score that they are to enter unnoticeably and are to go from piano to fortissimo. The effect is repeated for a similar passage of sustained notes a few bars later.

In order to achieve this effect, the concerto grosso must have had at least twelve players. To these one may add two violins from the concertino, plus at least one player of the concertino continuo; another

---

[34] Use was apparently made of two *cori* or groups of instruments in Rome, to judge from Apolloni's serenata *Fermate, o là, fermate armoniose corde*, which, in a manuscript of the text (I-Rvat, Chigi L.VI.193, fo. 43), is said to be 'con due cori di istrumenti'.

player is required when the voice has its own continuo. At the very least, *L'accademia d'Amore* required sixteen instrumentalists, and one feels certain that they would have been more since the three continuo parts would not have been played by just one instrument each. The simple indication 'Tutti li bassi', which appears at the heading of the Secondo Accademico's aria mentioned above, encourages one to conclude that Stradella's penchant for variety, extended here to the number of instruments to perform a continuo, would have included their quality and timbre as well. To the instrumentalists, whatever their exact number, must be added five singers. In all, twenty-one or more musicians performed the accademia, a statistic which clearly indicates that it was an important work. It may even have been the 'accademia di musica' which Gaspare Altieri organized for Carnival of 1675; this employed 25 instruments.[35]

The accademia *Il Damone* was entitled by its poet Sebastiano Baldini *L'alme* as well as *La forza delle stelle*. The work opens with the shepherd Damone inviting his beloved nymph Clori to come out to him under the starry sky. Their continual declarations of love—differentiated only by Damone bemoaning his suffering from passion, while Clori is simply happy—present nothing unusual in a normal seicento cantata, and when the couple finishes discoursing, the text could be considered complete. In fact, some copies of Baldini's manuscript (apart from a few added lines) end at this point. Stradella has two settings of the text, one in the Modena Biblioteca Estense (1.4–7) and another in the Turin Biblioteca Nazionale (1.4–6), which instead continue the plot in conformity with other copies of the literary source. In the Turin music manuscript, five other characters, a group of serenaders apparently not seen by Damone and Clori but only heard by them, take up the subject of love, arguing—in academic fashion—either that 'who follows Cupid never finds peace' or that 'who flees Cupid does find peace'. Damone asks Clori if she hears the 'amorous voices', but she replies that she is deaf to all voices but his. He then explains that it was he who prepared the 'improvised harmonies' so that in their songs she would hear his sighs instead of his cries. The serenaders continue and end with a madrigal which tells the stars that, if one becomes an *amante*, the glory goes to them although fortune blesses the lover. In the Modena version there are only three who discuss love, with comments along the way by Damone and Clori; the lovers end by admiring the brilliant stars from which their ardour descends, and praising Love who gives such happiness. This score, too, ends with a madrigal analogous to that in the Turin copy.[36]

[35] Filippo Clementi, *Il Carnevale romano nelle cronache contemporanee* (Rome, 1899), 590.
[36] The scores and several literary sources which I uncovered are listed in Gianturco–McCrickard, *Stradella Catalogue*.

The plot in the two musical sources is obviously similar; however, the Turin version seems the 'neater' of the two, with its first section for Damone and Clori, a second during which one hears the serenaders only, and then a final tidying-up section which explains the presence of the serenaders and offers the moral of the story. The Modena text, once the first section for Damone and Clori is over, has all characters carrying on their independent conversations until the end when the moral is given. It is interesting, but not quite as effective. One is tempted, therefore, to suggest that the Turin score is based on a subsequent poetic version.

All told, there are six literary sources for the two music versions, all affirming Baldini's authorship. However, another source suggests that it was Christina of Sweden who outlined the plot to the poet. As is known, Christina founded a literary and musical academy in 1674. The works of the members were performed at meetings, an activity she wanted to participate in personally and, to this purpose, she wrote a scenario for a serenata. The beginning of it is as follows:[37]

Serenata for five voices, two sopranos, a contralto, tenor, and bass, accompanied by the customary instruments and *sinfonie*.

While enjoying the silence and cool air of a beautiful and tranquil night on a balcony, Clori and Damone sing a dialogue full of tenderness and love, giving voice to their amorous passions for each other. Together they lament their misfortune which so often cruelly divides them and interposes so many difficult obstacles to their happiness.

While engaged in these affections, they hear from afar a *sinfonia* which interrupts them. After the *sinfonia*, three voices sing together, the tenor of which says that to live happily one must rather flee from Love. The contralto responds that in order to live happily together one must follow Love.

The bass says that Love, like death, cannot be escaped, that he who flees him is wise, but that he who is not captured and vanquished by him is fortunate, that one does not love by choice but by fate; and together they argue about this topic until they are interrupted by another *sinfonia*, after which Clori and Damone engage in another dialogue, singing at times simultaneously, at times pathetically alone. They let it be known that the serenata has filled them with doubts and suspicions, but that, nevertheless, these are required of lovers and not offensive to them, and they finish by thanking Love for all that he has made them suffer and enjoy. They are astonished that Love, that god so extolled, of whom everyone speaks and writes, should be so little understood in the world. With these reflections they thank him again for having wounded them with so noble a dart, for having inflamed them with such a beauteous love, for having revealed to them alone his most hidden and precious mysteries, unknown to the common herd; and

---

[37] Sven Stolpe published a version of Christina's scenario in *Kristina-Studier* (Uppsala, 1959), 204–8; the beginning was translated into English by Thomas E. Griffen in 'The Late Baroque Serenata in Rome and Naples: A Documentary Study with Emphasis on Alessandro Scarlatti' (Ph.D. diss., University of California at Los Angeles, 1983), 63–4, and his version is given here.

they boast that of those enjoying the kingdom of Love, none have suffered or desired as much as they.

While this is happening, the bass enters into their ensemble and in a recitative rejoices further in the happiness with which Love blesses those whom he deigns to make felicitous, and on this subject the two sopranos and bass sing. After this the three voices sing again in unanimity, and then another *sinfonia* is played, and finally a five-voice madrigal, the most tender and pathetic the composer can create, ends the work.

Christina's scenario, with its discussion of the merits and problems of love, could well have been proposed at a meeting of her academy. What is more, it clearly provided the basis for Baldini's text of the Modena score, the only real difference being the number of sinfonias: Christina requested five instrumental pieces, whereas Stradella wrote only four. The score even calls the work an 'Accademia'. Information gleaned from one of Baldini's manuscripts confirms a Rome performance of the Modena version. I-Rvat, Chigi R.III.68 gives the text on fos. 1026^r–1027^v; but previously, on fo. 1025^r, as though he were announcing the text, Baldini has written 'Here is the whole cantata.' He then continues with questions directed to whomever was in charge of the performance, which must have come from Stradella: 'One wants to know who the soprano will be, in order to have the music conform to the ability of the voice. Also, by when it must be composed, so that [your] very kind desires may be fulfilled day and night.' Another hand has written a partial answer: 'The sopranos are [Giuseppe] Vecchi and [Francesco Maria or Giuseppe] Fede, the tenors are Don Francesco, Isidoro, and the tenor of St Peter's.'

Vecchi (who sang Zeffiro in Stradella's *La Circe*, 'Se desio curioso') and both Fede brothers were castrati, and therefore would have taken the roles of Damone and Clori. The remaining 'tenor' serenaders were actually a contralto, tenor, and bass in Stradella's score, but it could be that 'tenor' was a term the writer of the above note used when he meant a non-soprano or a non-castrato. In any event, the only known 'Isidoro' is Cerruti, who, after beginning as a bass, sang tenor. 'D. Francesco' could have referred either to the bass Don Francesco, a cleric of Gallicano (31 km. outside Rome), or the contralto Don Francesco, a canon from Palestrina (both sang in *La comica del cielo* by Rospigliosi and Abbiati in 1668). It is not possible to speculate on the identity of the 'tenor at San Pietro' because of the uncertainty of the term 'tenor' and because it is not clear what voice part is lacking.

We now know some of the cast of the Modena version of *Il Damone*, and that the cantata had a Roman performance at some time between 1674 (when Christina founded her academy) and 1677 (when Stradella left Rome). Inexplicably and contrary to reason, it seems as though the Turin *Il Damone*—also related to Christina's scenario but with changes in structure, number of characters, and ending—was also performed in Rome. Evidence for this is suggested by the names of 'Giulia' and 'Antonia' written alongside the parts of Damone and Clori respectively. While there is no information that associates Stradella with singers by these names once he left Rome, Antonia may have been Antonia Coresi, one of the city's best sopranos. Until 1670 she was in the employ of the Colonna and then became part of Queen Christina's household. In the 1671 Tordinona performance of *Lo Scipione Affricano*, in which Stradella was also involved, Antonia took the role of Scipione, an example, in addition to that of *Il Damone*, of a woman taking a male role. There is no clue as to Giulia's identity. Further on in the Turin score, one finds the initials 'G' and 'V' alongside the parts for the two soprano serenaders (even when 'the two ladies'—Giulia and Antonia—are said not to sing any more, which means that the 'G' was not for Giulia). They also probably refer to names of singers, and two Roman sopranos who come to mind are Giovanni Francesco Grossi and Giuseppe Vecchi, the latter also part of Christina's cast. Grossi sang at the Tordinona during the years Stradella was active there, and in fact his superb performance in *Lo Scipione Affricano* made people refer to him ever after as Siface; he also took the role of Herod's wife in Stradella's oratorio *San Giovanni Battista*.

To have written two poetic and musical versions of Christina's scenario is strange, and—as in the case of the two versions of *La Circe*—no explanation for it can be given. It could be that, after Christina's version was performed, some other member or Baldini himself, as a true academic, offered his own treatment of the subject proposed by Christina: he left the initial situation as it was, kept some lines and added others, augmented the number of serenaders, and provided a motive for the serenade (Damone had organized it). Naturally any notice of an 'accademia in musica' offered by Christina, such as the successful one given at her palace at the beginning of 1676, is tantalizing, because it could refer to Stradella's composition.[38]

Even though there are two versions of *Il Damone*, there are enough similarities in the two scores to be able to discuss them together. For example, the duets for Clori and Damone 'Io se t'amo | t'adoro' and 'O stelle adorate' are textually and musically the same in both scores, as is the ATB trio 'L'amare è destino' (only words amounting to five syllables are different) and some recitative. Occasionally, there are pieces where the text is the same but the music different, such as Damone's aria 'Miri mai di me chi sia', Clori's aria 'Sospiri quanto sa', the trio for Damone, Clori, and bass (Modena) or the SSB serenaders (Turin), 'Grand'incanto d'una beltà', and the aria for Damone (Modena) or the bass serenader (Turin),

---

[38] I-Rvat, Barb. lat. 6381, *avviso* of 4 Jan. 1676.

'Del nume al potere', as well as a few lines of recitative. In these cases it is most interesting to compare the settings and observe that the Turin one is generally the more sensitive in its text-underlay and in capturing the mood (Ex. 8). Curiously, it also has a somewhat lower tessitura for the two main protagonists.

Ex. 8.

At the end of the Turin *Il Damone*, after 'fine' was written by the copyist, three other pieces follow which are perhaps discarded or alternative settings. These are an aria for alto and continuo 'Di smalto le mura' (which is the same text, except for the change of one word, as the alto–tenor duet with continuo in the Modena copy, 'Di ferro le mura'); the aria 'Se chi fulmina la terra' for soprano and continuo with a concerto grosso ritornello; and a soprano, alto, bass, and continuo trio, 'Stelle col vostro ardore' (which is the same text as the concluding five-part madrigal in the Modena *Il Damone*).

If the supposition is true that for the Turin *Damone* Antonia Coresi sang the part of Clori, that another equally gifted singer took the role of

Damone, and that the two excellent castrati Grossi and Vecchi assumed the roles of two serenaders, it is surprising that Stradella made so little of their capacity for virtuosity. This is not to say that their music is easy, but the complete lack of any brilliant fiorituras deprives them of opportunity to shine. A generally syllabic setting is what one finds in the Modena version of the serenata, too, and here one is certain of the expert ability of the singers. At the same time, there are attractive arias, such as Damone's expressive 'Miri mai di me chi sia' (Turin), with its lyrical ternary rhythm (3/2), suspensions, and falling perfect and diminished fourths, which encourages sympathy for the young man's plea for pity from his beloved.

Among the loveliest pieces in the *Damone* settings are the vocal ensembles: the ternary (3/2) 'Io se t'amo | t'adoro' for Damone and Clori (in both versions) based on gently curving phrases often begun after an octave skip to highlight the emotional intensity of the words; the sprightly contrapuntal trio 'Chi segue Cupido non trova la pace | Chi fugge Cupido ritrova la pace' for the serenaders (Turin), which distinguishes the music for the bass from that of the alto and tenor since his point of view is different from theirs; the closing five-part madrigal 'Stelle, voi ch'influite' (Turin), which has the voices enter in a continually changing order with each succeeding point of imitation, the whole pushing ahead until the moral of the serenata is reached; then there is a cadence for all parts, and with fresh impetus imitation allows the closing text to be heard repeatedly.

As usual in his larger serenatas, however, Stradella's greatest attention was given to the instrumental ensemble. Both the Modena and Turin scores ask specifically for concertino–concerto grosso ensembles. In Modena there are three arias accompanied by concertino solo (Clori's 'Sospiri quanto sa', the alto's 'Ma pur la cruda pregata', and Damone's 'Miri mai di me'), although a concerto grosso ritornello may be connected to it (as in the latter for Damone). No aria is accompanied by the concerto grosso, though. Instead, there is one aria which employs both ensembles (Clori's 'Questo nume non presume'). Perhaps to avoid covering the voices, direct accompaniment is mainly with just basso continuo and other instruments play only between vocal phrases. In fact, with all the possibilities that the concertino and concerto grosso could have offered, for the remaining four duets, three trios, and one quintet, as well as three other arias, only continuo accompaniment is provided in this score, and hardly ever even an instrumental ritornello.

In both scores the concertino consists of two violins and basso continuo, and the concerto grosso of two violins, viola, and continuo, which was to become the standard instrumentation for it. This latter ensemble plays two one-movement sinfonias during the course of the Modena serenata and, with parts doubled by the concertino and with a continuo 'lira', a two-movement sinfonia to open the work. While the internal sinfonias show no relationship to the Turin ones, the first 36 measures of the open-ing piece are the same in both scores, after which Modena makes a cadence and Turin continues for an imitative section of 48 more bars.[39] This same sort of distinction may be seen throughout the two scores, which is to say that, in general, Turin develops possibilities left unex-plored in Modena. It also adds elements which allow for further variety of sonority and disposition.

One of these is Stradella's employment of the concertino to accompany a line of recitative at two different points of *Il Damone*. Both times, two hendecasyllabic lines of text following an aria are given to the same char-acter; the first is set as simple recitative by Stradella and the second— always a line of particular impact—is set in arioso style with instrumental accompaniment. They are, therefore, examples of the composer's relatively frequent use of accompanied recitative and proof of his desire to distin-guish between ordinary and heightened text.[40]

The most significant element for achieving variety in the Turin *Damone*, however, is an additional concertino of two violins and basso continuo. One concertino is called that of the 'Primo Choro' and is employed in all three sinfonias, in the first two as a separate entity, and in the third to double lines of the concerto grosso; it also accompanies arias, either alone (as for the bass's 'Del nume al potere') or as an individual entity together with the concerto grosso (as in the first soprano's 'Chi viva godendo' and the second soprano's 'Disperarsi è vanità'). In addition, Stradella makes separate use of the Primo Choro continuo, both as an accompanying factor (the ATB trio 'Chi segue fugge Cupido' and the SSB trio 'Grand'incanto d'una beltà'), and as a reinforcement of the con-certo grosso (Clori's aria 'Sospiri quanto sa', Damone's aria 'Quante stelle nel ciel rimiro', and the ritornello to the trio 'Grand'incanto d'una beltà'). Although not named specifically, it must also be this continuo which is to be used for the alto–tenor duet 'Chi cerca farsi beato', the ATB trio 'L'amare è destino', and the final quintet 'Stelle, voi ch'influite'.

One is justified in supposing that all of the serenaders' music in the Turin score, including any recitative for them, would use the instruments of the Primo Choro, because Damone and Clori have a separate con-certino called—since their roles were to be taken by two women— 'concertino delle due Dame'. This second concertino alone accompanies Damone's aria 'Miri mai di me'; and, as a separate ensemble, together with the concerto grosso it accompanies his aria 'Quante stelle nel ciel

---

[39] In the Turin score, the concertino and concerto grosso are scored separately because, as the sin-fonia continues, the parts are not always doubled.

[40] They are after Damone's 'Miri mai di me chi sia', and after the bass serenader's 'Dal nume al potere'. In both these cases, Jander in 'The Cantata and the Opera', 96–106 mistook recitative for aria text, and believed that a line of regular recitative interrupted the aria, which was then concluded by a last line of text.

rimiro' and Clori's aria 'Sospiri quanto sa'. Its basso continuo serves to accompany the two duets for Damone and Clori, 'Io se t'amo | t'adoro' and 'O stelle adorate', as well as any recitative for these two protagonists.

In short, Damone and Clori had one concertino, and the serenaders had another, a practical solution to the problem of accompanying singers who were not standing together. The concerto grosso was used with either of these concertinos to form a larger ensemble; however, it was also employed alone, and in these moments it was reinforced with instruments from one or the other concertinos. In addition to the variety afforded to the Turin *Il Damone* simply by passing from one of the several possible groupings of instruments to another, is the variety Stradella achieves through employing them contrapuntally. An excellent example of this is the bass serenader's aria 'Disperarsi è vanità'. The four-line text of 8/4/4/11 syllables has been divided into two sections of one line and three lines respectively and set not continuously (as the text would imply) but as an ABB'A form, a choice calling for textual and therefore musical repetitions prompted by the composer's desire to create an extended piece. As far as the instruments are concerned, they are present through-out the aria, but with different material and different tasks: the contra-puntal concertino, distinguished by a figure of an eighth-note followed by two sixteenths, serves to accompany the voice directly; whereas the more homophonic concerto grosso, using a figure based on a dotted eighth fol-lowed by a sixteenth, comes in between vocal phrases. As the voice often has the dotted figure, another element of imitation is added as the motive is heard passing from the bass to the concerto grosso. It is in interesting, lively pieces such as these, filled with characteristic figures repeated insis-tently, as well as other more lyrical and seductive ones, that one sees why Handel was attracted to Stradella's music.

Other secular cantatas which Stradella scored for a large instrumental ensemble are not of the accademia type. The texts of two of these are also by Sebastiano Baldini and, although only one of them may be dated pre-cisely, they must both have been written for Rome. *Lo schiavo liberato* is a reworking by Baldini of an episode in Canto XVI of Torquato Tasso's epic poem *Gerusalemme liberata*. In 75 eight-line strophes of hendecasylla-bles, Tasso described the garden of the beautiful Armida where the cru-sader and warrior Rinaldo, 'a young man, more handsome and valiant than any other', has been made the sorceress's willing and loving prisoner; in the end Rinaldo returns to his senses through the efforts of his com-panions Carlo and Ubaldo, and escapes with them, much to Armida's vengeful anger.[41] Baldini's autograph, which he entitled *Lo schiavo d'amore*

[41] *Tutte le poesie di Torquato Tasso*, i: *Gerusalemme liberata*, Lanfranco Caretti ed. (Verona, 1957), 350–68. The quotation of Tasso's description of Rinaldo is on p. 670.

vengeful anger.[41] Baldini's autograph, which he entitled *Lo schiavo d'amore liberato* (and which he called a 'cantata'),[42] does not follow its model except in plot. Moreover, the seriousness of tone adopted by Tasso, reinforced by his constant repetition of long verses in a set poetic pattern, is absent in Baldini. Instead, for much of the poetry, on account of a predominance of shorter lines and frequent rhymes, there is a tendency towards banality. Only Armida's passionate outcry for her lost Rinaldo at the end of the cantata shows writing of some quality.

Comparison between Baldini's autograph and the text as it appears in Stradella's score reveals some interesting differences. In nine places, text of three to eight lines has been eliminated from the score. Some text now in the score, however, is not in the poetic source: these are the duet 'Non più prigioniero' for Carlo and Ubaldo, for which Baldini has a different text; and five lines from Armida's aria 'Almen dai claustri' beginning with 'Demoni e furie'. It is very possible that all of the changes were made by Baldini at Stradella's request. That the autograph is not the final poetic version is in fact suggested by the incompleteness of the aria 'Ozio si vile fugga da me', given in its entirety in the musical score.

This same aria illustrates yet another difference between the poetic source and the music: Baldini indicated that it was for Ubaldo, but Stradella set it for Carlo. Moreover, there are several other instances of similar differences between sources. For example, Baldini wrote 'Il vigor rendi agli spirti' as a duet for Carlo and Ubaldo, whereas Stradella has set it as an aria for Ubaldo; the poet intended the recitative beginning 'La fronte che d'usbergo' for Ubaldo, whereas Stradella has given it to Carlo; Baldini has assigned the recitative beginning 'Resta in pace' to Carlo, whereas Stradella scored it for Ubaldo. These changes can probably be explained by the need to provide Carlo and Ubaldo each with another aria. That the poet was quite aware of the necessity to please the singers by writing a sufficient number of closed forms for each is seen by his totalling them up for each character after he completed the first version of *Lo schiavo d'amore liberato*.[43] However, as Baldini's numbers differ from the final version (mainly because the four protagonists now have one more aria each), it is possible that Stradella, either alone or with the poet, had to take the situation in hand to keep peace with the cast.

Also to be gleaned from Baldini's text is the information that the placing of instrumental sinfonias in a serenata could have been indicated by the poet. For example, Baldini wrote that there should be one at the

---

[42] I-Rvat, Chigi L.VI.190, fos. 307ʳ–313ᵛ. The indication 'Serenata, o Academia' on Stradella's score of *Lo schiavo liberato* now in the Biblioteca Estense of Modena (Mus. F. 1156) is an incorrect addition to the manuscript by a later hand, and must be discounted.

[43] Fo. 134 of his manuscript.

[44] Before serenatas in I-Rn, Fondo gesuitico, 240 one reads indications such as: 'After a loud sinfonia by 15 strings and [other] instruments'; 'After a long chord by the instruments the bass says

cant is what Baldini had to say at the end of what is now Part I of *Lo schiavo liberato*: 'Here one can have a short sinfonia; after giving drinks and sweets to the Ladies, the sinfonia can be repeated.' He assures us that the *festa* was for an invited audience; he also reveals that the host expected to serve refreshments and wanted the moment to do so to be created during the musical entertainment. This very practical motive may be just why many of Stradella's cantatas with large instrumental forces are separated into two parts. Baldini's last order, that the sinfonia should have been repeated after the guests had been served, was only partly complied with by Stradella, who does begin Part II of *Lo schiavo liberato* with a sinfonia, but it is a new one.

The instrumentation of *Lo schiavo liberato* is similar to that employed in *L'accademia d'Amore*. Athough not used in as many combinations as in the work considered earlier, the same concertino–concerto grosso ensemble is still not employed as a single entity but rather in various combinations throughout the course of the serenata. This is evident just from indications in the score: before Armida's aria 'E dove t'aggiri' one reads, 'Concerted aria with only the concertino'; before 'Almen dai claustri' is written 'Armida's concerted aria with the concerto grosso follows'; at the beginning of 'Non chiuder quei lumi', is 'Armida's concerted aria with concertino and concerto grosso follows'. Carlo's aria 'Quell'intrepida virtù' is also accompanied by the concerto grosso, but the voice has its own continuo as well. Lastly, there are arias which have only continuo accompaniment, such as Armida's 'E tu, peregrino, errando ten vai'.

Affirming that a multiplicity of instruments played the basso continuo is the indication 'and all the basses of the concerto grosso play' which precedes Rinaldo's 'D'amarsi e mirarsi in braccio'. Stradella's careful control of sonority (and probably timbre, if each continuo line had different instrumentation) is noted again in the directions before 'Di senso già priva' not to have any bass instrument except the concerto grosso continuo; and before 'Raffrena i pianti e le strida' not to have any bass or accompaniment other than the concerto grosso.

As usual with Stradella, the accent in *Lo schiavo liberato* is on counterpoint, and one is aware of this as soon as the work opens. The first movement of the sinfonia offers a concertino proceeding imitatively in alternation with a more sustained homophonic concerto grosso; but then the larger group also takes up the imitative style, and from then on rapid scale passages are presented by both concertino and concerto grosso. The ensembles may be called upon to collaborate contrapuntally even when accompanying the voices, as seen in the concertino of Armida's 'Non chiuder quei lumi' and in the concerto grosso of her 'Di senso già priva'.

. . .'; 'It begins with a sinfonia by 30 instruments'; 'After a long sinfonia, which ends as a battle'; 'Another happier sinfonia is played'; 'A sad sinfonia is played.'

Accompanied by only basso continuo, 'E tu, peregrino, errando ten vai' offers yet another technique, that of the ostinato. Suiting the subject of the text, the bass 'wanders' from one level to another. Armida's part here is independent of the ostinato; she also has extremely demanding fiorituras to execute. Stradella's thorough schooling is perhaps best seen in the closing four-part madrigal 'Quanto fu vergognoso il viver tra pace'. It opens with an ascending and then a descending phrase in binary metre which are then taken up in imitation; a following section in ternary metre offers an ascending scale motif also used in inversion; the third main point of imitation begins with a sustained downward skip of a fifth which moves on gradually to become a rapidly winding, florid stretto. Moreover, Stradella's skill in word-painting responds to Baldini's suggestive text, a moral on the benefits of repentance.

Unfortunately, nothing is known about a performance of *Lo schiavo liberato*. It is particularly regrettable that the name of the singer of Stradella's Armida has not come down to us, because whoever performed the long scene for the sorceress when she realizes that she is to lose Rinaldo, must have been quite an artist. Passionate recitative, an expressive lyrical aria, angry recitative, a threatening aria all follow one upon the other, calling for dramatic conviction and refined musical ability.[45]

Fortunately, more information on its performances has come down to us for another of Baldini's texts. On the poet's manuscript the work is said to be a 'Serenata given by Signor Prince Don Gasparo Altieri for the Queen of Sweden in August 1674'. Entitled *Il duello*, it is for the characters 'Filli, Silvio, Amore, Sdegno'[46] and conforms to Stradella's score of *Vola, vola in altri petti*, a serenata for two sopranos (Filli and Amore), mezzo-soprano (Silvio), and bass (Sdegno), accompanied by a concertino–concerto grosso ensemble (two violins and continuo; violin, mezzo-clef viola, alto-clef viola, continuo, respectively). It is the earliest datable composition for concerto grosso. A contemporary reported that the 'most noble serenata' was performed on 15 August 1674, first at about 10 in the evening for Queen Christina of Sweden, in the street below her palace where many people gathered to listen and where Cardinal Azzolino attended from the balcony; and then later on the same night for the Duchess of Gravina, the cardinal's sister, where once again there was an 'excessive' crowd. On 20 August Don Gaspare had the work performed two more times, first for his wife, and then for the Duke of Anticoli on the Corso. These four performances were given with the musicians

[45] A facsimile of one of the two extant scores of *Lo schiavo liberato* (I-Tn, Giordano 14) is to be found in Gianturco, *Cantatas by Stradella*, no. 15, where the text is also given in poetic layout in the Appendix.

[46] Sources for the text are listed in Gianturco–McCrickard, *Stradella Catalogue*.

disposed in three coaches; besides serving as an outdoor stage, the carriages—lit by a 'great number' of flaming torches—also transported the cast.[47]

This sort of performance was not unique in seventeenth-century Rome. In addition to Marazzoli's *Vivere e non amare* for 15 instruments disposed in three coaches, we know of a musical entertainment given after supper from two coaches on the evening of 12 August 1668 by Duke Sforza to the Rospigliosi, at which Marquis Olgiati (a relative of Stradella's staunch supporter) was present.[48] In one were the singers Fidi (soprano), Vulpio (contralto), and Isidoro [Cerruti?] (bass) together with a harpsichord, and in the other were six violins, a viola, a violone, and two archlutes. Obviously the carriages were quite large if all of these string instruments could be accommodated in one of them, perhaps like the carnival floats familiar from engravings. In the same period Lelio Colista composed a serenata for Flavio Chigi which was performed by a 'great quantity of voices and instruments' from three coaches.[49] Since Marazzoli's serenata had more than one performance, Altieri's repeated presentations of Stradella's *Vola, vola in altri petti* are not surprising.

As Baldini's *Il duello* opens, Filli is lamenting that she has been betrayed in love. When Silvio reveals that this has been his fate, too, they agree to protest and not to love any more. With this, Amore and Sdegno (Disdain) appear, the former scolding them for their decision, the latter agreeing with them. After various exchanges—during which Amore affirms that no one can resist him, and Sdegno insists that, on the contrary, it is indeed possible to condemn a tyrant—they rush into battle, both claiming that 'Reason assures me that in the end I shall win.' For her part, Filli is quite certain that 'that blindfolded god who was wicked' will not be victorious, and the serenata concludes as she and Silvio renew their intent to oppose Amore with the help of Sdegno. Comparison between Baldini's text and Stradella's score shows several differences consisting of cuts in the poetry which then necessitated writing some new text. Since there is no reason to doubt that the poet and composer worked in close proximity, it is more than likely that it was Baldini who made the required changes to his text.

The three independent instrumental sinfonias are all for the concerto grosso. Two of them are programmatic: after Filli and Silvio agree to flee from love and thus to safety, there is a binary-form, triple-metre 'Balletto'; and when Amore and Sdegno fight at the end of the serenata (the 'duello' of Baldini's title), there is a binary-form 6/8 sinfonia. The

[47] I-Rc, MS 5006, 'Memorie diverse' by Don Giuseppe Contini, *Sacerdote Romano*, 15 and 20 Aug. 1674.

[48] I-Rvat, Chigi L.IV.94, fos. 102^r–104^r, 150^r–155^v, and I-Rc MS 5006, 12 Aug. 1668, respectively.

[49] Lionnet, 'Flavio Chigi', 298.

sinfonia which serves to open the work is also binary, a sprightly triple-metre movement introduced with slower common-time phrases.

As was Stradella's practice, the vocal pieces may be accompanied with continuo alone (Filli's 'Al campo si corra'); with continuo to accompany the voice but with either the concertino or concerto grosso playing ritornellos (Filli's 'Vola, vola in altri petti' and 'La speranza del gioir', Amore's and Sdegno's duet 'Tiranno tu sei'); with a continuo for the voice plus the concerto grosso (Filli's 'Più non ardo'); as well as with the complete concertino–concerto grosso ensemble (Silvio's 'Vieni a sciorre le catene' and Sdegno's 'Che lo Sdegno ceda ad Amore'). An imitative texture prevails for the instruments, with some quite difficult sections (see, for example, the series of sixteenth-notes tossed from one concertino violin to the other in 'Che lo Sdegno ceda ad Amore'). The vocal music, too, is demanding, and not only in the closed forms but also in the recitative: often quick, with skips, and broken into short phrases, all to simulate the excitement of the characters' heated discussions. In spite of the attractiveness of this style, however, the piece which was the most popular in *Vola, vola in altri petti* was Amore's and Sdegno's duet, 'La ragion m'assicura'. Eleven copies have thus far come to light of this easy-flowing, ternary-metre intertwining of soprano and bass lines. As many sources even omit the occasional interventions by the concerto grosso, one must conclude that it was the simple, consonant vocal music itself, with its recurring presentation of a repeated-note descending phrase, which pleased singers.

Qual prodigio è ch'io miri? is a Stradella serenata which is undated, without a poet's name, and without a poetic source. The plot is simple but not without interest and charm. A naïve lover is enthralled by the starlit night and wishes his beloved's eyes would wake and shine on him. A bitter lover says that it is dangerous to arouse love, which he likens to the sleeping basilisk, a mythical, lizardlike monster whose glance could kill. Their talk wakens the very object of their discussion, a lady (called simply 'Dama') who, from her window, asks who they are. The first gentleman says he is one who begs her help to rid his heart of smouldering flames; the second says he is one who ignores her scorn and coldness. She tells them to be quiet, and offers them some advice: since love is accustomed to prostrate itself before cruelty and disdain in its adoration of beauty, they should seek that heart which bows down before disdain or inflames love. She herself will not give in: the greatest victories of a woman's valour are achieved through disdain and love. The first lover vows that, loved or scorned, he will continue to search for love; the second resolves instead not to look any longer, since without the weapon of scorn one cannot win. They agree that to despise a woman is bad, but to love her is worse.

Qual prodigio è ch'io miri? was performed with two concertino ensembles plus a concerto grosso,[50] resources which were similar to those required in the Turin version of *Il Damone*. One of the concertinos was in a 'cocchio', a gentleman's coach, and was associated with the lovers; the second concertino's location is not specified beyond the fact that it is separate from the first, but since it is called the 'concertino della Dama', it may even have been near the window from which she sang, possibly also in a coach; the concerto grosso, too, was in a coach. From the example of *Vola, vola in altri petti*, the reason for the coaches is easily explained. If the lady in Stradella's *Qual prodigio è ch'io miri?* was to sing from a window, the chances are that the performance took place out of doors; coaches offered a solution to the problem of where the others could be positioned in order for the instruments to be adequate supports for the voices and yet be heard by the audience. Although it is not known on what occasion the serenata was presented, it is likely that it would have been in Rome since all of Stradella's datable concertino–concerto grosso cantatas were for Rome.

Several aspects of *Qual prodigio è ch'io miri?* are worth noting. For example, both concertino continuo parts call for lutes, whereas the concerto grosso continuo seems to have been taken by a violone or cello.[51] Moreover, a lute continuo alone accompanies recitative, the duet 'Amiche | Nemiche, a pietà', the second sections of the arias 'Io pur seguirò' and 'Seguir non voglio più'. Both concertinos are made up of two violins and continuo, and the concerto grosso consists of one violin, two violas (reading alto and tenor clefs respectively), and continuo. The only closed forms which employ a concertino alone are the arias 'Amor sempr'è avvezzo' and 'Io pur seguirò', and the second section of the aria 'Su, mie stelle'. The concerto grosso alternates with a concertino in the arias 'Basilisco, allor, che dorme' and 'Mio petto inerme'; however, in the latter piece its parts are doubled by the other concertino. This reinforced concerto grosso is what accompanies the aria 'Seguir non voglio più' and the opening section of 'Su, mie stelle'. Clearly, and as is usual for Stradella, each successive closed form presents variety and surprise through its different combination of instruments.

All the voices—soprano first lover, bass second lover, soprano lady—are afforded attractive music. Supposing a Roman performance of *Qual prodigio*, one wonders if the part of the second lover was taken by Francesco Verdoni, for whom Stradella wrote such fine bass music as Erode in *San Giovanni Battista*. In the aria 'Basilisco, allor, che dorme' one appreciates the skill required to execute the insistent rapid phrases,

---

[50] See Gianturco–McCrickard, *Stradella Catalogue* for all sources.
[51] The score indicates the instrument with just the letter 'V', the abbreviation used to indicate simply a bowed string instrument.

the occasional fiorituras, the frequent large skips. The same technique is needed for the first section of his aria 'Seguir non voglio più'; the second section, in contrasting ternary metre, is more lyrical, but control is needed all the same to sing the eight similar four-measure phrases, each of which rises and then descends, often ending with a skip.

Perhaps the most striking role of the three is that of the lady. Not only does she begin singing from a window (not at all a usual location, especially not in a cantata), but she is kept apart from the other characters throughout. The poet further emphasized her singularity by allotting the entire central section of the work to her: first a recitative, then a tripartite aria; after a sinfonia she returns with another aria, simple recitative, and finally accompanied recitative. Her determination and strength are adequately portrayed in the energetic, passionate phrases Stradella has given her.

The music for the first lover also requires an accomplished singer since, although not especially filled with fiorituras, it goes up to the second B♭ above middle C, a singular pitch in the seicento. His enthusiasm is communicated in phrases of repeated rhythmic patterns and lines, where telling use is made of arpeggiated figures, sustained notes, and occasional trills.

When accompaniment is by the basso continuo or concertino, they tend to accompany the singer directly; but when the concerto grosso is employed, it plays only between vocal phrases and thus does not cover the voices, which it could easily do in an outdoor performance. Again profitable use is made of counterpoint. This is seen perhaps somewhat more in the vocal closed forms than in the instrumental sinfonias which, instead, rely more on the repetition of short rhythmic figures, alternation between concertino and concerto grosso, and sonority for their effectiveness.

As is known, Handel made use of sections of Stradella's *Qual prodigio è ch'io miri?* in his oratorio *Israel in Egypt*.[52] Naturally any discussion of Handel's use of Stradella's music would say more about Handel than Stradella, but the borrowings are proof that at least one work by Stradella was known to Handel. It offered him an example of Italian vocal and instrumental style, of the large cantata or serenata, and of possible ways to employ a concertino–concerto grosso ensemble.

The two remaining Stradella serenatas, *Chi resiste al dio bendato* and *Il barcheggio*, although accompanied by concertino–concerto grosso ensembles, do not make complete use of the terminology. In the former example, 'Concerto Grosso' appears next to lines for violin, mezzo-clef viola,

---

[52] For a detailed comparison of the two scores, see Taylor, *The Indebtedness of Handel*, 53–75, 87–9.

alto-clef viola, and continuo. No smaller group of strings is ever employed; however, there is an additional continuo line, one which is associated with the voice even when the concerto grosso is scored for (as in the arias 'Chi resiste al dio bendato' and 'Chi vive con amor vive beato', and in the duet 'Fra lacci e catene'). It is conceivable that the concerto grosso was intended to be in opposition not to a smaller group of strings, but to the second group of continuo instruments. At the same time, with the term 'grosso' Stradella could have meant that the ensemble was to be made 'large' by doubling the parts. Another interesting use of terminology appears in the aria which closes the serenata, the 'Chi vive' mentioned above, which calls for 'the concert of instruments'. This piece is said to be based on the 'Tarantella', and indeed the 6/8 music (Ex. 9) is similar, not to the traditional folk-dance of southern Italy but to Athanasius Kircher's example in compound duple metre of a song used to cure tarantism (probably more a form of hysteria than a poisonous bite) published in his *Magnes sive de arte magnetica* (Rome, 1641). The theme is given both to the voice and to the first violin.

Ex. 9.

The text of *Chi resiste al dio bendato* offers the usual discourse about Love: whoever resists him knows no joy, but whoever does not resist suffers. In spite of this dilemma, Amore is invited to show his 'amorous fire', since whoever has love is blessed and lives among roses and lilies. The words could have easily been sung by one person, but have been divided between a main protagonist (soprano), heard in three arias, and two others (soprano, bass), whose single duet and some recitative mainly offer advice. In the duet each successive phrase is related but yet different, a good example of Stradella's subtle way of varying material. The strophic aria 'Chi del bendato arcier' also shows his inclination to manipulate material: the text of each strophe is stated twice, but the music is not repeated (except for the fioritura on 'piacer', which is virtually the same).

The opening sinfonia is in two movements. The first is a ternary 'Spiritoso', 33 measures of imitative music which call for the dynamics, still rare at this time, 'piano', 'forte', 'legato piano'. The second movement is more unusual. The binary form exhibits the usual modulations, from the tonic to the dominant at the end of the first section (A major to E major), and back to the tonic at the end of the second section. The first section is imitative, in ternary metre, and only 25 measures long; however, the second section is 86 measures long, and comprises four alternations between 3/4 and 3/8 'Presto' tempo within which there are inner modulations from the dominant to the subdominant, to the tonic, to the dominant, and finally to the tonic. Even though the text of *Chi resiste al dio bendato* is relatively short and uncomplicated, Stradella managed to render it in an interesting manner, albeit on a small scale.

The occasion which prompted *Il barcheggio* demanded a dramatic and brilliant work.[53] To celebrate the marriage between Carlo Spinola and Paola Brignole, from two of the most notable Genoese families, the spouses' fathers decided to offer a boating *divertissement*. The diplomatic resident from Modena reported that it was first planned to invite guests for 8 June 1681:

If the weather on the sea is good tomorrow, an entertainment is scheduled to be given on the bay in the afternoon for the ladies and gentlemen, a musical concert with splendid refreshments on the occasion of the marriage of the Signori Giovanni Benedetti [read Carlo] Spinola and Paola Brignole, the former a child of Signor Giorgio and the latter of Signor Ridolfo, who are paying the expenses.[54]

The weather, unfortunately, must not have been good that day, because the festivities did not take place until 19 June:

Towards evening on Thursday the ladies and gentlemen of this city had a sumptuous diversion on the bay, having been taken round the harbour by four galleys, besides a very great number of smaller boats, and then conducted aboard a special construction [made] of barges, [which] formed a hall covered by lightweight silk and richly adorned. Here they were entertained with a mixture of harmonious voices, poetry, and instrumental music accompanied by the most exquisite food and refreshments of all sorts, the whole [affair] offered to them as a prelude to their forthcoming marriage by Signori Carlo and Paola . . .[55]

Although it is not known what music was performed for the marraige itself, celebrated in the aristocratic church of S. Maria Maddalena in Genoa on 6 July 1681,[56] evidence indicates that Stradella was the composer of the delightful sea entertainment. His title, *Inventione per un barcheggio* or simply *Il barcheggio*, indicates music for a 'boating'; moreover, one of the copies is dated 16 June 1681,[57] just prior to the actual performance. In addition, in a letter Stradella wrote to Flavio Orsini on

[53] Some of the material presented here on *Il barcheggio* appeared in Carolyn Gianturco, 'Music for a Genoese wedding of 1681', *Music and Letters*, 63 (1982), 31–43; corrective note in 64 (1983), 321; corrections and additions have been made here without comment. For a performing edition of the serenata, see Harry M. Bernstein, 'Alessandro Stradella's Serenata "Il barcheggio" (Genoa, 1681): A Modern Edition and Commentary with Emphasis on the Use of the Cornetto' (2 vols.; DMA diss., Stanford University, 1979).

[54] I-MOas, Cancelleria ducale, Avvisi dall'Estero, busta 63, 7 June 1681.
[55] Ibid., 21 June 1681.   [56] Catelani, *Delle opere*, 37.
[57] The date probably indicates that the performance was postponed once again.

24 May 1681, he mentioned that he would soon be involved in 'un barcheggio', a big celebration to be put on at sea for two 'spouses'.[58] Most conclusive are the references to the young couple in the text: 'Long live Carlo united forever to Paola' is set four times; Paola is called 'the Brignola Minerva'; the name Spinola is connected to Carlo; and reference is made to the writer Anton Giulio Brignole, the girl's grandfather.

The author of the epithalamic text is not known, but either Benedetto Pamphili, whose sister Anna, to whom he often sent texts for music, was living in Genoa (married to Giovanni Andrea Doria), or Giannandrea Spinola, a relative of the groom and author of a number of *commedie per musica*, would be reasonable candidates. As the work opens, Anfitrite (Amphitrite, soprano), a nereid married to Nettuno (Neptune, bass), is voicing her good fortune in being his consort. She and the King of the Sea then invite the nymphs to join them in celebrating their marriage. Next Proteo (Proteus, alto; in mythology the shepherd of Amphitrite's seals) arrives and invites everyone to rejoice in another wedding, that of Carlo and Paola. At this Anfitrite becomes jealous, and in her piqued state declares: 'from the horrible Aeolian grottoes I will arouse whistles and hisses; with a thousand furies of strong whirlwinds I will avenge my injuries.' Nettuno, concerned that his beloved has been disturbed, asks Proteo 'for which Paola, for which Carlo, presumptuous shepherd, is the sacred applause?' Upon hearing the answer, he convinces Anfitrite that she, too, should sing the praises of the two virtuous heroes. The work ends as all three do so 'with the clamour of a thousand trumpets'.

The 'Cantata, o Serenata', as the copy of *Il barcheggio* now in Turin calls it, is a long composition. Divided in two parts, it has 15 arias, five duets (one of which is performed three times, albeit twice abbreviated), two trios, and three sinfonias. Accompaniment is by a concertino–concerto grosso ensemble although the terminology does not appear. In order to evaluate this statement, the instruments called for or implied must first be discussed. The most puzzling question with regard to instrumentation comes from the request in the two extant copies of the serenata to use either 'Tromba o Cornetto', a bewildering choice until one understands the nature of the two winds.[59]

The seventeenth-century trumpet was a valveless metal tube which could play only a restricted number of notes, the harmonics, but for a range which went from two octaves below middle C to two octaves above it; at the same time, a performer was not expected to play the entire range. It is known, though, that virtuoso trumpeters managed to execute

[58] I-Rasc, Arch. Orsini, I. 279, no. 487 (see no. 23 in App. 2a for the whole text). From the letter, one is led to believe that the serenata was completed in May.

[59] The following information on the two winds is taken from *The New Grove*, 'Trumpet' by Edward H. Tarr and 'Cornett' by Anthony C. Baines.

diatonic and chromatic passages through lip control. At the same time, two basic and limiting factors connected with trumpet playing were always taken into consideration by composers: the difficulty of playing at length due to the strain on the lips, and the difficulty of playing in the upper range.

The cornetto, on the other hand, had no such disadvantages. While also having a cup-shaped mouthpiece, it was a curved wooden instrument covered with leather; it also had fingerholes (similar to those on a recorder) which afforded it a complete chromatic range of two and a half octaves. Instead of the brilliant sound of the trumpet, it had a more lyrical quality. In fact, during the first half of the seventeenth century, the violin and cornetto were considered alternatives although the violin eventually replaced the cornetto.

To sum up the situation, by 1681, the date of *Il barcheggio*, the trumpet was more in vogue than the cornetto, and had a more unique sound; but it was not able to be played continuously, and it had problems with its upper register. I believe that it was for these practical considerations that Stradella left the choice of instrument entirely up to the performers without even stating when the two were to alternate: when problematic wind passages occurred (and they occur frequently in *Il barcheggio*) or if the trumpeter found he was tired, the cornetto could replace him. In any event both instruments would have been suitable for *Il barcheggio*, since their supposed maritime ancestor, the conch, was traditionally played by Triton, the son of Amphitrite and Neptune.

Another wind instrument, the trombone, is also named in the score. The aria 'Chi mi scorge ad Anfitrite?' requests 'All the basses with a single trombone' for the continuo, and the sinfonia before Part II is to be played by 'basses with trombones'. It is therefore clear that there was more than one trombone, and that they played in smaller or greater number. One finds this same sort of unequal grouping for the violins. Throughout the serenata, there are often two separate parts for violins: this is true for the opening Sinfonia, for the closed vocal forms 'A Proserpina e Giunone', 'Son lieta, o fortuna', 'Scherzi, rida, e brilli il mar', and so forth. Sometimes, however, the violins are to play in unison, as in 'All'impero de' germani', 'Con la sposa del nume', 'Mille vezzi, mille amori', the two sinfonias in Part II, etc. From this information, it is still not certain, however, if there were only two solo violins or whether more played each part. The question is resolved from the statement which precedes 'Con la sposa del nume': 'One plays this aria that follows for Neptune with two solo violins in unison when the part [i.e. voice] sings, and when it does not sing all play with the trumpet, which begins first, and trombone.' During the aria there are indications of 'play' and 'tacet' to confirm that vocal phrases are to be accompanied by trumpet, two solo violins in unison, and the continuo with trombone, and that the music between the vocal phrases requires trumpet, additional violins, plus the continuo possibly with more trombones. One could easily call these groups a concertino and concerto grosso, especially since there is frequent use of 'soli' and 'tutti' with regard to the violins throughout the serenata.

In other moments of *Il barcheggio* combinations of instruments other than those already discussed are called for. They are given here in an order which reveals not only their variety but also their different sizes. In the repeated duet 'Agl'applausi più festivi', for example, the voices are accompanied by continuo alone (with a ritornello of trumpet/cornetto, two violins, and continuo). The situation is the same (with the difference that in the ritornello the violins are in unison and there is a trombone on continuo), for example, in the arias 'Per porger tributo' and 'Che la bocca di perle e coralli'. There are also pieces where the voice is accompanied by two violins and continuo, such as the arias 'A Proserpina e Giunone' and 'Del splendor degl'avi suoi'. Trumpet/cornetto, two violins in unison and continuo are employed in the aria 'All'impero de' germani'; trumpet/cornetto, two violins in unison, and continuo with trombone are used in the sinfonia to Part II; trumpet/cornetto, two distinct violin parts, and continuo accompany the aria 'Son lieta, o fortuna'.

The alternation of groups within a single closed form, as well as the varying of forces in the course of a work—both of which one finds in *Il barcheggio*—were typical procedures for Stradella in serenatas scored for concertino–concerto grosso. The composer simply experimented here with winds in addition to the usual strings. *Il barcheggio* is, then, the earliest known work in which a wind instrument participated in a concerto grosso ensemble.

The texture of *Il barcheggio* is definitely contrapuntal, occasionally in a manner generally associated with a later period. This is true of Nettuno's aria 'Chi mi scorge ad Anfitrite?', where the instruments continually present a musical motif in which the voice does not participate. However, the opening sinfonia is more typical of Stradella's technique: here the trumpet/cornetto brightly announces a D major chordal theme, which is immediately taken up by the continuo, tossed to the first violin, and then answered by the second violin. The sinfonia sets the style for the whole serenata, a brilliant work which delights in imitation and echo effects, and which capitalizes on the special (and still unusual) timbre of the wind instrument and in the possibilities for virtuosic display when the trumpet/cornetto and voice are paired and pitted against one another, as in Proteo's difficult and marvellous aria 'Agl'applausi risveglisi il cor' (Ex. 10).

One knows nothing about the singers or the instrumentalists of *Il barcheggio*, but they must have been exceptional to have performed the

Ex. 10.

serenata so well that the Modenese diplomat described it enthusiastically as 'a mixture of harmonious voices, poetry, and instrumental music'.[60] Stradella obviously felt he could demand a great deal from them, a conclusion one draws not only from the notes but from several requests for subtlety of interpretation (such as 'Adagio'; 'Presto'; 'mezzo tempo'; 'Allegro assai staccato'; 'Adagio e staccato'; 'Adagio, forte, e staccato'; 'Presto e staccato'; 'All the basses with a single trombone, but the trom-

[60] In Stradella's letter to Orsini cited above (no. 23 in App. 2*a*), he mentions the willingness of the Genoese to hire good singers from elsewhere. He also says that 'Margherita di Bologna' and her sister are in the city at present, both much appreciated, and it is possible that one of them sang in *Il barcheggio*.

bone must play rather staccato and with little breath'). The instructions also reveal Stradella's carefulness, and his concern for a correct understanding of his music and proper performance of it.

That the opening sinfonia of *Il barcheggio* was his last sinfonia, suggested to some by the phrase 'L'ultima delle sue Sinfonie' written on the copy now in Modena, or that the serenata was his last work, understood from 'L'Ultima Composizione' on the same manuscript, seems highly unlikely. There were more than eight months between June 1681, the date of *Il barcheggio*, and February 1682, when Stradella died, and a composer as prolific as he, in good health, and sought after by patrons as he was, would not have remained idle during them. For example, in his letter of 24 May 1681 to Orsini, he wrote of composing a 'cloak-and-dagger operetta' for the following summer.[61] The remarks on the Modena manuscript of the serenata probably meant that, at the time the copy of *Il barcheggio* was made, it offered Stradella's 'last' or 'latest' (no distinction is made in Italian between the two) sinfonia and 'last/latest' composition. We know that in February 1681 Goffredo Marino had sent Stradella's opera *Il Trespolo tutore* to Francesco II d'Este; as a consequence, Stradella received a commission from the court for an oratorio, *La Susanna*, which was presented in Modena in April. It could very well be that either the composer himself or someone else in Genoa kept sending the duke copies of Stradella's music, and that *Il barcheggio* was simply another of his efforts, his 'latest', to be sent to the Este court.[62]

Sacred and Moral Cantatas

A dozen of Stradella's cantatas are not settings of secular poems; rather, they are based on texts of a sacred or moral nature.[63] His five sacred cantatas were intended for three different occasions: two were for Christmas; two were most likely intended for the Feast of All Souls celebrated on 2 November; and one was meant to be sung during Lent, perhaps on Good Friday.

The two Christmas cantatas, *Si apre al riso ogni labro* and *Ah! troppo è ver*, both have instrumental accompaniment other than basso continuo. Beyond this, though, the former work is an example of a small-scale cantata, whereas the latter is similar to Stradella's serenatas. The three characters

---

[61] In Stradella's letter to Polo Michiel dated 21 Dec. 1681 (I-Vmc, PD C. 1067, no. 359), he implies that he has been and wants to continue writing for the Venetian (for the whole letter, see no. 24 in App. 2*a*), another confirmation of his compositional activity.

[62] For similarities between music in *Il barcheggio* and other Stradella compositions, see Gianturco–McCrickard, *Stradella Catalogue*.

[63] See Carolyn Gianturco, '*Cantate spirituali e morali*, with a Description of the Papal Sacred Cantata Tradition for Christmas 1676–1740', *Music and Letters*, 73 (1992), 1–31.

of *Si apre al riso ogni labro* (soprano, alto, and bass accompanied by two violins and continuo) simply comment on the marvel of Christ's birth. As the opening text says, 'Every lip opens to smile, and every eye closes to tears'; later on it is said that 'every word becomes song' due to His coming, 'the reason of every joy'. The whole first section of the cantata reminds one of early liturgical dramas: the soprano tries to tell his companions the reason for his joy and they ask in bewilderment, 'Why?', 'How?', 'Who?', allowing him to continue his description of the birth each time. Once they have understood, all three participate in recounting the wonders of the Nativity. The work features a series of arias, a single duet, and three trios, the music of which is generally syllabic but with the occasional moment of virtuosity. The overall impression is of great vitality and enthusiasm, qualities which are generated especially through the imitative, rhythmic style employed.

A sense of movement is encouraged also by sometimes beginning a closed form in one key and ending it in another: the alto aria 'All'ignudo redentore' begins in E minor and ends in G major; the bass aria 'Con quel gel ch'il sen gl'agghiaccia' begins in D major and ends in G Major; the soprano–alto–bass trio 'O gran bontà' begins in G major and ends in D major. This is common practice for Stradella in his recitatives, but not in closed forms, which habitually begin and end in the same key. Since other set pieces in *Si apre al riso* are handled in his normal fashion, one is inclined to see the three variants as his attempt to achieve direction at these moments of the cantata. An analogy could be made with Stradella's treatment of 'transitional' movements of sonatas.

In five especially pregnant moments of the score, Stradella created accompanied recitatives. The first occasion is at the very opening of the cantata; later on it is for the soprano's line 'at the appearance of the Sun, every shadow disappears'; describing Christ's birth in a chilly stall, the alto encourages all to burn for Him—and goes on in accompanied recitative—'Who freezes for you'; the soprano takes up the same topic, saying that with the warmth of his sighs (and now in accompanied recitative) 'I will warm His cold limbs'. An especially splendid accompanied recitative, quite dramatic and full of fiorituras, with imitation between voice and instruments, is sung by the bass as he beholds the enthroned Child and sees 'He has swords in hand, and is shaking [them]!' (Ex. 11). So many accompanied recitatives coupled with modulatory closed forms are indications that the composer wanted to make something alive and unusual out of a rather ordinary text.

Ah! troppo è ver, Stradella's other Christmas cantata, is more dramatic. The Nativity story is here amplified by an opening scene between Lucifero (Lucifer, bass) and his Furie (Furies, SSAT), all desperate that

Ex. 11.

the devil's evil intentions may soon be thwarted. Next the arrival of the Heavenly Child is announced by the Angelo (Angel, soprano) to a Pastore (Shepherd, tenor), who in turn calls all to come with him. His surprise at what he sees directs one's attention to Maria Vergine (soprano), devotedly and lovingly accepting her dual role as mother and servant. Another Pastore (soprano) pays homage to the Child; he is assured by Giuseppe (Joseph, alto) that the gates of heaven will open to them. All (SSATB) join in a song of praise and wonder.

What strikes one first in *Ah! troppo è ver* is the instrumentation, a concertino (two violins plus continuo)–concerto grosso (violin, alto-clef viola, tenor-clef viola, continuo) ensemble of the sort Stradella employed in several important secular serenatas. In addition, three instruments are called for specifically by name, and given idiomatic music. In the second movement of the opening sinfonia, together with the two concertino violin parts there is a part for lute and another for harpsichord. These latter two alternate and are used as melody instruments to present motivic phrases of sixteenth-notes in imitation with the strings. The harpsichord ends the section alone with a long rapid passage, like a cadenza, which uses both upper and lower registers of the keyboard;[64] this leads without pause to the entrance of the concerto grosso alone, which, in contrast with the preceding spirited common time, offers sustained chords of suspensions in ternary metre. After a second similar alternation of concertino and concerto grosso sections, the concertino with lute and harpsichord returns, to be joined by the larger group for the closing phrase of the movement. When Stradella died, he owned three lutes, and Pitoni said the composer was an excellent harpsichordist. It is quite possible, then, that one of the two parts was written for himself.

The third instrument called for by name in *Ah! troppo è ver* is the harp. To accompany the shepherd's request that their homage be accepted by the Child ('Deh, ricevi i nostri voti'), the Modena copy of the cantata calls for 'arpa doppia'.[65] In the bipartite aria (binary and then ternary metre) the voice and instrument are at first independent, the sustained vocal line accompanied by the harp in scalar figures repeated so often as to constitute a quasi-ostinato. In the second section, the voice's arpeggiated phrases as well as its weaving florid ones (especially appropriate as the shepherd asks to benefit from the world's 'turnings') are imitated by the instrument.

Another striking feature of *Ah! troppo è ver* is the dramatic way in which the voice is introduced. Just when the lively third movement of the opening sinfonia, scored for both concertino and concerto grosso, is coming to its expected conclusion, Lucifero interrupts the final cadence crying out angrily that the stars are against him. He goes on, accompanied by only continuo, to sing a wonderful five-measure fioritura which describes the 'fiery' disasters he foresees. The excitement continues into Lucifero's aria, 'E sarà chi non s'accinga', where cascades of sixteenth-notes pass from voice to first and second concertino violins. As usual, Stradella has written particularly fine music for the bass voice.

---

[64] On the importance and uniqueness of Stradella's treatment of the harpsichord here and elsewhere see Arnaldo Morelli, 'La tastiera concertante all'epoca di Corelli', in Pierluigi Petrobelli and Gloria Staffieri (eds.), *Studi Corelliani IV: Atti del Quarto Congresso Internazionale (Fusignano, 4–7 settembre 1986)* (Florence, 1990), 196–9.

[65] The double harp had two ranks of strings, one diatonic and the other chromatic; one simply extended one's finger slightly beyond the first row of strings to play a chromatic alteration. For more information, see Ann Griffiths and Joan Rimmer, 'Harp: Double Strung Harps', *The New Grove*. An interesting discussion of the instrument which includes several good illustrations of it is by Cristina Bordas, 'The Double Harp in Spain from the 16th to the 18th centuries', *Early Music*, 15 (1987), 148–63. Filippo Albini's *Il secondo libro dei musicali concenti da cantarsi nel cembalo, tiorba, o arpa doppia, ad una, e due voci* (Rome, 1626) and Monteverdi's *Orfeo* are two other examples of scores which call for the instrument. One knows, too, that Marco Marazzoli was a harpist, as was Costanza, the wife of Luigi Rossi; and Orazio dell'Arpa obviously got his name from the instrument.

One must also remark on the exquisite beauty of the soprano aria 'Sovrano mio bene' for Maria Vergine. The entire instrumental ensemble is involved in the alternation of a 3/2, suspension-filled, 'pathetic-style' section, intended to depict Mary's deep love for the Holy Child, with a graceful and lovely 3/8 section which expresses her joy. Notable, too, are the two vocal ensembles of *Ah! troppo è ver*. The first is an SSAT quartet for the Furies, 'Al cenno orribile del Re dell'Erebo', as they fly about doing the devil's bidding; and the second is an SSATB quintet called a 'Madrigale' in the score, 'Or che luci sì belle', which closes the cantata with an affirmation of Heaven's supremacy. Both are excellent examples of 'stile antico' contrapuntal technique applied to a newer motivic, rhythmic baroque style; they are, moreover, difficult vocally but they would have been executed by the cantata's soloists.

Ah! troppo è ver was probably a Roman work. Although the poet or patron are not known, this sort of Nativity tale set as a cantata was popular in Rome.[66] What is more, Stradella wrote several works for voices and concertino–concerto grosso there in the 1670s. This date could find confirmation in the cantata's phrase 'della clemenza sua' repeated in a distinctive way three times and which might refer to Pope Clement X who reigned from 1670 to 1676.

Stradella's two sacred cantatas for 'the Souls of Purgatory', *Crudo mar di fiamme orribili* and *Esule dalle sfere*, differ in a way similar to his two Christmas cantatas, with the former being on a smaller scale than the latter. Whereas nothing precludes *Crudo mar* being composed for Rome, the date 1680 on the Modenese copy of *Esule dalle sfere* places it in Stradella's Genoa period.

One understands why Pompeo Figari, the Genoese clergyman who was the author of both texts, was to become a founder of Arcadia. Dominating *Crudo mar* is his clear and vivid imagery of the soul being in purgatory's tremendous sea of flames, suffering terribly and unable to find respite. Only when he believes himself unable to resist any longer does the soul remember that it is the will of the Eternal Maker that he be in purgatory, and that therefore he will be saved. His happiness causes him to conclude: 'Inconceivable comfort: the wilder the sea, the sweeter the port.'

Figari laid out his text in lines for recitative, and four closed forms which deserve comment. Normally the closed forms offered verses of an even number of syllables with strophes composed of lines of equal length. Such a structure was said to be preferred by composers, who could write regular, not over-extended phrases for it. However, except for the last aria, Figari does not follow convention. Whereas the concluding

[66] See Gianturco, '*Cantate spirituali e morali*'.

'Allegrezza! Già la speme mi conforta' offers a normal 4/8/8/8–syllable plan, the other three arias do not. The opening 'Crudo mar di fiamme orribili', instead, is 8 *sdrucciolo*/8/8 *tronco*/8 *sdrucciolo*/8/8 *tronco*/5/11 (where *sdrucciolo* indicates an accent on the antepenultimate syllable and *tronco* indicates an accented last syllable) which is repeated for the second strophe of text; the second aria 'Astri rigidi, se collassù' is structured 10 *tronco*/8/8/8 *tronco* in the first strophe, and 4 *tronco*/8/11 in the second strophe; and the third aria in the cantata, 'In mar sì rio', follows the scheme 5/5/5 *tronco*/5/5 *tronco*/5 *tronco*/8 in the first strophe, and 8/4/11 *tronco* in the second strophe. The irregularity of the lines in these three examples, the fact that they are frequently of an odd number of syllables, and often end with a manneristic accented syllable, are all signs of Figari's poetic sophistication. These characteristics, coupled with his skilful use of the language, undoubtedly heightened the interest the sacred cantata would have held for the cultured Italians for which it was intended.

Stradella's setting of the text maintains the feeling of restlessness and anxiety achieved by Figari. For bass voice, two violins and basso continuo, the cantata opens with a sinfonia. Its single movement is divided into two sections, the second of which presents, in imitation, the theme of 'Crudo mar di fiamme orribili', normal practice in an overture of a later period, but still rare in the seicento. The vocal and instrumental lines of the aria are angular and consist of phrases of different lengths and on various pitch levels, in a contrapuntal texture. The impression is one of controlled irregularity, the same quality one can attribute to the poetry. It is only for the last, poetically regular aria, 'Allegrezza! Già la speme', that another atmosphere is created, one of joyous assurance. The bass voice is called upon here—as it is throughout the cantata—to execute difficult music, and in rapid alternation with the violins.

The section which is most surprising in *Crudo mar di fiamme orribili*, however, is the concluding one. The last two lines of text, which sum up the soul's sentiment and Christian belief (cited above), are of recitative text: a 7-syllable line followed by an 11-syllable one. However, after such a brilliant performance by the bass voice, supported in all the previous arias by the violins, two lines of simple recitative would not have been satisfying. Or at least Stradella desired something more. In fact, the sacred cantata ends with a splendid accompanied recitative.[67]

Pompeo Figari's other text about purgatory which Stradella set is *Esule dalle sfere*. Christian doctrine is again set forth in a compelling manner. It begins with Lucifero venting his anger that he and the other devils have

---

[67] *Crudo mar* may be seen in a facsimile edition in Gianturco, *Cantatas by Stradella*, no. 14; the text is offered in poetic layout in the appendix to the volume.

been banished from heaven. He is determined that the souls in purgatory feel his jealous revenge. Either singly or in chorus the Anime (suffering souls) beg God to relieve their terrible agony. Finally an angel arrives (no doubt the Archangel Gabriel) as a 'messenger of comfort', their pain stops immediately, and they are invited to go to heaven. Lucifero protests that their alleviation and removal is unjust if he is to be doomed to eternal exile. He is told that any punishment would be too light for his terrible sin; what is more, it is the prayers of mortals which have been able to remove the slight blemishes from these beautiful souls. Lucifero's chagrin at his defeat makes him flee; the angel and the souls rejoice that 'after a short cry, laughter is eternal'.

Figari did not implement the contorted structures of *Crudo mar di fiamme orribili*, but only strophes with lines of four syllables ('Troppo avari') or six syllables ('Crude voragini' and 'A cor supplicante'), for example. Interest is achieved, instead, through vivid language and varied verbal rhythms, and through the overall plan of the drama. Approximately the first third of the text is organized with ritornellos: after an opening section of recitative, Lucifero's first closed form, 'Mie schiere severe', repeats its opening lines of text to achieve an ABA structure; next the Anime, the souls in purgatory, utilize a ritornello in 'Da mostri sì crudeli', an exchange between one of them and the rest; then a single soul offers the closed form 'Troppo avari', once again repeating text. After this tightly organized section, during which the devil torments the souls, the middle part of *Esule dalle sfere* offers less frequent alternations as the single souls beg for aid (recitative text and a single closed form, 'Crude voragini'). However, to show the continual infliction of pain by the devil and the desperation of the Anime, the section continues in several interchanges between the two, culminating in the interruption of the agony by the angel. In the last section of the cantata, the tension of the drama is relaxed, and there are two lively closed forms for the Angelo ('Su, su spariscano' and 'A cor supplicante') and a final ensemble for him and the souls ('Alle gioie, ai contenti, al Paradiso'). In *Esule dalle sfere* Figari was an able dramatist, one capable of using language, form, and style with sufficient creativity to render a very simple tale and ordinary doctrine captivating.

Stradella reflected and heightened this interest. As in *Ah! troppo è ver*, Lucifero is set for bass, a suitable voice for the sinister and powerful devil, made more terrible through his frequent fioriituras (that at the end of his first recitative is more than six measures long). Underlining his contrast with the devil, the Angelo is a soprano; the Anime are SATB, with an aria each assigned to the soprano and bass souls. The music for all voices, even the chorus, is generally more angular than not; through their obligatory efforts to sing the intervals, the singers give due emphasis to the meaningful text. *Esule dalle sfere* is introduced by a sinfonia for two violins and basso continuo. The two movements, plus two others, are also found in purely instrumental music sources and were published by Marino Silvani in his *Scelta delle suonate* of 1680. While the cantata cannot be dated precisely, it was probably not composed later than 1680.[68]

Da cuspide ferrate on the 'Crucifixion and death of Our Lord Jesus Christ', although by an anonymous poet, could well have been written by Pompeo Figari.[69] Its simple structure of *versi sciolti* for the narrator, a single closed form for the protagonist, and further *versi sciolti* for the narrator is enriched through striking imagery and sophisticated versification. The scene described is of Christ dying in 'bloody agony' on the cross. He expresses His willingness to accept His fate in the lines, repeated at the ends of both strophes, 'the time has arrived; come then, my heart, you die'. The narrator returns to comment that Christ proved His love by dying, and ends by asking the listener to comment on His words.

Stradella has set the sacred text for alto, two violins, and basso continuo. Even though not long, the work must have been for a somewhat important occasion—perhaps for a confraternity's special Good Friday service—because the strings not only accompany the voice for the closed form, but introduce the cantata with a two-movement sinfonia. Stradella's handling of the narrator's first recitative takes full account of the meaning of the text, but it is the beauty of Christ's two-strophe aria, 'Già compìto è de' tormenti', which strikes one. It is one of Stradella's loveliest examples of the 'pathetic style', in which strings and voice interweave in easy imitation to create poignant suspensions reflecting the sufferer's torments.

The end of *Da cuspide ferrate* is also noteworthy. The poet was obviously questioning the listener about his faith, and therefore, although only a single line, the question is of enormous importance. Stradella realized both facets: since it is a question, he ended it not in G minor, the central key of the cantata, but on the dominant D major, strikingly approached by a Phrygian cadence; and since the line is a weighty one, he heightened it by scoring it as an accompanied recitative.

Together with sacred and secular cantatas, there was also a moral or didactic repertory in the seicento,[70] and Stradella contributed seven works

[68] A modern edition is by Eleanor F. McCrickard, *Alessandro Stradella, 'Esule dalle sfere', A Cantata for the Souls of Purgatory* (Early Musical Masterworks; Chapel Hill, NC, 1983). I am not in agreement with Aldo Scaglione's transcription and poetic layout of the text included in the volume. Also see McCrickard's article, 'Stradella's *Esule dalle sfere*: A Structural Masterpiece', in Carolyn Gianturco and Giancarlo Rostirolla (eds.), *Atti del Convegno di studi 'Alessandro Stradella e il suo tempo', Siena, 8–12 settembre 1982, Chigiana*, 39, NS 19 (1988), 347–69.

[69] See Gianturco, *Cantatas by Stradella*, no. 13 for a facsimile of the cantata; the text in poetic layout is in the appendix to the volume.

[70] See Gianturco, 'Cantate spirituali e morali'.

to the genre. Their poetry varies in subject and in length, but all urge the listener to reflect upon his behaviour; often the brevity of life is considered as well. *Apre l'uomo infelice*, Stradella's most 'classic' text because it is by that classic master Giovanni Battista Marino (set earlier by Alessandro Grandi), insists that man is born to misery, that he has tears before he sees the sun; it also reminds one that 'from the cradle to the tomb is but a short step'. Stradella's setting of the poetry is for a virtuoso soprano and basso continuo. Its single aria, 'Fanciullo poi che non più', and recitative are filled with long and frequent fiorituras; this style characterizes the opening, too—one of Stradella's most distinctive (Ex. 12).

Ex. 12.

Giovan Filippo Apolloni laments in his 'Moralità per Musica' set by Stradella, *Quando sembra che nuoti*, that just when one thinks all is going well, problems arise. He refers in particular to love and its trials on one's constancy. Stradella organized the three strophes of poetry into several internal ABB' structures within a large closed form, and wrote the closing lines as recitative followed by arioso. The work, which exhibits a fine sense of tonality and intelligent use of insistent rhythmic patterns, is scored for contralto and continuo.

Voi ch'avaro desio nel sen nudrite, for soprano and basso continuo, is another moral cantata with only one aria plus recitative. Here Midas vainly tries to stop his hand from turning everything into gold, and sadly concludes, 'Because I obtained too much, I lose myself.' The many lines of recitative text are handled with insight by Stradella, who frequently shifts into arioso style as Midas' desperation increases.

In *Dalla Tessala sponda scese d'Argo la prora* the Greeks are looking for the Golden Fleece. Dawn tells them that she cannot quench their thirst for treasure, and the concluding moral is that the troubles of the soul are calmed if desire is checked by poverty. Recitative introduces the three arias in this work for contralto and continuo. The arias themselves are sectional, exhibiting frequent changes of time signature to reflect the various strophes of poetry, and are developed simply by repeating text and modulating to related keys.

The advice in *Mortali, che sarà* is that one should not wait till it is too late, but should be aware of the signs from God and act accordingly. Stradella began by calling out to 'mortals' as if to get their attention, and then set the question put to them about the meaning of a comet in the sky more rhythmically. The line is repeated twice more in the course of the work as a ritornello. The cantata is for bass and continuo, and, as in all his works for this voice, abundant use has been made of fiorituras both in arias and recitative, a style quite suitable for a text which orders all to cry, to turn pale, and to tremble in the face of flames and thunder. *Mortali, che sarà*, besides being a 'singer's cantata', is also tonally competent (with closed forms in the tonic, dominant, relative minor, and supertonic keys) and internally well organized (for example, there are often phrases of characteristic rhythmic patterns repeated sequentially).

A friend and admirer of Marino, Francesco Balducci, was the author of Stradella's cantata *Spuntava il dì*.[71] The poem describes the loveliness of a rose, but also points out that the flower must die; human beauty, which the world so admires, must also fade, and therefore one should not be haughty. The lines are for a narrator who occasionally leaves off his description to address questions of morality to the rose; however, Stradella has assigned the text to an SSB vocal ensemble accompanied by basso continuo. The trio offers five closed forms in the course of the cantata, two of which bring back the final section of the opening piece in which it is asked to what advantage is beauty (lines beginning 'Ma che pro'?'), and one of which repeats the same section but without the opening line; another trio ends with the whole *intercalare*. The text of this latter trio, beginning 'Per valletta o per campagna' (but without the *intercalare*), is also heard in a soprano aria, its repetition decided upon by Stradella probably so that he could write a second-soprano aria to balance the first-soprano aria, 'La vagheggiano gl'albori', and thus satisfy both soloists. In the a 3 sections both lyrical homophony and imitative counterpoint are employed; in solo sections, there are few fiorituras but they require a fine technique.

The largest of Stradella's moral cantatas is *Alle selve, agli studi*, a setting

---

[71] Balducci (Palermo, 1579–Rome, 1642) was renowned both for his turbulent life and for his poetry which enabled him to become a member of several literary academies. His *Rime* were first published in Rome in 1630, but were reprinted several times (such as in Venice, 1662–3). Among them are those labelled 'Rime morali' which include the text set by Stradella. (He is also the author of Stradella's secular cantata *Di tal tempra è la ferita*.)

of a long text by Benedetto Pamphili.[72] Stradella would have known him in Rome, but since *Alle selve, agli studi* is dated 1680, one can place its composition in Genoa, where one of Pamphili's sisters, Anna, was married to Prince Giovanni Andrea Doria, and another, Flaminia, to Prince Nicolò Pallavicino. The work is called a 'Cantata morale' and bears the Latin theme 'Otia si tollas periere Cupidinis arcus' (If you become idle, you will perish by Cupid's bow.) As it opens, Diana is going off to the woods, Apollo to study, and Marte (Mars) to take up arms. When Amore appears and asks them what new desire moves their hearts, they tell him he is arrogant and proud and that they repudiate him. He insists that he will still be able to make them fall in love. Long discourses follow about Amore and about the three gods' individual intentions to resist him, during which *otio* is often cited as something to flee: who stays far from idleness, laughs at Amore; if idleness does not open one's heart, Amore cannot enter it; where idleness does not reign, Amore is defenceless. In the face of such determination Amore must admit defeat, and in the end he gives up his arrows and his fire.

Pamphili's spirited argumentation is set by Stradella for two sopranos (Diana and Amore), and two contraltos (Apollo and Marte), the whole accompanied by basso continuo. Of the sixteen closed forms, nine have two similar strophes of poetry, and therefore Stradella set them as repeated strophes of music ('Tu che sei più delle belve' for Marte, 'Le muse canore non curan' for Apollo, etc.); and when Pamphili differentiated his strophes in their verse-structure, Stradella also changed his music from one strophe to the next ('Vinto Amore? O bel pensiero' for Amore, 'Non è più tempo Amor' for Marte, etc.). Again, when the characters each say something different in a stretto-type recitative, the music reflects their diversity; but as soon as they verbally agree on something, the music seconds them with the same material.

The overall impression of *Alle selve, agli studi* is of a mature composition for virtuoso performers. True, fiorituras, although occasionally present, do not abound; at the same time, the insistent, dynamic rhythm for all voices requires excellent musicians with good vocal techniques and the ability to interpret the cantata's spirited arguments. A large part of the atmosphere is achieved through the collaboration of the instrumental bass with its difficult, continually active, lively, often ostinato lines (as in Amore's 'Volarò, ferirò'). The duet for Amore and Marte, 'Così va s'amor con beltà', is a fitting and musically splendid way to relieve Amore of his 'bow, arrow, torch, and frivolities' and thus close Stradella's most significant *cantata morale*.

---

[72] The son of (ex-cardinal) Camillo Pamphili and Donna Olimpia Aldobrandini, Princess of Rossano, Benedetto Pamphili (Rome, 1653–1730) was left a large fortune by his great-uncle, Pope Innocent X, which enabled him to occupy his leisure writing poetry for music. His several oratorios, operas, and cantatas were set by composers such as Alessandro Melani, Alessandro Scarlatti, Bernardo Pasquini, and Handel.

7

Theatre Music

During his years in Rome and Genoa, and perhaps in Venice and Turin, Stradella had occasion to write music for the theatre. This was not as frequent as his opportunities to compose chamber music, but among his extant works there are a sufficient number of operas, prologues, intermezzos, and substitute arias, as well as incidental music for a play, to enable us to evaluate his ability.

Operas[1]

Letters from Settimio Olgiati to Polo Michiel from 30 June 1677 to 1 April 1678 refer to an opera Stradella was to compose for Venice on a libretto by the Florentine Gianfrancesco Saliti.[2] Unfortunately, no title or subject is named. It is not certain what eventually happened to the score since it is neither mentioned in later extant correspondence, nor does it seem ever to have been performed in Venice.

In Genoa Stradella was immediately involved with the Teatro Falcone, at first just directing the opera orchestra and coaching singers; but by 30 April 1678 the management had put the 1678–9 season into his hands. He wrote to Polo Michiel that Genoa usually presented an old and a new opera each year and he wanted to do Sartorio's *Seleuco*.[3] In the end Stradella set a revised version of the libretto himself, and presented it under the title *La forza dell'amor paterno*.

Act I. Antioco, son of Seleuco, King of Syria, is to marry Lucinda; however, he has fallen in love with the unknown girl in a portrait he found on a field of battle.

---

[1] Earlier studies of Stradella's operas are: Hess, *Die Opern*; Carolyn Gianturco, 'The Operas of Alessandro Stradella (1644–1682)' (2 vols.'; D.Phil. thesis, Oxford University, 1970); id., 'Caratteri stilistici delle opere teatrali di Stradella', *Rivista italiana di musicologia*, 6 (1971), 211–45; Paolo Fabbri, 'Questioni drammaturgiche del teatro di Stradella' in Carolyn Gianturco and Giancarlo Rostirolla (eds.), *Atti del Convegno di studi 'Alessandro Stradella e il suo tempo'*, Siena, 8–12 settembre 1982, *Chigiana*, 39, NS 19 (1988), 79–108.

[2] In chronological order they are: I-Vmc, PD C. 1064, nos. 201, 192, 190, 278, 265, 299, and PD C. 1065, nos. 385, 400, and 377. See also Saliti's letter to Michiel (undated but probably Mar. 1678: I-Vmc, PD C. 1065, no. 282) in which he refers to the Venetian taste in opera.

[3] Nicolò Minato had originally entitled his libretto *Antioco* and, as such, it was first set to music by Cavalli in 1658; but in 1666 the opera was heard again, this time with Antonio Sartorio's music and now entitled *Seleuco*. On this occasion it was dedicated to the Genoese Duke Paolo Spinola, and it could be that it was this local connection which suggested a revival in Genoa.

She turns out to be Stratonica, Queen of Asia, already engaged to Seleuco. Faced with this reality, Antioco becomes ill and Stratonica falls in love with him. Seleuco decides to postpone both weddings until his son recovers. A further complication is that Arbante, a prince of the court, loves Lucinda and she begins to succumb to his persistent attentions. Serious scenes are interspersed with comic ones in which the old servant Rubia declares that she is available for whomever wants a wife, adding that under the cover of marriage all things are honourable. Another servant, Silo, says he is also available for whomever wants a husband. Rubia suggests he choose her.

Act II. The court physician, Ersistrato, has a musician try to revive Antioco's spirits with song, but the prince becomes worse. Stratonica and Lucinda come to see him but he is aware only of the queen. Rubia flirts now with the courtier Eurindo who tells her she is too old. Arbante continues to pursue Lucinda. In his delirium Antioco goes about the palace breaking things; he even mistakes Rubia for Iole and Ariadne, and then, thinking her the rapacious eagle of Jove, attacks her.

Act III. Ersistrato finally finds a way of telling Seleuco that his son is sick because of his love for Stratonica, but when confronted with the truth by his father, Antioco denies it; despondent, the prince raves madly. His father then sends him a letter he is to give to Lucinda; it says she is to marry the bearer. Not knowing this, Antioco has Arbante deliver it. Lucinda and Arbante are ecstatic. Silo also declares his love to Rubia. Ersistrato reveals Antioco's love for Stratonica to Seleuco who relinquishes her as *The Force of Paternal Love* dictates.

Who made the revisions to Nicolò Minato's libretto for Stradella is not known.[4] Act I of the Genoese version follows Minato's original libretto quite closely, any differences being mainly those of omission plus the addition of two comic scenes, one for Rubia and another for Rubia and Silo. Act II, however, is very much altered, with new scenes (the humorous scene 7, and Eurindo's scene 15), arias (in scene 6 for Antioco, in scene 14 for Arbante) and lines added, and others omitted (the 20 scenes of 1666 are reduced to 17 in 1678).[5] Actually, a whole new shape is given to the act by allotting more time to Rubia's humour and by making less of Seleuco's foolish and undignified infatuation with the young Stratonica. The plot of Act III again conforms more closely to the original libretto.[6] As Gentili has pointed out, the events proceed without constraint, and the characters are clearly and decisively drawn.[7]

[4] According to Francesco Saverio Quadrio, *Della Storia, e della Ragione d'ogni poesia*, iii/2 (Milan, 1744), 514 Lonati had revised the text for Milan in 1671, but this version was not the one Stradella used.

[5] Stradella incorrectly numbered sc. 7 of Act II as sc. 6, and thus his score has two scenes with the same number 6. He continued to misnumber the scenes throughout the rest of the act. Any references here to Act II will use the proper, corrected number.

[6] Throughout the opera, several second strophes of text in the printed libretto are not in Stradella's score; however, they are in a volume of arias from the opera in I-MOe, Mus. G. 325, which means they were intended to be sung but were simply not written out in the score. For more details, see Gianturco–McCrickard, *Stradella Catalogue*.

[7] Alberto Gentili, 'Un'opera di Alessandro Stradella ritrovata recentemente', *Il pianoforte*, 8 (1927), 210.

From Stradella's music it is obvious that the cast was excellent. Examining the list of singers he sent to Michiel,[8] one can attempt a listing of the roles they took: Marcantonio Orrigoni, *primo soprano*, Antioco; Caterina Angela Botteghi, soprano *prima donna*, Stratonica; Francesco Rossi, *secondo soprano*, Eurindo; Francesco Vallerini, contralto, Arbante; Francesco Guerra, tenor, Seleuco; Giacomo Filippo Cabella, bass, Ersistrato; Federico Generoli, contralto, Rubia; Giovanni Battista Petriccioli, *buffo* bass, Silo.

As for the *seconda donna* in the soprano role of Lucinda, Stradella wrote some music first for a Neapolitan singer who was reported to be excellent but on arrival was judged unacceptable. She was quickly substituted by a local castrato, Granarino, who did the opening night, albeit unsatisfactorily. It was then decided to have Annuccia (surname unknown) come from Rome and do the part. Stradella commented that in the meantime *La forza* was performed with only one female. One deduces that Granarino also did the soprano role of the musician, and Stradella's autograph score confirms his inadequacies. For the aria 'Troppo misero cor mio', first sung by the musician and then repeated and extended by Antioco, he wrote two versions: a florid one and a much simpler one. A second aria for Musico and Antioco, 'Quel ch'al core', was eliminated altogether.[9]

Apart from this one instance, Stradella was able to write florid lines for all the serious characters. However, the voice is not exploited alone; rather, it is dealt with as part of a concerted whole, as a force of one line pitted against those of the two violins and continuo which accompany the opera. Stradella does this in two effective ways: either the voice remains static, sustaining one note over several bars of instrumental activity; or the voice alternates with the instruments in stating and restating rapid phrases. This same predilection for a contrapuntal texture is revealed in the instrumental ritornellos, and in the violin accompaniments to arias: practically all rely upon imitation rather than a doubling of a melody in thirds or sixths as their mode of expression, and generally it is imitation of ideas which may be considered more rhythmic than melodic.

In fact rhythm is the essential character dominating the whole opera: rhythm that insists, that drives, that repeats. Connected to rhythm is the motif, since it is often the repetition of a particular motif which creates propulsive rhythm. However, there is also interest in the motif for itself, as a means of generating a whole aria and becoming its theme. For example, in 'Sulla nave della vita' for Stratonica (Act I, sc. 2) Stradella repeatedly used a rocking motive made by a skip of a fourth in the bass to suggest the rocking motion of a ship, and even the voice occasionally pre-

---

[8] Letter of 27 Jan. 1679, I-Vmc, PD C. 1066, no. 577 (no. 15 in App. 2*a*).

[9] On the several changes in the score, see my article 'The Revisions of Alessandro Stradella's *Forza dell'amor paterno*', *Journal of the American Musicological Society*, 25 (1972), 407–27.

sents it. In Arbante's 'Amoretti all'armi' (I. 5), a rapid four-note motif is used throughout like a rallying cry to Cupid's archers. Comedy, too, is served by motifs as in Rubia's aria 'Il marito è una coperta' (I. 7) where awkward rhythm serves to point up the *buffo* side of her personality. Together with a competent manipulation of rhythm and motives, Stradella—perhaps as an extension of these two—also took advantage of the sequence. One example is a recitative where it is coupled with a chromatic bass (Ex. 13), but the opera has several instances of sequences in closed forms as well.

Ex. 13.

One of Stradella's favourite ways of organizing an aria, apart from contrasting sections, is through the basso ostinato; in fact, 15 arias are composed on such a plan while others show a tendency towards it. What is more, in several instances the same ostinato is used in all sections of an aria, such as in the ABA arias for Arbante, 'Con voi femmine chi ci riesce' (II. 14) and 'Senza speranza, ohimè' (I. 12). The ostinato is such an integral part of Stradella's technical equipment in the opera that he uses it even in a recitative for Antioco: in Act II, scene 17 beginning at 'No, no, errai, mia bella', a scalar bass figure is repeated six and a half times for a section in arioso style where the voice breaks out into florid phrases on the word 'cantar'. The ostinato in Rubia's aria 'Credere a' giovanotti è vanità' (III. 17) is so simple as to be almost banal (Ex. 14), but it is probably just this dumb insistence Stradella wanted in order to point up the narrow-minded foolish servant. In fact, several of her arias are based on similarly unsophisticated ostinatos.

As is to be expected, the closed musical forms in *La forza dell'amor*

Ex. 14.

paterno mirror the poetic forms. Here as elsewhere in Stradella's vocal music, similarly structured strophes of poetry result in strophic music (as in 'Chi non ha d'aquila gl'occhi' for Stratonica, I. 4), and two different poetic structures in succeeding strophes result in two different musical sections (as in 'Amoretti all'armi' for Arbante, I. 5). Poetic structure often dictated internal musical form as well, and as a result ternary form predominates: see for example, the music for 'Quanto tardate, o quanto' for Stratonica (II. 12) where a languid A-section in triple metre is followed by a spirited B-section in common time which is quite extended as well.

An interesting scene, and one which illustrates Stradella's response to text and drama, is Act III, scene 9. Seleuco has just left Antioco after hearing him deny his love for Stratonica. The young man is at once despondent and angry with himself for having lied. His 19 lines of *versi sciolti*, instead of being set as a section of simple recitative by Stradella, are treated individually so as to underscore Antioco's various emotional states, with ternary rhythm alternating with binary rhythm, and lyrical, melodic phrases alternating with more rhythmic ones where repeated notes dominate, and with string accompaniment alternating with just basso continuo. In short, the scene is treated as a true accompanied recitative, exactly as it would be conceived in the eighteenth century.

Other particular responses to text are the two mad scenes for Antioco in Act II, both added to Minato's libretto for Genoa.[10] Following the tradition of such scenes, it is Antioco's sadness (over his problematic love of Stratonica) which causes his madness. However, the scenes are not traditional monologues. In Act II, scene 16 Antioco is with his servant Silo, and believes that they are both fighting the gods Jove, Mars, and Pluto, who are trying to take his beloved away. In the next scene (II. 17) Antioco is joined by Rubia (Silo having exited), and passionately declares his love for her; amusingly, she doesn't realize he is raving and is inclined to believe him. While scene 16 is rather dramatic with its imagined battle, scene 17 is frankly humorous, and thus two different sorts of mad scene

---

[10] Deriving from Ludovico Ariosto's famous and influential poem of 1532, *Orlando furioso*, the first theatrical mad scene in Italy seems to have been in *Pazzia d'Isabella* performed by the Gelosi, a *commedia dell'arte* company, in 1589 in Florence. Operatic mad scenes are to be found early in the history of the genre, for example in Venice in 1641 in Benedetto Ferrari's *Ninfa avara*, Giulio Strozzi's *Finta pazza*, and Gian Francesco Busenello's *Didone*. By 1643 Giovanni Faustini was able to affirm that such scenes were common in the theatre, and that he had been asked to include one in his opera *Egisto* in order to reveal the special qualities of the actor-singer who was to do the part. In general, the character usually goes mad from sadness; in a monologue, he or she sees things which are not there and mistakes what is present for something else.

1. The Stradella Coat of Arms (red lion rampant on a field of yellow crossed with a white band).

2. Document dated 20 June 1638 in which the composer's father, Marc'Antonio Stradella, is said to be from Nepi and his uncle from Fivizzano. Marc'Antonio requests here to have his son Giuseppe made a Cavaliere di Santo Stefano.

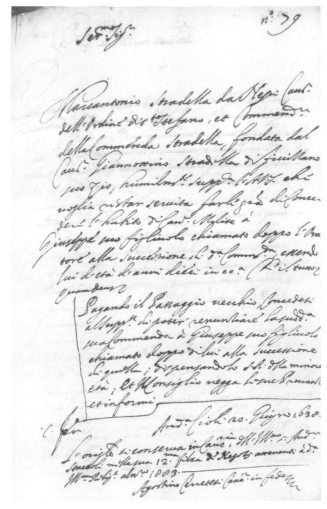

3. Fortress of *Vignola*, where Marc'Antonio Stradella was *Vice-Governor* and lived with his family in 1642–3.

4. Palazzo Lante, Rome: (*left*) façade, (*right*) inner courtyard. Alessandro, his mother, and his brother Stefano lived here *c*.1652–60.

6. Musical fountain of Mount Parnassus in the Apollo Salon of Villa Aldobrandini, Frascati, Rome. It provided the setting for Stradella's *La Circe* of 1668.

5. Anonymous caricature of Sebastiano Baldini, poet of several Stradella cantata texts.

7. Letter from Alessandro Stradella to Cardinal Flavio Chigi dated 27 Nov. 1670 in which he urgently requests a loan of money: (*left*) beginning of the letter, (*right*) close, with Stradella's signature.

8. Church and
Convent of SS.
Domenico e Sisto.
Stradella's motet
*Pugna, certamen,
militia est vita* was
performed here in
1675 when Angelica
Lante became a nun.

9. Queen Christina
of Sweden. She
devised the scenario
for Stradella's *Il
Damone.*

0. An autograph page of Stradella's *Forza dell'amor paterno* of 1678.

1. Expenses for Stradella's burial dated 26 Feb. 1682.

12. Inventory of Stradella's belongings at the time of his death.

13. Francesco II d'Este, a patron of Stradella and early collector of his music.

are presented in the same opera. Stradella handled them only adequately, but perhaps it was because Antioco's rather routine madness, stated in predictable recitative–aria text, did not stimulate his imagination. (Less than two months later, he was to have a better opportunity of responding to a character's wild imaginings in his comic opera, *Il Trespolo tutore*.)

A curious practice not yet fully appreciated is also to be found in *La forza dell'amor paterno*. While it is known that successive performances of an opera in another theatre could offer different arias—sometimes new settings of text from the original libretto but also occasionally pieces with new text as well—it has usually been thought that such additions were either newly composed or taken from other operas. In *La forza*, however, one of the arias comes from a Stradella cantata. In Act II, scene 6 Antioco, who has just declared himself to be 'too miserable', cries out to the stars that he will die of his love. The aria he sings, 'Morirò, stelle perfide', is exactly the same, both text and music even to key, as appears in his soprano–continuo cantata, *A' pie' d'annoso pino*. While it suits the situation in the opera only in a general way, in the cantata the idea of death is introduced prior to the aria and commented upon afterwards. Therefore, the cantata was composed first, and later, when Stradella (or perhaps the Genoese Antioco) felt *La forza dell'amor paterno* required a good piece which would complain about love in attractive music, the aria was lifted from the cantata and inserted in the opera.

On the whole, *La forza dell'amor paterno* is a serious opera which emphasizes the serious. Of the ten characters, only two are comic and their scenes, although amusing, do not exhibit true *buffo* character. The various *cori* called for in the libretto—of soldiers, spear carriers, cavaliers, pages, and black slaves—never sing. Added to the visual interest of such groups are the several indoor and outdoor scenes presented during the course of the opera, ranging from the 'countryside at night, with the moon and a starlit sky' to a 'scene of the sea in the distance' to a 'salon in the palace' and so forth.

The 15 performances of *La forza* were greatly applauded according to Stradella,[11] and Della Corte, one of the first twentieth-century historians to examine the score, concurred that it was an interesting work of beauty and taste.[12]

As soon as *La forza dell'amor paterno* was over, *Le gare dell'amor eroico* opened (on 1 January 1679). The plot is again based on ancient history, and the libretto is again an anonymous revision of one by Nicolò Minato. In spite of the author's fame, Catelani, perhaps overly harsh in his

---

[11] His letter to Polo Michiel of 27 Jan. 1679 cited in n. 8 above (no. 15 in App. 2*a*).
[12] Della Corte, '*La forza d'amor paterno*', 391.

judgement, considered the poetry simply 'bad'.[13] Originally entitled *Mutio Scevola*, the libretto was first set by Cavalli in 1665 and after Stradella it would be composed by Bononcini, Handel, and Draghi.[14] Stradella's version follows Minato with some cuts (such as Act III, scene 5 and part of scene 6) and additions ('Sì, che l'ucciderò' for Muzio, I. 5). However, a change of emphasis was effected in Act III whereby Ismeno's savage treatment and implied raping of Elisa are greatly toned down and all succeeding references to it eliminated. In addition, in Stradella's score 6–8 lines of text are cancelled in 11 different moments of the opera.

Act I. The Roman warrior Orazio and the Roman Consul Pubblicola are fighting against the King of Etruria, Porsenna, on a bridge in Rome. The Roman warrior Muzio bemoans the loss of the Janiculum and the outer limits of the city to the enemy, as well as the capturing of his beloved Valeria, Pubblicola's daughter. Orazio's wife Elisa and daughter Vitellia have also been taken prisoners. Muzio determines to find and kill Porsenna or die in the attempt. Tarquinio, former King of Rome, anxious to rule again, urges Porsenna to attack but the Etruscan cautions against haste. The head of his army, Ismeno, brings Valeria, Vitellia, and Elisa before Porsenna who keeps Valeria and tries to win her over to him by allowing her maid Porfiria to remain with her; the other two are given to Ismeno. An Etruscan soldier, Floro, is willing to give his life to help Valeria but she refuses, enraging him. By now Orazio, Muzio, and Milo (Orazio's servant) have entered the enemy camp. Pretending to be on the enemy's side, Muzio declares his support to Tarquinio; Valeria decides he is a traitor. By mistake, Muzio kills Publio, a soldier, instead of Porsenna. He tries to escape and Porsenna is reluctant to take revenge against someone from his beloved's country.

Act II. Ismeno persists in his declarations of love to Elisa, Valeria tries to rid herself of her love for Muzio, and Porfiria offers herself to Floro. Muzio has been captured and Porsenna condemns him to death by burning; he is willing to exchange Muzio's life for Valeria's love but she refuses. After Muzio wilfully burns his right hand for having failed to kill Porsenna, and after he lets the King know that 300 men will follow him in the same attempt, Porsenna offers Rome, prisoners, and his condemned life to Muzio in exchange for Valeria. Muzio agrees, although hesitantly. Rebuffed by Floro, Porfiria offers her love to Milo who tells her she is too old and wrinkled! Ismeno threatens Elisa with the death of Vitellia; she still does not succumb and so he takes her child away. Valeria, aided by Floro and Porfiria, manages to escape, but when she arrives expecting protection from her father, he—convinced of the wiseness of Muzio's agreement with Porsenna—chides her for not considering the fate of her country. Muzio tells Valeria he loves her but must do his duty by bringing her back to Porsenna to marry him.

Act III. Tarquinio tries to dissuade Porsenna from peace, but he is told to leave.

[13] Catelani, 'Delle opere' (1865), 346.

[14] For a discussion of the changes made to the libretto each time, see Harold S. Powers, 'Il *Mutio* tramutato, i: Sources and Libretto', in Maria Teresa Muraro (ed.), *Venezia e il melodramma nel seicento* (Florence, 1976), 227–58.

Ismeno's cruel insistence with Elisa is rewarded with death: she gives him a sleeping-potion and kills him. Porfiria proves her love to Milo by giving him her portrait encircled with gold and jewels. When Porsenna realizes Valeria's deep love for Muzio and his for her, he renounces his right to the girl: virtue rules over love in a royal heart. As Orazio states, 'At the end of every torment there is happiness.'

According to the libretto, *Le gare* was performed with the following succession of scenes, each representing a location in Rome: the River Tiber with the Pons Sublicius; the Roman Forum; a camp on the Tiber where the Tuscans have weapons and tents; a wood; a garden in Trastevere; Porsenna's gallery of paintings and statues; an isolated place with a view of the walls of Rome, and of the Tiber; a city square; a palace courtyard in Trastevere; the soldiers' quarters in Trastevere; a royal salon in Rome. Several of these (the woods, garden, gallery, courtyard, salon, and perhaps also the scene with a view) could have been used in *La forza*; but they probably still delighted the audience, as well as helping them follow the intricate plot. Another bit of economy could have been the costumes for the various *cori*, the very same groups of 'extras' as had been called for in *La forza dell'amor paterno*.

The roles of *Le gare dell'amor eroico* were increased by one soprano and one bass over those of *La forza dell'amor paterno*, and therefore it is not known who in addition to Caterina Angela Botteghi, Marcantonio Orrigoni, Annuccia, and Granarino took the soprano roles of Valeria, Muzio, Elisa, Floro, Ismeno, and Vitellia; or who beyond Giacomo Filippo Cabella and Giovanni Battista Petriccioli did the bass roles of Milo, Pubblicola, and Tarquinio; one assumes, however, that Francesco Guerra took the tenor part of Porsenna, and Francesco Vallerini and Federico Generoli the contralto parts of Orazio and Porfiria. The instrumental ensemble accompanying the opera was once again composed of two violin parts and basso continuo.

In the 59 arias, three duets,[15] and one trio of *Le gare dell'amor eroico*, all of the common seicento forms are fairly equally represented. The ABA arias are mostly short with simply a return of the opening phrase at the end. Only six of them exhibit a clear change of key when a second idea is presented; modulation to the dominant, subdominant, or relative minor is indiscriminate. Indubitably, they are a far cry from the fully developed late seventeenth- and eighteenth-century da capo arias, but they are also only a shadow of what Stradella wrote in other works.

Neither did he give the ABB' form particular treatment; rather, he deals with it as was usual earlier in the century. Occasionally such arias are in only one key, thus blurring any true sectional separation, but modulation

---

[15] The Gianturco–McCrickard *Stradella Catalogue* incorrectly lists the duet 'Non si move | Non sussurra' (II. 18) as an aria.

at B is also to be found. Generally, however, modulation takes place during the second section with no particular preference for key; two or three keys are visited in each aria. 'S'il veder piacer arreca' (II. 2) for Porfiria illustrates his usual handling of the form. Once again these arias are neither extended nor well developed.

Together with this surprising series of rather short and formally simple arias, is the equally uncommon insistence on an older style of part-writing. For example, even though they are not many, considerable attention is given to the four ensembles. They are generally quite expressive because of the dissonance treatment, but in a polyphonic language which is closer to the *stile antico* than to the newer, more instrumental seventeenth-century one. Other sections, too, bear witness to an earlier style, such as Elisa's arias 'Dure glebe, io pur vi frango' (II. 3) and 'Dolce gioia del mio core' (II. 5), where violins and voice skilfully interweave each other's lines.

Another indication of Stradella's technical training is his particular use of the basso ostinato in *Le gare dell'amor eroico*. The aria 'E qual delitto, o ciel' for Elisa (II. 5) is an example which one might consider 'classical' since it employs exact repetitions of the traditional four-note descending ostinato figure. Stradella merely filled it in chromatically and rounded it off cadentially. No attempt is made to disguise the ostinato, for the repetitions are presented separated one from another by rests enabling each statement to stand out. In addition, the ritornello appearing after the aria takes up the idea in imitation. It is one of Stradella's most orthodox uses of an ostinato, quite different from his more frequent free use of it.[16]

On the whole, *Le gare dell'amor eroico* gives the impression of being an early work. The simple arias, not only short but generally undeveloped, the use of rather tightly organized counterpoint in the ensembles and for the two violins and continuo which accompany the opera, and the employment of the strings mainly between vocal phrases all give the impression of an opera written before *La forza dell'amor paterno*.

There are, of course, noteworthy moments in *Le gare* which reveal its composer to be aware of drama. For example, the writing is especially fine in those sections depicting war or aggressive sentiments, such as the opening of the Act I three-movement sinfonia meant to portray the battle between the Romans and the Etruscans; or Pubblicola's cries of 'Si rompa, si franga' (I. 1) as the bridge falls during the opening battle; or Porsenna's aria 'Miei pensieri all'armi' (I. 19) sung when he is uncertain he can punish his enemies if they are friends of his beloved. There is also the line of recitative which introduces Elisa's determination to kill Ismeno (expressed in her aria 'Alla vendetta, all'armi', III. 11): in Stradella's hands, 'Misera, che farò?' becomes an expressive, adagio-accompanied recitative (suitably

---

[16] Floro's only aria, 'Fortezza, mio core' (II. 15), is certainly a 'grand' example of the ostinato, although not typical of Stradella's handling of the technique in *Le gare*.

based on descending tetrachords reiterated imitatively by each of the instruments and voice) which leads beautifully into the fiery aria.

However, these are only a few scattered moments in the otherwise unexceptional opera. That his music was effective is clear from Stradella's affirmation that at times it was difficult to continue the opera due to the tremendous applause.[17] Moreover, one of the very simplest of the arias, Elisa's 'Se nel ben sempre incostante' (I. 14), was frequently copied and published after Stradella's death,[18] a proof of its charm.

At the end of January 1679, either the 30th or the 31st, Stradella's comic opera *Il Trespolo tutore* opened at the Teatro Falcone in Genoa. The composer said it was simply an 'amusement', but yet 'bellissima'; besides, as he wrote to Michiel, the Genoese liked 'comic things'.[19] The libretto was a reworking by Giovanni Cosimo Villifranchi of a play by Giovanni Battista Ricciardi.[20] According to his friend Angelo Fabroni, Ricciardi published *Il Trespolo tutore* in 1669;[21] in 1679 Villifranchi published his adaptation for music, calling it *Amore è veleno e medicina degl'intelletti o vero Trespolo tutore*. In his dedication to Ricciardi, Villifranchi explained that he had published the libretto not in connection with a specific performance but merely to prove his and Ricciardi's authorship, since the work had already been set to music and given in Rome, Genoa, and Naples. He complained that in the first and last cities characters, scenes, and arias by another author had been added; only in Genoa was the work given as he and Ricciardi had written it. Although Villifranchi named no poets or composers, the brief history of *Trespolo* may now be set forth and Stradella's role in it clarified.

[17] Stradella's letter to Polo Michiel of 27 Jan. 1679 cited in n. 8 above (no. 15 in App. 2*a*).

[18] For all copies and editions, see Gianturco–McCrickard, *Stradella Catalogue*. It is always possible that Stradella had composed *Le gare dell'amor eroico* before arriving in Genoa. Unfortunately, the fact that there is similarity of material in the last movement of the Act I sinfonia and the sinfonia to his 1681 oratorio *La Susanna* (also found as the fourth movement of his C major trio-sonata, 7.3–1) is not an aid in dating the opera.

[19] Stradella's letter to Polo Michiel of 27 Jan. 1679 cited in n. 8 above (no. 15 in App. 2*a*).

[20] Born in Volterra in 1645, Villifranchi began his studies in Siena. He continued to pursue philosophy in Pisa and in fact published a philosophical work when only 16. He returned to Volterra as a medical doctor, but was called to Florence as *medico fiscale* to Grand Duke Ferdinando. Here he wrote prose comedies, operas, and prologues and finales for both musical and prose works, especially for the *Percossi*. Among those of the society were the good friends Giovanni Battista Ricciardi and Salvator Rosa. Ricciardi was the natural son of a Florentine couple and, although born in Pisa, lived most of his life in Florence. He was esteemed not only as a writer of poetry and prose comedies but also as a brilliant conversationalist. In 1673 he became professor of moral philosophy at the University of Pisa. (On Villifranchi see Raffaello Maffei, *Tre volteranni Enrico Ormanni, Giovan. Cosimo Villifranchi, Mario Guarnacci* (Pisa, 1881); and on Ricciardi see Negri, *Scrittori fiorentini*, and Aldo de Rinaldis, *Lettere inedite di Salvator Rosa a G. B. Ricciardi* (Rome, 1939), xl–xliii.)

[21] Although Ricciardi's libretto, published in Bologna, is undated, Angelo Fabroni, *Historiae Academiae Pisanae* (Pisa, 1791–5), iii. 131 gives 1669 as the date of publication. A copy of the libretto is at I-MOe.

The altered libretto was most likely the work of Lorenzo Beatucci, a Florentine contralto who took comic roles of old women, and it was set to music by Bernardo Pasquini. The opera was given first in Rome on 14 February 1677, in Contestabile Colonna's theatre. The Pope was very disturbed by the performance because he had heard that the boxes had been constructed in such a way that one could go from one to the other, thus encouraging licentious behaviour among the ladies and gentlemen; in fact he sent two priests to Beatucci to make a formal protest since he had requested specifically that the boxes be separated.[22] The same poet and composer were also involved in the other performance of *Trespolo* which disturbed Villifranchi. In 1678 the impresario Orazio Salvatore invited the Florentine composer Giovanni Bonaventura Viviani to Naples. Viviani brought with him a company of singers, among whom were Lorenzo Beatucci and the Roman singer Stefano Carli, and they gave two operas at the Teatro di S. Bartolomeo. The next year Salvatore sublet the theatre to Giovanni Liguori who kept the same company to do *Il Trespolo tutore*; on 26 April 1679 Beatucci hired the Livornese *musico* Stefano Bussi as an extra singer for the comedy which was given that Spring.[23] This would have been the second comic opera performed in Naples, the first being *Il Girello* at the same theatre in 1673.

Stradella had left Rome for Venice just before *Trespolo* was performed and therefore would not have known Beatucci's and Pasquini's work.[24] In any event, it was the original Ricciardi–Villifranchi libretto which he set to music. The few changes to it concern the cutting of occasional lines, and the addition of the aria 'La speranza d'un dolce contento' (III. 11), and the recitative beginning 'Dicendo con mia madre' together with the following aria 'Se tuo fato invariabile' (III. 5), all for the role of Despina.

The main character of the opera and cause of continual comedy is Trespolo (bass), the foolish *tutore* or guardian. The rest of the cast includes his ward Artemisia (soprano) who is in love with him, Nino (contralto) who loves her, Ciro (soprano) his initially crazy brother who also loves Artemisia, Simona (tenor) their old, foolish nurse, and Despina (soprano) her shrewd daughter. The company of singers Stradella had at the Teatro Falcone could easily have covered the roles, but who did what part is not known. The instrumental ensemble accompanying the voices, two violin parts and basso continuo, is the same as in all Stradella's operas.

---

[22] I-Fas, Mediceo del Principato, fo. 3658, *avvisi* dated 13, 16, and 20 Feb. 1677. At the time of my article 'Il Trespolo tutore di Stradella e di Pasquini: Due diverse concezioni dell'opera comica', in Maria Teresa Muraro (ed.), *Venezia e il melodramma nel settecento* (Florence, 1978), 185–98, I mistakenly read Beatucci as Bertucci.

[23] See Ulisse Prota-Giurleo, 'Notizie inedite intorno a Gio. Bonaventura Viviani', *Archivi d'Italia e Rassegna*, 2nd ser., 25 (1958), 225–38.

[24] For a comparison of both composers' settings, see my article 'Il Trespolo tutore'.

Act I. Simona encourages the reluctant Despina to marry Trespolo. Nino then asks the girl to pretend to love Trespolo so that he can woo Artemisia. The mad Ciro passes Artemisia and seeing she is sleeping, suggestively decides to lie down next to her, but Trespolo sends him away. Artemisia then tells Trespolo that she has chosen a husband and after adding, 'Other than he there is none, and he is here present', runs into the house. Confused, Trespolo spies Ciro and decides it is he. But when the tutor knocks at Artemisia's door with her 'husband' Ciro, she is revolted. Ciro, however, is delighted at the idea of marrying her. Still too embarrassed to name her beloved, Artemisia dictates a letter for him to Trespolo in which she repeatedly says, 'It is you!' Unfortunately, Trespolo still does not understand, and when Nino arrives he now believes him to be her beloved and hands him Artemisia's letter.

Act II. Simona is giving Ciro a lesson in proper behaviour. Despina taunts Trespolo as he declares his love for her. She gives him Nino's letter of reply which he misreads and concludes Nino to be vulgar. Even so, Trespolo tells Nino that if he gives him Artemisia, he should be given Despina in return. Artemisia overhears the conversation and realizes her guardian has not understood her. Nino is rejected by Artemisia and cries out against cruel Fate. Artemisia tells Trespolo that before he can marry, he has to give her a husband. She tells him that the one she loves is his age, has three syllables in his name, is as tall as he is, and has a great deal to do with him. When she gives him a mirror saying it is a portrait of her beloved, Trespolo does not recognize the face. Instead he sees Simona and decides now that she is the object of Artemisia's affections.

Act III. Trespolo convinces Simona to consider a union with Artemisia. When the girl thinks Simona understands she loves Trespolo, she gives the servant a ring for him. But Simona decides she will have Artemisia for herself. Ciro, now sane, declares madness can be cured by love; Nino, now mad, rants on about his lost love. Simona gives Artemisia's ring to Trespolo as Despina's dowry. When she asks about the ward's inheritance, Trespolo tries to understand the girl's father's testament but misinterprets everything because he does not know Latin. Ciro tries to correct him. Trespolo next makes a secret appointment with Despina. When Ciro furtively enters the house that night in order to defend Despina's honour, he is discovered by Artemisia and Trespolo, both armed with swords against the intruder. Unwittingly, Artemisia's sword puts out Trespolo's candle and when he leaves to relight it, Artemisia continues to speak of her love for her guardian but Ciro thinks she means him. They leave to get married. Simona sings that although one's teeth are missing, the appetite grows. In the end, Artemisia is married to Ciro and Despina will wed Trespolo. Nino is now completely mad. Ciro sings that Love can make every heart and every mind either crazy or sane (hence Villifranchi's title), that this blind baby gives and takes liberty; he ends exclaiming that love is a 'great unhappiness!'

By the time Stradella wrote *Il Trespolo tutore* comic operas—both Tuscan and Roman—were young but not new. How many he had heard is impossible to know. At the same time, it was his prologue of 1668 (*O di Cocito oscure deità*) which travelled with *Il Girello*; in addition, he had composed other comic prologues and intermezzos for the Teatro

Tordinona in 1671–2. Therefore, he had had experience with comedy long before setting *Trespolo*. In Ricciardi's play the characters are ordinary people made to speak an everyday language. The comedy is sometimes light but more often borders on slapstick, and it makes use of erotic innuendoes and vulgarity. As regards the title-role, Ricciardi often had a character named Trespolo in his comedies. Actually this is not a true name but rather a word which means 'a tripod'; however, it is commonly used to mean something rickety and falling apart, and actually not able to support anything: in short, an apt definition of the protagonist.

The 59 arias and 3 duets of the opera come in every form, metre, and length, with or without a ritornello, and accompanied or unaccompanied by the instrumental ensemble. The sort of arias given to Trespolo, one of the first *buffo* basses in operatic history, are typical of Stradella's comic style here. 'O Despina, tanto bella' (Act I, sc. 8) is written almost completely in non-stop eighth-notes (Ex. 15) and 'Che musica bella' (III. 12) is a triple-metre aria with a rather square and folk-like melody. As well as through its simplicity, Trespolo's personality and silliness is apparent there in the phrases 'qui suona il mio core' ('here sounds my heart', which must have been sung in falsetto) and the contrasting 'e qui le budella' ('and here the guts') (Ex. 16).

Ex. 15.

Ex. 16.

Stradella's ability to sustain and shape comedy is apparent also in the recitative of *Il Trespolo tutore*. Eighth- and sixteenth-notes predominate—many on repeated tones—with an occasional quarter-note on syllables of more stress, a 'patter' style which encourages rapidity of execution. One of the especially long amusing scenes of recitative is for Artemisia when she dictates a letter intended for her beloved to Trespolo (I. 11). Not only is the text funny, especially since Artemisia tries desperately to let her guardian know that she loves *him*, but Stradella succeeds in having Trespolo's irritation come through as he insists he has already written 'It is you!', 'Siete voi!'—missing the point completely—as well as Artemisia's frustration. Rests punctuate ideas and show impatience, imitation illustrates the repetition of Artemisia's sentences by Trespolo, and the breaking off of the imitation points up their discord. Equally effective is the long scene (II. 8) when Trespolo attempts to decipher Artemisia's father's will.

As relief to the comedy, there are occasionally scenes of a more serious tone. Such is scene 4 in Act I for Artemisia which also provides examples of two well-developed arias. The first, 'Quando mai fra tanti duoli', is a lyrical, triple-metre AB aria where the sections are separated by the restatement of the opening instrumental ritornello. Dissonances are used in the first section to express Artemisia's sadness at not being able to communicate her love to Trespolo; in the second section a bit of word-painting intensifies 'amoroso', and imitation between the voice and continuo helps to extend a sequential idea. The aria is lovely, slow, and quiet; it is accompanied by continuo alone. Immediately following, in sharp contrast and in response to new ideas expressed in her lines, is Artemisia's aria 'Cieli, dunque, che farò?' in which she asks the Heavens what she should do. The violins are present as a concerted force playing between short vocal phrases, the metre is duple, and the music spirited. The use of the Neapolitan sixth on the word 'morte' and the following chromatic bass are all part of *opera seria* equipment.

Two scenes in *Il Trespolo tutore* are part of another tradition, that of operatic 'mad scenes'. As Villifranchi stated in the preface of his libretto, they were not in Ricciardi's play but had been added by him. While Stradella had already tried his hand at such scenes in *La forza dell'amor paterno*, Villifranchi's text gave him opportunity for greater dramatic and compositional scope. In Act III, scene 5 Nino is alone. He is sad over being rejected by Artemisia and, distracted, keeps talking about the many suns he sees, saying that his sun (Artemisia) is not there. He believes he sees Astolfo (the character in *Orlando furioso* who goes to the moon on a winged griffin looking for Orlando's brain) and asks him what he is doing. He wants Astolfo to find his mind, too, which his beloved made him lose. Nino also talks of flames and hears an owl. He doesn't know whether to laugh or cry, and tells all he sees to flee as he will soon more likely cry. Scene 15 of the same act presents Nino again alone, and even madder. He begins by calling out 'Tarapatà, tarapatà, tarapatà', urging invisible armed horsemen to war, to take away cruel Artemisia's heart. Battle makes him tired, and he believes Artemisia is with him sweetly telling him to sleep, and that she will sleep with him. But Nino is unable to rest, he is disturbed by the Furies and monsters; he then sees several characters from Hell. In the end he believes Artemisia will love him in spite of herself.

As Nino's imagination presents him with one vision after another, and he reacts to all of them, Stradella continually changes the music. In scene 5 accompaniment is by basso continuo with the violins playing just ritornellos between sections, but in scene 15 they accompany the voice directly. However, in both cases the vocal line alternates between simple recitative and arioso including an occasional fioritura, the metre between binary and ternary, the tempo from adagio to spiritoso—all in response to the text and Nino's imagined world.

The success enjoyed by Stradella's *Il Trespolo tutore* prompted the Genoese nobleman Goffredo Marino to write to Francesco d'Este about the comedy on 23 February 1681.[25] He noted the different and unusual style of Ricciardi's text and Stradella's music. Marino clearly hoped that the opera would be given in Modena, and even offered to bring Stradella there himself. By 8 March Francesco II had the score of *Trespolo*,[26] but no performance of it was arranged. That the music interested him is certain, though, since Stradella was invited instead to compose an oratorio, a genre closer to the duke's pious nature.

In the following year of 1682, a version of *Trespolo* closer to Pasquini's than to Stradella's was given in Bologna under the title *Il Trespolo balordo*. Only in 1686 was Modena to hear Stradella's opera at the Teatro Fontanelli. While he is not mentioned as the composer of *Il Trespolo tutore balordo*, the Modenese libretto is very similar to that used in Genoa, the only real difference being the elimination of some lines. In general these regard recitative; however, many lines from Nino's two mad scenes were also cut, perhaps revealing a change of taste regarding the genre; moreover, Artemisia's short aria 'Ah, se visibile fosse dall'Erebo' (III. 17) was removed. The most conclusive proof that it was Stradella's music which was used in Modena is the inclusion there of Despina's aria 'La speranza d'un dolce contento', cited earlier as not being in the Ricciardi–Villifranchi text but only in his score.

After *Il Trespolo tutore*, Stradella's operatic career in Genoa declined. Within the year the Adorno family sold the Teatro Falcone to Eugenio Durazzo, and perhaps because he had been favoured by the previous administration, Stradella was no longer engaged by the theatre. Only a year and a half later did he have occasion to write another opera, this time not for Genoa but for Rome. An old patron, Flavio Orsini, Duke of

[25] I-MOas, Archivio segreto estense, Carteggio e documenti di particolari, busta 654; for a translation of the letter see Ch. 4, n. 39.

[26] Ibid.

Bracciano, sent him a libretto he had written entitled *Moro per amore;* Stradella finished the music by 24 May 1681.[27]

From what Orsini says in his libretto, published under the anagram of Filosinavoro after Stradella's death, it is clear that *Moro per amore* was never performed in a public theatre.[28] Orsini refers to Stradella as 'that noteworthy great genius', but feels that in the several years since the opera was composed taste had changed from its 'good former style' and the music might now be found tedious. Actually, it offers some of Stradella's best operatic writing.

Act I. After the death of Ormondo, King of Sicily, his daughter, Eurinda, is crowned queen. Durante, King of Cyprus, is preparing to invade Sicily, but his son, Floridoro, having heard of Eurinda's beauty, decides to disguise himself as the Moor Feraspe and, together with his servant Fiorino, penetrates the court at Messina as a slave. Rodrigo, Eurinda's guardian and head of the army, insists that she marry, whereas Eurinda is determined not to. Lindora, the queen's servant, is attracted to the Moor and Eurinda assumes him as her personal slave so the two servants can be together.

Act II. Fiorino acts as the servant of Filandro, Ambassador of Naples, who brings a proposal of marriage for Eurinda from his king, an alliance which would gain her a valuable ally in Sicily's conflict against Cyprus. Eurinda has fallen in love with Feraspe but his low station precludes marriage; he too loves her but is silent. Other cross-purpose situations are created by the love of both Lucinda, a Sicilian princess, and Lindora, Eurinda's servant, for the Moor. Furthermore, Filandro declares his love to Lucinda and Fiorino flirts with Lindora.

Act III. Eurinda continues to resist pressure from Rodrigo and Filandro to marry the King of Naples. She hedges, saying that while her men die in battle against Cyprus, she cannot think of a union. She learns that the Moor, on his way to deliver a letter from her to Rodrigo at the army camp, was taken prisoner by the Cypriots. She rants against the Furies who torment her. Luckily Feraspe/Floridoro is recognized by his men, and returns to explain who he is and that he loves Eurinda. Their marriage brings peace between the warring countries. The practical Lucinda forces her heart to turn to Filandro, and Fiorino and Lindora happily sing of Love's victory.

Orsini's libretto—its title a play on words meaning either 'A Moor for love' or 'I die of love'[29]—was not an altogether new concept. Giovanni Faustini proposed the same disguise-for-love situation earlier in *La virtù*

[27] See Stradella's letter to Orsini of 24 May 1681 in I-Rasc, Archivio Orsini, I. 279, no. 487 (no. 23 in App. 2*a*).

[28] A copy of the libretto is in I-Lbs, a facsimile of which is in *Italian Opera Librettos: 1640–1770*, vol. vi no. 7, ed. Howard M. Brown (New York and London, 1979). A manuscript copy of Orsini's preface is in I-Fas, Miscellanea Medicea, 506, 'Carte di lettere, che sono nella Segretaria del Serenissima Prencipe Duca di Bracciano'.

[29] Enrico de Angelis, 'L'idea di potere nell'opera lirica del seicento', in Carolyn Gianturco and Giancarlo Rostirolla (eds.), *Atti del Convegno di studi 'Alessandro Stradella e il suo tempo'*, Siena, 8–12 *settembre 1982*, Chigiana, 39, NS 19 (1988), 109–24, sees, in its conflict between love and power, similarities between *Moro per amore* and G. A. Cicognini's libretto of *Orontea*.

de' strali d'Amore of 1642 and again, with a Moor, in *L'Alciade* performed
in 1667. The duke's libretto also shows similarity with the very popular *Il
Girello*, wherein the character Mustafà is an *innamorato*, is a king's son,
and is disguised as a Moorish slave. Moreover, a throw-back to earlier
pastoral operas is evident when Eurinda discusses her frustrating position
uselessly with an echo (Act III, sc. 4). As for the score, *Moro per amore* is
the only one of Stradella's operas which exists in several copies, four to be
exact,[30] rather unusual for a work never performed publicly. One manuscript is largely autograph; two others are excellent, professional copies,
one of which is covered in lovely flowered satin damask, and they could
have been made for Orsini; the fourth copy, inaccurate and incomplete, is
in Modena and was probably made quickly for Francesco II.

   Not only is *Moro per amore* chronologically Stradella's latest extant
opera, but stylistically it is his most consistent. Nothing appears awkward
or forced, all proceeds easily and regularly. This impression of maturity
and unity is achieved first and foremost through its assured handling of
tonality. To begin with, there is no preference for one mode or the other,
the arias being almost equally divided between major and minor keys. The
beginning of an aria typically establishes the chosen key immediately, often
through an arpeggiated motif (Ex. 17): the tonic chord is thus exposed and
a characteristic motif established. Within the course of arias basic chordal
progressions are used to strengthen the opening orientation. As for modulations, Stradella almost without exception exhibits what are now common
tonal procedures: in major keys he goes first to the dominant and then to
the subdominant or relative minor keys; in pieces in the minor, he modulates first to the relative major, then to the dominant or subdominant.

Ex. 17.

Recitatives and arias may be connected by being in the same key, or
they may be bridged with a dominant–tonic relationship in the key of the
aria (the concluding key of the recitative becoming the dominant of the
key of the following aria), or a subdominant–tonic relationship (the tonic
of the aria seeming to be the dominant in the key of the recitative but

----

[30] See my 'Sources for *Moro per amore*'.

then modulating). The scheme is used so consistently in *Moro per amore* that any other occasional relationship causes surprise.

Within the recitatives themselves a tonal plan is likewise imposed. Two recitatives in Act I may be cited to illustrate this. In scene 6 between the aria 'Sì, del Moro la figura non mi spiace' for Lindora and the duet 'Vogliamoci bene' for Lindora and Feraspe/Floridoro, the recitative proceeds from E major to A major, D major, G major, and to C major, ready for the duet in that key. Under the control of the cycle of fifths the recitative moves easily and with direction. The recitative which opens scene 7 of the same act also follows the cycle of fifths but with a single interruption, since the aim here is not to modulate but simply to create movement during the recitative and yet return to the key of departure: A major, D major, G major, (skip to) B major, E major, arriving at the following aria 'Mai gioir, ah non potea' for Lindora in A major. No such easy handling of the harmonic cycle would have been possible without a sure sense of tonality and an understanding of its usefulness.

Other consistent features of the opera may also be noted. For example, a favourite way of beginning an aria is that in which a single phrase is repeated several times through imitation between instruments and voice. One sees this in 'Dolce Amor, nume bendato' for Filandro (Act III, sc. 2) where a phrase is stated first in the basso continuo, then in the voice, the continuo repeats it again, and finally the voice presents it going on to other material. This method of construction characterized by a sort of false or hesitant beginning by the voice (Riemann's *Devisenarie*) was to become 'an almost unconscious mannerism of style' by the end of the century;[31] in *Moro per amore* it was a unifying feature.

As for the preferred type of texture in the opera, it is a contrapuntal one. Instruments and/or voices generally proceed imitatively creating a full, concerted texture. Occasionally this serves to heighten the meaning of the text. For the aria 'Fugga il pianto' for Lucinda (III. 5), the violins and continuo are in very close imitation with one another and with the voice throughout the piece, and as a result they and the voice musically depict the verb *fugga*. Of course the motif offered by Stradella here, with a scalar figure of sixteenth-notes on the strong beats, gives impetus to each point of imitation and thus encourages the sense of fleeing. In the aria 'Afflitta, trafitta quest'alma' (III. 1) the instrumental ensemble again interprets the text but in a more subtle way. Eurinda sings here of the affliction in her breast, for which she sighs and is delirious ('sospira, delira'). Through a halting ostinato, a line interrupted by rests, her lack of tranquillity and her uncertainty are poignantly depicted. The basso continuo line of her aria 'Col mio sangue' (III. 6) represents Eurinda's sobs: the rests interrupt

---

[31] Donald J. Grout, *A Short History of Opera* (2nd edn.; New York, 1965), 105.

the line as her tears interrupt her speech. The affective vocal motive associated with the main textual idea of her aria 'Seppellitevi nel core, ciechi
affetti' (II. 6) is taken up by the instrumental ensemble and is its only
musical material. Through imitation which continues in all sections of the
aria, the phrase becomes the instrumental 'theme' of the piece: the hope
of the protagonist that her feelings hide themselves is with her from
beginning to end, and it is non-verbally communicated by the instrumental statements of this desire-motif. In all these examples the instrumental
ensemble is more than an accompaniment and more than a concerted
force in the music. Rather, it is a participant in, and interpreter of the
drama.

In this same vein, there are two instances in *Moro per amore* where
Stradella broadens his musical organization to serve a dramatic purpose.
'Stelle ingrate' (II. 3) and 'Afflitta, trafitta' (III. 1) both end with Eurinda
worriedly questioning her fate with the words 'Che, che sarà?' In the first
instance they are used as part of the A-section of the ternary aria which,
therefore, returns at the restatement; in the second case the phrase is a
recurring refrain. Significantly, Stradella set the text to exactly the same
music in both arias, implying that for him this textual–musical phrase
typifies Eurinda's concern for the future.

In two other arias he uses a musical phrase to convey the same meaning
but in one case drops the text. For Eurinda's insistent aria 'Dimmi Amor,
che fia di me?' (II. 3) the basso continuo presents, in the minor mode, a
vigorous figure as an ostinato on various pitch-levels. It is heard throughout the aria and is developed imitatively in the succeeding ritornello. After
the duet for Filandro and Lucinda 'Quando un core in amore' (III. 5) the
same figure, but now in the major, is the main idea of the ritornello. It
has no motivic connection with the duet and seems curiously out of place
unless one associates it with the earlier aria to Amor. The change in mode
may be merely because the duet is in the major and a smoother connection is achieved by altering the figure to conform with it; or, more sophis-
ticatedly, it may be that the concern expressed in the aria has been
resolved by the hope of the duet and, therefore, a shift in mode was
appropriate. At any rate one does recognize that the same material is used
in both references to Amor, once with an enunciated text, another time
without it.

Form is another interesting feature of *Moro per amore*. Due to
Stradella's mirroring of poetic form, through-composed and bipartite
pieces are rare whereas strophic arias (of two strophes) abound. Orsini,
however, made great use of refrains, either as part of a single-strophe aria
(for example in 'Nume Amor, fammi gioir', 'Stelle ingrate, e che sarà?'
and 'Dimmi, Amor, che fia di me?' in Act II, scene 3) or as part of each
strophe of a two-strophe aria (as in 'Muta stil se vuoi gioire' and 'A con-

siglio, amorosi pensieri' in Act II, scenes 4 and 7 respectively). These, then, result in tripartite (ABA) musical pieces, some of them developed sufficiently by Stradella to merit being considered true da capo structures.

More noteworthy, however, are those cases where Stradella decided not to adhere to Orsini's outline, such as in 'Bellezza che in sdegni', 'Quante forme strane e varie', and 'Mio core respira' (in Act II, scenes 3, 6, and 9 respectively) where he set two similarly structured strophes of poetry (AA) to different music (AB); and in 'Non ho forza che resista' (Act I, scene 3) where he, not the poet, decided to repeat text and thus create a tripartite structure. Stradella also sometimes elaborated and/or sectionalized musical strophes, thereby making patterns not offered in the poetry (for example, strophes of abb' in 'Oh, che caso stravagante', abc in 'Tu dovresti contentarti', as well as aba in 'Dammi spirto da resistere' (Act III, scenes 7, 5, and 1 respectively). All of his changes attest to the composer's desire to offer greater structural variety than the poet had planned, as well as to his aesthetic and dramatic need to have forms which were more defined than the poet provided in order to be able to write extended and better-developed musical sections.

The splendid but difficult music of *Moro per amore* was conceived for a cast of two female sopranos (Eurinda, Lucinda) and a castrato soprano (Fiorino), a female contralto (Lindora) and a castrato contralto (Feraspe/Floridoro), and a bass (Rodrigo), to be accompanied by Stradella's usual orchestra of two violin parts and basso continuo.

When Stradella wrote to Flavio Orsini about the opera in late spring 1681, he also mentioned an untitled 'operetta' of the 'cloak-and-dagger' type, meaning by this a tale of adventure about *cavalieri*. Six singers are being recruited, and it is to be an excellent cast including Margherita di Bologna (surname Salicola) and her sister Angiola; either the castrato Cortoncino (Domenico Cecchi), employed by the Empress of Vienna, or Gioseppino di Baviera (Giuseppe Maria Donati); the *buffo* Giovanni Battista Petriccioli of Rome; from Milan a 'vecchia', that is a tenor specializing in old women's roles, and one who was 'considered rather good'; and last the tenor Canavese. They had wanted Pietro Santi of Vienna, but the Emperor would not release any of his musicians.

In all, the new opera was to be for two women, a castrato, a 'normal' tenor and a comic tenor, and a comic bass. The only known possibility could be the opera Mario Tiberti found in Rieti in the 1930s entitled *Doriclea*.[32] Although Flavio Orsini is said to have written a libretto with the same title, it could not be his text which Stradella referred to, otherwise there would have been no need to describe it to the duke. According

---

[32] Tiberti, '*Doriclea*'.

to what Tiberti has written, the unavailable or lost *Doriclea* (upon enquiry, Tiberti was not clear about its present whereabouts) has the sort of plot which could have been described as 'cloak-and-dagger'.

Doriclea (soprano) is supposed to marry Olindo (who never appears on stage), but she actually loves Fidalbo (castrato contralto) and runs off with him. At some point his jealousy is needlessly aroused, but he is prevented from giving vent to it against Doriclea by the arrival of Lucinda (soprano) and Celindo (tenor), who explain the misunderstanding to Fidalbo and all ends well. Comic diversion is provided by the servant Delfina (contralto), desperately in love with Giraldo (bass), a courtier.

Even the voices, with the exception of the contralto Delfina instead of the comic tenor (a change which could have been necessitated by the unavailability of the desired singer), fit Stradella's description. Moreover, the opera is accompanied by an instrumental ensemble of two violins and continuo, the usual instrumentation in Stradella's operas. Unfortunately, until the opera is able to be seen by someone other than Tiberti its authenticity cannot be determined nor its music evaluated.

The only other extant Stradella opera is *Corispero*, unfortunately incomplete in its single source.[33]

Act I. Armondo, King of Rhodes, is in his army camp. Just before he dies by the hand of an assassin, he gives his unwilling daughter Almestilla in marriage to Prince Crudarte who killed the assassin, indicating him as his successor. Princess Clorimira, next in line to the throne after Almestilla and not averse to the latter's death, is wooed by Tradonte; but she loves the astrologer Corispero, who in turn loves Almestilla. Unaware of this, Crudarte urges Corispero to try to effect Almestilla's change of heart; if he is successful, Crudarte, as king, will always obey him. Cosmiro (Almestilla's servant), Nubesta (Clorimira's servant), Lustrino (another servant), and Golone (court jester) offer comic diversion to the complications of the lords and ladies.

Act II. Cosmiro gives Almestilla two jewels taken from the assassin's pocket. Since they had been given to Crudarte as a gift by her father, they implicate him in the king's murder. She relates the discovery to Corispero and asks him to find her a more suitable husband. She orders troops to be ready and at her disposal. Clorimira begins to entertain thoughts of having Crudarte as her lover; he—tired of rejection by Almestilla—considers returning her love. Tradonte tells Crudarte that Corispero is his rival for Almestilla's heart and that he accuses him of having killed the king. Crudarte now accuses Corispero of being a traitor and imprisons him, but he is released by Almestilla. Crudarte threatens to have Corispero killed if Almestilla continues to refuse him. However, the people and soldiers rush on stage crying, 'Death to Crudarte, long life to Corispero.' Several scenes of comedy are provided by the various servants.

---

[33] As Fabbri rightly pointed out in 'Questioni drammaturgiche', 98–9.

For one female (Almestilla) and one castrato soprano (Corispero), one female (Clorimira) and one castrato contralto (Tradonte), one tenor (Crudarte), and one bass (Armondo) in the *serio* cast, and a female contralto (Nubesta), one tenor (Golone), and two basses (Lustrino and Cosmiro) in the comic cast, *Corispero* includes two four-part choruses of soldiers and people; it is accompanied by an instrumental ensemble of two violin parts and basso continuo. It could be that this is the opera by Saliti Stradella was to have set in or before 1677, but whether it is or not, it is unfortunate Stradella never finished it because it offers fine music. Three aspects of the score may be singled out to demonstrate the composer's sense of organization and consistency at the time of composition: his use of the basso ostinato, the concerto style, and the arioso.

Even though the ostinato principle is employed frequently in *Corispero*, a motif or phrase is never repeated in the same way on the same pitch throughout an aria. 'Per mio regno' for Almestilla (Act II, sc. 3) comes close to this, however: the one-measure figure is used 21 times in the course of the piece, and all but seven begin on the same pitch. A five-note scalar motif is repeated almost without interruption in Crudarte's 'Debil piazza cui richiede' (II. 12), but on various pitch-levels which outline harmonic progressions; occasionally only three of the five notes are sounded, and three times the motif is given in a descending rather than an ascending direction. Appearing in all sections of the AABA aria for Almestilla, 'Specchiatevi nel pianto' (I. 11), is a phrase which generally appears together with its 'answer', the same figure on the dominant. Variety is achieved either by changing the pitch-levels or by stating the ostinato on the same level two or three times in succession. In all, the phrase appears 31 times in the course of the aria. All of these examples represent rather traditional handling of the ostinato; but Stradella also makes use of a freer treatment of the technique.

In several arias one motivic figure—sometimes alone, sometimes with other material—may be said to permeate and to generate the entire piece. A case in point is 'Fida pure alla speranza' (II. 5) for Crudarte which uses a short scalar idea of five notes in ternary rhythm. It appears repeatedly not only in the basso continuo but also in the two violins and, though less frequently, in the voice. (In one place the voice takes off with a rare fioritura of 19 notes which ends with the motif.) It is employed in exact imitation, in contrary motion and its imitation, and in simultaneous thirds in the violins. Crudarte's 'Soffrirà, spererà quest'alma' (I. 13) is intensely unified by the repeated use of a rhythmic–melodic figure (Ex. 18) on various scale degrees. It does not appear in the bass, but there is hardly a measure where it is not heard either in the violins or the voice. The melody which is tossed from the continuo to the voice in Crudarte's 'Tra cruci funesti' (II. 14) (sometimes in invertible counterpoint) is the only

Ex. 18.

idea in the short aria (65 measures in triple metre). None of these is an
example of a basso ostinato aria; however, it is obvious that the basic principle of repeating a phrase or motif is the underlying plan of the composition. It would be reasonable, therefore, to consider these arias as
extensions of the ostinato principle: Stradella was familiar with this means
of organizing the bass; in *Corispero* he applied it to other lines as well.

Evidence of still other kinds of ostinato are to be found in two other
arias. Clorimira's attractive 'Fortuna, non mi tradir' (I. 6) is an ABA aria
with not just one basso ostinato, but six. Each of the figures is repeated
anywhere from two to six times, leaving a total of only six free measures
in the piece which are needed to accomplish two modulations.[34] The patterns succeed one another, only the first returning after its statement in
the instrumental introduction to the aria and again at the end when the
A-section comes back. Most often repetition occurs at the same pitch, but
the fourth pattern begins on a different level each time. The entire ostinato phrase is repeated in each case, except the fifth pattern where the
two-measure idea is used only twice and only the beginning three-note
figure of it is used four more times. The total effect of the aria is one of
insistence, quite suitable for Clorimira's command to Fortune not to abandon her.

In 'Nel liceo del Dio sagace' (I. 6), also for Clorimira, the bass is
derived from a figure which has ostinato rhythm and direction rather than
pitch. It is a two-measure idea in ternary metre, which begins stepwise
usually upward but occasionally downward, and which changes direction
after the third note and then continues in a more angular manner.
Admittedly, the phrases are not identical, but the essential characteristics
are always there and presentations are interrupted only five times in order
to bridge phrases. The ostinato also appears in the opening vocal phrase,
in canon with the bass.

Certainly related to the ostinato principle are those arias accompanied
by violins and continuo in which a single motif is tossed from part to
part, with an emphasis on regularly recurrent pulsations and in an idiom
where voice and instruments compete on equal terms. An example of this
'concerto style' is Corispero's 'La mia mente è un labirinto' (I. 4) where
one short, rhythmic idea permeates the voice, violins, and instrumental
bass (Ex. 19). The stepwise and energetic figure is used so frequently in

---

[34] They also coincide with the only fioritura vocal phrases in the piece, and these on the name
'Amor'.

Ex. 19.

all parts that it is heard as the single characteristic motif of the aria. Other such examples are 'Chi crede ch'io voglia penare' (II. 8) for Almestilla and 'Fida pure alla speranza' (II. 5) for Crudarte.

Ariosos are often employed by Stradella to interrupt long passages of recitative in *Corispero* and, thus, to provide some relief from them. For example, the ten measures of arioso for Nubesta in Act I, scene 2 are preceded and followed by pages of recitative. Stradella does this about 15 times in the two acts left to us of the opera. More importantly, there are at least a dozen places where an arioso is used as a bridge between a recitative and an aria. At the end of most seventeenth-century recitatives, the rhythm of the bass picks up and the voice has a rather formula-like phrase, all designed to end the recitative in a definite manner and prepare for a clearer beginning of the following aria. This is not what is intended here by the arioso-bridge. Rather, it is a more extended passage, often with a new metre indication, of a melodic–rhythmic character. Stradella employed such an arioso just before several arias (such as those preceding Corispero's 'Affrettate il girar' (II. 3; Ex. 20) and Almestilla's 'Specchiatevi nel pianto' (I. 11)) with the result that there is a flow from recitative to aria rather than the more usual abrupt change in style between them. The arioso is used so often in *Corispero* that it would seem that Stradella was striving for some sort of hybrid connection between the two styles.

Ex. 20.

Prologues and Intermezzos

There are extant sources for eleven of Stradella's prologues and nine of his intermezzos.[35] When the Teatro Tordinona opened as a public theatre, Stradella was invited to collaborate on four of the five productions of 1671 and 1672, contributing prologues and intermezzos for operas previously heard in Venice, two by Cavalli and two by Cesti.

Nicolò Minato's libretto of *Lo Scipione Affricano* performed first in Venice in 1664 recounts the Roman proconsul Scipio's period in Africa, specifically when he captured Syphax, King of Numidia (modern Algeria). For the Venetian production there was no prologue, and only a ballet at the end of each act. The same format was maintained in Florence, 1669, when the opera was dedicated to Cardinal Leopoldo de' Medici. For Rome, however, Stradella composed a prologue and two intermezzos to texts

---

[35] Not included here are the prologue and intermezzos Stradella composed for the prose comedy *Il Biante*. This entire work is discussed in the following section. Corrections to prologue and intermezzo sources in Jander, 'Prologues' are made in Gianturco–McCrickard, *Stradella Catalogue*. These and other corrections may not be noted here.

probably all by Giovan Filippo Apolloni.[36] The prologue *Fermate, omai, fermate* is actually a condensed version of Apolloni's *Marte placato* for Innsbruck in 1655, written to celebrate Christina of Sweden's conversion to Catholicism,[37] and which Cesti probably set to music. The stage directions for the prologue indicate, 'Venere (Venus) and Amore (Love) in a cloud drawn by two doves. Marte (Mars) in a chariot drawn by two lions.'

It begins with Venere telling her doves to stop in Rome so that she can contemplate its glories. When Marte says he would like to bring back the triumphs of Scipione, Venere doubts that there are theatres worthy and able to give the hero the necessary setting. Amore flies off to find one. Marte asks the 'proud and clement stars' to help (a reference to the Altieri Pope Clement X whose coat of arms featured stars); Venere turns instead to the 'points of gold' (on the coat of arms of Christina of Sweden, to whom *Lo Scipione Affricano* was now dedicated). Amore soon returns and says that all is ready, explaining that his speed was due to the 'beautiful goddess of the River Tiber'. He concludes 'Viva, viva, viva, viva Scipione, viva, viva!', thus allowing the opera proper to begin.

The prologue serves to set the scene, reminding the audience that it is a theatrical returning to the past. None of the three characters, in fact, takes part in the opera. However, Amore's last words are the very words of the rejoicing crowd sung at the opening of the opera and thus connect the present with the past. The prologue is comprised of recitative, two arias, and two duets, and while not at all dull, it is not musically important either. The real interest would have been visual, what with lions and doves pulling chariots of heavenly characters across the sky, and then stopping to look down on Rome; Amore's mechanically manipulated 'flights' off and on stage would have added to the spectacle. In short, *Fermate, omai, fermate* is an entertaining introduction to *Lo Scipione Affricano*.

Stradella's two intermezzos for the same opera, *Su, su, si stampino* and *Amanti, che credete?*, were equally entertaining.

In *Su, su, si stampino*, intended to be performed between Acts I and II, Amore returns, this time in a scene with Vulcano (Venere's one-time husband here implied to be Amore's father) and three Ciclopi (Cyclopes). The one-eyed giants are busy forging arrows for Amore (stage directions tell them to beat the metal in time to the music). However, Vulcano assures him that Scipione, as Venere desires, will stay in love with Ericlea because of her beauty and, hence, that the arrows are not necessary. When Amore leaves, Vulcano tells the Ciclopi to stop their tiring work, at which suggestion they dance.

As usual, the intermezzo refers to the opera proper and adds a light touch to it. Two different versions of it are extant, although the only aria ('Compagni non più' for Vulcano) is the same in both.

---

[36] For all literary and music sources, see Gianturco–McCrickard, *Stradella Catalogue*. Cametti, *Tordinona*, 326 says the Vatican score of *Scipione Affricano* is catalogued Chigi Q.V.41, but it is actually Chigi Q.V.60.   [37] For information on Apolloni and his poetry for music, see Morelli, 'Apolloni'.

The stage directions for *Amanti, che credete?*, to be performed between Acts II and III of *Lo Scipione Affricano*, read: 'Bellezza (Beauty) on a chariot drawn by many of her slaves, and a chorus of them.' The goddess warns lovers not to think that just because they are beautiful they will be free: Amore ties everyone to her chariot! (At this point the slaves are to leave the chariot and sit about the stage.) Bellezza (who could be equated with Venere) states that Scipione, 'who has conquered the universe', is hers; but the slaves disagree and say that he is free of her chains. Although Bellezza threatens revenge, the chorus sings of the joy of being free from her.

Comprising recitative, three trios, and dances, the intermezzo also refers to the plot of the opera, commenting on the story and provoking the audience's curiosity about Scipio's outcome.

Chi mi conoscerà is another Stradella intermezzo which may originally have been intended to be done between Acts II and III of *Lo Scipione Affricano*. Both Amore and Vulcano are in the scene, and since they were present in the opera's Act I–II intermezzo, it could be that the intermezzo was written as a sequel to *Fermate, omai, fermate*.

Bugia, Goddess of Lies, explains that Venere, who swore eternal fidelity to Vulcano, was found in someone else's arms; she excused her guilt by saying that every defect of love is contrived by Bugia. Vulcano is also furious with Bugia, but she affirms that deceit is a virtue, and that whoever can lie will be successful. Vulcano wants to find Amore, too, to tie him up and kill him. Disguised as a shepherd, Amore sings that he is looking for Bugia, a good companion for those who need to pretend they are dying of love. The intermezzo ends with all three characters advising 'live and let live'.

Chi mi conoscerà contains recitative, five arias, two duets, and the closing trio. If it were written for *Lo Scipione Affricano*, it was much more extended than either the prologue or Act I–II intermezzo, and perhaps for this reason was discarded in favour of the simpler and more relevant (since it refers to Scipio's plight) *Amanti, che credete?*[38]

The second opera of the Teatro Tordinona's first season was Cavalli's *Il Giasone*, now intitled *Il novello Giasone*. The original libretto was by the Florentine Giacinto Andrea Cicognini, who had been influenced by Spanish 'cloak-and-dagger' drama. In *Giasone* he had little respect for the original Greek legend of Jason's quest for the Golden Fleece, the witch Medea's help in his endeavour, and his marriage to her; and instead refused a truly noble hero and delighted in irony and exaggerated language. In fact, Cicognini declared in his preface to *Giasone*: 'I write for

[38] Alfred Loewenberg, *The Annals of Opera, 1597–1940* (Geneva, [1955]), states that an intermezzo *Lesbo e Ceffea* was composed by Stradella for *Lo Scipione Affricano*, but there is no proof of this.

mere fancy, my fancy has no other end than to delight.' Giovan Filippo Apolloni's prologue for *Il novello Giasone, Questo è il giorno prefisso*, prepared the audience admirably for what was to come.

It begins seriously enough with lines from Cicognini's original prologue, in which Sole (the Sun) outlines the plot of the opera. Stradella went along with the ruse and used Cavalli's music for them for fifteen measures. But suddenly, 'While Sole is singing, Sole's chariot and the whole stage set collapses, and all at once everything disappears, and a [new] scene appears.' Now Sole is joined by Musica, Poesia, and Pittura, who are frantic that the whole opera is now ruined. Their exclamations follow quickly one after another as they curse the rhymes, colours, paintbrushes, and music paper as all being wasted. At this point, Architettura arrives and tells them they are complaining uselessly and—wonderfully—brings order to the stage. All realize that their preparations for the opera are finished, except Poesia who would like to try a song by Musica. The score says that an aria (any aria at all) is to be performed here, after which all agree they must not rehearse any longer, and cry 'Viva Giasone!' as an introduction to the opera.[39]

One can only imagine the audience's surprise and delight at a whole stage set falling apart, and then all being replaced before their eyes; one must also appreciate the excellence of the Tordinona engineer, machinery, and stage hands. It does not seem that Stradella composed any intermezzo for *Il novello Giasone*, but he did write new arias.[40] Acciaiuoli gave the opera again in 1678, this time with his marionettes,[41] and it is possible that Stradella's music was heard on this occasion as well.

The second season of the Teatro Tordinona began on 31 December 1671 with Cesti's setting of Apolloni's *La Dori*, performed first in Florence in 1661 but also in Venice in 1671. In Rome (where the opera was said to have been done 'middlingly well')[42] Stradella was asked to set the prologue, *Dormi, Titone, addio* (probably also by Apolloni). Stage directions for it read: 'Aurora, who rises in a cloud. Zeffiro in another cloud on the right-hand side, and Euro in another on the left-hand side.' The plot is quite simple.

Aurora, Goddess of Dawn, leaves her husband, Titone, sleeping in order to attend to her duty of beginning the day. Zeffiro (the West Wind) and Euro (the East Wind) ask why she has summoned them. She explains that it is the wedding-day of the beautiful Dori (daughter of the King of Egypt) with the King of Persia, and tells the winds to spread the news to the Rivers Tigris, Euphrates, and Nile, and to the Red Sea. In a closing trio, 'Alle gioie, ai contenti', they sing to joy, contentment, delight, pleasure, Persia, Egypt, and the hemisphere.

---

[39] Some lines are omitted in Jander's transcription of the text ('Prologues', 95–6).

[40] For a discussion of these pieces, see Ch. 9. Cametti, *Tordinona*, 328 says that Giasone is a contralto but he is actually a baritone.

[41] Clementi, *Il Carnevale Romano* (1899), 603.   [42] Ibid. 586, quoting an *avviso* from Rome.

Apolloni wrote very little recitative text, but four closed forms: two arias, a duet, and a trio. Stradella extended the music by composing instrumental ritornellos which take up in imitation the themes heard in the closed vocal forms. The lovely images of dawn, winds, clouds, and the prospect of a happy marriage between good-looking rulers, all presented in the poetry and reinforced in the lyrical music, would have been displayed visually before the audience through the stage sets and machinery. It is interesting to note that the opera was dedicated to Don Gaspare Altieri, one of Stradella's patrons.

The libretto for *La Dori* says that a comic intermezzo was presented after Act II, but no text for it has been included. It might have been a work such as Stradella's *Che fai, Dorilla mia?*

Here two servants, Dorilla and Lisetto, sing for each other the ariettas their respective mistress and master have been singing and which they find ridiculous. The pieces are not included in the score; instead there are only indications to sing four 'old but known' songs.

An intermezzo of this type, with just a pretence of a plot and so little text, would not have merited inclusion in the libretto. Stradella's contribution to *Che fai, Dorilla mia?* was the recitative of the two servants' brief conversation and a short, two-section opening sinfonia. It is doubtful that he would have chosen his own arias as examples of 'old but known' music to make fun of.

On 12 February 1672 the second opera of the season opened. It was Nicolò Beregan's *Il Tito*, also to music by Cesti. The real Titus was emperor of Rome from AD 79 to 81. He conquered Israel, destroying Jerusalem, and was memorialized in Rome's Arch of Titus. Although he was a wise and clement ruler, his brother, Domitian, poisoned him. In the opera, among the various episodes recounted is the love affair of Tito and Marzia, and it is this which gave Filippo Acciaiuoli the idea for his prologue, *Aita, numi, aita.*

Marzia, concerned about Tito's love for her, has sent her nurse, Cencina, to the underworld to ask the help of Plutone (Pluto). The servant (who also appears in the opera itself) arrives there astride a large goat, and cries out hysterically for help to all the gods and her dead relatives. Devils threaten her, as does their leader, Scacazzur, who wonders if she intends to seduce Plutone. The old woman is flattered, and begins to flirt with Scacazzur. The king of the underworld, on a flaming throne which rises out of the ground, now appears. In answer to Cencina's request that Tito be kept faithful to Marzia, Plutone sends for Apollonio. In the libretto he is called a 'a famous magician' (referring to a certain Apollonius of Tyana, a philosopher from the first century AD said to have performed miracles and made prophecies). Apollonio agrees to assist Marzia, and he and Cencina both ride away into the air on the goat.[43]

Obviously, the prologue was full of visual marvels: characters arriving and leaving astride a big goat; hell; a chorus of threatening devils; Pluto and his flaming throne. However, it was also great fun; moreover, the comedy is so 'low' at times that it is positively vulgar, particularly when Cencina is involved. As far as the music is concerned, besides responding to each comic–dramatic situation, Stradella made judicious use of the orchestra in aiding the drama and distinguishing between roles. The trio of devils is accompanied by basso continuo only; Cencina has continuo accompaniment to her two arias, but instrumental ritornellos are added to them; Pluto, the most important and serious character of the prologue, has his aria accompanied by two violins and continuo throughout. For added interest, Stradella increased this ensemble in the opening sinfonia to include a trumpet and two viola parts.

At the end of Act II of *Il Tito*, one reads the following directions in the libretto: 'Here a ship arrives from the sea, and lets off on shore the Re del Congo (King of the Congo), who comes to render tribute to Tito; his servants do a dance and end the second act'.

From Stradella's intermezzo *Oh, ve' che figuracce!* one learns that the king was a pygmy and that his followers (Caramoggi) were small and deformed. In the libretto's list of machines to be used in the opera, they were mistakenly called 'Indians'. To greet the Re del Congo is Cencina, astonished at the sight of these strange characters. The pygmy king is attracted to her and comically offers to make her his queen. Before being taken by her to Tito, he has his subjects give her a demonstration of 'Indian' dancing.

Stradella set the conversation between the king and Cencina in recitative; the dances, however, are not included in his score and one cannot be sure that they were his contribution.

The Venice 1666 performance of *Il Tito* had been dedicated to Maria Mancini, her husband Lorenzo Onofrio Colonna, and her brother Filippo Giuliano, the Duke of Nivers, and Maria Mancini said she was so delighted with the opera, she saw it five times.[44] The Rome 1672 production was once again in her honour, as *Il novello Giasone* had been the year before. Several years earlier, the Colonnas had been connected with another of Stradella's prologues, *O di Cocito oscure deità*. It was presented in their palace during Carnival 1668 together with Acciaiuoli's comedy *Il*

---

[43] In the Rome production, while it is true that Cencina does not appear in the original libretto (Jander, 'Prologues', 98), she replaces the earlier character Lucindo and therefore does not constitute exactly an 'additional' role.

[44] Her diary as quoted by Loewenberg, *Annals*, under the year 1666.

Girello set to music by Jacopo Melani. The opera was performed before 26 cardinals and many other guests, including Christina of Sweden, and was praised as a 'novelty, all beautiful; very beautiful scenes, . . . Quite superb costumes, well acted'.[45] Robert Weaver defines the work as 'a frankly political satire directed against absolutism in the time of the first flourishing of the absolute monarchs' and suggests that it could have been tolerated only in Italy 'where the independence of the Church and of the petty republics, dukedoms, and principalities was threatened by the monarchs of the surrounding nations'.[46]

The opera is about Girello, the king of Thebes' gardener. When he catches his wife together with one of King Odoardo's counsellors, Ormondo, the annoyed nobleman manages to get him banished. While in exile Girello meets a magician who gives him a cloak which will make him appear to be Ormondo, and a root which can cause the king to look like the gardener. Naturally, Girello then returns to Thebes and the fun begins!

The prologue for *Il Girello* was entrusted to Giovan Filippo Apolloni, and he invented a lively and dramatic piece to introduce the very comic opera.

It takes place in the underworld where Plutone and Proserpina (Persephone) urge the Erinyes, those 'obscure deities' of the River Cocytus, a tributary of the Styx, to infest the earth with war. Vendetta (Revenge) and Inganno (Deceit) then complain of the unjust goings-on in the Kingdom of Thebes, and ask that they be allowed to wield their punishment against Ormondo. It is agreed, and all four call the spirits to come out of hell, to populate Earth, and 'reform behaviour'.[47]

There are connections here with *Il Giasone*, and specifically with the scene in which Medea casts a magic spell to help Jason obtain the Golden Fleece. In the earlier libretto, Cicognini offered lines of six syllables, each a *verso sdrucciolo*, that is with the accent on the third-last syllable (and not on the more common penultimate syllable), beginning 'Dell'antro magico'. At the end of the prologue to *Il Girello*, when Plutone, Proserpina, Vendetta, and Inganno also, in a sense, conjure up all spirits to have them invade the world, Apolloni employed the same unusual poetic structure. What is more, Stradella imitated Cavalli's repeated-note setting and rhythm (Ex. 21).

The opening duet for Plutone and Proserpina, 'O di Cocito oscure deità', is an interesting handling of their lines. Apolloni has given Plutone and then Proserpina two strophes, each strophe different in structure (four verses and then three verses, of five and seven syllables alternately);

---

[45] An *avviso* from Jan.–Feb. 1668 quoted by Clementi, *Il Carnevale romano*, 578; also see Weaver, '*Il Girello*'.

[46] Weaver, '*Il Girello*', 152.

[47] As comparison will show, Weaver's summary of the plot of the prologue, 153, is quite different.

Ex. 21.

[S-Proserpina; A-Vendetta; T-Inganno; B-Plutone]

then they share another strophe (four verses of six syllables). Stradella set the first pair of strophes in a traditional AB musical structure; but when Proserpina presents her pair the music is not identical to Plutone's: instead she sings a melodic inversion of his music (Ex. 22). When next they have the same text and both call on the 'Tremendous spirits,

Ex. 22.

condemned to groans', Stradella overlaps their running lines of eighth-notes in imitation. It is interesting to consider how the scene was created on stage. One set of suggestions comes from *La caduta del Lucifero*, an anonymous seventeenth-century sacred play: 'While the mouth of hell is open one hears sounds of chains and drums, with frightening cries and shouts, and flames of fire which one makes by taking two covers from boxes of sweets, with two or three lighted wax candles, and behind a lot of rosin powder, and that thrown in the air will have an admirable effect'.[48]

Another Stradella work, the amusing intermezzo *La ruina del mondo*, is a complaint against such pieces by one of its performers.

Milo complains that he cannot face having to do another intermezzo: no new ideas come to him, and he is fed up with the usual comic situations. Fortunately, three excellent musicians arrive, one of them a Spanish guitarist from Castile. He decides to have them serenade his love, Rubia. At this point the 'serenata' within the intermezzo takes place, and one of the musicians, Nano, sings the aria 'Aure placid'e vezzose'. This is followed by a Spanish song and guitar sonatas, which are not included in the score. As dawn is approaching, Milo—calling the musicians 'bats'—sends them away.

Because there is a comic character named Milo in Stradella's opera *Le gare dell'amor eroico*, it is possible that *La ruina del mondo* was composed for it. At the same time, Rubia was a comic character in *La forza dell'amor paterno* (where she is paired with Silo), and therefore it could be that the intermezzo, a serenade for someone with that name, was intended for this opera. In either case, the intermezzo would have been heard in Genoa during the 1678–9 season.

While the examples discussed thus far are either definitely or most probably datable, other Stradella prologues and intermezzos are less certain. In four cases one might suggest at least the main operas with which they may have been associated. On 15 January and 3 February 1667 Antonio Sartorio's double opera *La prosperità d'Elio Seiano* and *La caduta d'Elio Seiano* was produced in Venice. The librettist Nicolò Minato expected that the two works would be performed on successive evenings, but the cast refused the strenuous task of learning and performing them almost simultaneously. The real Aelius Sejanus was an Etruscan minister for Tiberius, who ruled Rome when the emperor was in Capri. He was so ambitious that he had Tiberius' family killed, and expected to marry Livia, Tiberius' daughter-in-law. The emperor finally had him put in prison and killed in AD 31.

[48] A copy of the play, but with its title-page damaged and therefore without date or author, is in I-Rc.

Aelius Sejanus's 'rise and fall' was clearly a good topic for operas, and one of Stradella's prologues also refers to him.

At the beginning of *Lasciai di Cipro il soglio*, Venere says she has left Cyprus (in the foam of whose sea she was supposedly born) to come to Rome with her Grazie (Graces) in order to spread peace and happiness. After a dance (missing in the score), she and the four Grazie tell Seiano to remain crowned with laurel.

The text would seem appropriate for the 'prosperità' part of the Etruscan's career, but associating Stradella's prologue with a specific performance of Sartorio's opera is not easy. The Venetian 1667 production seems not to have had a prologue, and the Genoa 1668 and Rome 1672 productions have different prologues from Stradella's.[49] At the beginning of 1676, however, letters from Settimio Olgiati to Polo Michiel, as well as several diplomatic dispatches, mention that *La prosperità d'Elio Seiano* was done in Lorenzo Onofrio Colonna's house, certainly on 21, 25, and 31 January and seemingly every day of February until the 22nd.[50] Moreover, Acciaiuoli wrote the prologue. Since Stradella was connected with all of these gentlemen, it is reasonable to suppose that he was asked to set the prologue performed with the opera. Olgiati also mentioned that the Colonna children were to dance in an 'intermedio' and it is possible that the ballet called for in his prologue was performed by them. In May of 1676 Olgiati wrote to Michiel that he would send him some excerpts from *Seiano* 'newly done by Stradella', which could suggest that the composer set some of the arias as well.[51]

Domenico Filippo Contini's *Gli equivoci nel sembiante* is about Eurillo who loves Clori, and Clori who loves Eurillo, but who become confused by the arrival of Armino, Eurillo's unknown twin; added to this is the jealousy of Lisetta. The opera was the first Alessandro Scarlatti set.

It opens with Eurillo, who says, 'Follow me, O hopes; Leave me, O suspicions,' referring to his love for Clori. Having to write an introductory prologue to precede these lines, a librettist could reasonably imagine them as being directed not just to 'suspicion' in general, but to an entity called Sospetto (Suspicion); he could, therefore, have decided to make Sospetto the protagonist of his prologue. Since Stradella's *E dovrò dunque in solitaria stanza* is indeed a monologue for Il Sospetto, it is conceivable that it was performed as a prologue with Scarlatti's *Gli equivoci nel sembiante*. What is more, the first of its two arias has textual

[49] Cametti, *Tordinona*, 332, says that the Vatican score is catalogued Chigi Q.V.44 but it is actually Chigi Q.V.63.

[50] The Olgiati letters are dated Rome, 13 and 26 Jan. 1676 and are in I-Vc, PD C. 1063, nos. 362 and 295 resp. Relevant *avvisi* are: I-Rvat, Barb. lat. 6381 dated 25 Jan., 15 Feb., and 22 Feb. 1676; I-Fas, Mediceo del Principato, fo. 3942 dated 25 Jan. and 1 Feb. 1676.

[51] Olgiati's letter in I-Vmc, PD C. 1063, no. 83 (the day of the month is not legible). It should be recalled that Stradella set a cantata by Apolloni, *Son prencipe, son re*, subtitled *Il Seiano*.

connections with the title of the opera: 'Il sospetto, o quant'è caro a chi adora un bel sembiante'.

Another aspect in its favour is that the prologue is in the key of D major, the tonality of the opera, and it would, therefore, have connected with it most easily.

Scarlatti's opera was first performed privately in Contini's house and at the Collegio Clementino in Rome on 5 February 1679, but afterwards it was presented at Rome's Teatro Capranica, Bologna's Teatro Formagliari, in Naples, Vienna, and so forth—a real success. It would seem most logical that Stradella's prologue was written for the Rome performances even if he were no longer in the city. However, the same prologue would appear to have been 'adjusted' for use with another opera. This is suggested by a Turin manuscript which has some different text for the second strophe of the aria described above, and—more importantly—adds an accompanied recitative and a ritornello which modulates to the key of C major. As one reads on the score, this closing instrumental section serves 'to modulate to the key of the beginning of the comedy of four [characters]'. Which 'commedia' in the key of C major with four characters is intended, is not known.[52]

Another of Stradella's prologues, *Dal luminoso impero*, although the text does not say so, is sung by Leda. It was for her that Zeus took the form of a swan, through which two eggs were produced: Helen (later of Troy) was hatched from one egg, and Castor and Pollux from the other.

In Stradella's prologue Leda laments the fate of her children, specifically that of Helen. She ends by wishing that her daughter will be protected and enjoy glory.

The work is called a prologue on Stradella's autograph of it, but it is not surprising that a later hand wrote on the Modena copy 'cantata', since the outline of a long recitative, two-strophe aria, recitative, another aria, much recitative ending in an arioso, gives the impression of being a cantata. The fact that it is for solo soprano and basso continuo, the most typical cantata scoring, reinforces the impression.

There were two seventeenth-century operas for which this prologue might have been conceived: Aurelio Aureli's *Helena rapita da Paride* set by Domenico Freschi, and Nicolò Minato's *Elena* (on a subject by Giovanni Faustini) set by Cavalli. Since Stradella was in Venice in 1677 when Freschi's opera was first performed, it could be that he was asked to do a prologue which was then not performed. At the moment, however, *Dal luminoso impero* cannot be associated with any specific opera or performance, even though both of the operas mentioned were given many times.

[52] Both Turin sources are autographs, but say nothing in themselves about which was done first or last.

Stradella's intermezzo *Su, miei fiati canori* is also for soprano and continuo only.

The character Fama (Fame) is seated on a cloud, and orders her 'melodious breaths' to make trumpets sound in praise of Ciro, in the battle between him and the cruel tyrant ruler of Babylon.[53] She hurries off to make his name known 'at the other pole', at which point the opera proper would have begun.

The most likely work with which *Su, miei fiati canori* could have been associated was Francesco Provenzale's *Il Ciro* performed in Naples, 1653 and, with musical additions by Cavalli, in Venice, 1654. Perhaps Stradella's intermezzo was intended for some later performance of the opera. Stradella wrote several pleasant fioturas for the soprano, and encouraged an interplay between voice and continuo. Although there is recitative and two arias, the second strophe of the first aria, 'Sì, che tra lucide schiere', is missing from the score. The only extant copy of the intermezzo, because of its decorated first initial, was probably intended as a presentation copy.

Rome celebrated the signing in 1668 of the Peace Treaty of Aix-la-Chapelle with entertainments of all sorts: masses sung by several choirs, banquets, public fountains of wine, elaborate contructions showing, for example, the Church with War and Peace kneeling on each side, or Peace under an arch of triumph, from which fireworks were set off, and so forth. The *avvisi* from May to September are filled with notices of such celebratory events,[54] and since Stradella's prologue *Che nuove? Oh, ragionevoli* has one of its characters say that there is to be a hunt 'now that peace has been made between the French and Spaniards', it is reasonable to assume it was connected to one of them.

The prologue takes place in Rome, in a public bath where, as well as using this service, men also come in to get shaved, to have their calluses or teeth removed, to exchange gossip, enjoy a prostitute, eat, drink, play cards —all of which goes on off-stage and is commented upon during the scene. What one actually sees is a cittadino (citizen or city-dweller), who comes in to get shaved and to learn the local goings-on (his opening line translates as 'What's new?') from the stufarolo (one who attends a stove or furnace, and meaning here the one in charge of the bath). They are interrupted from time to time by a fattore (servant), who comes in for more playing-cards, to complain that a customer has stolen his tips, to report the arrival of the young lady Catera, and finally to warn that a fight has broken out. As the bath attendant describes this last episode, all the customers try to dress quickly and run away (perhaps in fear of the arrival of city guards). In their rush, they take the wrong clothes and are seen by the attendant, citizen, and

---

[53] The historical Cyrus was King of Persia and conquered Babylon in 539 BC.

[54] For example, see the *avvisi* for this period in I-Rvat, Barb. lat. 6369. For two sketches of firework constructions in Rome, June 1668, see Bjurström, *Feast and Theatre*, 50–1.

servant as masqueraders; they tell the frantic customers that if they are, they should run, jump, and dance!

Che nuove? Oh, ragionevoli offers a wonderful slice of seventeenth-century Roman life. The text is lively, with distinctions of class made through the characters' language; local habits are also portrayed. Stradella has scored the roles of the stufarolo and the cittadino for two tenors, a voice often reserved for comic parts, and that of the fattore for soprano, thereby suggesting he is a young boy. The main character is the stufarolo, who is assigned four arias, two with accompaniment, by two violins, and two with just continuo accompaniment, although there are instrumental ritornellos. His music is generally lively and syllabic, except, for example, when he waxes more lyrical on the preference for Spanish doubloons instead of chickens from Romania as bribes. The delightful prologue has as its climax the closing trio 'O, che piacere' for the three onlookers of the ridiculously transvested crowd.

While it is not known for which work *Che nuove? Oh, ragionevoli* was intended, it is clearly an amusing commentary on contemporary behaviour, particularly that of the male members of society. One of Stradella's intermezzos, *Soccorso, aita, ohimè*, criticizes women in a comic manner.

It opens with the cry of Gola (Hedonism) for help against Modestia (Modesty), who is angry with her for the 'many parties and balls' which are held everywhere. Moreover, Modestia finds that the women of Holland, Sweden, Paris, Venice, and even Peru are wearing clothing and jewellery which are too extravagant. Gola responds that customs have changed, that a woman who doesn't know how to behave according to the times loses her reputation for beauty. When Modestia says she cannot suffer such behaviour, Gola tells her to come back in Lent! She agrees and leaves, but Gola stays to enjoy it all.

Stradella's recitative, three arias, and one duet offer simple, syllabic, and rhythmically lively music suitable for the comic scene.

Because of the reference to Holland and Sweden, members of the Triple Alliance which caused France to sign the Treaty of Aix-la-Chapelle, it is possible that *Soccorso, aita, ohimè* was also written at the time of the peace. In addition, its subject suggests it could be paired with *Che nuove? Oh, ragionevoli*. The unusual reference to Peru in the intermezzo could also relate it to the prologue, where in the trio it is repeated often that 'beautiful Catera without a skirt is worth Peru'. As stated earlier, however, it is not known with which work the prologue and intermezzo were associated.

In 1666 Flavio Orsini, Duke of Bracciano, had one of his comedies performed, and he had it repeated on 4 December 1668. Since his brother the cardinal had been in France from October 1665 to June 1666,[55] it could be that his return was the occasion for the first performance; at the revival of the comedy, the ambassador of Venice and his wife were the special guests. It would seem that this second performance was in the home of the ambassador of France.[56] It may be that Stradella's prologue, *Reggetemi, non posso più*, by Flavio Orsini was composed for this very comedy. The prologue gives several clues about the main work, by mentioning France, Prince Alfonso, the Infante of Hungary, Gismena (the Infante's beloved?), and Gustavo, a father and king (Christina of Sweden's father?)—all references to what one assumes are characters in the comedy proper. However, it has not been possible to determine anything more about the main work.

Stradella's prologue is a discussion between Capriccio (Caprice) who says he cannot resist love, and Costanza (Constancy), who says she will help him, agreeing that to suffer in a tempest is difficult. After these lines, reference is made to several other people (those mentioned above) and their ability or inability to be constant. The invitation is extended to see whether Capriccio or Costanza is victorious in the end, meaning at the end of the comedy.[57]

The tenor Capriccio has been given one aria, but the soprano Costanza has three. The generally simple vocal writing has been enhanced by much use of two violins in addition to the continuo, instrumental parts which—as is usual for Stradella—are generally in imitation.

Stradella's *Chi me l'avesse detto* is also comic but, uniquely among his intermezzos, it is on a sacred subject. In the New Testament, Acts 13 one reads of Saul (later known as Paul) going with Barnabas to Cyprus, where they met a magician named Bar-Jesus, a Jew who claimed to be a prophet and magician. He was a friend of the governor Sergius Paulus. When the governor showed interest in the Christians, Bar-Jesus tried to turn Sergius Paulus away from them. Saul called Bar-Jesus the son of the Devil, and for trying to turn the Lord's truths into lies, made him blind. This episode is reworked in *Chi me l'avesse detto* to become an amusing, lively, and contemporary enactment of it.

A Napoletano, who speaks in his colourful dialect, marvels at the wonders which Bariesù has worked: statues who speak, men who fly, etc. However, he is also a bit wary and feels one should keep a certain distance from such unusual happenings. (Stage directions say that he walks and plays an instrument as he considers the miracles.) Bariesù arrives for an appointment with Sergio; the 'presidente' (promoted in the intermezzo from governor) is late because he has been talking

---

[55] *Avvisi*, I-Rvat, Barb. lat. 6368, 10 Oct. 1665 and 12 Jan. 1666 respectively.

[56] An *avviso* cited by Ademollo, *I teatri di Roma*, 103.

[57] In the Modena copy (but not in the Turin autograph), the last recitative has been assigned to a new character, Costume (Habit), but this may be a mistake.

with San Paulo and is impressed with him. Bariesù is furious and says that only he, the magician, is to be believed. When he shows Sergio and the Napoletano hell as an example of his power, the southern Italian is frightened, and the President is so saddened at the sight of suffering souls that he wants the vision removed. The gloating Bariesù says that San Paulo should disappear, but at this point he arrives saying that Bariesù, the son of the Devil, must be punished with blindness. San Paulo and Sergio say that 'He who gets in heaven's way on earth, should not receive the light of heaven.' San Paulo then banishes Bariesù, Sergio asks San Paulo to instruct him in the new faith and goes off with him, and the Napoletano says one should never trust sorcerers.

The characters (alto, two tenors, and bass) are accompanied by continuo only in the four arias and two duets, but it interacts in a lively and interesting manner with the voices. Suitable for the comic style, the music is generally syllabic and rapid. One can imagine the intermezzo as being a useful and amusing didactic tool between the acts perhaps of a sacred play, but one does not know with what other work it was performed.[58]

The author of Stradella's prologue *Con meste luci* is Francesco Maria de Luca Sereni, to give him his full name. An 'accademico umorista', Sereni wrote prose plays[59] which occasionally would have a spoken or even a sung prologue.[60] In November 1672 one of his plays, a *tragicomedia*, having already been performed with success in Rome (as the dedication explains), was presented in Bologna. It was entitled *Il Purismondo*, the name of the Prince of Rhodes, one of the protagonists. The play takes place in Cyprus, and at the end of it the King of Cyprus extols the peace which now reigns between his country and Rhodes due to the coming marriages between his children and the prince and princess of Rhodes. To introduce his play, Sereni wrote a 'Prologo per Musica' with the stage directions: 'Peace enchained, sleeping; She awakes and says, "Con meste luci".' The prologue corresponds exactly to one of Stradella's.[61]

Here Pace (Peace) explains that she has been chained by Amore in Cyprus. As she rebels at the injustice of her plight, she spies an arrow, that which has made her a prisoner. Recognizing its 'magical worth', Pace uses the arrow to break her chains. In her person, Peace and Love have joined forces, and together they will be victorious against Disdain. The prologue ends with her cry, 'Long live only liberty'.

---

[58] It does not seem to have been the practice to offer intermezzos between parts of an oratorio.

[59] Such as *L'Armelindo* (Rome, 1664), *Il Fausto overo Il sogno di D. Pasquale* (Rome, 1665), *L'Amore vince lo Sdegno* (printed in Ronciglione but dated Rome, 1673), *L'Oronte overo Le corone fra le catene* (Bologna, 1681), *La Rosina overo La fortuna tra le sventure* (Rome, 1687), *Don Pasquale nel soglio overo Nella guerra la pace* (Rome, 1687), *La Colpa innocente overo Il Fidamiro* (Rome, 1690), and *La Carlotta overo Il piacere nel dispiacere* (Rome, 1695).

[60] For example, *L'Amore vince lo Sdegno* had a spoken prologue and *L'Oronte* had a sung prologue (beginning 'Che stravaganza è questa!'); *L'Armelindo* had two prologues, one spoken and one sung (the latter beginning 'E pur udir degg'io').

[61] The stage directions are also written on the two extant scores.

Con meste luci offers recitative and five arias for Pace, a soprano, with only basso continuo accompaniment. Sereni wrote a two-strophe structure for the first and fourth arias 'Con meste luci' and 'No, non si creda un core') and a three-strophe structure for the second one ('Con larve apparenti'), and Stradella followed his lead exactly. In the latter example he increased the effect of already-heard material, augmenting its insistency by employing a rhythmic figure repeatedly in the bass (Ex. 23). The third aria, 'Deh, perché sì crudo Amore', is structured on a return of the opening section: ABACA. The vocal style is syllabic until the fifth and last aria, 'Prigioniera io non son più', when Pace's exultation of liberty takes off in florid phrases.

Ex. 23.

When Sereni's play *Il Purismondo* was first performed in Rome is not known, but one assumes that the libretto for Bologna, including the prologue, was what was heard at that time. His other works were dedicated to members of the Roman aristocracy (the Rospigliosi and Pamphili families, to name but two), but neither he nor Stradella seems to have been connected to one particular patron. For this reason it is impossible to speculate on the original sponsor of *Il Purismondo–Con meste luci*.

Incidental Music

On 5 February 1671 Filippo Colonna married Cleria Cesarini.[62] Filippo, Contestabile Lorenzo Colonna's brother, had been a cleric and was already on the way to becoming a cardinal. However, the possibility of gaining the Cesarini fortune of more than two million scudi[63] made him renounce the ecclesiastical life. It was a great advantage in overcoming bureaucratic obstacles that Pope Clement X, an Altieri, was a close friend of both families.

The marriage was one of the two most important of the season, the other being that of Anna Pamphili and Giovanni Andrea Doria. Once

---

[62] I-Rvat, Barb. lat. 6373, *avviso* dated 7 Feb. 1671. On the Cesarini family, see Ademollo, *Livia Cesarini*.

[63] I-Rvat, Barb. lat. 6373, *avviso* dated 31 Jan. 1671.

contracts were signed, the families of both marriages celebrated 'almost every evening [with] parties, operas, and comedies'.[64] After the Colonna–Cesarini wedding ceremony, Filippo again offered a 'comedy, and most splendid supper' to the guests.[65] It is quite possible that the spoken play *La Laurinda overo il Biante* (commonly referred to simply as *Il Biante*), with music by Stradella interspersed, was one of the comedies presented in celebration of the marriage. This is suggested by references in the comedy to the places and people involved.

It is necessary to an understanding of the *argomento* of the play to realize that the Cesarini owned, in addition to property in Rome, the nearby area of Ardea and the Principality of Genzano, and that this latter name was assumed by some to be derived from Cinzia (Cynthia), alias Diana, since a temple found in Genzano was believed to have been dedicated to the Goddess of the Hunt.

Il Biante takes place in Oriolo (of which the Altieri were princes). Laurinda, the daughter of the Prince of Ardea (Cesarini territory), together with her servant, Biante, has come here for refuge (a reference to the protection offered to the Cesarini by Clement X). She is escaping from assassins sent by her father, who was told by the evil priest of the Temple of Diana (a reference to Genzano) that she would be the cause of his death; he convinced the father to make the priest's brother heir to his fortune. Laurinda is in Oriolo disguised as a young man, Tiresio. She is engaged to Delio, Prince of Cintiano (a reference to Filippo Colonna who agreed to assume the name and rights of the Cesarini of 'Cintiano' or rather Genzano). Delio thought that Laurinda was on a hunting trip, but when he was told that she had been killed (as the soft-hearted assassins who let her go falsely told her father), he determined to avenge her death and, therefore, has also come to Oriolo.

Prologue. The character Gloria (Glory) is seen suspended above a column (a symbol found in the coats of arms of both the Colonna and Cesarini families), surrounded by six Virtues, each with a star on its head (thus representing the Altieri coat of arms with its six stars). She is to judge who is the best courtier of three diversely dressed characters who introduce themselves. They are the Genio della scherma (the Spirit of Fencing), the Genio del ballo (Spirit of Dance), and the Genio del cavallo (Spirit of Equitation).

Act I. Biante and Laurinda/Tiresio, in need of food and shelter, come upon Lindoro and his servant Squarcetta, to whom Biante tries to sell medicinal cures. As they leave, the Genio del ballo comes along dressed as a foreign knight. Lilla arrives and asks if he has seen Delio, for whom she has an invitation from her mistress, Almirena (formerly in love with Lindoro and now with Delio). The Genio goes off to look for him. At that moment Delio arrives, explaining about Laurinda to his servant Nisillo. Lilla gives him Almirena's invitation, an action seen by Lindoro who is furious. As the act proceeds, Almirena assumes Tiresio as

[64] I-Rvat, Barb. lat. 6373, another *avviso* dated 7 Feb. 1671.
[65] Ibid., the first *avviso* of 7 Feb. 1671 cited above.

a servant; she also accuses Lindoro of making love to her servant and declares she is through with him. Biante convinces Almirena's father, Pollione, a decrepit and miserly old noble, he can cure his gout; to do so, he puts powder on the old man's legs and ties his stockings in such tight, painful knots that he cannot get them off unless he pays Biante to do so. Through a ruse, Biante manages to get the key to Pollione's money, and helps himself to it. He gives his accomplice Squarcetta some money, too, but then manages to get it back by selling him a ring.

First intermezzo. The Genio del cavallo praises himself; a ballet follows.

Act II. Almirena is singing an 'arietta' she has had composed. Lilla is desperate because Almirena wants her to give a love-letter to Lindoro, telling him that Almirena caught her writing it and dismissed her; in this way Almirena will be free to love Delio. Lilla is afraid her love, Squarcetta (who has given her Biante's ring), will believe it is all true. Lindoro meets the Genio della scherma who is looking for a *cavalier* willing to meet his challenge that evening before a certain lady. Lindoro will try to gather some friends for the Genio, and in return asks him to sing that same evening in a garden. When Almirena sees her father, she gives him a watch which Delio has given her. Biante convinces Pollione to visit a lady that evening, and gets the nobleman's watch (the same Almirena gave him) so that he will be on time to pick him up. He arranges for Squarcetta to come into the room pretending to be the lady's husband, rip all Pollione's clothes off, and beat him up in feigned anger; Biante then tells the old man that in the fray he lost the watch. Realizing that love is blooming between Almirena and Delio, Laurinda/Tiresio sends her betrothed a jewel and a letter which let him know she is alive.

Second intermezzo. The Genio della scherma boasts in song of his worth, after which four pages perform a mock battle.

Act III. Delio shows Laurinda's letter to Almirena. As he is leaving, he recognizes Laurinda/Tiresio, entrusts her to Almirena's care, and goes off to seek justice. The would-be assassins beg to be spared. In the end Almirena will marry Lindoro. The Genio del ballo finally meets up with Delio and gives him the message, now late, from Almirena. It is agreed that both weddings will take place in Rome. When Pollione complains about the expense, Delio offers to pay for Almirena. He says that he would have already left for Ardea (supposedly to explain all to Laurinda's father), but 'certain Princes who vacation in Oriolo' invited him to a fête which will take place shortly. All are delighted to attend.

Third intermezzo. Gloria says that all three Genii have won. Praises are sung to the gods who are 'altieri' (noble) and 'clementi' (clement), an obvious reference to the Pope.

The comedy is more of an entertainment than a true drama, and has a mixture of characters taken from various sources. Tiresio recalls the prophet Tiresias of classical literature who changed sex, as does Laurinda through her disguise. 'Delian' is actually an epithet of Apollo, so 'Delio' could simply stand for Apollo, one of the greatest gods, and the play's beloved is thus associated with all that is good and desirable. Lindoro, by contrast, is a character from the *commedia dell'arte*, a secondary-role lover just as the young man is here. In addition, two characters are taken from the seventeenth-century lower class: Biante, not a proper name but the way a tricky, dishonest person—which the servant proves himself to be— would have been called; similarly, Squarcetta's name means to 'break up' everything. Adding to local colour, Squarcetta uses Roman dialect frequently.

The prologue and three intermezzos are set almost entirely to music, whereas the play is in general spoken, but with musical moments interspersed. These are all introduced as actual 'music', not simply as lyrical expressions rendered more affective through a musical setting. For example, in Act I Biante decides to while away the time singing, and the result is his aria 'Chi non sa che sia disgrazia' (sc. 1); he then asks Laurinda/Tiresio to sing to get people's attention so that he can sell them medicine, and she performs the aria 'Come posso cantar' (sc. 3). The Genio del ballo pretends that he is just walking by, singing, and offers the aria 'Bel nume di Gnido' (sc. 4). Almirena sings the aria 'Datti pace, o Fileno' (sc. 9), a piece she says was recently given to her, as an example of one which expresses her present sentiments. Laurinda/Tiresio sings the aria 'Delio infido, empio padre' (sc. 10) without an excuse but, overhearing the music, Almirena decides that the young servant is singing for his amusement.

In Act II the practice continues. At Lilla's request, Almirena sings the aria 'So ben che mi saettano' (sc. 1) which a 'virtuoso' has composed for her. The Genio della scherma's aria 'S'in petto unirò' (sc. 3) expresses his inner sentiments, but it is assumed to be simply a song by Lindoro who envies the beautiful voice. When the momentarily rejected lover asks the Genio if he will sing for him that evening, the Genio sings the aria 'Dal rigor d'un'empia sorte' (sc. 4) to see if Lindoro likes it as a piece of music for the occasion. While they are waiting to visit Pollione's non-existent lover, to pass the time Biante asks him if he sings, and proceeds to teach him; the delightful comic duet 'Begl'occhi, dormite' is the result (sc. 12).

In Act III Almirena's aria 'Canta il labbro' (sc. 1) is offered as yet another example of her musical repertoire. Biante's aria 'Finiscono, svaniscono' (sc. 6) is thought to be a song by Pollione. Tiresio says he/she has learned a duet on Almirena's harpsichord, and the two sing 'Non sa mai amor ferir' (sc. 7).

The times that music is sung during the course of the play without being introduced or considered as actual 'music' are exceedingly few. Three examples are for the Genii (Act I, sc. 5 Genio del ballo, 'Sento in seno una speranza'; Act II, sc. 4 Genio della scherma, 'Già parmi veder'; and Act III, sc. 9 Genio del ballo, a repeat of his 'Bel nume di Gnido'); however, they are not characters of the play proper but of the prologue and intermezzos (they simply 'pass by', as it were, in the play), and as such are 'fantastic' characters and part of the purely musical cast. Biante breaks into song, but it is only a line of arioso, 'Chi sa far da biante è un bel mestiere' (If you know how to be a *biante*, it's a good job), once in Act II and once in Act III: it is obvious that he does so because he cannot contain his delight with himself. Perhaps only two closed forms may be considered truly 'operatic'. The first is Almirena's Act III aria, 'Sì, sì, mio cor, narralo tu', a serious expression of her state which she offers in music without any excuse to do so; and the comic aria 'Lasciate correre', which has four strophes sung in alternation by Biante and Pollione, and during which the two comic characters argue about money.

The author of the text is not known. He was quite cultured, because of all the allusions to people, places, literature, and tradition that are so cleverly introduced. He was also capable of dealing with comedy, and able to imitate a *commedia dell'arte* scenario which intertwined comedy, complex situations, and excuses for music with such skill. Moreover, he was someone familiar with the musical theatre. Two candidates come to mind. One is Filippo Acciaiuoli, author of the very popular operatic comedy *Il Girello*, a type of burlesque which has several characters from the *commedia dell'arte*, and for which Stradella wrote the prologue discussed earlier. The other possible author of *Il Biante* is Giovanni Andrea Lorenzani (1637–1712), an esteemed artisan in brass whose poetry for music was in constant demand by Roman nobles. He was especially gifted in comedy, and delighted in using dialect, especially his own Roman language.[66] Unfortunately, at present *Il Biante* may not be assigned to any writer.

As may be inferred from what has been said thus far, recitative plays almost no role in *Il Biante*. Of the twenty arias, two duets, and two trios (these latter for the Genii), five are strophic, even though the repeat may not be immediate (as in 'Come posso cantar' (I. 3) which has spoken dialogue separating the strophes, and 'S'in petto unirò' (II. 3) which has another aria and spoken dialogue between strophes). Ternary structures dominate the music, both simple ones such as 'Sento in seno una speranza' (I. 5) and longer, more complex sectional pieces as 'Datti pace, o Fileno' (I. 9). Much of the music is 'serious' and, either in the pieces for the earnest Genii or in the arias and duet performed as musical selections, offers typical examples of Stradella's operatic and chamber music styles, as in Almirena's aria 'Canta il labbro' (III. 1) (Ex. 24).

At the same time, there is also music which reveals Stradella's ability to write comedy. These moments all involve the character Biante, and are specifically his arias 'Chi non sa che sia disgrazia' (I. 1) and 'Finiscono,

---

[66] On Acciauioli, see Thomas Walker in *The New Grove*. Giorgio Morelli's 'Giovanni Andrea Lorenzani: Artista e letterato romano del seicento', *Studi secenteschi*, 13 (1972), 194–251, is an excellent biography of Lorenzani and also provides a list of his works.

Ex. 24.

svaniscono' (III. 6), as well as the one he alternates with Pollione, 'Lasciate correre' (III. 11). In each of these, Stradella lets Biante's over-active, scheming temperament emerge by writing long, non-stop phrases of eighth-notes where the text is sung syllabically, thus imitating the character's constant chatter (Ex. 25). Biante's seemingly serious duet with Pollione, 'Begl'occhi, dormite' (II. 12), is rendered humorous both by the music-teacher situation in which Biante puts himself, and by Stradella's request that old Pollione sing first in falsetto when imitating Biante, and then as the bass that he is. The simple two-part lines also offer pleasing harmony.

Il Biante is scored for two violins and basso continuo, as are Stradella's operas. Continuo arias may have string ritornellos associated with them. The instruments are also employed in a single-movement, two-section sinfonia before the prologue, and a two-movement ballet in the third intermezzo. Two other instrumental sections are also called for, but the music is not included in the sources: they are in Intermezzo 1, a ballet for the Genio del cavallo which most likely was meant to accompany a feigned

Ex. 25.

exhibition of his riding; and in Intermezzo 2, a battle for the Genio della scherma. In both cases a trumpet not called for elsewhere in the score is requested. It could be that the instruments simply improvised the music for these sections, perhaps even playing something familiar. While there are six soprano, two contralto, and two bass roles, it is possible to perform *Il Biante* with only two singers for each voice-part (S, S, A, A, B, B); the cast is completed by the three non-singing roles of Delio, Lilla, and Nisillo, and several 'extras'.

In 1679 Girolamo Pignani edited a collection of Italian songs, *Scelta di canzonette italiane de più autori*, for publication in London. He included two pieces from *Il Biante* in it: 'Non sa mai amor ferir', a duet for Almirena and Laurinda/Tiresio (III. 7), and 'So ben che mi saettano', an aria for Almirena (II. 1).[67] Neither could be considered an example of vocal bravura, but the continual employment of the voice(s) in a syllabic setting with interesting rhythms and pleasing harmonies has its charms. In fact, 'charming' is the adjective which one could most aptly apply to all of *Il Biante*.

While other seicento operas had occasional expressions in dialect (such as *Chi soffre, speri* with text by Giulio Rospigliosi and music by Virgilio Mazzocchi and Marco Marazzoli, which used the dialects of Bergamo and Naples) or spoken texts (*Finta pazza* with text by Giulio Strozzi and music by Francesco Sacrati),[68] the historical significance of *Il Biante* lies elsewhere. It is perhaps the only extant work which illustrates what a

---

[67] The collection was published by Godbid and Playford. Pignani also included another Stradella duet, *Care labbra che d'amore* for soprano, bass, and basso continuo.

[68] See Henry Prunières, *L'Opéra Italien en France avant Lully* (Paris, 1913; repr. New York and London, 1971), 74 n. 3 on the use of spoken lines in the Paris production of 1645.

commedia dell'arte production must have been like: a spoken play of low comedy, disguise, love, and complicated situations, with music interspersed. The music heard in *commedia dell'arte* productions may not all have been as fine as Stradella's, but the way it is inserted here recalls the same practices.

8

Oratorios

The Arciconfraternita del Santissimo Crocifisso, one of Rome's most prestigious confraternities, took its name from a crucifix unharmed in a terrible fire at San Marcello, and built an oratory dedicated to it in a square about a block behind the church in 1568. Documents from 11 February 1667 name Stradella as the composer of an oratorio heard there on the second Friday of Lent, that is on 4 March. The account adds that it was to be 'with words by Lotti'.[1]

Unfortunately, the oratorio on which Giovanni Lotti and Stradella collaborated—possibly the composer's first—is lost, and not even the title is known. However, since it was to be performed at the Crocifisso, it must have been in Latin, the usual language of their oratorios.[2] Moreover, considering their habit of separating the instrumentalists in *palchi*, that is in stands or boxes, it is not difficult to see herein at least the makings of a concertino–concerto grosso ensemble, exactly the accompaniment Stradella adopted some years later for another oratorio, *San Giovanni Battista*.

To celebrate the Holy Year 1675, the confraternity of the church of the Florentines in Rome, San Giovanni dei Fiorentini, which met in the Oratorio della Pietà,[3] decided to offer a series of fourteen oratorios to be performed between January and April.[4] The composers were among Rome's best: Antonio Masini, Maestro di Cappella at the papal Cappella Giulia; Giuseppe Antonio Bernabei,[5] organist at the oratory; Bernardo Pasquini, in great demand by Queen Christina of Sweden; Alessandro Melani, Maestro di Cappella at the French church of San Luigi. In

[1] Reported by Domenico Alaleona, *Storia dell'oratorio musicale in Italia* (Milan, 1945; previously published (with different pagination) as *Studi su la storia dell'oratorio musicale in Italia* (Turin, 1908)), 342.

[2] On music at the Crocifisso, see Owen Jander, 'Concerto Grosso Instrumentation in Rome in the 1660's and 1670's', *Journal of the American Musicological Society*, 21 (1968), 171. My first investigations of all Stradella's oratorios were presented in 'The Oratorios of Alessandro Stradella', *Proceedings of the Royal Musicological Association*, 101 (1974–5), 45–57.

[3] The oratory, founded by members of Filippo Neri's group and called by various names (including Sant'Orsola della Pietà, Oratorio dei Fiorentini, Oratorio del Consolato, Oratorio della Pietà), was demolished in 1888 when the present Corso Vittorio Emanuele II was built.

[4] Documents related to this series of oratorios were found by Casimiri and presented in 'Oratorii'.

[5] Since he was in Munich at the time, it could not have been Ercole Bernabei, as was supposed by Casimiri, 'Oratorii', 158.

addition, the little-known Giovanni Battista Mariani (called 'di Pio' because he worked for Cardinal Carlo Pio of Savoy) composed an oratorio, as did Stradella. While records indicate payment to instrumentalists mentioning 'concertino' and 'concerto grosso' in such a way as to suggest comparable accompaniment for the whole oratorio series, only the score for Stradella's *San Giovanni Battista* has survived.

It is an exceptional work. Stradella himself considered it his best composition to that date,[6] and one can suspect he wisely gave great care to writing music in honour of John the Baptist, patron saint of Florence, which had been requested by a group of Florentines. One should remember, too, that Stradella's father had been a member of the Medici order of knights, the Cavalieri di Santo Stefano, a title his older brother Giuseppe now held. Burney, who possessed a copy of the oratorio score, described it at length in his *General History*, saying he was 'interested and surprised . . . by the new and unexpected beauties of Stradella's compositions, compared with those of his contemporaries'.[7] Surer proof of its success is that it continued to be performed even after Stradella's death.[8]

The libretto by Ansaldo Ansaldi presents the well-known New Testament story of John the Baptist who, in trying to turn Herod from worldly pleasures, arouses the anger of his wife's daughter, which results instead in John's decapitation. The text is based on the New Testament gospel according to Mark, Chapter VI, verses 17–21; in fact, occasionally whole lines are quoted from the Bible.

There are five characters: besides San Giovanni Battista, there is Erode (King Herod), his wife called Erodiade la Madre, her daughter Erodiade la Figlia (known more commonly as Salome), and the Consigliere (the king's counsellor); in all, two sopranos, a contralto, tenor, and bass. These same voices join together in various vocal groupings to take on the added ensemble roles of Giovanni's disciples and Erode's courtiers. The oratorio was performed on Passion Sunday, 31 March 1675 by 32 musicians: 27 instrumentalists to accompany the five singers.

Although the singers are named in the accounts, the role each assumed is not. Knowing their voice-ranges, however, it is most likely that the parts, and payment, were distributed as follows. 'Gioseppino di Baviera' (Giuseppe Maria Donati) would have taken the alto role of Giovanni (3 scudi); Francesco Verdoni, the bass role of Erode (2 scudi); 'Siface' (Giovanni Francesco Grossi), the soprano part of the daughter (1.50

[6] According to his first biographer Giuseppe Ottavio Pitoni in 'Notitia de' contrapuntisti e compositori di musica' [compiled *c*.1695–*c*.1730], ed. Ruini, 324.

[7] Charles Burney, *A General History of Music*, ed. Frank Mercer (London, 1935), ii. 580. *San Giovanni Battista* is discussed in detail on pp. 578–80. Also see Smither, *History*, i. 314–26 on Stradella's oratorios and in particular *San Giovanni Battista*.

[8] For information on librettos and music sources of all the oratorios, see Gianturco–McCrickard, *Stradella Catalogue*.

scudi); Giovanni Matteo Leopardi, the tenor role of the Consiglere (1.50 scudi); and 'Peppino soprano d'Orsino' (Giuseppe Ceccarelli) probably took the small soprano role of the king's wife (0.90 scudi).[9]

To accompany them were a number of non-specified instrumentalists (ten played for all the oratorios, another ten were hired specially by Stradella and one of these was a harpsichordist from Cortona), plus two extra 'violette' or violists, two violinists (Carlo Ambrogio Lonati and Carlo Mannelli), a lutenist (Lelio Colista), and two contrabass players (a certain Simone, and a Francesco Maria employed by the Altieri family). Probably the specifically named, and separately paid, violinists and lutenist and perhaps one of the contrabass players formed the concertino while the concerto grosso (to judge from a list of instrumentalists employed in Antonio Masini's *Sant'Eustachio* performed earlier in the same series),[10] was probably composed of six violins,[11] four first violas, four second violas, four violoncellos, and one contrabass.[12] The harpsichord may have been used by either ensemble although it is called for specifically only in the concertino.

Since similar instrumentation is to be found in his serenata *Vola, vola in altri petti* of August 1674 and in his motet *Pugna, certamen, militia est vita* of January 1675, *San Giovanni Battista* was not Stradella's first experience with a concertino–concerto grosso ensemble.[13] All the same, one wishes that his oratorio of 1667 were available because, since it may have had a similar orchestra, one would then be in a position to evaluate Stradella's approach to its use in oratorio from the age of 27 to 35. As it is, there is an absolutely competent handling of the two groups in *San Giovanni Battista* to achieve maximum variety. Of the fourteen arias in the oratorio, six are accompanied by basso continuo alone,[14] and seven by the orchestra. Of these latter, one aria ('Io, per me, non cangerei') is accompanied by the concertino only; two ('Sorde dive', 'Vaghe ninfe') are accompanied by the concerto grosso only; one ('Tuonerà tra mille turbini')

---

[9] It is not clear why Rostirolla, 'Istituzioni religiose', 590 decided to give Giovanni's alto role to a tenor, and the counsellor's tenor role to a soprano. The payments make no sense this way either.

[10] Casimiri, 'Oratorii', 167–8.

[11] Including 'Il Bolognese', most likely Arcangelo Corelli, who played for the whole series, and therefore also for Stradella's oratorio (Casimiri, 'Oratorii', 167).

[12] Burney, *General History*, ii. 578, while thinking 'the accompaniments very ingeniously contrived', supposed the orchestra to be the same as used in 'Corelli's Concertos, for two violins and violoncello *del concertino*, and two violins, tenor and base *del concerto grosso*'. Proof that this would be possible in performance is the 19th-c. English copy of the oratorio now in the Royal College of Music, London (MS 600). For a discussion of the string instruments employed in Stradella's concerto grosso ensembles, see my 'Corelli e Alessandro Stradella', in Giulia Giachin (ed.), *Nuovi studi corelliani, Atti del Secondo congresso internazionale, 1974* (Florence, 1978), 55–62.

[13] It is also possible that the undated cantatas *L'accademia d'Amore, Il Damone, Qual prodigio è ch'io miri?, Lo schiavo liberato*, and 'Cantata per Natale' *Ah! troppo è ver*—which also employed concertino–concerto grosso instrumentation—were from this same period.

[14] For their titles, see Gianturco–McCrickard, *Stradella Catalogue*.

has its first part accompanied by concerto grosso and its second section (beginning 'Di cieco carciere') accompanied by concertino; one ('Soffin pur rabbiosi') is accompanied by the two combined groups.

Two other arias show still further manipulation of the entire orchestra. When the daughter in 'Queste lagrime e sospiri' laments she will never be happy unless Erode decapitates Giovanni, the orchestra consists of only one ensemble: a first violin part (where the two concertino violins would also play), a second violin part, all violas now on one part instead of the usual two, and basso continuo. A second and separate continuo part (certainly intended for those instruments usually assigned to the concertino) is written under the voice and is clearly a direct support for it. Different from this orchestra (of two violin parts, one viola part, plus continuo) is that which accompanies Erode's reluctant, worried answer to the girl, 'Provi pur le mie vendette': again the voice is provided with its own continuo, but the orchestra consists now of two violin parts, two viola parts, and continuo.

As regards the continuo instruments, apart from what one is able to glean from payments to individual players, something may be learned from indications in seventeenth-century copies of the score.[15] That the concerto grosso would have had more than one continuo instrument is suggested by the expression 'With all the basses of the Concerto Grosso', which one finds before the Consigliere's aria 'Anco in cielo'; that among its instruments the concertino employed both harpsichord and lute for the continuo is deduced from indications in Erodiade la Figlia's aria 'Sorde dive'. Here accompaniment is by the concerto grosso only; there is no second continuo line assigned to the voice, and furthermore the indication is 'and the other bass does not play'.[16] But later on, at the second section, one reads 'Here the bass of harpsichord and lute enters'.[17] At this point, in addition to the concerto grosso and its continuo, a second and separate continuo line accompanies the voice directly, clearly to be played by harpsichord and lute.

In all the arias where, in addition to the concerto grosso, there is either a concertino or simply a second continuo part, the 'Concerto Grosso delle Viole' (as the ensemble is called) does not usually play directly with the voice but serves to alternate with the singer plus concertino and/or continuo. Occasionally in these cases the concerto grosso writing is imitative (as in 'Soffin pur rabbiosi'), but generally it is homophonic between vocal

---

[15] GB-Lbl, Add.45882; I-MOe, Mus. F. 1136; from a later date but also exhibiting performing indications is the incomplete score at F-Pn, Rés. V.S. 1396.

[16] London and Modena MSS; Paris reads 'e si sono un Basso solo'. A basic difference between the London and Modena copies is that when only the concerto grosso is called for in Modena, London indicates that the concertino is to become part of this ensemble.

[17] All three cited copies.

phrases. For example, the first section of the above-mentioned 'Sorde dive' (62 bars in common time) is 'concertata con il Concerto Grosso delle Viole'.[18] The orchestra, warned to play softly,[19] offers a rich contrapuntal accompaniment directly with the voice. But at the second allegro section (102 bars), where the voice has its own continuo, often in imitation with it, the concerto grosso plays only between vocal phrases and now in homophony. A similar employment of forces is to be found in Erode's aria 'Tuonerà tra mille turbini', 'a magnificent blustery base song', as Burney described it,[20] where the first section is accompanied by the combined concertino and concerto grosso. Here the king rages that his power will thunder as a thousand hurricanes against Giovanni for having dared to disturb his court. As usual, the concertino accompanies the voice directly while the concerto grosso joins in between vocal phrases. Once again the writing is contrapuntal for the concertino, and chordal for the tuttis. The quite different and calmer mood of the second section (beginning 'Di cieco carcere'), in which the king sends Giovanni to prison, is reflected in the more flowing accompaniment provided now by the concertino alone.

The orchestra also introduces the oratorio with a well-developed and imitative-style sinfonia written in three sections for the concerto grosso alone, and plays ritornellos before and/or after vocal numbers. Although they are not as frequent as in Stradella's operas, ritornellos similarly present a theme of the vocal piece and usually in imitative counterpoint. An unusual ritornello is attached to 'Su, coronatemi'. The aria is constructed over a basso ostinato, a brief idea jubilantly reiterated throughout both strophes of the stepdaughter's exultation over Giovanni's decapitation, which breaks off only at moments of vocal fiorituras. In the concerto grosso ritornello which follows, it is the ostinato which is selected for development and which is heard passing back and forth from violin to continuo while the violas provide harmonic filling to their counterpoint. 'Anco in cielo' is another continuo aria based on a basso ostinato, in this case presented on various levels. Once again it is the ostinato which continues into the following orchestral ritornello. (Although it does not have ritornellos, mention might be made here of 'Volin pure lontano dal sen', since it is yet another continuo aria based on a basso ostinato.)[21]

Of the various vocal ensembles, the duets for Erode and Erodiade la Figlia are especially outstanding, and to judge from the eighteen pre-twentieth-century copies of 'Nel seren de' miei/tuoi contenti', this was quite a popular one, especially in England. Even Burney felt it worthy of inclusion in his *General History*, noting that he did so because 'the harmony, modulation, and contrivance, are so admirable', it being 'a

---

[18] Modena MS.   [19] Modena and London.   [20] Burney, *General History*, ii. 579.
[21] Burney, ii. 578–9, felt that when there was just continuo accompaniment there was no need to realize the harmony of a basso ostinato.

speciman of the perfection to which this species of writing was brought by Stradella'.[22] *San Giovanni Battista* closes with yet another father–stepdaughter duet, 'Che gioire/martire'. Here Stradella joined two characters of different mind. He gave the girl rapid phrases to express her joy, and Erode sustained notes for his awful doubt that perhaps he had made a mistake in killing Giovanni. Even though the two sing simultaneously, one finds 'Allegro' written over the girl's part and 'Adagio' over that for the king, certainly intending mood rather than tempo. As the D major duet proceeds, they begin to wonder about their feelings, and to ask why one is happy and the other not. During this section Stradella modulated to the dominant. Since the questions go unanswered, he ended the ensemble in A major, thus leaving the musical discourse also unresolved.[23] Another duet in the oratorio, 'Morirai, uccedetelo/Uccidetemi pur' for the gloating Erodiade la Figlia and the willing martyr Giovanni, is a bravura piece for both singers who are called upon to execute series of sixteenth-note fiorituras, often in imitation.

Also worthy of note is the 'Madrigale a.5', 'Dove, Battista, dove' for Giovanni's followers. When the saint decides to leave his family and disciples, three of these excitedly ask where he is going. When he tells them 'to the court of Erode', the writing is expanded to a five-part madrigal for their repeated warnings. As was usual in seventeenth-century oratorio, the above-mentioned lines of three-part recitative (which also begin 'Dove, Battista, dove'), the five-part madrigal, as well as the trio 'Non fia ver che mai' and repeated quartet 'S'uccida il reo' both for Erode's courtiers, would have been sung by the principal singers, free to regroup or assume other parts as needed in the unstaged drama. It is no doubt exactly because of the absence of scenery and costumes and in the desire to simulate dramatic movement that the practice was to locate performers in various places in the oratory, and that Stradella attempted to create so much variety through his accompaniments.[24]

In addition to the arias and ensembles, the vocal writing includes not only the expected simple recitative but many sections of highly charged text treated as ariosos. They often appear at the end of a recitative and serve to provide a stylistic bridge to an aria. An especially effective example occurs when Erodiade la Figlia, at the end of her recitative beginning

[22] Burney, ii. 579. Padre Martini used the duet as an example in his *Esemplare o sia saggio fondamentale pratico di contrappunto sopra il canto fermo* (Bologna, 1774; repr. Ridgewood, NJ, 1965), ii. 17–20.

[23] For a discussion of this and other examples of musical rhetoric in Stradella's oratorios, see Howard E. Smither, 'Musical Interpretation of the Text in Stradella's Oratorios', in Carolyn Gianturco and Giancarlo Rostirolla (eds.), *Atti del Convegno di studi 'Alessandro Stradella e il suo tempo'*, Siena, 8–12 settembre 1982, Chigiana, 39, NS 19 (1988), 287–316.

[24] Burney, ii. 579, noted: 'Yet, notwithstanding the attention necessarily given to fugue and imitation at this time, Stradella has introduced a greater variety of movement and contrivance to his oratorio, than I ever saw in any drama, sacred or secular, of the same period.'

'Deh, che più tardi a consolar la spene | di questo afflitto core', insists that she cannot live while Giovanni lives, that she cannot go on hearing and seeing that 'monster'. After this moment of increased emotional tension, expressed in an arioso, she sings her 'pathetic' aria, 'Queste lagrime e sospiri', a skilful and extraordinarily beautiful study in dissonance control (Ex. 26). Another typical use of arioso is during recitative, such as that for mother and daughter when they discuss Giovanni's decapitation and where, as their excitement increases, the recitative twice becomes more lyrical; when Erode joins them, he too turns to arioso as he begs the girl to ask whatever boon she will of him, not suspecting the horrible favour she desires.

In general, *San Giovanni Battista* presents the same characteristics to be found in Stradella's operas. It shows masterly handling of all the techniques employed, and all within a definitely tonal setting.[25] It is true that here the da capo structure is not the main one (in fact, it appears only once, in 'Io, per me, non cangerei'), but this factor is due as much to the librettist and his choice of poetic forms. However, Stradella's use of the ostinato, frequently and in a free manner, can be associated with opera. Two other aspects of the writing in *San Giovanni Battista* also suggest a 'dramatic' interpretation of the text. First is the recitative, filled with repeated notes and sung over static basses of long-held notes—all conducive to a rapid execution which allows one to get on with the plot rather than encouraging one to sing. Mainly, though, Stradella's dramatic style is evident here in his rhythm: it is motivic, repetitive, insistent, whether in a slow tempo or a fast one. Certainly the ostinato often provides just these characteristics. However, the style is not limited to the bass but, especially through the counterpoint at which Stradella was so able, it permeates all lines and gives the sense of drive found in late seventeenth-century opera, and in much music of the eighteenth century.

La Susanna, probably Stradella's last oratorio, conveys the same impression as *San Giovanni Battista*. Written for Modena and dedicated to one of the century's most generous patrons, Duke Francesco d'Este II, *La Susanna* was performed at the Oratorio di San Carlo in Modena on 16 April 1681, less than a year before Stradella was murdered and six years after *San Giovanni Battista*. Most of Stradella's operas were composed in the interval between these two oratorios, and if one were to open the score of *La Susanna* at random and not notice the role of a narrator, one would see no difference in form and style here from *La forza dell'amor paterno* or *Moro per amore*. First of all, accompaniment in the oratorio is

---

[25] According to Burney, ii. 580, 'the recitative is in general excellent; and there is scarce a movement among the airs in which genius, skill, and study do not appear. This is the first work in which the proper sharps and flats are generally placed at the clef.'

Ex. 26.

provided by two violin parts plus continuo, exactly the scoring for all of Stradella's operas. As in the operas, one finds the da capo form[26] and the two-strophe aria.[27] Of the fifteen arias, only six are accompanied by the orchestra, but seven of the remaining basso continuo arias have opera-style ritornellos played either before and/or after, taking up in imitation the principal motif of the aria.[28] For example, 'Ma folle è ben chi crede' has the same ritornello before and after as does 'Belle fonti a me sareste'; but 'Ma costanza miei fidi pensieri' and 'Sventurata, e sarà vero'[29] have different ritornellos before and after, the preceding ritornello being related thematically to the first half of the aria, and the one after to the last part of the aria.

Most importantly, every closed form of *La Susanna* presents an insistent motif from which the music develops and which characterizes it. Several times this results from repetition of a basso ostinato. For example, 'Da chi spero aita, o cieli' presents a figure which is repeated exactly throughout the two strophes of the aria, changing level only for modulations (Ex. 27). The ostinato in 'Così va, turbe insane', a sixteenth-note figure used sequentially for long or shorter phrases finishing off at cadences with eighth- and quarter-note dominant–tonic skips, runs insistently throughout the whole aria (Ex. 28). 'Vecchio nefando, io so' also has an all-permeating ostinato, which is taken up by the voice as well.

Ex. 27.

Ex. 28.

'Voglio amare e che sarà' does not have a true ostinato, but rhythmic drive is achieved through a simulated ostinato, running quarter-notes which create the effect of repeating while not actually exactly doing so; here, too, the voice participates in the figure. In 'Ma folle è ben chi crede' a scalar figure is presented repeatedly, and a constantly moving bass in 'Quanto invidio il vostro stato' and 'Belle fonti a me sareste' achieves the same rhythmic drive.

---

[26] The arias 'Voglio amare e che sarà', 'Così va, turbe insane', and the ensemble 'Fu sempre letale impuro amor'.

[27] 'Ancor io d'Amor fui colto', 'Belle fonti a me sareste', 'Da chi spero aita, o cieli'.

[28] On instrumentation and placement of ritornellos, see Gianturco–McCrickard, *Stradella Catalogue*.

[29] Also the duet 'Chi dama non ama'.

Accompanied by orchestra, 'Zeffiretti che spiegate' exhibits another type of ostinato, in this case short motifs passed from violin to violin to voice, clearly to depict the 'zephyrs' but thereby providing the aria with a characteristic motif. Through imitation other numbers also insist on a typical figure: for example, the second section of the closing quintet 'Chi contro l'innocenza', the duet 'Dell'opra nefanda', and the trios 'Se dall'Erebo si scatenò' and 'La bellezza è un puro saggio'.

The libretto for *La Susanna* was the work of Giovanni Battista Giardini, the Este duke's secretary,[30] and it would seem to have been his first oratorio. Giardini's source was the Old Testament Book of Daniel, Chapter 13.

Susanna, Joachim's wife, decides to take a bath in her garden one day. Waiting for her to undress are two of the old men who are supposed to act as wise judges for the Jews: Primo Giudice, Secondo Giudice. When they hungrily ask her to make love with them, she cries out, bringing her servants, husband, and townspeople to the scene. The wily judges say she had a young lover with her who ran away before they could catch him, and they convince everyone that Susanna should be stoned to death. At this point the young Daniele takes it upon himself to question the judges separately, and when they give different versions, Susanna is saved and the judges condemned to death.

The musical cast is composed of two sopranos (Susanna, Daniele), a tenor and bass (the two Giudici), and a contralto (the Testo or narrator). A chorus (made up of the five soloists) always enters after the Testo with a moral summing-up of the situation he has just described.

As was typical of Stradella, the arioso appears in *La Susanna* at moments of increased emotion: for example, when the Primo Giudice gets carried away thinking about Susanna at the end of his recitative 'Arde il mio seno'; or when her natural beauties, revealed as she is taking her bath, are described by the Testo. In general, however, there is little arioso and, as was Stradella's practice in his operas, alternation is generally between simple recitative and real closed forms. The voices, while occasionally called upon to execute fioriituras (such as those the narrator has in 'No, non va, senza i suoi disastri' and Susanna in 'Quanto invidio il vostro stato' and 'Belle fonti a me sareste'), usually have syllabic music. It is not through *virtuosismi* that Stradella has made their parts interesting, but rather through music which allows them to be participants in the drama.

---

[30] According to Girolamo Tiraboschi (*Biblioteca Modenese* (Modena, 1781–6), ii. 404), historian of the Modena court, Giardini wrote 12 oratorios, one opera, and other 'componimenti'. Seven of the oratorios were dedicated to the subject of Moses and spanned the years 1682–91 (see Crowther, 'Oratorio Tradition', especially his Appendix, 'A Chronological List of Oratorios Performed in Modena, 1677–1700', 59–62, extended to 1665–1702 in his *Oratorio in Modena*, 192–200). Tiraboschi also notes that *La Susanna* was performed again in 1687, but the only other extant libretto for Modena is from 1692. For a discussion of both the text and music of *La Susanna*, see Crowther, *Oratorio in Modena*, 40–57.

For example, the lyrical style, interesting harmony, and ternary (3/2) metre are right for the Primo Giudice to express his uncontrollable amorous feelings for Susanna in 'Freddo gelo e fiamma interna'; as is the contrasting simplicity of 'Quanto invidio il vostro stato' suitable to Susanna as she expresses her desire to be as pure as the 'dear limpid waters'; and the descending slow lines of 'Da chi spero aita, o cieli' are illustrative of her dejection and tears at having been condemned to death because falsely accused of infidelity.

San Giovanni Battista was a New Testament story and *La Susanna* comes from the Old Testament; and while the earlier oratorio evolved its drama with only direct dialogue, *La Susanna* has a narrator who—in fourteen interventions totalling about 200 lines—describes, in recitative and aria, the various scenes, the judges, Susanna, and so forth. But otherwise, both oratorios show structural similarities which are present in all of Stradella's six extant oratorios and which were typical of middle and late seventeenth-century oratorios in general.

All but one of Stradella's oratorios call for what Arcangelo Spagna considered the 'safe' maximum number of five soloists (*Santa Pelagia* is for four singers),[31] and assign them arias, duets, trios, quartets, and quintets both as individual characters and as part of a group called upon to comment or to respond in the drama.[32] The oratorios also reflect the difference of contemporary opinion concerning the use of a narrator, since three have a narrator and three are without one. By the 1660s and 1670s, there does not seem to have been a preference for a particular voice-range for the role either[33] and, in fact, Stradella gives the part of narrator to all voices: once to an alto (*La Susanna*), once to a tenor (*San Giovanni Chrisostomo*), and in his oratorio *Ester*, to a bass in Part I, and then to a soprano in Part II.[34]

His oratorios also illustrate seventeenth-century discussion about whether there should be only real characters and not personifications.[35] As

---

[31] 'Discorso intorno a gl'oratori', introduction to *Oratorii overo melodrammi sacri* (Rome, 1706); also included in Alaleona, *Storia*, 313 ff., and translated into German in Arnold Schering, 'Neue Beiträge zur Geschichte des italienischen Oratoriums im 17. Jahrhundert', *Sammelbände der internationalen Musikgesellschaft*, 8 (1906–7), 49 ff. A summary with some additions is to be found in Quadrio, *Della Storia*, iii/2. 496–7; Burney, *General History*, 582, derived his section on Spagna from Quadrio. Spagna proposes 5 singers on p. 16.

[32] Some confusion arises between the number of roles and the number of singers. *Santa Editta* has six different roles (Umiltà appears only at the very beginning and very end), but they could be taken by five singers; a similar situation arises for *Ester, liberatrice del popolo ebreo*, where the role of narrator may be assumed first by an already present bass and then by an already present soprano; and for *San Giovanni Chrisostomo*, where a soprano courtier could become the narrator.

[33] Spagna, 'Discorso', 4, says that the narrator had originally been assigned most frequently to a tenor.

[34] For complete scoring details, see Gianturco–McCrickard, *Stradella Catalogue*.

[35] Spagna, 496.

has been seen, both *San Giovanni Battista* and *La Susanna* have only real people. The characters in *San Giovanni Chrisostomo* are also all real people, in this case out of church history.[36]

Eudosia, Empress of Byzantium, is delighted that the people pray to the new statue of her. Giovanni Chrisostomo (John Chrysostom), already exiled once before for going against the Empress, risks a second exile by telling her she is not divine and insisting that she should not be worshipped. Although one courtier tries to defend the bishop, he is exiled and dies.

Ester, liberatrice del popolo ebreo tells the Old Testament story[37] of Mardocheo (Mordecai), a Jew in Babylon who refused to bow before the minister Aman (Haman) and so was condemned to death together with all the Jews. He sends his niece, Ester the wife of Re Assuero (King Ahasuerus, who is not aware that she is a Jewess), to beg her husband for pity, which she does successfully and as a consequence Aman and his whole family are put to death instead. Throughout, the 'unreal' character, Speranza Celeste (Divine Hope), helps the Jews keep up their spirits.

The two remaining oratorios, *Santa Pelagia* and *Santa Editta, vergine e monaca, regina d'Inghilterra* (St Edith, Virgin and Nun, Queen of England) have a great deal in common, including their great reliance on characters which are not real but are personifications of abstract qualities. Both oratorios refer to women popularly believed to have been saints. That not much was known about them as historical figures is clear from the librettos. The real Pelagia was a beautiful and rich courtesan of Antioch. She was also an actress. It was said that—'beauty having been united with perversity'—she was able to spread corruption throughout the city. One day, due to the persuasions of Bishop Nonno of Antioch, she was blessed by Divine Grace, left off her worldly ways, and converted to Christianity. In fact, she ended her days in a monastery in Jerusalem.[38]

---

[36] John Chrysostom (b. Antioch *c*.344) was from a wealthy family and studied the liberal arts and law. He became a hermit, but returned to Antioch in 381, was made a deacon of the church and then a priest. After some years spent preaching, he was appointed Bishop of Constantinople. His austere manner and severe interpretation of Christian morality brought him into direct opposition with the Empress of Byzantium, Eudoxia, wife of Arcadius, which caused John's exile and subsequent death. Stradella's oratorio dwells on this conflict.

[37] Taken from the Book of Esther, chs. 3 and 4.

[38] The citation is from Piero Bargellini, *Nuovi Santi del Giorno* (Florence, 1960), 261. In the Roman church of Sant'Apollinare Nuovo, Pelagia (much honoured in the Middle Ages) is represented in the procession of virgin martyrs. For another dramatic interpretation of her story, see the play of the same title by Antonio Nucci (Bologna, 1677), which included members of the family, servants, and so forth. According to Joseph-Marie Sauget, 'Pelagia', *Bibliotheca Sanctorum* (Rome, 1968), 432–7, the source for Pelagia's life was John Chrysostom (Homily 67 of his Commentary to St Matthew's Gospel), who called her simply a 'penitent from Jerusalem'; the name of Pelagia, that of a martyr from Antioch, was added by a later author known simply as Giacomo. Both Pelagias celebrate their feast on 8 October. Because of the connection between John Chrysostom and Pelagia, one wonders if the two librettos and/or oratorios were conceived as a pair.

In the oratorio, however, Pelagia's occupation is not mentioned, and she is simply tempted by Mondo (The World) and a group of Mondani (Worldly Spirits); Nonno (not called a bishop) invokes the warrior Religion to save her (rather than relying upon his own skill as a preacher).

The Editta referred to in Stradella's libretto must be Edith, the wife of Edward the Confessor,[39] but the plot invented by the librettist, Lelio Orsini, is a very general one applicable to any saint.[40]

We learn that Editta has heeded the counselling of Umiltà (Humility) and has ignored the pleasures of the world. Thereafter, there are arguments by Bellezza (Beauty), Grandezza (Greatness), Nobiltà (Nobility), and Senso (the Senses), who try to persuade her to follow them. However, Editta is convinced that they offer only passing pleasures and she prefers to remain firm in order to obtain the lasting joys of Paradise. Umiltà appears at the end to say that Editta gained happiness through sorrow.

The librettos of *Santa Pelagia* and *Santa Editta* offer little in the way of drama, being intellectual moral discussions. No one changes his position, not even his moral one, from what it was in the beginning. Neither Pelagia nor Editta is converted, or confused; no conflict really touches them. There is, in short, no 'action' of any kind. One can couple the other four librettos comparably. Both Ester and Giovanni Chrisostomo are in conflict, but not imminently and not personally. Giovanni's fate, if he loses against the Empress, is going to be only exile, not death; and when he argues with her he is not representing himself, but merely voicing a moral position; it is all a bit impersonal. Ester, too, is not pleading for herself but for the Jewish people. Moreover, it is not certain even if she does not persuade the king to be merciful that she will be killed. However, not just impersonal moral questions are raised: the fate of human beings is also touched upon. Action is implied by Giovanni's exile, and by Assuero listening to Ester and changing the fate of the Jews and of Aman. In both oratorios there is danger, but it is one step removed, as it were. *Ester* and *San Giovanni Chrisostomo* are definitely more dramatic

[39] Other Queen Ediths appear in English history, for example the one whose name was changed to Matilda, and they might even be able to be called 'nuns', but since Edward the Confessor had no children and let it be believed it was because his marriage had not been consummated, his wife is the only one who might have been thought a 'virgin'.

[40] Don Lelio Orsini, Prince of Vicovaro and brother to Flavio, Duke of Bracciano (whose texts Stradella also set), wanted to become a Capuchin but the rigours of monastic life proved too much for him. He was dedicated to spiritual exercises to the point of being a zealot, if not a bigot, until the dire financial problems of his family convinced him to marry the nun Livia Cesarini. However, the young woman preferred Federigo Sforza, and so Lelio remained celibate (see Ademollo, *Il Livia Cesarini*). A member of the Accademia degli Umoristi, his piety encouraged him to write mainly sacred texts for music. Spagna, 'Discorso', 20 lists him among those who preferred oratorios with a narrator; Mandosi, *Biblioteca Romana*, ii. 188–91, states that several of his oratorio texts were printed in Germany. According to Litta, *Famiglie celebri*, Lelio Orsini died on 20 May 1696; he left his belongings to the Arciconfraternita delle Stimate, of which he was Guardian.

plays than either *Santa Pelagia* or *Santa Editta*; but *San Giovanni Battista* and *La Susanna* are the most dramatic of all Stradella's librettos: in both, one is dealing with a life-or-death situation, and for the principal (human) characters themselves.

It was suggested earlier that *San Giovanni Battista* and *La Susanna* were also 'dramatic' musically. Does it follow that *San Giovanni Chrisostomo* and *Ester* are less dramatic, and *Santa Pelagia* and *Santa Editta* least dramatic of all, as their respective librettos would indicate? The answering of these questions is rendered problematic by the fact that two of the scores are incomplete, both *Ester* and *Santa Editta* calling for ritornellos which are not in the scores.[41] In the extant manuscripts, these two oratorios are accompanied by basso continuo alone, but since Stradella's ritornellos were always played by an orchestra, one is certain that instrumental parts are also missing. The scores were probably copies made for singers who needed only the continuo in order to rehearse. Besides the ritornellos, indications in *Ester* suggest that it lacks some of the closed forms as well.[42] However, even if deciding something about the music of Stradella's remaining oratorios may be problematic, it may at least be attempted.

In greatest contrast with the mature 'operatic' style of *San Giovanni Battista* and *La Susanna* is *Santa Pelagia*. Of the twenty-nine vocal pieces in the oratorio, one is a duet and one is a quartet, and both are extremely contrapuntal. The especially rich texture of the ensembles is maintained in the arias as well, something not typical of the operas. Another indication of Stradella's intent to create a style eminently contrapuntal is to be found in his treatment of the bass-line. Rather than providing a continuous support to the instruments or instruments and voices, the bass adds yet another independent melodic line to the texture, appearing or dropping out irregularly, as it does, for example, in 'Saette e fulmini' where accompaniment is by full orchestra. The bass frequently has rests of one or two bars, apparently so that when it is to respond imitatively to the strings its entry may be more clearly heard. An interesting employment of accompanying continuo instruments, again to achieve maximum diversity from them, is in 'Ah, sfere guerriere'. Here the voice is given one musical line; the harpsichord a different line of continuous triplets; the 'Violone' a third line which, although it follows the harpsichord, is simpler (Ex. 29).

The orchestra of *Santa Pelagia* is composed of two violins, viola, and continuo, but there are also instrumental accompaniments which exclude

---

[41] Twenty-two ritornellos are missing from *Ester*, and 18 from *Santa Editta*, several of which are to be played more than once. Attention was first called to the incompleteness of these scores in Gianturco, 'The Oratorios'.

[42] An aria for Aman and a duet or trio.

Ex. 29.

the viola, and thus there is a greater variety of instrumental forces than one finds in the operas (full orchestra or just continuo). The orchestral music is not easy either, not only because its style is imitative, but also because the parts in themselves are relatively demanding, their rhythm often irregular, and tempos brisk.[43]

Santa Pelagia is not conceived in a dramatic or operatic vocal style either, but rather in a generally lyrical style. Phrases are long, winding their way stepwise, avoiding cadences in order to spin out to greater length and encourage a calmer, cantabile rendition. *Santa Pelagia* is 'lyrical' also in that it is occasionally simply a show-piece for the title-role. At the end of Part I, Pelagia sings a series of four arias ('Quanto è cara, quanto è bella', 'Godo, sì, di gemme e d'ori', 'Sono i crini aurati', 'Le pupille son faville'), interspersed with recitative by the same protagonist alone. The result is one long *scena* for soprano.[44] This is, of course, due to Pelagia's inner conflict at this moment, and her need to express her various states of mind; but for whatever reason, rather than showing connection with opera, the oratorio seems to be a cantata at this point. Even the frequent use of long arioso sections within recitatives is more typical of the latter genre.

The fact that the writing, although not typical of opera, is capable both in the recitatives and closed forms is disconcerting, and makes it impossible to decide that *Santa Pelagia* is an early work simply because it is less dramatic.[45] It may be that here his cast, patron, and librettist—all unknown factors—requested a concert rather than a drama in music.

---

[43] The opening 4-section sinfonia certainly is not Stradella's best instrumental writing, being rather too emphatic and less imaginative than was usual for him. Since it is in a hand different from that which appears in the rest of the only extant manuscript, one wonders if it really is by Stradella. Among other strange characteristics is the dotted figure in the Largo and the balance between the movements, neither of which is typical of Stradella.

[44] Pelagia sings a grand total of 7 arias in Part I and 5 in Part II.

[45] The only extant libretto is from Modena, 1688, after Stradella's death.

Santa Editta presents similar problems of evaluation, but here they are due to the incompleteness of the manuscript. As already stated, the extant score contains only continuo accompaniment,[46] and therefore considerations on the actual texture of the oratorio or its instrumentation[47] are impossible. Discussion must therefore be limited to form and vocal style. Several compositional features would suggest *Santa Editta* to be an early work. First there is the often unclear harmonic movement which gives the impression somewhat of rambling, as do the duet 'Chi può le nostr'alme' and the aria 'Dunque il ciel tanti contenti'. There are also the unadventurous tonic–dominant–tonic modulations which predominate in the closed forms. Such features could indicate that the composer is inexperienced in adopting a tonal language: he is unable to achieve definite direction in his music through chord progressions, and he is confined to simple modulations.

Of course, the plot of *Santa Editta*, with its long academic discourses, not dramatic in any sense of the word, does not call for energetic, incisive, surprising music for its realization. Lyricism suits it best (for example, there is a predominance of the ternary 3/2 metre, usually reserved in opera for amorous/lyrical moments). Recitative, although it sometimes has phrases of repeated notes, gives the general impression of being rather slow due to a more melodic contour. The occasional fioritura, such as in the imitative duet which concludes Part I, 'Chi può le nost'alme', and Editta's 'Così fuggite un piacer quaggiù', is notably long for Stradella, another sign of a tendency to 'sing'. While conceding that the high number of ensembles (nine) was a contribution of the librettist, it must be admitted that the score as a result is for this reason, too, not like the contemporary theatrical musical genre. What is more, Stradella gave them contrapuntal (cantata) settings, much more rewarding for singers than simple (operatic) homophony would have been.

Ester, liberatrice del popolo ebreo, because it too is extant in only an incomplete score lacking ritornellos and possibly closed forms as well, may also be evaluated only partially,[48] considerations on texture or instruments being impossible here as they were for *Santa Editta*. While Stradella once again strove for continuity within a lyrical 'cantata' frame, here his technique appears to be more mature. Although only one aria of the nineteen in the oratorio exhibits a ternary structure, 'No, non disperate', a piece for Speranza Celeste, it is handled in a masterly way. The form which appears in eleven arias and which, therefore, predominates in *Ester*, is that

---

[46] Even this is lacking for the trio 'Mal nato è 'l desire'.

[47] Ten arias and several ensembles call for ritornellos, sections which Stradella always assigns to instruments other than just those in the basso continuo.

[48] Some text is also missing; and no libretto exists for *Ester*.

in two sections. While sometimes this was suggested to the composer by the text (two structurally different strophes of poetry), it is not always the case. Three examples, which constitute a *scena* for Ester in Part I, may be cited as examples of both procedures.

After Ester has been told by her uncle Mardocheo that she must save his life and beg the king, her husband, for mercy, her first reaction is to think of the danger to her own person: she risks disapproval by daring to go before Assuero unsummoned; and then death in declaring to be, as the niece of Mardocheo, a Jewess. But in a series of three arias and recitatives she manages to get control of herself and resolves to be courageous and ask for justice no matter what the consequences. Each of the arias—'Miei fidi mensieri', 'Su dunque a ferire', 'E perché il mio re'—is in two distinct sections. The poet wrote two strophes for each of the three closed forms, structured AA, AB, AB. However, Stradella composed different music for the identically structured as well as non-identically structured strophes (AB, AB, AB), thereby imposing an element of unity on the scene. One should also note the unusual descending modulations effected by Stradella as he passes from one aria to the next: the first is in E minor, the second in B flat major, and the last in A major. It is an extended scene during which Ester presents continually new thoughts, and Stradella tried to reflect these in his music. However, he also strove for unity, even more than was implied in the text.

This long soliloquy for Ester is followed by two choruses for the Jewish people, an SSB trio, 'Deh', pietoso in noi si volga', and an SSABarB quintet, 'Chi da sì gran ruina' (with intervening recitative), both well-developed ensembles of imitative polyphony as are all the ensembles in the oratorio (two trios, one quartet, and one quintet). They continue to the dramatic climax of Aman's refusal to subdue his pride and release Mardocheo, an AB aria which is brisk, bright, and full of interestingly organized fiorituras as he tells Ester to cry ('Piangete pur, piangete'), that her tears mean nothing to him (Ex. 30).

Even with *Ester*'s greater competence in form, tonality, and direction,[49]

Ex. 30.

---

[49] Occasional lapses into 'rambling' are still to be found though, such as one notices in the two arias, separated by recitative, for Esther in Part II when she appears before Assuero, 'Supplicante e prostrata' and 'Se agl'occhi tuoi giammai'.

it is still not a 'dramatic' work: rhythmic insistence, while present in the oratorio (as was seen in 'No, non disperate'), does not characterize *Ester*, nor does the related ostinato. Emphasis is on lyricism, as it was in *Santa Pelagia* and *Santa Editta*; but in *Ester* it is given somewhat more shape than in *Editta* through what would seem to be (allowing that one is judging from incomplete scores) simply Stradella's acquired greater technical skill.

San Giovanni Chrisostomo appears to be from the same period as *Ester, liberatrice del popolo ebreo*, if not actually a bit later, since it too suggests its composer was more competent than *Santa Editta*'s. Immediately evident are the long vocal phrases of generally syllabic music, typically without rests, accompanied by an active continuo in constant eighth- and quarter-notes. Stradella was perhaps compensating for the absence of strings by requesting a more ever-present participation from the existing forces of voice(s) and basso continuo in order to create as full a sound as possible. However, one does not find the rhythm motivically organized, nor are there related ostinato figures either, although there is a tendency towards such organization of material.

At the same time, the da capo form is present in the oratorio and, in fact, four of the fourteen arias and one duet ('Della vita il fragil legno') are well-delineated da capos. Most of the closed forms in the oratorio, however, are through-composed, such as the SST trio 'Benché giuste tempra l'ire' sung by Eudosia's courtiers who urge punishment for Giovanni. A similar striving for continuity is also seen in several scenes, such as the one beginning 'La morte n'addita' for Giovanni (bass) and an unnamed (alto) courtier, during which they expound alternately on the passing of this world's vanities and the joys of death. Directions in the manuscript at the beginning of the scene indicate that it is a 'Solo [bass] aria but taken up immediately by the contralto'. After the two voices have sung, one reads 'Basso subito'; and after him the alto sings again. In this way, the ternary (3/2) metre is not interrupted, but each singer keeps it going by entering immediately. It is an aria, but for two alternating singers.

Similar organization is encountered in Part I, where an SAB trio of courtiers in 'Se teme chi regna' affirms in imitative counterpoint that a coward is not fit to rule. The soprano of the group, in a following solo section (beginning 'Da grave periglio'), insists with lyrical calm that one must not be slow to make decisions; after which the trio is repeated. Now the bass, in a spirited section (beginning 'Rigori prudenti'), argues that it is not always wise to pardon offenders; after which there is a repeat of the same trio.

This same sense of continuity is evident in a large portion of Part II of the oratorio, because little or no recitative separates the closed forms, and there is a build-up to the closing SB duet, 'Giocondo nel mondo chi gode', where for the last time one hears of the joys of death and the strifes of life. This piece is more extended than the other ensembles (in all five duets, three trios, and one quintet): there are 78 measures of 6/8 metre in two strophes of music, a setting where, in addition, embellishments are introduced at the second strophe.

Because of the predominance of aria-style music, and of the quality of the music itself, *San Giovanni Chrisostomo* also shows more affinity with cantatas than with operas. Responsibility for much of the structure of the oratorio must, of course, be shared by the anonymous librettist[50] and Stradella.

As stated earlier, a Latin oratorio from the early part of Stradella's career is lost; an Italian oratorio, from perhaps the end of his life, is also lost. A notice regarding it was found in records of a Florentine confraternity, the Compagnia di S. Bernardino e S. Caterina, dated November 1683, which stated that they had heard a Stradella oratorio about St Catherine.[51] Since the confraternity heard an oratorio about the saint also in 1687 and again in 1690, it is possible that it was the same work by Stradella.[52]

Several Catherines are revered by Christians: Catherine Fieschi of Genoa[53] and Catherine of Siena[54] are two. However, whereas the feast-day of Catherine Fieschi is celebrated on 15 September and that of Catherine of Siena on 30 April, Catherine of Alexandria is honoured on 25 November, and therefore she would most likely have been the subject of the oratorio which the Florentine confraternity heard that month. The legend about this Catherine of Alexandria began in the sixth or seventh century. She was a virgin tortured and decapitated for resisting the advances of the Emperor Maximinus, and her body was buried by the angels on Mount Sinai. Since at the touch of her body the torture wheel fell apart, she was known as Catherine of the Wheel.[55] While no oratorio

---

[50] Possibly Lelio Orsini, since Mandosi, *Biblioteca Romana*, ii. 189 lists a *San Gio. Crisostomo* among his works; however, no libretto has yet come to light.

[51] I-Fas, Comp. rel. sop. 254, no. 3, fo. 89ᵛ, cited by Guasconi, L'Oratorio', p. xxxii and Hill, 'Oratory', 137.   [52] Hill, 'Oratory', 153–4.

[53] Catherine Fieschi (Genoa, 1447–1510), with whose family Stradella was in contact (he dedicated *Le gare dell'amor eroico* to Bianca Maria Spinola Fieschi in 1679), was married to Giuliano Adorno. The marriage of convenience was not happy due to his wayward behaviour, but her religious devotions effected his conversion. They lived thereafter in great simplicity and helped the sick. Catherine wrote a treatise on Purgatory. When her body was exhumed it was intact, and this encouraged devotion to her. She was officially canonized in 1735. (See Fausta Casolini, 'Caterina da Genova', *Enciclopedia Cattolica* (Città del Vaticano, 1949), iii. 1145–8.)

[54] A Dominican nun from the age of 16, Catherine at first worked with the sick; but her greatest efforts were directed at bringing the Pope from Avignon to Rome in 1377. Catherine received the stigmata in 1374; she was canonized in 1471. (See Innocenzo Taurisano and Enzo Carli, 'Caterina da Siena', ibid., 1151–8.)

[55] A. Pietro Frutaz and Giovanni Corandente, 'Caterina d'Alessandria', ibid., 1137–42.

by Stradella on any St Catherine has come to light, there is an anonymous *Oratorio di Santa Caterina* in the Vatican Library (I-Rvat, Barb. lat. 4209) about this very saint, and its supposed librettist, Lelio Orsini, was closely associated with Stradella.[56] If this very score is not his (it has tentatively been attributed both to Luigi Rossi and to Marco Marazzoli), he may have set the same libretto for Florence. However, further evidence is needed before any conclusion may be reached.

In summary, Stradella is known to have composed eight oratorios. In 1667, he wrote a Latin oratorio (now lost, title unknown) for Rome; in 1675 *San Giovanni Battista*, also for Rome; and in 1681 *La Susanna* for Modena. Dates of composition for his other oratorios are not known, but for thirteen years after his death, Stradella's oratorios continued to be performed. They were heard in 1682, 1684, 1687?, 1688, 1690, 1692, 1693, and 1695, a most unusual occurrence in a period when new works were constantly being written. Only performances of *San Giovanni Chrisostomo* and *Ester, liberatrice del popolo ebreo* are undocumented.

[56] See Smither, *History*, 191–4 for a summary of the plot and a discussion of the music. Among Lelio Orsini's works, Mandosi, *Biblioteca Romana*, ii. 189 lists the libretto *Santa Caterina*.

9

Arias, Duets, Trio

Occasionally, single closed forms are extracted from a larger vocal composition, and are found in manuscript sources independent of the complete work. Since such copies are extant today due to a variety of reasons, their number cannot tell us anything certain about the popularity of a work; it is, nevertheless, interesting to notice which Stradella pieces became excerpts.[1] For example, of the four arias from *Il Biante* found separately, one of these—'So ben che mi saettano'—was even published in 1679, and a duet for two sopranos from the same comedy, 'Non sa mai amor ferir', appears in four different sources. Soprano arias from Stradella's operas *La forza dell'amor paterno* and *Le gare dell'amor eroico*, respectively 'Così Amor mi fai languir?' and 'Se nel ben sempre incostante', are each found in five sources. Two arias and two duets from the serenata *Vola, vola in altri petti* also circulated as excerpts, the soprano–bass duet 'La ragion m'assicura' appearing in as many as 11 manuscripts. The number of copies is surpassed only by the soprano–bass duet 'Nel seren dei miei/tuoi contenti' from the oratorio *San Giovanni Battista*, which is found in 13 copies. Without passing judgement on other selections, the inordinately large number of sources containing these last two duets does attest to their appeal. In truth, all excerpts are usually indicative of a desire to perform a favourite composition on its own as chamber music.

In addition to these pieces which Stradella conceived as part of one of his own larger compositions, we possess 36 arias, 13 duets, and one trio which he wrote to isolated texts. Some were intended, either definitely or probably, for insertion into other composers' operas; others seem to have been composed directly as chamber entertainment. Among the examples of theatre music are four arias intended to be used in the 1671 Tordinona presentation of Cavalli's setting of Cicognini's *Il Giasone* (entitled *Il novello Giasone* in Rome). 'Delizie, contenti' for the character Giasone replaced Cavalli's Act I, scene 3 version. Although the role was given in Venice to a contralto and in Rome to a baritone, both composers opted for a simple, ternary-metre (3/2), syllabic setting in D minor, with accompaniment by two violins and basso continuo (Ex. 31).

Two other arias, 'Che mi giovan le vittorie' and 'Dormite, occhi,

---

[1] On all sources, see Gianturco–McCrickard, *Stradella Catalogue*.

Ex. 31.

dormite', were also for Giasone, but their text is not in the earlier libretto
and, therefore, they were written especially to be inserted during the
Rome presentation of the opera (I. 3 and III. 14 respectively). Both arias
are furnished with string accompaniment, but in the second aria this
assumes theatrical relevance. In this particular scene, the comic servant
Demo has been sent by his master to kill Giasone. He decides to see if,
by playing the violin, he can make the prince fall asleep so that he can
attack him more easily. It is to his playing that Giasone sings 'Dormite,
occhi, dormite' (Sleep, eyes, sleep), a true violin–voice duet. When
Giasone finally sleeps, Demo is tempted to break the violin over his
head![2] 'Destatevi, o sensi, risvegliati, onore', on the other hand, is a new,
additional aria for the character Isifile (II. 14).[3]

Because three other arias are found in sources which contain Stradella's
prologues and intermezzos, it is assumed that they were also intended to
be inserted in other composers' operas. They are 'Chi mi disse che amor
dà tormento', 'Torna, Amor', and 'Deh, vola, o desio', the last written
over a bass-line which, because of its motivic organization, is almost an
ostinato (Ex. 32). The employment of string ritornellos in the contralto
aria 'Speranze smarrite' and the duet 'Aure fresche, aure volanti' for
mezzo-soprano and baritone, typical of larger genres (operas, oratorios,
cantatas), gives support to the supposition that they, too, are part of a
more complex composition.[4]

The soprano–baritone duet *Ardo, sospiro e piango*, although its text is

---

[2] The entire scene for Demo and Giasone, beginning with the text 'Dovunque il pie' rivolgo' and
composed of recitative, the aria 'Dormite, occhi, dormite', and more recitative, had been added to
Cavalli's opera for the production in Rome. In the original libretto of 1649, a recitative begins
'Ovunque il pie' rivolgo', but the rest of the text is not the same, nor does it introduce an aria.

[3] Jander, 'Prologues', 96 read the title as '. . . *risvegliatevi*'.

[4] For the Rome 1672 production of Cesti's setting of Apolloni's *La Dori*, Stradella wrote the prologue *Dormi, Titone, addio*. Several new arias were added to the opera and it is likely that Stradella
composed them, too, even though his settings have not as yet come to light. As listed at the end of
the libretto, they are entitled: 'Se l'anima mia'; 'Regio manto'; 'Si prepari le cadute'; 'Ch'io più creda
alla fortuna'; 'O costanza gradita'; 'O Bagoa, sei pazzo a fe'; 'Dolcissime pene, ch'il cor m'affigete';
'All'armi, o pensieri, ch'il nume d'amore'; 'D'ogni duol mi prendo gioco'; 'Non vi credo, speranze
bugiarde'. An added duet was 'Celinda, tu non degni?'.

Ex. 32.

from Nicolò Minato's opera *Artemisia* (set by Cavalli in 1662), was probably not composed for insertion in the opera, because in the original libretto the text is assigned to the single character Artemisia as an aria: the plot would not have allowed her first-person words to be expressed by two people.[5] Luigi Rossi was attracted to Minato's distinctive words and, earlier than Stradella, considered them suitable for a chamber duet.[6] One is tempted to say that Stradella knew Rossi's setting, especially because both versions use dotted rhythms, a feature which is not typical of Stradella (Ex. 33). However, Rossi's attention is directed to the voice and to creating a lovely musical sound, whereas Stradella is preoccupied with having the text understood. His duet presents the voices in continual imitation, in a sectional composition organized with internal repetitions of a 35-measure section beginning 'Che farci poss'io'.

In fact, imitation is the prevalent technique also in Stradella's chamber duets and trio composed to text not apparently taken from a larger work, and, as in the example cited, it sometimes dominates the closed form. For example, *La bellissima speranza che nutrisce*[7] is in four sections which alternate binary and ternary metres, but in each section the soprano and bass are in imitation. *Sarà ver ch'io mai disciolga*, instead, is in two strophes, but here again the soprano and bass are in constant imitation. *Trionfate, invitti colli*, Stradella's only chamber trio (its single source is an autograph), is also organized on the principle of imitation. Its two strophes of poetry, one of five lines and the other of six lines, have been translated into the expected two-section composition (AB). Both musical sections offer continual imitation for the two sopranos and bass, imitation in which the two violins and basso continuo also participate. The richness of the resulting texture suits the words of praise for 'il sol clemente' (the clement sun), also referred to as 'la stella' (the star): in other words Emilio

[5] The opening sentiments 'I desire, I sigh, and I cry' are common in musical literature although the exact words are not so common. Perhaps the first to write them was Remigio Fiorentino in a poem he published in his *Rime* (Venice, 1546). It could be that Minato was referring to Fiorentino when he began Artemisia's aria. After the opening line, Minato's text does not, however, continue to follow Fiorentino.

[6] I-Nc, c.I.1, fos. 69[r]–72[v], but incomplete.

[7] This duet is also to be found in the sources as *La dolcissima speranza*; in these cases the opening music is an embellished version of *La bellissima speranza*.

Altieri, Pope Clement X, who had stars in his coat of arms. Since he reigned from 1670 to 1676, the trio must have been composed during these years.

Other Stradella chamber duets, although they rely on imitation when both voices are present, alternate such sections with those for just one voice. *Fulmini quanto sa quel sembiante* for soprano, bass, and continuo offers much two-part vocal music, but also a section for each of the voices alone. *Occhi belli, e che sarà del mio duol* has music a 2, then a 1 for one of

Ex. 33.

the sopranos, next a 2, a 1 for the other soprano, and lastly a 2. *Dietro l'orme del desio* also begins a 2, then has an a 1 section for soprano, an a 1 section for contralto, and then closes with both voices singing again together.

Clearly there is no single musical structure which Stradella preferred or which seems to have been imposed on him either by contemporary taste or by the text. As a matter of fact, it is not apparent why one plan (continual imitation, or alternation of ensemble music with solo music) was

Ex. 33. *(cont.)*

used instead of another. The closed poetic form which served as the basis for a chamber duet or trio expresses the sentiments of one person, and could just as easily have been set as an aria. The number of singers to participate in its expression was, therefore, not predetermined by the poet.

Stradella's composition of chamber arias is documented not only through his music but also through letters. In July 1676, Settimio Olgiati was, as usual during Stradella's Roman years, strengthening the young musician's contact with the Venetian Polo Michiel. Apparently Michiel had asked for some of Stradella's music, and Olgiati had passed on the request. Before composing, however, Stradella wanted to know 'what little aria [*arietta*] does he mean and therefore to send the words of the aria'.[8] Stradella himself later wrote to Michiel that he had possibilities to do chamber music in Genoa,[9] which could also mean the composition of vocal music. Stradella's clearest reference to the genre, however, is in his letter to Michiel of 11 June 1678. In it he responded to the Venetian's interest in *canzoni*, saying that he will send him some of his own as well as pieces by Lonati; if Michiel wants, he can also ask friends in Rome to send him theirs. Later on in the same letter Stradella returns to the *canzoni*, and asks if Michiel wants 'little arias [*ariette*] or chamber cantatas', and whether he wants them 'long, bizarre [i.e. unusual or amusing], or even sad'.[10]

Stradella's phrase confirms that the cantata and the aria are two distinct genres.[11] What is more, arias to be found singly in music sources exhibit the same formal characteristics as those incorporated into cantatas, operas, and oratorios. The simplest structures are those composed either of a repeated strophe, as one finds in the soprano–continuo arias *Chi avesse visto un core* and *S'Amor m'annoda il piede*; or of two different sections (AB), as in *Non fia mai, ah no, ch'io speri* (S, bc); or of two different sections but with a repeat of the opening (ABA), as in *Quanto è bella la mia stella* (S, bc); or of three different sections (ABC), as in *Il mio cor che è infelicissimo* (S, bc). One also finds examples of arias which have an *intercalare*, some repeated phrase or section: for example, in *Fedeltà sinché spirto in petto avrò* and *Da Filinda aver chi può* (both S, bc) the opening phrase is presented three times which results in an ABACA structure. This same plan is extended further in *Adorata libertà, dal mio core non partir* (S, bc) to become ABA'CA'ABA.

The subject of Stradella's chamber arias is always love. 'Eyes' as representing the beloved, so frequent in baroque poetry, are clearly the point of

---

[8] Olgiati's letter to Michiel in I-Vmc, PD C. 1063, no. 146.

[9] Letter of 30 Apr. 1678 from Stradella to Michiel: I-Vmc, PD C. 1065, no. 218 (no. 11 in App. 2*a*).

[10] I-Vmc, PD C. 1065, no. 260 (no. 12 in App. 2*a*).

[11] For a more detailed analysis of the question, see Gianturco, 'The Seventeenth-Century Cantata'.

reference in pieces such as *Avete torto, occhi miei cari*; *Begl'occhi, il vostro piangere*; and *Le luci vezzose volgetemi, o Clori*. The constraints of love, their making a prisoner of the lover, are noted among other arias in *Bel tempo, addio, son fatto amante*; *S'Amor m'annoda il piede*; and *Adorata libertà, dal mio core non partir*. Occasionally the text is more ambitious and imaginative, such as that of *Deh, frenate i furori* which compares love to a storm and shipwreck, where the suffering heart has need of a quiet port. It is also possible to find examples of a lighter treatment of love: in *Pria di scior quel dolce nodo* someone (Silvio?) tells Filli to wait before breaking the knot which ties their hearts. However, if she decides to try other 'chains', since he has managed to live without his heart, he won't die with it back!

As is usual for Stradella, his treatment of the voice in these chamber arias is generally syllabic with some use made of fioritura 'madrigalisms' on appropriate words. Especially interesting is the behaviour of the instrumental bass. In most cases it is an active collaborator with the voice, a true partner in making the music. Examples such as *Quanto è bella la mia stella* (Ex. 34) and *Parti, fuggi dal mio seno* (Ex. 35) encourage one to

Ex. 34.

believe that, in an intimate gathering of aristocratic friends and acquaintances, it would have been quite possible to accompany the voice with just lute, harp, or violone/cello. Since Stradella is known to have possessed three lutes at his death, one can imagine that he himself often accompanied singers of his chamber vocal music.

Ex. 35.

Par-ti,   fug-gi   fug-gi dal mio se-no   par-ti,   fug-gi

fug-gi dal mio se-no

10

Madrigals

As the seventeenth century wore on, fewer madrigals were written in comparison with those of the previous century. However, the genre did not die out[1] and poetry manuals continued to discuss it. For example, in 1691 Giuseppe Gaetano Salvadori wrote in his treatise: 'The Madrigal is a short [piece of] poetry, which is contained in a single stanza of six, eight, or ten verses, or more if the Author likes, and with those corresponding rhymes, which in the same way please him.'[2] However, he counselled the would-be author of madrigals not to leave any line unrhymed. As for the subject of the poetry, it could be anything at all.[3] The texts of Stradella's four a 5 independent madrigals usually conform to Salvadori's definition.

Piangete, occhi dolenti has six lines and his other three madrigals—*Clori, son fido amante*; *Pupillette amorose*; *Tirsi un giorno piangea*—have eight lines. All are a mixture of 7- and 11-syllable lines. Rhyme-schemes range from strict couplets in *Pupillette amorose* to a more interesting interlinking structure in *Tirsi un giorno piangea*. In each case the subject is love denied, twice by Filli, once by Clori, and once by a beloved affectionately called 'little loving eyes'. The treatment is always uncomplicated, unmanneristic, and typical of early, light madrigals.

Similar to these pieces are the ones that appear in Stradella's larger vocal compositions, each time called a madrigal. At the end of his Christmas cantata *Ah! troppo è ver* is a 6-line poem, 'Or che luci sì belle', intended as a general moralistic conclusion in praise of the eternal lights of heaven. Concluding the cantata *Lo schiavo liberato* is a 6-line madrigal, 'Quanto fu vergognoso', which applauds Rinaldo's decision to quit the pleasures of Armida and return to a life of virtue and soldiering.

These examples follow a practice quite typical of seicento oratorios which often ended with a didactic moralistic madrigal. At the same time, a much shorter and atypical example is to be found in one of Stradella's

---

[1] See Gloria Rose, 'Polyphonic Italian Madrigals of the Seventeenth Century', *Music and Letters*, 47 (1966), 153–9; Frederick Albert Hall, 'The Polyphonic Italian Madrigal: 1638 to 1745' (Ph.D. diss., University of Toronto, 1978), and Margaret Mabbett, 'The Italian Madrigal 1620–1655' (Ph.D. thesis, King's College, London, 1989).

[2] *Poetica toscana all'uso Dove con brevità, e chiarezza s'insegna il modo di comporre ogni Poesia, cioè Sonetti, Canzoni, Madrigali, Ottave rime, Poemi Eroici, Tragedie, Commedie, et anco per Musica* (Naples, 1691), 35.

[3] Both remarks are on p. 36.

own oratorios, *San Giovanni Battista*. Also called a madrigal, the text has only three lines of poetry, and they appear not at the end of the oratorio but during the course of Part I. Here, in 'Dove, Battista, dove?', John the Baptist's disciples worry about his decision to go to Herod's court 'where only deceit and thievery reign'.

At the end of Stradella's cantata *L'accademia d'Amore*, the character Amor, acting as judge in a debate between Beauty and Courtesy, is lauded as an 'erudite master' in 'Dotto maestro è Amore'. The 'madrigal' is again a general moralistic affirmation, albeit less serious than the examples cited thus far. The madrigals which end the two versions of the cantata *Il Damone* are similarly 'amorous'. They are both general comments about fate which creates lovers, and are thereby closer in subject to traditional Renaissance madrigals.

All of these examples, both those found as independent madrigals and as integral parts of larger vocal works, are for five voices, except the one in *Lo schiavo liberato* which is for four voices. The poems of Stradella's remaining madrigals are four independent compositions which are set for only three voices. *È pur giunta, mia vita* has the simplest and most regular text, the declaration of a lover reluctant to take leave of his beloved. *Sperai nella partita*, a madrigal of seven lines, a less common structure, could have been intended as a sequel to *È pur giunta*, since a lover laments that departure has not lessened his pain. Another 7-line madrigal, *Colpo de' bei vostr'occhi è la mia piaga*, presents a lover in the first enthusiastic flush of passion and begging for a kiss.

However, these texts—as well as those Stradella set for five voices—pale by comparison with that of his remaining a 3 madrigal, another one which has to do with kissing. *Feritevi, ferite* is by Giovan Battista Marino, and was published first in Venice in 1602, in Part 2 of *Le Rime* as no. 8 in the section 'Madrigali e Canzoni' where it is entitled 'Guerra di baci'.[4] It was soon set to music and the list of printed settings is impressive.[5] It was neither the unusual length of nine 7- and 11-syllable lines nor the interesting but yet not exceptional rhyme-scheme which attracted attention; rather, it was Marino's marvellous manneristic skill with words:

Feritevi, ferite	Wound yourselves, wound,
viperette mordaci,	biting little snakes,
dolci guerriere ardite	sweet arduous warriors
del Diletto, e d'Amor bocche sagaci!	of Delight, and wise mouths of Love!
Saettatevi pur, vibrate ardenti	Throw arrows at yourselves too, thrust burning

---

[4] p. 447.
[5] For a catalogue of printed settings of all of Marino's poetry, see Roger Simon and D. Gidrol, 'Appunti sulla relazione tra l'opera poetica di G. B. Marino e la musica del suo tempo', *Studi seicenteschi*, 14 (1973), 81–7.

l'armi vostre pungenti!	your piercing weapons!
Ma le morti sian vite,	But let deaths be lives,
ma le guerre sian paci,	but let wars be peace,
sian saette le lingue e piaghe i baci.	tongues be swords, and kisses be sores.[6]

Marino's exhortation to those 'sweet arduous warriors of Delight', the lips, to wound and be wounded is a mastery of metaphor, its sense made still more delightfully ambiguous at first hearing through tripping rhythms and syllables which are repeated but with new sense: note the use, for example, of *vi* in lines 1–2 where it first means wound 'yourselves' and then immediately after is the beginning of 'little snakes'; and in line 5 where it first means throw arrows at 'yourselves' and then is the beginning of 'thrust'. The language is concise, the tempo lively, superbly suitable for a situation where one pleads 'but let deaths be lives, but let wars be peace, tongues be swords, and kisses be sores'.[7]

Charles Burney, who possessed *Piangete, occhi dolenti*, as well as the score of *San Giovanni Battista*, considered Stradella's madrigals (together with those of Marenzio and Alessandro Scarlatti) 'learned and pleasing in modulation, and more fanciful and agreeable in the traits of melody that are used as subjects of imitation'.[8] In fact, he felt that Stradella was one of only a handful of composers after Domenico Mazzocchi who distinguished themselves as madrigalists.[9] He singled out the *Battista* madrigal as being 'truly admirable' and discussed it in the following terms: 'It begins with eight or ten bars of excellent counterpoint, in which is a very early, if not the first, use of the extreme sharp sixth; and then bursts into a fugue on two excellent subjects, which are reversed and otherwise admirably treated. Except Handel's, I never saw a better vocal chorus, for its length.'[10] David Allen, who edited Stradella's 5-part independent madrigals, considers them 'a charming Baroque view of a Renaissance style'.[11]

In his madrigals, as in all his music, Stradella shows himself to be an able contrapuntalist, as both Burney and Allen noted. In true cinquecento polyphonic fashion, point after point is presented and imitated usually at the fifth above or fourth below, or at the octave or unison, and most commonly a voice enters before the previous one has completed the point. What is new and peculiar to the seicento is Stradella's completely tonal

---

[6] The translation is mine.

[7] For other considerations on the text and also on Stradella's setting, see Gian Paolo Minardi, 'G. B. Marino e il madrigale *Feritevi, ferite viperette* di Stradella', in Carolyn Gianturco and Giancarlo Rostirolla (eds.), *Atti del Convegno di studi 'Alessandro Stradella e il suo tempo', Siena, 8–12 settembre 1982, Chigiana*, 39, NS 19 (1988), 191–200.

[8] Burney, *General History*, ii. 749.   [9] ii. 421.   [10] ii. 578.

[11] 'The Five-Part Madrigals of Stradella', in Carolyn Gianturco and Giancarlo Rostirolla (eds.), *Atti del Convegno di studi 'Alessandro Stradella e il suo tempo', Siena, 8–12 settembre 1982, Chigiana*, 39, NS 19 (1988), 189.

language. The 14 pieces are divided equally between major and minor keys: F major is used for both *Feritevi, ferite* and *Clori, son fido amante*, and D major for *Colpo de' bei vostr'occhi* and 'Or che luci sì belle', whereas C major, E major, and A major are used only once; the minor keys employed are D (three times), E, F, G, and A.[12] All madrigals modulate, some only to the dominant such as *Colpo de' bei vostr'occhi*, but usually to more keys, as *Piangete, occhi dolenti* which also vacillates between modes as it proceeds from E minor to G major, B minor, D major, A minor, C major, and G major, to end up at the opening key but with the third raised. By contrast, in 'Or che luci sì belle' and *Feritevi, ferite* only major keys are touched upon: D, A, G, D, B, A, D and F, G, D, F respectively. In short, all the madrigals, in whatever key and exhibiting whatever modulations, are clear proof of Stradella's competent handling of tonality, as well as his mastery of the polyphonic tradition.

In addition, he is interested in interpreting and communicating the meaning of the poetry. First, the settings are syllabic with an occasional fioritura only on words such as 'love' or 'death', thus allowing for comprehension of the words. Secondly, musical structure takes its cue from the texts. For example, *Sperai nella partita* is separated into two sections: lines 1–4 express what had been the lover's hopes; lines 5–7 his desperation. Stradella follows the same structure, repeating the text for lines 1–4 twice, and that of lines 5–7 twice. In *E' pur giunta, mia vita* the structure is similar: in lines 1–4 the lover states his situation, and in lines 5–6 his feelings about it; and Stradella maintains the division, repeating each part twice.

Marino's *Feritevi, ferite* offers another structure, presenting its ideas in three couplets until the closing three lines which are a separate group: in lines 1–2 the lips are told what to do, in lines 3–4 they are described, in lines 5–6 they are again told what to do, and in lines 7–9 there is a series of conclusions. Here again Stradella follows the poet: lines 1–2 are maintained as a unit, and are repeated three times; lines 3–4 are another section, and the text is stated twice; lines 5–6 comprise the next section, and are repeated three times. While the three concluding lines of text do comprise the final section of music, Stradella varied his pattern of repeating all the text of a section equally and stated line 7 only once and lines 8-9 twice.

The number of times a line of verse is stated is an indication of Stradella's personal understanding of the text. *Tirsi un giorno piangea* opens with a description of Tirsi crying (l. 1) as well as the reason for his tears (l. 2). Stradella states both verses twice, but he then offers what he considers the more important line 2 twice more. Tirsi's desperation, his wanting to pull Cupid's arrow from his breast (ll. 3–5), is stated only

---

[12] To accommodate the *chiavette* system of clefs used, Allen transposed both *Tirsi* and *Pupillette* down a third in his edition, *Alessandro Stradella: Four Madrigals for Five Voices* (London, 1981).

once; whereas the distraught lover's longing for 'sweet repose' is seen by Stradella as a focal point of the text and he states it three times. Although each line in *Colpo de' bei vostr'occhi* is treated as an entity by Stradella, he states the opening text—the true subject of the poem ('your eyes') and the reason for the lover's plight—three times before going on. In *Clori, son fido amante* line 4, with the reason why the lover is desperate (because Clori won't pity him), is stated more than any other.

Stradella's independent madrigals are seventeenth-century musical settings of a sixteenth-century poetical genre. The texts are not outstanding examples of what poets were capable of, with the exception of Marino's *Feritevi, ferite*, but they are certainly no worse than what other composers set. Stradella gave them adequate attention, revealing competence in counterpoint and tonality, and his usual attention to text. For whom they were written is not known. One expects that they were composed on request for performance by aristocratic dilettantes and the professionals in their employ, perhaps at meetings of academies with musical interests.[13] The indication 'a Tavolino' which appears on the scores certainly implies that they were performed in the manner of earlier madrigals, that is with the singers seated about a table. Judging from the large number of extant sources in England, Stradella's independent madrigals—from the short, 44-measure *È pur giunta, mia vita* to the longer 104-measure *Piangete, occhi dolenti* and 110-measure *Tirsi un giorno piangea*—continued to be performed, probably in the same manner, into the eighteenth century. In fact, both *Clori, son fido amante* and *Piangete, occhi dolenti* were apparently sung at the first meeting of the Academy of Ancient Music held at the Crown Tavern in London in 1726.[14]

The scoring for the a 5 settings, even those which are part of larger works, is SSATB, except for *Pupillette amorose*, which is SSMezAT. 'Quanto fu vergognoso' from *Lo schiavo liberato* is SATB; two of the four a 3 madrigals are set for SSB, whereas *Colpo de' bei vostr'occhi* is for SAB and *È pur giunta, mia vita* for SAT. Two of the madrigals have alternative endings. Those for *Feritevi, ferite* offer a choice between a high and syllabic setting or a lower more florid one. In *Pupillette amorose* the difference is mainly one of texture: one ending proceeds in the same regular, quarter-note pattern as the rest of the madrigal, continuing to present the point of imitation already introduced for the last phrase of text; the other offers eight measures during which the four lower voices are in imitation while the upper part reiterates only the note b' in long sustained tones.

Except for *Pupillette amorose*, all of the madrigals have continuo

[13] Domenico Dal Pane, a successful castrato and Maestro di Cappella of the Sistine Chapel from 1669 to 1679, had some of his madrigals performed at the musical academy founded by Abbatini: see Wolfgang Witzenmann's article on Dal Pane in *The New Grove*.

[14] For information on all of Stradella's sources, see Gianturco–McCrickard, *Stradella Catalogue*.

accompaniment.[15] On the score of *Clori, son fido amante* one reads, 'with Basso Continuo if one wants to sing with a harpsichord'. This is surprising since the part is not simply a basso seguente, but obviously Stradella intended to be helpful to those who either preferred or needed instrumental support as they sang. Other independent continuo parts are furnished for *Piangete, occhi dolenti, Sperai nella partita,* and *È pur giunta, mia vita*; whereas the remaining works have simply basso seguente lines.[16] In either case, whether to use continuo or not would seem to have been a choice left to the performers, since the works are satisfying even a cappella.

[15] The phrase 'senza Instromenti' written on sources for *Clori, son fido amante* and *Tirsi un giorno piangea* does not refer to the basso continuo, but means that the madrigals were not scored for instruments other than the continuo and that, moreover, they were intended to be performed without instruments doubling the vocal parts.

[16] The basso continuo part of *Tirsi un giorno piangea* is not complete, but as it begins with rests one assumes it was not a continuous independent support but simply a basso seguente.

11

Sacred Vocal Music with Latin Texts

No settings of complete liturgical services—Mass, Vespers, Compline, or others—are to be found among Stradella's sacred music with Latin text, but there are 18 settings of single Latin texts: some are to words which occur in the liturgy; others have texts which, even though they may refer to a particular feast-day, are non-liturgical motets.[1]

Of the four liturgical settings, *Ave regina coelorum* is a Marian antiphon invoking the Virgin in her role as Queen of Heaven, and is used at Compline from 2 February to Wednesday of Holy Week. *Tantum ergo* expresses veneration and is sung whenever there is Benediction of the Blessed Sacrament, for example at that most popular devotion of Forty Hours[2] favoured by the Jesuits and Filippo Neri as a way of encouraging devotion to Christ in the Eucharist. The text of *Benedictus dominus Deus* is the Canticle Zacharias sang when his son, the future John the Baptist, was born.[3] It is called for in the liturgy at various times: at Lauds on Christmas and on Maundy Thursday; at the Office for the Dead; and at Burial Services.

The biblical text of *Vau: Et egressus est* is from the Old Testament Book of Lamentations.[4] The Lamentations were sung at Tenebrae (Matins and Lauds) on Maundy Thursday, Good Friday, and Holy Saturday. Each verse or group of verses begins with a Hebrew letter (*Aleph*, *Beth*, *Ghimel*, *Daleth*, *He*, *Vau*, and so forth). Stradella's motet indicates that it is for 'il Mercordi Santo', meaning that it was for the Maundy Thursday service traditionally anticipated the previous afternoon. It is specifically for the Second Lesson of the First Nocturn of Matins and offers the sixth, seventh, eighth, and ninth verses (beginning respectively *Vau*, *Zain* (omitted in the score but intended), *Heth*, and *Teth*) of the first poem in the

---

[1] For recent discussions of what constitutes a motet, see for example Anthony M. Cummings, 'Towards an Interpretation of the Sixteenth-Century Motet', *Journal of the American Musicological Society*, 34 (1981), 43–59, and Jerome Roche, 'Alessandro Grandi: A Case Study in the Choice of Texts for Motets', *Journal of the Royal Musical Association*, 113 (1988), 274–305.

[2] This is a service which commemorates Christ's period in the tomb by exposing a consecrated Host in a monstrance for forty hours.

[3] As reported in Luke 1.

[4] This is a collection of five poems traditionally attributed to Jeremiah (but no longer believed to be by him) lamenting the destruction of Jerusalem in 586 BC and the subsequent ruin and exile of its people.

Book, plus the verse 'Jerusalem, Jerusalem, convertere ad Dominum Deum tuum' which concludes liturgical readings.

Stradella's remaining sacred works have non-liturgical texts, and four of these were written by the composer himself. They suggest he had a good formal education and was familiar with classical Latin literature.[5] He intended each motet for a different occasion. *Care Jesu suavissime* is in honour of Filippo Neri, who was 'entirely devoted to the love of charity', and was perhaps intended to be sung on the saint's feast-day, 26 May. Stradella's call to sinners to kneel before Mary in *Dixit angelis suis iratus Deus* is suitable for performance at any of the Virgin's feasts, whereas *Exultate in Deo, fideles* is for Christmas and effectively describes the ills of the world which the star of Jesus dispelled. The opening seven words of *O vos omnes, qui transitis per viam* are to be found in Responsory 5 of Matins and Antiphon 1 of Lauds on Holy Saturday, but the text which follows is Stradella's own, mainly a tribute to the gentle qualities of Jesus and an invitation to celebrate Him in joyous song.

The rest of Stradella's motet texts are anonymous. *Convocamini, congregamini* and *Sinite lacrimari, sinite lamentari* are both for the feast of Mary's Immaculate Conception:[6] in *Convocamini* the Devil fears that his power will be weakened by Mary, conceived without sin, who will be the 'medicine' and 'protection' of all men; and in *Sinite lacrimari*, all is light and joy due to her immaculate conception, and everyone is urged to put his trust in her. *Nascere virgo potens* commemorates Mary's birth celebrated on 8 September, and ends with a call to sing her praises. In *In tribulationibus, in angustiis*, also dedicated to Mary, she is metaphorically referred to as a 'mountain', as she often is in Christian poetry, to which 'mountain of delights, . . . of succour, . . . of justice, . . . of charity' all peoples are called.[7] *Sistite sidera, coeli motus otiamini*, with its affirmation that all creatures sing the triumph of Mary, is intended to be used generally 'For feasts of the Blessed Virgin Mary', as the Modena source declares. *Plaudite vocibus* encourages great rejoicing and singing for the feast of Easter, whereas *Oh maiestas aeterna* is a soul's passionate desire for the peace resulting from Christ's birth. *Locutus est Dominus de nube ignis* would seem to be a soliloquy by an unnamed female saint and was probably intended for her feast-day. *Surge, cor meum* is a multi-purpose motet with its general plea to the soul not to languish but to rise up.

Fortunately, we know exactly what occasion prompted Stradella's motet

---

[5] See App. 2c. for a transcription of Stradella's motet texts as well as English translations of them.

[6] Although the doctrine stating that Mary was not touched with Original Sin was officially defined only in 1854 by Pope Pius IX in his encyclical *Ineffabilis Deus*, it was popularly believed by Christians from the 9th century on and celebrated regularly on 8 Dec. beginning in the 11th century.

[7] The wording of the text makes one wonder if it refers to an actual place, perhaps called 'Mount', or whether it has to do with height in some way, as would be the Sanctuario di S. Maria dell'Assunzione in the Chigi town of Ariccia.

Pugna, certamen, militia est vita humana. When Angelica—of the respected Roman family Lante with whom the boy Alessandro, his brother Stefano, and their mother had lived—became a nun in the convent of SS. Domenico e Sisto in 1675, the event was celebrated with a Latin dialogue set by Stradella (the poet is unknown): Maria Christina (Angelica's name as a nun) vies with and wins over the Flesh, the World, and the Devil.[8]

As for the music of these sacred works, Stradella accompanied nine of them with basso continuo alone.[9] Of these, four are for solo voice, four are for two voices, and one is for three voices. Eight compositions have parts for two violins in addition to the continuo: four such works are for solo voice, while there is a single setting each for two, three, five, and six voices. Singularly, *Pugna, certamen* has an even larger instrumental ensemble of concertino and concerto grosso to accompany the four singers.

Stradella's sacred Latin works may be divided into three stylistic categories, each category indicating a different compositional approach: either a 'polyphonic approach', a 'duet–trio approach', or a 'cantata approach'. These were not unique to him alone, but they have not previously been described or given specific terms. That showing most connection with traditional church music is the 'polyphonic approach', and Stradella used it appropriately to set two well-known and beloved liturgical texts, *Ave regina coelorum* and *Tantum ergo*, scoring both for soprano, alto, and continuo. The antiphon is divided into two sections, the first in binary metre (26 measures) and the second (beginning 'Gaude virgo gloriosa') in ternary metre (95 measures). *Tantum ergo* follows the same plan, first a binary section (27 measures), then a ternary section (beginning 'Genitori genitoque'; of 64 measures). Within each section of the motets, however, there is continuous imitation between the voices. True, it is in the seicento lyrical style, very florid and demanding vocally; and the phrases are made up of typically short, rhythmic figures (Ex. 36). However, the continuous flow and overlapping of the two voices is reminiscent of earlier cinquecento practice.

The second approach is that wherein solo sections are alternated with those for more parts. This is the usual practice in contemporary chamber duets and trios and two of Stradella's Latin compositions are of this type. For two sopranos, bass, two violins, and continuo, the motet *Sinite lacrimari* opens with a long, florid, imitative section for the two upper voices accompanied with continuo alone. Next, sixteenth-note phrases by

---

[8] On the score her surname is given as 'Lanti'. For a similar event, see payments made for musicians who performed when a girl of the Chigi family became a nun in 1675: I-Rvat, Arch. Chigi, 2687.

[9] For complete details on the scoring of Stradella's motets, see Gianturco–McCrickard, *Stradella Catalogue*.

Ex. 36.

only one soprano are shared through imitation with the two violins (beginning 'Conturbantur dissipantur'); a bass voice and continuo section ('Optata sum spirata') follows; then a section for all three voices and continuo ('Tota pulchra speciosa'); again for bass and continuo ('Sub immani servitute'); now for the second soprano and strings ('Inter homines et caelum'). A soprano, bass, and continuo section ('Tellus gaude orbis plaude') and a section for all three voices and continuo ('Vox iucunda laude munda') conclude the motet. Throughout, binary and ternary metres alternate. The florid style announced at the beginning is maintained, as is the principle of imitation. The only difference between this work and a chamber trio is the language of its text. The canticle *Benedictus dominus Deus* exhibits the same characteristics, although on a somewhat smaller scale since it is for soprano and alto only, and has only continuo accompaniment.

The overwhelming majority of 14 of Stradella's extant sacred Latin compositions, however, follow a 'cantata approach'. For one voice (*Vau: Et egressus; O vos omnes qui transitis; Dixit angelis; Exultate in Deo, fideles; Sistite sidera; Surge, cor meum; Plaudite vocibus; Locutus est Dominus de nube ignis*), or two (*Care Jesu; O maiestas aeterna*), three (*Nascere virgo*), four (*Pugna, certamen, militia est vita*), or five voices (*In tribulationibus, in angustiis*), as well as five solo voices plus an added 'ripieno' soprano part (*Convocamini, congregamini*); and with simply continuo accompaniment or with two additional parts for violins or a still fuller concertino–concerto grosso ensemble, these works—liturgical and not—all offer an alternation of recitative with closed musical forms.

To understand what sort of Latin poetry would encourage the application of a 'cantata approach', the motet *In tribulationibus, in angustiis cordis mei* may be examined in some detail.

In tribulationibus,	In the tribulations,
in angustiis cordis mei,	in the difficulties of my heart,
levavi oculos meos in montem,	I lifted my eyes toward the mount
unde venit auxilium mihi.	from which my help came.
5 Mons iste qualis est?	What is this mountain like?
Dicito mihi, qualis est?	Tell me what it is like,
Ut in opportunitatibus meis	so that [I may] in my need
petam auxilium mihi.	ask help for myself.
Mons iste	This mountain is
10 inter omnes sublimior,	highest above all,
inter omnes excelsior,	raised up above all,
omnes excedens	exceeding all other
altitudine montes.	mountains in height.
Narra mihi	Tell me
15 qualis est iste mons,	what is this mountain,
cuius altitudo	whose altitude
omnes trascendit montes.	goes beyond all other mountains.
Mons iste	This mountain
in vertice montium	first among mountains
20 Maria est,	is Mary,
quia altitudo Mariae	because the sublimity of Mary
supra omnes sanctos refulsit.	outshines all the saints.
Ad montem venite,	Come to the mountain,
accurrite gentes!	run, all people!
25 Non fructus doloris,	Not fruits of pain,
sed cibos dulcoris,	but sweet food
gustabitis vitae.	of life will you taste.
Ad montem venite.	Come to the mountain.
Ad floridum montem,	To the flowering mountain,
30 o filia Sion,	O daughter of Sion,
ad gratos lepores,	to enjoyable pleasures,
ad thuris odores,	to the scents of incense,
ad balsami fontem,	to the fountains of balsam,
ad floridum montem.	to the flowering mountain.
35 Hic spirant leniter	Here breathe lightly
et flant suaviter	and blow gently
aurae dulces, aurae molles,	the sweet breezes, the soft breezes,

	aurae laetae Zeffiri.	the fecund breezes of Zephyr.
	Ubique mel, ubique flos,	Everywhere honey, everywhere flowers,
40	ubique fluit celestis ros.	everywhere heavenly dew is displayed.

O mons delitiarum,
o mons auxilii,
o mons, iustus es,
iustitiae sol.

O mountain of delights,
O mountain of succour,
O mountain of what is right,
sun of justice.

45 Pro nobis ipsum deprecare
nostra salus, nostra spes,
si charitatis mons Maria tu es.

Pray to him for us,
you are our salvation, our hope,
our mountain of charity, Mary.

O gratum montem,
o caeli fontem,
50 non spinae dolentes,
sed rosae rubentes,
tuam regalem
coronant frontem,
o gratum montem.

O pleasing mountain,
o fountain of heaven,
not painful thorns,
but red roses
crown your
royal forehead.
O pleasing mountain.

55 Eamus egentes,
curramus gementes.
In valle doloris
si opem petamus,
montem istum ascendamus.

Let us go, wretched people,
let us run, lamenting.
In the valley of grief
if we ask for help
we may climb this mountain.

A Latin text may be based on either a quantitative or an accentuated system. In the former, which is that of classical Latin, the unit is the 'foot' (dactylic, iambic, trochaic, etc.), an organized succession of long and short syllables. In the latter system the unit is the syllable, and syllables are so placed that the tonic accents of the words coincide with the rhythm or rhythmic accents of the words. The quantitative system began to weaken around the third and fourth centuries AD, when vulgar Latin was used, for example, in religious hymns of a popular nature. Together with traditional metric Latin, accentuated Latin was also employed. By the late Middle Ages, this second system began to be adopted also in Latin poetry of a more erudite nature; and it was the only system of poetry applied to vulgarized Latin and Italian.

In the case of *In tribulationibus*, no use at all is made of the metric feet of quantitative classical Latin; instead, the motet is written completely according to syllabic accentuation. Therefore, one may determine its structure by applying the rules which govern contemporary Italian poetry. In so doing, one realizes that there is the same alternation of poetry for musical recitative with poetry for closed musical forms (arias, duets, and so forth). The motet, in fact, opens with recitative: 22 verses which, although of various lengths (and therefore without a clear structure), are most often of seven syllables; there is no rhyme-scheme; and the rhythm is close to that of spoken speech.

Verses 23–34 (beginning 'Ad montem venite'), on the other hand, exhibit an extremely regular structure: two strophes, each strophe of 6-syllable lines and the same rhyme-scheme (axbbaa). These poetic closed forms were translated by Stradella into a duet and a trio, the first accompanied by continuo plus violins, the second by continuo alone. Verses 35–40 (beginning 'Hic spirant leniter') are not as perfectly organized but are nevertheless clearly structured, with lines coupled through the repetition of first words (*aurae* and *ubique*) and through their length (5 *sdrucciolo*/5 *sdrucciolo*/8/6 *sdrucciolo*/9 *tronco*/9 *tronco*); in addition, the same rhyme is applied to lines of equal length (aabcdd). The poetic strophe was set as a duet with basso continuo by Stradella.

Verses 41–7 are only somewhat more structured than the opening ones, but not yet into what one could call a closed poetic form. The seven lines (beginning 'O mons delitiarum') show only a slight tendency toward a pattern of length (6/5/6 *tronco*/5 *tronco*/9/8 *tronco*/11 *tronco*), and the only rhyme is for the third and last two lines. It is clearly a hybrid section and Stradella responded in like manner: he set the text as recitative in aria-style music—in other words, as an arioso—for a trio of voices plus continuo, further declaring it not to be a closed structure by beginning in one key (G major) and ending in another (E minor).

The remaining lines of text are in two organized strophes. Verses 48–54 (beginning 'O gratum montem') exhibit the rhyme-scheme aabbxaa for lengths of 5/5/6/6/4/5/5 syllables, and Stradella set them as a duet with string accompaniment. Verses 55–9 (beginning 'Eamus egentes') follow the rhyme-scheme aaxbb for lengths of 5/6/6/5/8 syllables, and here Stradella employed all five voices (SSATB) plus the parts for two violins and basso continuo to conclude the motet.

Obviously, the anonymous poet of *In tribulationibus* was born after the invention of dramatic poetry for music. He had a Latin vocabulary, but used the words with an understanding of Italian poetry, and more specifically of poetry for music. Stradella, as usual, noted the characteristics of the text and reinforced them through his music. In addition, he distributed the verses—which could easily have been pronounced by only one or two persons—among five protagonists, thus enlarging their interpretative dimensions. By also varying the voices and instrumentation, he rendered the execution of the motet still more interesting.

Pugna, certamen, militia est vita, another motet by Stradella which adopts the 'cantata approach', even calls for specific characters. As stated earlier, it was written to celebrate the occasion when Angelica Lante took her vows and became the nun Maria Christina. The motet opens with the affirmation that 'Human life is a battle, combat, warfare', but then Maria Christina, 'a meek virgin' but 'terrible, formidable', is seen to enter the enemy camp and be victorious against Satan (the Devil), Caro (the Flesh), and Mundus (the World). Articulated in several sections—recitative, an aria for each of the four protagonists, two trios, and four quartets (one of which is repeated)—it is similar to Italian cantatas composed for particular guests or events. The singers were likewise *virtuosi*, as is seen from their solo music filled with difficult phrases of continuous sixteenth-notes, and from their ensembles based on frequent entrances in imitation of lines often comprised of short, rhythmic motifs.

Pugna, certamen, performed on 28 January 1675, is one of the earliest datable works employing concertino and concerto grosso, and is certainly the earliest motet of this type. In the main, the concerto grosso (one part for violin, two for viola, and another for continuo) plays ritornellos attached to closed forms accompanied by basso continuo alone. The concertino (two parts for violin, plus continuo), however, is never used on its own. The combined ensemble is called upon only once, in the aria for the heroine, 'Non gladio et telo'. Here the imitative concertino usually accompanies the voice directly, whereas the homophonic concerto grosso plays between vocal phrases and occasionally at the ends of vocal phrases to reinforce a cadence. The style is a vigorous one, suitable for the lines which describe the 'Roman girl' calling the enemies out to fight, armed 'not with sword or dagger, not with armour or shield', but only with 'a consecrated veil'.

Quite different from Stradella's other sacred Latin works set according to a 'cantata approach' is *Vau: Et egressus est* whose text is from the Old Testament Book of Lamentations. A Latin translation of the Scriptures was first prepared by Jerome near the end of the fourth century AD, therefore the motet text cannot exhibit those features characteristic of dramatic Italian and Italianate poetry for music. As for the liturgical Gregorian chant rendition of the Lamentations, it is similar to psalmodic recitation, with repeated use of a single reciting-tone preceded by a short intonation and followed by a cadential figure. The only departure from syllabic chant is offered by a neume repeated on each of the Hebrew letters which precedes each verse or group of verses of the Lamentations and which thus serves to signal their succession.

Regardless of the original format of the expressive and poignant text, Stradella set it as though it were a cantata while still adhering to the broad outlines of a traditional liturgical rendition. In his composition, most verses are still recited, but now in the discursive, undulating style of seicento recitative. A non-syllabic setting is maintained for the Hebrew letters, but the fiorituras assigned to them are expanded four, five, or more times beyond the few notes of the original neume (Ex. 37). In addi-

Ex. 37.

tion, Stradella has made an aria of the section beginning 'Teth: Sordes eius in pedibus eius' and concluding with the line 'Jerusalem, Jerusalem, convertere ad Dominum Deum tuum' (which ends each liturgical presentation of the Lamentations). Apart from the Hebrew letter *Teth*, the rest of the A major aria is in 3/2 metre, a lovely lyrical setting which is mainly syllabic except for the exhortation to return to God. The musical style of the entire alto and basso continuo motet is definitely seventeenth-century; since it utilizes a 'cantata approach', the genre of the Lamentations is also a modern one.

A few remarks relevant to the performance of Stradella's sacred Latin music would be in order. While it was the practice in the seventeenth century to indicate violin parts through the use of the treble clef, no such equivalent guide is available for continuo instrumentation. One may assume, however, that the likely performance of these works in a church, a chapel, or an oratory would have included an organ.[10] The various members of the lute family (archlute, theorbo, chitarrone) could also have

[10] This is confirmed by the parts made in Modena for Stradella's motets and which are now in the Biblioteca Estense (see Gianturco–McCrickard, *Stradella Catalogue*).

been used, as well as violone, cello, harpsichord, and harp.[11] Throughout Stradella's period, the voices would normally have been one to a part, but it was also possible to increase this number in ensembles for special occasions.[12] While a liturgical setting could have been sung at its appropriate liturgical moment, and any sacred composition performed during services of devotion such as those held by confraternities, motets were normally sung during the Offertory of a Mass.[13] Apart from *Pugna, certamen*, however, it is not known exactly when or where Stradella's sacred Latin works were heard.

[11] On the use of these instruments in sacred music, see the following studies: Frederick Hammond, 'Musicians at the Medici Court in the Mid-Seventeenth Century', *Analecta Musicologica*, 14 (1974), 151–69; Jean Lionnet, 'André Maugars, Risposta data a un curioso sul sentimento della musica d'Italia', *Nuova rivista musicale italiana*, 4 (1985), 681–707; Lionnet, 'Flavio Chigi'; John Burke, *Musicians of S. Maria Maggiore, Rome, 1600–1700*, *Note d'archivio*, NS 2, supplement (1984), esp. 77–87.

[12] Lionnet, 'Flavio Chigi' and Burke, *S. Maria Maggiore*.

[13] Jean Lionnet, 'Performance Practice in the Papal Chapel during the 17th Century', *Early Music*, 15 (1987), 3–15.

12

Instrumental Music

The first mention of Stradella's instrumental music is in a letter from Abate Settimio Olgiati to Polo Michiel dated Rome, July 1676.[1] Olgiati passed on Stradella's question about which instruments were to do a 'concerto' requested by the Venetian. It is also possible that Stradella's further comment that 'one never composes in eight [parts], rather it will be in four with the parts doubled' also concerned an instrumental composition. On 21 August of the same summer, Olgiati wrote to Michiel that 'Stradella has not finished your sonata'; however, immediately thereafter the composer arrived with his 'efforts' together with a recommendation concerning performance: 'He tells me that everything depends on having the instruments play well together.' Olgiati ended by advising the Venetian to 'make use of the warning'.[2]

When in Genoa, Stradella continued to compose instrumental works for Michiel, and in a letter of 11 June 1678 he not only said he would send some sonatas to Venice, but asked whether they were to be 'for harpsichord, organ, lute, harp, violins in two or three parts, or string concerti grossi',[3] thus confirming that he and others wrote sonatas for a wide variety of instruments. This is especially significant since it suggests that wider use was made in Italy at this time of solo lute, harp, and keyboard sonatas than has perhaps been realized. Final mention of a sonata written for Michiel is in a letter dated 26 June 1679, when Stradella promised to send one in the next post.[4]

Stradella's extant instrumental music found in sources where it is independent of a vocal work divides itself as follows: twelve solo sonatas for violin and basso continuo; two duo-sonatas for violin, bass, and continuo; nine trio-sonatas for two violins and bass with continuo; three sonatas for large ensembles; and one keyboard toccata.

Keyboard Works

The one toccata extant today cannot be the only keyboard work Stradella composed. His willingness to write harpsichord and organ sonatas for

---

[1] I-Vmc, PD C. 1063, no. 146. The exact day is not legible.
[2] PD C. 1063, nos. 152 and 151 respectively.
[3] PD C. 1065, no. 260. See no. 12 in App. 2a for the entire letter and its translation.
[4] PD C. 1066, no. 251 (no. 21 in App. 2a).

Michiel serves as proof to the contrary, as do the lost volumes of his *Toccate da Cimbalo* and *Sonate da Cimbalo*;[5] what is more, his written-out solo passage for harpsichord in the Christmas cantata *Ah! troppo è ver* shows an intimate familiarity with the keyboard idiom. This is confirmed by Pitoni, who praised Stradella for his talent 'in handling the keys with velocity'.[6] The comment is not associated with any particular instrument, but a seventeenth-century keyboard player would have been competent on both harpsichord and organ.

The same ambiguity prevails with Stradella's *Toccata* itself, given that no instrument is named in its single surviving source.[7] Although one does find toccatas for lute in this period, and although Stradella was probably a proficient lutenist, it seems certain on stylistic grounds that the work was intended for keyboard. However, which keyboard instrument cannot be determined since there is no part for pedals and no passage that would not be equally effective on organ or harpsichord. We know that composers such as Frescobaldi wrote toccatas for both organ and harpsichord; therefore, it is best simply to assign Stradella's *Toccata* to the general category of keyboard music.[8]

While not difficult when compared with later German examples of the genre, Stradella's *Toccata* cannot be said to be simple. This is due principally to its 'perpetual-motion' rhythm: 85 of the 87 measures offer continuous sixteenth-notes for either one hand or both hands simultaneously (only the first and last measures are chordal). In addition, the figures are not all arpeggios and scales, but also contain particular melodic designs which require greater attention for their execution. Two of these constitute an element of unity in the piece—a 'rocking' motif and the skip of a third coupled with a scalar pattern in the opposite direction which are heard throughout the *Toccata* (Ex. 38). A further unifying feature is tonality. This is made clear right at the beginning where several measures are devoted to the delineation of the key of A minor. Tonality is reinforced by frequent dominant–tonic cadences, by a clear plagal modulation to D minor, by usually sounding some one of the notes of the tonic chords (A minor or D minor) on strong beats throughout the work.

The result is not at all an undirected piece in the manner of early Renaissance examples of keyboard music; nor do we have here a generally

[5] See Gianturco–McCrickard, *Stradella Catalogue*, Sect. 9: Lost Works.

[6] Pitoni, *Notitia*, 'Alessandro Stradella'.

[7] For this and all sources see Gianturco–McCrickard, *Stradella Catalogue*. For an edition of the music itself, see McCrickard, *Alessandro Stradella: Instrumental Music* (*Concentus Musicus*, 5; Cologne, 1980); also see the same author's 'Alessandro Stradella's Instrumental Music: A Critical Edition with Historical and Analytical Commentary' (2 vols.; Ph.D. diss., University of North Carolina at Chapel Hill, 1971).

[8] Lute toccatas by composers such as Kapsberger, d'Aragona, and Piccinini offer a more generally chordal texture in alternation with scalar passages in one voice at a time, characteristics more suited to the capabilities of the lute.

Ex. 38.

chordal style with runs heard against a chord as was typical of the works of Merulo and Padovano. Neither is Frescobaldi's rhythmically varied, rhapsodic style, clad in a complicated or fugal context, imitated. The insistence on certain figures in a continuous style has prompted Willi Apel to consider it the earliest known example of the type of toccata from which the eighteenth-century étude was to evolve.[9]

Curiously, two sources present the fourth movement of Stradella's Violin Sonata 7.1–2 as a work for keyboard.[10] The single-note melody line with supportive bass of the binary 12/8-metre piece could easily be played on a harpsichord or organ; moreover, it is an indication of contemporary performance practice which has not been fully realized. While it is the only example of its kind among Stradella's compositions, it should encourage the playing of other violin sonatas of his on a single keyboard instrument.

Sonatas for Large Ensembles

Stradella's three extant works for larger ensembles illustrate baroque imitation of Renaissance *cori spezzati* works. In his *Sonata a 4* (7.4–1) two groups of instruments are divided as 'Primo Choro' and 'Secondo Choro'. The first chorus is composed of two violins and basso continuo, and the second chorus of two cornetti and continuo. A much longer and more developed work than Gabrieli's *Sonata pian e forte*, the D major *Sonata a 4* offers both binary and ternary metres in its three movements (₵, 3/2, 3/8). The somewhat strident quality of the cornetti alternates with the more singing sound of the violins, both in the same range like equal pairs of voices, in a brilliant setting that is tonal, clearly organized, and with easy-to-follow imitation.

Stradella's *Sonata a otto viole con una tromba* (7.4–3) is more akin to a vocal composition where, in addition to the choruses, there is a soloist. The instruments, all strings, are again divided into 'Primo Choro' and 'Secondo Choro' with a basso continuo added to the second chorus 'si placet'. The two groups, treated imitatively as well as homophonically, alternate or come together in phrases of varying lengths. Either participating in their imitation, or seemingly independent of it, is the instrumental soloist, the bright and forceful baroque trumpet. Each of the four move-

---

[9] *The History of Keyboard Music to 1700* (Bloomington, Ind., 1972), 694.
[10] Numbers referring to Stradella's instrumental works are those assigned to them in Gianturco–McCrickard, *Stradella Catalogue*.

ments (₵, ₵, ₵, 6/8) is in D major, with modulations to the dominant and subdominant keys.

Another example of the use of alternating ensembles is Stradella's *Sonata di viole*. In the second half of the sixteenth century, when voices and instruments were joined together the composition was known as a *Concerto*, signifying that a 'unity' had been accomplished with 'diverse' elements. When accompanying a vocal work with instrumental groups of different sizes, Stradella named the ensembles according to their size: small concerto or 'concertino' and large concerto or 'concerto grosso'. Even when such instrumental groups played alone in a vocal work, the terminology was maintained. One finds the same designations in the *Sonata di viole*, a work apparently not conceived in connection with a vocal composition but as an independent piece of instrumental music.

The concertino is made up of two violin parts and lute, and the concerto grosso of violin, two viola parts, and basso continuo (perhaps archlute, theorbo, or bowed string, and possibly reinforced with keyboard). Although the two groups usually play music of equal difficulty and therefore their main difference is generally one of sonority, in the third movement the concertino is spotlighted with two extended passages of sixteenth-notes for both violins, phrases which are not given to the concerto grosso, and thus a distinct, soloistic role is assigned them here.[11] Its alternation of metres, forms, and tempos, and the breadth of the work (179 measures not counting repeats), based on a skilful handling of tonality, as well as the high level of technique demanded of the players, point to the *Sonata di viole* (7.4–2) as being one of Stradella's most mature instrumental works.

Concerti Grossi Connected to Vocal Works

The *Sonata di viole*, however, should not be considered Stradella's only concerto grosso. In 1689 Corelli composed an 'Introduzione' (two movements) and 'Sinfonia' (three movements) to be performed with Giovanni Lulier's oratorio *Santa Beatrice d'Este*. They were scored for concertino and concerto grosso. Later on, Corelli used the penultimate movement of the sinfonia as the third movement of his Op. 6 No. 6.[12] In the light of this information (and because some of Stradella's non-concerto grosso instrumental pieces once connected with vocal works were similarly used

---

[11] Jander, 'Concerto Grosso Instrumentation', 179 did not notice this movement and mistakenly says that Stradella gave soloistic music to the concertino only when it accompanies bass arias.

[12] Adriano Cavicchi, 'Una sinfonia inedita di Arcangelo Corelli nello stile del concerto grosso venticinque anni prima dell'opera VI', *Chigiana*, 20 (1963), 43–55, and Gianturco, 'Corelli e Stradella'.

as separate compositions), his sinfonias scored for concertino and concerto grosso, although connected with vocal works, should be considered part of the instrumental repertory and performed separately.[13]

Stradella employed a concertino–concerto grosso ensemble to accompany one oratorio, one motet, and eight cantatas,[14] a total of ten works. Not all, however, use the two groups in an opening or intermediate sinfonia; and not all sinfonias are of sufficient length (at least 100 measures) to warrant being acknowledged as more than introductions to vocal works. At the same time, four instrumental sinfonias may be considered genuine concerti grossi: the sinfonias introductory to the cantatas *Il Damone* (in the Turin version), *Ah! troppo è ver*, *Qual prodigio*, and *Lo schiavo liberato*. Here one finds two or three movements, in alternating binary and ternary metres, and alternating allegro and adagio tempos, in which homophony predominates in the slower sections and imitative counterpoint in the quicker ones. Within each tonally organized movement—and some are binary dances—the two ensembles rarely play as one entity, alternation being preferred by Stradella. While all parts are generally treated equally, the concertino occasionally emerges with greater virtuosity, notably at the beginning of the sinfonia to *Lo schiavo liberato* and in various moments of the sinfonia to *Ah! troppo è ver*. In short, one can say that Stradella's extant concerti grossi are actually five in number: these four sinfonias plus the *Sonata di viole*.

None of the large ensemble works discussed thus far is a series of only dances or rather *sonate da camera*. Instead all follow the pattern of the *sonata da chiesa*, where slow and fast movements alternate and where together with these one may also find a binary dance. This is true of Stradella's remaining sonatas for smaller ensembles (excluding a set of variations).

Solo Violin Sonatas

Excepting the Variations, which will be discussed separately, the majority of Stradella's eleven solo sonatas are in four contrasting movements, while two[15] contain six movements. In all cases the sonatas are clearly tonal: F major is used for three works; D major, A minor, and D minor in two; and E minor and G major for one work each. All sonatas begin and end

---

[13] Regarding the concerto grosso repertory, the beginning of movement III of the opening sinfonia of *Il barcheggio*, for example, is related to the beginning of the Sonata a 4; and movement III of the opening sinfonia of *Qual prodigio* is like movement IV of the *Sonata di viole*.

[14] Respectively: *San Giovanni Battista*, *Pugna, certamen, militia est*, *Ah! troppo è ver*, *Chi resiste al dio bendato*, both versions of *Il Damone*, *L'accademia d'Amore*, *Lo schiavo liberato*, *Qual prodigio è ch'io miri?*, *Vola, vola in altri petti*. Although not noted on the score as such, under certain aspects *Il barcheggio* could also be said to be accompanied by a concertino–concerto grosso ensemble.

[15] 7.1–6, 7.1–11.

in the same key, and in six of them[16] all movements are in the same key. However, five movements begin in one key and end in another: when there are four movements, this occurs in the penultimate one[17] and where there are six movements, it takes place in the fourth.[18] It is interesting to note that these movements begin in the key a third lower than the rest of the sonata, modulating to the home key by the end of the movement. They are clearly transitional movements, sometimes organized sequentially (the third movement of Sonata 7.1–2 is a typical example of how Stradella spins out a connecting section). Their aim is to provide, three-quarters of the way through the sonata and after so much insistence on the same key, harmonic interest and direction and thereby prepare one, through the novel interlude, to listen refreshed—as it were—to the final section(s) again in the principal key.

Naturally, modulations occur also during the course of other movements, most often to the dominant, subdominant, and related minor and major keys. Further interest is offered by 'affective' sections, those characterized by chromatic lines or more angular ones, as one finds in the fourth movement of Sonata 7.1–11. The structure of non-transitional movements may be binary or through-composed; one also finds two (unrepeated) sections in a non-dance movement, such as the opening of Sonata 7.1–1, where twelve bars provide a pensive introduction to the rest, a spirited Allegro.

Both violin and bass parts are conceived for technically competent performers, evident in the series of sixteenth- or faster notes to be found in all sonatas. Unfortunately, the sources never indicate the instrument(s) of the lower part. The problem is further complicated because the bass is not designed simply as a harmonic support. Rather, it is frequently in discourse with the solo violin, even rising to the treble register (as in movement III of Sonata 7.1–11, Ex. 39). The imitative style of the music therefore requires that the bass assert itself in a bright and lively manner comparable to the violin. Doubtless, a member of the lute or bowed string families was assigned the melodic part.[19] It is possible that the continuo was not realized in some movements in order to allow the contrapuntal dialogue between the two parts to emerge clearly. However, when desired, a realization would have been accomplished by either an organ, harpsichord, or theorbo–chitarrone–archlute, as was usual in such sonatas. As for the violin, its entire range is not called into play. Stradella (and Corelli

---

[16] 7.1–1, –3, –4, –7, –9, –10.   [17] 7.1–2, –5, –6, –8.   [18] 7.1–11.

[19] On the differences between violone, violoncino, and violoncello and their employment in Italy at the time of Stradella, see Stephen Bonta, 'Terminology for the Bass Violin in Seventeenth-Century Italy', *Journal of the American Musical Instrument Society*, 4 (1978), 5–42, and 'Corelli's Heritage: The Early Bass Violin in Italy', in Pierluigi Petrobelli and Gloria Staffieri (eds.), *Studi Corelliani IV: Atti del Quarto Congresso Internazionale (Fusignano, 4–7 settembre 1986)* (Florence, 1990), 217–31, as well as Stefano La Via, '"Violone" e "Violoncello" a Roma al tempo di Corelli', ibid., 165–91.

Ex. 39.

after him) tended to avoid the lowest string of the instrument (made of unwound gut at the time), and employed mainly the first three positions; exceptional examples of the fourth position are to be found in the first and second movements of Sonata 7.1–1.[20]

Sonata 7.1–2 can serve to illustrate the various sorts of figures typical of Stradella's style in the violin sonatas. Quite common is the arpeggio, to be played either slowly or quickly; scalar patterns are favoured, as are repeated notes, and 'rocking' figures. Naturally, a motif in itself does not comprise the whole of the musical interest. Rather, it is the way it is presented, and repeated—either exactly or in a sequential pattern—coupled with others, broken into still smaller units, and so forth. Generally, Stradella does not prefer exact repetition but delights in variations. To cite frequent and obvious examples, in the second section of dance movements it is not uncommon to find the same material inverted, as is the case in the second movement of Sonata 7.1–9. In the fourth movement of Sonata 7.1–1[21] the opening idea of the second section (an inversion of direction rather than of the exact notes of the beginning of the movement) undergoes several variations as the movement proceeds (Ex. 40). Another example of progressive variation is the first movement of Sonata 7.1–2, where the scalar line ends its descent each time in a different way (Ex. 41). This penchant for change is found everywhere in Stradella's music and constitutes one of its most striking characteristics.

Another work for solo violin is Stradella's set of Variations (7.1–12). Instrumental variations were popular in seventeenth-century Italy, and among those who tried their hand at the task were Kapsberger, who wrote a set for chitarrone over the line known as the *Romanesca*, and Corelli, who used the violin to decorate the oft-used *Folia*. In Stradella's sonata there are 25 variations in A minor over a bass-line not presently identifiable, although it could well have been invented by the composer (Ex. 42). The first 18 are in binary common metre, and the last seven in ternary 3/4 metre; in all of them the bass phrase of 13 sustained tones is the

---

[20] The 4th position is also called for in the 3rd movement of the *Sonata di viole* (7.4–2).

[21] Motivic material used here also appears in movement IV of the opening sinfonia of *Il barcheggio*.

Ex. 40.

Ex. 41.

Ex. 42.

same. The solo violin, by contrast, changes completely with each presentation of the bass, its variations becoming more complex and technically
more difficult as the sonata proceeds (Ex. 43). One can imagine two different scenarios for the writing of this piece: Stradella wanted to prove his
compositional ability by finding 25 different melodic solutions upon the
same bass; and/or a performer wished to manifest his mastery over the
violin and his skill at executing scales, arpeggios, double-stops, changing
bow direction quickly, legato and spiccato styles, and so forth.[22]

[22] Perhaps one should keep in mind that in an era in which multiple abilities were taken for
granted, composer and performer could have been one and the same. Alberto Gentili's affirmations in
'Alessandro Stradella', *Miscellanea della Facoltà di Lettere e Filosofia* [University of Turin], ser. 1
(1936), 165–6 about thematic connections between Vitali's Opus 2 No. 6 and Stradella's Violin Sonata
7.1–9, and about certain thematic relationships within movements of Stradella's violin sonatas, cannot
be verified. My thanks to John Suess for kindly sending me his transcription of the Vitali work, and
for having examined all of Opus 2 for some connection with Stradella.

Ex. 43.

Trio-Sonatas

Nine of Stradella's *sonate da chiesa* are for that most popular of baroque instrumental ensembles, the 'trio'. As in the solo violin sonatas, four movements is the norm (only 7.3–3 has a fifth movement). All trio-sonatas begin with a binary-metre movement, thereafter alternating binary and ternary metres. The preferred tonality is D major (three sonatas), with F major and A minor close behind (two each), followed by C major and G major (one each). Normally all movements are in the same tonality, but—as was the case in the solo violin sonatas—a penultimate movement may be transitional and modulatory (7.3–2 and –5).[23]

There are a few surprises in these sonatas. That in C major (7.3–1) is a fine work which exhibits characteristics already noted in the *sonate da chiesa* for solo violin and continuo. The first movement begins with nine measures of rather serious adagio music full of held notes and suspensions, actually a long phrase presented first in the tonic and then again in the dominant; immediately following this is music of a different style, faster, more spirited, and dominated by pulsing lines tossed from one part to the other in imitation; the movement ends with six measures marked 'Adagio'. The second movement is a Presto in binary form, also imitative but simpler; the third is again imitative; and so is the last, a dance movement.

One would say it is a typical trio-sonata; the only trouble here is that the same four movements were used by Stradella as the sinfonia for his oratorio *La Susanna*. Whether the work was composed first for the oratorio (1681) or as an independent instrumental piece is impossible to determine. It is true that in the Turin manuscript the work is called a 'Sinfonia', and it would be convenient to be able to conclude that therefore it was originally connected with a vocal composition. However, the same work was published around 1700 in Bologna as the second one in a collection entitled *Sonate a tre di vari autori*, which leaves the question of origin and terminology still unresolved. For what comfort it may bring, it must be admitted that such confusion reigns over the entire repertory of baroque sonatas and sinfonias.[24]

The Trio-Sonata in D major (7.3–2) is another case in point. Probably while in Genoa, Stradella composed the sacred cantata, *Esule dalle sfere*, and began it with a two-movement instrumental 'Sinfonia'. In 1680, Marino Silvani in Bologna provided the piece with two additional movements and published it in a collection entitled *Scielta delle suonate*; again

---

[23] The modulation in 7.3–2 is different from that in the transitional movements in the solo works: here the opening tonality is the overall one (D major) and modulation is to the supertonic (E minor).

[24] There is similarity between the last movement of this sonata and the last movement of the opening sinfonia to Stradella's opera *Le gare dell'amor eroico*.

as a sonata, it is also found in manuscript sources of independent works. It is not possible to say which music was composed first, the sonata or the sinfonia.[25]

A problem of another sort arises with Stradella's Trio-Sonata in D major (7.3–3). The undated cantata *Furie del nero Tartaro* is for bass voice accompanied by two violins and continuo. When the work begins the voice is silent; the very same instrumental music is what opens the trio-sonata. Since one is not able to decide whether the sonata or the cantata came first, it is not possible to determine whether the opening of the sonata suggested the entrance of a voice to Stradella, or whether he realized that his initial instrumental cantata phrases could be developed along other lines.

Characteristics of Stradella's style not mentioned in connection with other works may be illustrated with his Trio-Sonata in A minor (7.3–8). A performer's virtuosity is of course delightful, and lively imitative counterpoint interesting; however, there is the danger that they become too familiar to be continually enjoyable. To them, Stradella adds moments which take one by surprise because they are uncommon. One stylistic characteristic regards voice-leading. Throughout the Renaissance and Baroque, it was established that after an interval of more than a third (when not in a proper arpeggio), a melody would change direction. (This was a necessity in vocal music, where the effort of a skip was to be relaxed afterwards.) Composers did this so regularly that, unless the music is interpreting an emotion-filled text, one comes to expect it. Therefore, in the third movement of Trio-Sonata 7.3–8, when Stradella continues after such an interval in the *same* direction, it causes surprise (Ex. 44). This sort of figure is not heard just a few times, it is a principal one of the movement, and there are thus several moments where a fresh sound breaks forth in an otherwise rather orthodox, tightly contrapuntal piece.

Ex. 44.

vn. 1

Another characteristic of Stradella's style is the way a seemingly unimportant figure can take the upper hand. The stepwise turn made by notes 2–5 of the above example appears as an integral part of it; moreover, it is not its most crucial element, given that novel skips follow. At the same time, it is just this motif, separated from the rest of the phrase, which is

---

[25] In its two English sources, movements II and III are reversed (see Gianturco–McCrickard, *Stradella Catalogue*). Movement II is also used for eight measures at the beginning of the fourth movement of the sinfonia before Part II of *Il barcheggio*.

heard repeatedly from m. 19 on. Another example of this procedure may be noted in the first movement of the sonata which abounds in sixteenth-notes strung together in scales and turns. One would say, in fact, that the 21 measures are dominated by them. However, what the ear picks up are the inserted patterns of three, four, or more quarter-notes in stepwise motion: innocent as they seem, they provide the audible points of reference amidst so much constant activity.

One of these units helps create yet another of Stradella's hallmarks, an unusual chord progression. This occurs in mm. 12–13. Up to this point the harmony has been straightforward A minor and not at all chromatic. But now, by moving the second violin down and the bass up, both chromatically, an unexpected seventh chord is created, and not on the dominant which might be justified. More surprisingly, it is not resolved but is followed by still another seventh chord. The stepwise movement of the parts causing 'difficulty' removes any 'guilt' on the part of the composer, but the harmony stands out, something Stradella is never afraid of doing.

These sonatas are not mere 'soprano duets' with continuo support but true SSB trios. While it was common in chamber sonatas to play such a bass part with just a melodic instrument (bowed or plucked), church sonatas most commonly added chordal realization.[26] In the printed part-books of Sonata 7.3–1 'Violon Continuo' is called for, and both the British Library copy and the printed source of 7.3–2 request a keyboard on the bass part; but in general it is difficult to decide in these works (as it is in the violin sonatas) whether to realize the bass or not. Corelli's published church sonatas offer two bass parts, one melodic and the other for realization, even when they are almost identical; however, Stradella's sources provide only a single bass part.[27] Perhaps all instrumentalists are to read from the same part, each using the notes adequate for his role (as would be suggested by those occasional moments, such as in 7.3–5, where the bass-line divides into two parts). Even though the bass can be shown to vacillate in the trio-sonatas (as it does in the solo sonatas) between taking a melodic role and a supporting one—in the same movement it can enter into motivic imitation with the strings, and then drop out in order to balance the texture or complete the harmony—it is primarily melodic.

Duo-Sonatas

Two of Stradella's other *sonate da chiesa* highlight the same problem of bass role and instrumentation, which in turn influences the categorizing of

---

[26] See Sandra Mangsen, 'The Trio Sonata in Pre-Corellian Prints: When does 3 = 4?', *Performance Practice Review*, 3 (Fall, 1990), 138–64.

[27] In fact, by stating that Sonatas 7.3–7 and –8 are 'A 2 Violini e Basso', the Modena sources would seem to preclude a continuo.

such works. Both sonatas in question are scored for violin and two bass parts, one of which assumes a melodic function and the other a supporting harmonic role (indicated by an unusual number of figures in the single Modena source). The two works cannot be trio-sonatas, even though there are three parts, because these are not equal in role or function. They might at first be thought to be violin sonatas where the bass line has been divided in two, one a concertante elaboration of the other. However, closer examination reveals that this cannot be the case either. When parts are derived one from another they are continually related, with one simply 'richer' than the other. In these two sonatas, instead, while this happens occasionally, in general one of the basses participates thematically and imitatively whereas the other is consistently merely supportive (Ex. 45). These two works are, then, duo-sonatas: two melodic parts (SB) are accompanied by continuo. Who is to play the bass parts is not stated on the music. A plucked stringed instrument might be used, but a cello would be a better duet partner for the soprano violin; and the continuo could then be realized with organ.

The music of both duo parts requires excellent players. There are, of course, the expected scales, arpeggios, repeated-note figures, and so forth; but the continually skipping passages such as open the Sonata in D minor (7.2–1), and as one finds in the fourth movement, are unusually demanding. The sonatas are, atypically, in six movements. That in D minor follows a more traditional pattern by having all movements but the penultimate in the same key (the fifth is in A minor); but the one in B flat major (7.2–2) shows three transitional movements: the second modulates from B flat major to F minor; the third returns from F minor to B flat major; and the fifth movement goes from B flat major to F major. As far as their metres are concerned, both sonatas begin in binary time, and although they include ternary movements as well, their alternation is neither regular nor indeed the same.

Structurally they are not regular either. In the D minor sonata, for example, movements 3, 4, and 5 are quite short (from 10 to 17 measures), whereas the sixth—strangely based on four repeating sections (as though it were an early dance-form)—is 57 measures long (114 when repeated). On a more detailed structural level, the B flat major sonata shows Stradella working with musical ideas as though they were building blocks. The first movement begins in the manner of an adagio introduction to an allegro section, such as one finds in many other of his sonatas: a 4-measure phrase is presented on the tonic and then repeated on the dominant. However, no new section follows. Instead, the thematic material already heard is broken up into two units of a measure each (Ex. 46); these are presented together or repeated singly, without any evident pattern, up to the final cadence of the 32-measure movement. The two quite different

Ex. 45.

Ex. 46.

ideas are heard throughout the movement, but their unpredictable repetition and alternation relieves any possible monotony.

A similar concentrated working-out of material is evident in the same sonata's third movement, where the interval of a fourth dominates almost every measure of the first 18. It is usually described by step, but is also found as an open interval (Ex. 47*a*). During the rest of the movement, it is the fifth which asserts itself in the same way (Ex. 47*b*). It cannot be by chance that intervals related by inversion were chosen. The surprise is that they do not seem too simple as motifs, nor do they bore by repetition; interest is provided by shifting the rhythmic accent which delineates the intervals, and by combining the figures with other material.

Ex. 47.

Sinfonias Connected to Vocal Works

Discussion of Stradella's instrumental music cannot end without considerations similar to those which were made earlier in regard to his works for concerto grosso. It was suggested there that sinfonias scored for such an ensemble but part of vocal works be considered as belonging to Stradella's repertoire of instrumental music. Several examples of this seventeenth-century practice (such as the publication of introductory sinfonias as sonatas), and not just with regard to those for concerto grosso, have already been cited. It remains only to indicate which other Stradella sinfonias connected to vocal works could be performed in their own right.

Obviously, a single-movement sinfonia does not exhibit the necessary sectional structure of the contemporary sonata, and therefore should perhaps not be taken into consideration here.[28] A better case, however, could be made for sinfonias with two movements.[29] The great majority of these

[28] This then excludes the sinfonia to the opera *Moro per amore*, the third sinfonia to the cantata *Il barcheggio*, the second, third, and fourth sinfonias to the Modena version of *Il Damone*, the second sinfonia to *L'accademia d'Amore*, the second and third sinfonias to *Lo schiavo liberato*, the second sinfonia to *Qual prodigio è ch'io miri?*, the second and third sinfonias to *Vola, vola in altri petti*, the second sinfonia to *Ah! troppo è ver*, and the opening sinfonia to *Crudo mar di fiamme orribili*.

[29] Sinfonias to the cantatas *Chi resiste al dio bendato*, *Il Damone* (Modena version), *Infinite son le pene*, *L'accademia d'Amore*, *La Circe* ('Se desio curioso il cor v'ingombra'), *Lasciate ch'io respiri*, *Lo*

are scored for two violins and continuo, and exhibit the customary contrasts of metre and 'atmosphere' in a tonal and generally contrapuntal context.

Of Stradella's three-movement sinfonias, that which opens the opera *Le gare dell'amor eroico* is scored for two violins and continuo in the first movement, but the strings double the same part in the other two. Still, several features suggest its relationship to the eighteenth-century Italian symphony—it is tonal (D major), metres are alternated (3/4, c, 6/8), and the writing is imitative—and it would be an interesting piece to perform on its own.

There should be no reserve, either, about performing Stradella's four-movement sinfonias as independent works. They appear before Parts I and II of his cantata *Il barcheggio*. Although exhibiting some of the same features as noted in his *sonate da chiesa*,[30] they are of another type. Due to its subject and its performance in the bay of Genoa, the cantata made great use of cornetto/trumpet.[31] Therefore, in addition to two violin parts there is also a wind instrument, as well as basso continuo (including one or more trombones). The results are two brilliant works of the genre given impetus by Maurizio Cazzati in Op. 35, his Sonatas for trumpet and strings. In the *barcheggio* sinfonias, the wind instrument is made to vie in agility with the strings, and to interweave its wonderful sound among them: at one point the ensemble is even requested to play 'with enthusiasm'.

Peter Allsop places Stradella both formally and stylistically in the Roman School as a follower of Lelio Colista.[32] This is not surprising, given what is now known of Stradella's life and career; but it is the first time that a scholar has analysed enough Roman instrumental music to be able to realize Stradella's greater affinity with this repertoire rather than with that of Venice or Emilia, areas with which he has usually been associated.[33] Allsop also affirms that 'Rome rather than Bologna was in the forefront of developments in violin technique in the second half of the century'[34] and

schiavo liberato, Or ch'alla dea notturna, Per tua vaga beltade, Sciogliete in dolci nodi, Solitudine amata della pace, Da cuspide ferrate, to the operas *Il Trespolo tutore* and *La forza dell'amor paterno,* and to the oratorios *San Giovanni Battista* and *Santa Pelagia.*

[30] Both sinfonias are in D major; both have movements in binary and ternary metres (the first follows the sequence c, 3/2, c, 3/8, and the second 3/4, c, c, 3/8); and both are based on imitative counterpoint.

[31] The question of which instrument is to be used in the cantata is discussed in Ch. 6 under 'Secular Cantatas with Instrumental Accompaniment'.

[32] *The Italian 'Trio' Sonata* (Oxford, 1992), 199–203.

[33] For example, William S. Newman, *The Sonata in the Baroque Era* (New York, 1972), 131: 'Alessandro Stradella . . . probably belongs among the Venetians by virtue of his style'; and Arthur Hutchings, *The Baroque Concerto* (New York, 1965), 52, although not assigning Stradella to any school, says 'he was certainly influenced by the trend of music in that city [Bologna].'

[34] Allsop, *'Trio' Sonata,* 201.

finds that such virtuosity was also required of bass strings, features which have been noted here in Stradella's works. In fact, Stradella's 'treatment of the instruments themselves is far more ambitious than most of his contemporaries', and exhibits technical difficulties on a par with those found in Lonati's trio-sonatas.[35] Allsop's considerations hold true for other categories of Stradella's instrumental music as well and, therefore, his evaluation that, in his trio-sonatas, Stradella made a 'major contribution to Roman instrumental music of the late Seventeenth Century' may also be applied to his other instrumental works.

[35] Allsop, *'Trio' Sonata*, 203. Six of Lonati's trio-sonatas have been edited by Peter Allsop in *Italian Seventeenth Century Instrumental Music*, Series I: *Rome*, nos. 1 and 3: Carlo Ambrogio Lonati, *Sinfonie a 3* (Crediton, Devon, 1990 and 1988 resp.).

13

Pedagogical Work

There are several indications that Stradella was also a teacher of music. The first comes in a letter of 21 August 1676 from Settimio Olgiati to Polo Michiel in which he mentions that Stradella is now teaching 'for money', but the abate does not say to whom, or what he teaches.[1] The second comes from his unlucky association with Agnese Van Uffele in the autumn of 1677,[2] although it is not known which branch of music Alvise Contarini asked him to impart to her. Once in Genoa, Stradella was immediately put to work at the Teatro Falcone, and his duties included 'giving some help to these women who perform', as he wrote in a letter dated 8 January 1678.[3] This implies that he acted as a vocal coach, rehearsing the women in their parts and probably giving them advice on singing technique. He must have had some success at the theatre, because several Genoese noblemen convinced him afterwards to stay in the city and even supported him financially. Stradella augmented what they gave him by teaching six ladies of the aristocracy, who paid him generously for the lessons; and later on he also had gentlemen students.[4] Unfortunately, it is not known whether he taught them voice, an instrument, or simply the rudiments of music. The bass-baritone Giacomo Filippo Cabella was also trained in Genoa by Stradella, probably both in voice and music theory; in fact, Tosi said the singer came from the 'school of the famous Stradella', implying that the composer had many students and on a regular basis.[5]

While we have no contemporary reference either from Stradella or from one of his pupils as to his teaching methods, a manual does survive. Now in Bologna, the manuscript is entitled: 'Libro de Primi Elimenti [sic] del Sig:r Alessandro Stradella. 1694'. The date cannot, of course, be when Stradella wrote it, but rather when its anonymous owner acquired or used it. In fact, this latter seventeenth-century hand has headed the first page:

---

[1] I-Vmc, PD C. 1063, no. 151.

[2] According to Matteo del Teglia, Florentine ambassador, in a letter to Abate Marucelli, secretary to the Grand Duke, dated Venice, 30 Oct. 1677, and cited by Baccini, 'Il Maestro Stradella', 277.

[3] I-Vmc, PD C. 1065, no. 348 (no. 10 in App. 2a).

[4] Letter dated 30 Apr. 1678 in I-Vmc, PD C. 1065, no. 218 (no. 11 in App. 2a).

[5] Bologna, Accademia Filarmonica, MS 244, Notizie degli Accademici Filarmonici, under the biography of Cabella.

'Primi Elementi del Sig:r Alessandro Stradella', and therefore one is reassured that the contents of the manuscript are indeed by the composer.

The 'First Elements' of music are divided into nine chapters: Chapter 1, 'On harmonic consonances and how they are formed'; Chapter 2, 'Explanation of tone and semitone'; Chapter 3, 'On the octave, and the way to employ it in passages'; Chapter 4, 'On the perfect fifth, and the way to employ it in passages'; Chapter 5, 'On the fourth, and the way to employ it in passages'; Chapter 6, 'On the major and minor third and sixth'; Chapter 7, 'On the third, and the way to employ it in passages'; Chapter 8, 'On the major and minor sixth, and the way to employ it in passages'; Chapter 9, 'Explanation of the unison and the way to employ it in passages'.

In short, it is a series of lessons in counterpoint (that is, composition) for the beginner, and all consonant intervals have been described and their correct treatment explained. Stradella's ability as a teacher may be realized from several aspects of the manual. The first is its logical organization: it begins by explaining the term 'consonance' and then proceeds to treat such intervals one by one according to their complexity. The second is its abundance of musical examples: the intervals and the 'ways of employing' them result in more than 100 examples in two, three, and four parts; these are labelled 'good', 'bad', 'very bad', or 'tolerated' according to the correctness of the voice-leading in each case.

Certain expressions in the manual are charming, although simplistic today, such as: 'The octave is a perfect consonance, above all other consonances'; 'The fifth is a perfect consonance, the most noble in music after the octave for its perfection and beauty'; 'The unison is a privileged sound, but perfect.' At the same time, other expressions are useful for our understanding of baroque thinking. One concerns the octave, which is said not to give 'armonia' or harmony. The same word appears in the title of Chapter I, where the consonant intervals are said to be 'harmonic'. The noun 'harmony' and its adjective mean, then, the sound which results when two or more different tones are put together. It was a technical term, which it can still be today, and not simply an aesthetic evaluation of the 'harmoniousness' of a piece of music.

Other interesting expressions appear in regard to the fourth, octave, and fifth. In Chapter 1 the fourth is listed among consonant intervals; but in Chapter 4, which deals exclusively with the fourth, it is said to be 'one of the dissonances of music', although 'the least dissonant' and the 'most used'. Stradella then goes on to explain how it is 'saved' by the third or sixth. While one may have a series of fourths, one cannot have 'two, one after the other' octaves or fifths. In order to avoid parallel motion of these intervals, at least half a measure of consonant music must come between them; if, instead, there are dissonances between the two octaves or fifths, they do not eliminate the effect of parallel motion. A series of alternating octaves and fifths is only 'tolerated'.

It is most likely that, although all consonances have been touched upon, Stradella's manual as we now possess it is not complete. He must have intended to deal at least with dissonances as well, if not other aspects of composition; but whether he did so is not known.

In the next century Stradella continued to serve a didactic purpose. In 1774 Padre Martini used a piece of Stradella's music to illustrate his own manual, *Esemplare o sia Saggio fondamentale pratico di contrappunto fugato*. As an example of 'Fuga a due voci', Martini cited the soprano–bass duet 'Nel seren de' tuoi contenti' from Stradella's oratorio *San Giovanni Battista*. The points he wanted the student to notice are clearly numbered and described:

In this duet we have a good opportunity to learn the various artifices with which it was composed by the author, a man of renown in the last century. At the very beginning, at the proposal by the bass at no. 1 [bar 1], the soprano replies in contrary motion at no. 2 [bar 2]; and then the bass at no. 3 [bar 3] replies again, joining in the reply of the soprano but in syncopation; and the soprano at no. 4 [bar 4] takes up his reply, however inverting the chord at the upper fifth; and here in brief ends the first subject proposed. At no. 5 [bar 6] he proposes another subject, most suitable to express the sense of the words: 'da più venti è combattuta la mia nave' [my ship is beaten by many winds]. At the proposal of the subject the soprano replies at no. 6 [bar 7] at the octave above, and at no. 7 [bar 9] leads to the fourth of the key, where the bass takes up the subject. But since the intent of the author is to highlight the sense of the words 'combattuta è la mia nave', making the two parts compete with one another, he brings in the subject in various keys, now ascending, now descending, thus letting it be known how far one can go in the art of moving the affections of the listener. Having arrived at the regular cadence of the third, which of its nature in minor keys is major, he changes this major third to minor, in order to give more force to the words, which one meets at no. 8 [bar 19]: 'sdegno, amor, pietade, ed ira' [disdain, love, pity, and anger], which, being opposed to one another due to their mixture of affections, offer a good opportunity to the author of the music, for there is always more, by a turn of imitation, of modulation, to excite the diversity of the affections indicated by the words, and to show young composers how abundant and rich is their art in the means to move the same [affections] in the listeners, as circumstances require.[6]

Padre Martini, probably the most famous teacher in all of music history, saw in Stradella a composer of technical ability and of emotional communicability, and advised students to study him for these reasons. His is a judgement applied specifically to one duet, but one may urge that Stradella's entire repertoire be so examined and enjoyed.

[6] Reference to Stradella in Padre Martini's *Esemplare* is in vol. ii, Ex. VI, pp. 17–20; the translation of the passage is mine.

Appendix 1:
List of Works

Numbers refer to Gianturco–McCrickard, *Stradella Catalogue.*

Appendix 1

1.1–32	Dopo incessante corso di lagrimoso umore (S, bc)
1.1–33	Dove aggiri mia vita (S, bc)
1.1–34	Dove gite, o pensier? (S, bc)
1.1–35	Dove il Tebro famoso fa degli argentei flutti (S, bc)
1.1–36	Dove l'ali spiegate, ove indirizzate il volo (S, bc)
1.1–37	Ecco chi già nell'Asia (S, bc)
1.1–38	Eccomi accinto, o bella (Bar, bc)
1.1–39	Empio Amor, tiranno arciero (S, bc)
1.1–40	Eppur sempre a' miei desiri (S, bc)
1.1–41	Ferma, ferma, il corso (S, bc)
1.1–42	Fermatevi, o bei lumi (S, bc)
1.1–43	Figli, amici, Agrippina (S, bc)
1.1–44	Figli del mio cordoglio (S, bc)
1.1–45	Forsennato pensier, che far poss'io (S, bc)
1.1–46	Fuor della Stigia sponda (S, bc)
1.1–47	Genuflesso a tue piante (S, bc)
1.1–48	Già languiva la notte (S, bc)
1.1–49	Già le spade nemiche del trionfante Augusto (B, bc)
1.1–50	Giunto vivo alla tomba (S, bc)
1.1–51	Il destin vuol ch'io pianga (S, bc)
1.1–52	Il mar gira ne' fiumi (S, bc)
1.1–53	Il penare per te, bella, m'è caro (S, bc)
1.1–54	Il più misero amante ch'in amorosa fiamma (S, bc)
1.1–55	Il più tenero affetto che mai destasse Amore (S, bc)
1.1–56	In quel sol che in grembo al Tago (S, bc)
1.1–57	In sì lontano lido a che dunque m'aggiro (S, bc)
1.1–58	Io che lasciato fui più che dagl'occhi altrui (S, bc)
1.1–59	Io non vuo' più star così (S, bc)
1.1–60	Io vi miro, luci belle (S, bc)
1.1–61	L'anima incenerita ai rai del mio bel sole (S, bc)
1.1–62	La speranza del mio core sol voi siete (S, bc)
1.1–63	L'avete fatta a me! (S, bc)
1.1–64	Lontananza e gelosia son tormenti (S, bc)
1.1–65	Mentre d'auree facelle adornavan le stelle (S, bc)
1.1–66	M'è venuto a fastidio lo sperare (S, lute?, bc)
1.1–67	Noiosi pensieri, fuggite dal seno (S, bc)
1.1–68	Non avea il sole ancora dall'algosa magion (S, bc)
1.1–69	Non disserrate ancora avea le porte d'oro (S, bc)
1.1–70	Non me ne fate tante (B, bc)
1.1–71	Non mi curo di fedeltà (B, bc)
1.1–72	Non più piaghe al mio cor (S, bc)
1.1–73	Non sei contento ancora, o dispietato arciero (S, bc)
1.1–74	Non si creda alla fortuna (S, bc)

1.1–75	Non sperar, beltà lusinghiera (S, bc)
1.1–76	Ombre, voi che celate dell'Etra i rai (S, bc)
1.1–77	O mio cor, quanto t'inganni (S, bc)
1.1–78	Or che siam soli, Amore (A, bc)
1.1–79	Per molti anni è stato occulto (S, bc)
1.1–80	Per pietà, qualche pietà (S, bc)
1.1–81	Piangete, occhi, piangete lungi da me (S, bc)
1.1–82	Pietà di Belisario, cieco, ramingo (T, bc)
1.1–83	Presso un rivo ch'avea d'argentato cristal (Mez, bc)
1.1–84	Pria di punir, crudele, chi mai sempre t'amò (S, bc)
1.1–85	Privo delle sue luci (S, bc)
1.1–86	Qual di cieca passione (S, bc)
1.1–87	Quando mai vi stancherete (S, bc)
1.1–88	Quando stanco dal corso (S, bc)
1.1–89	Sciogliete pur, sciogliete i vostri accenti (S, bc)
1.1–90	Scorrea lassù negli stellati campi (S, bc)
1.1–91	Se Nerone lo vuole, se lo soffron gli dei (S, bc)
1.1–92	Se Neron pur mi vuol morto (B, bc)
1.1–93	Se non parti, o gelosia (S, bc)
1.1–94	Se t'ama Filli, o cor (S, bc)
1.1–95	Sì, ch'io temo e non disamo (S, bc)
1.1–96	Si salvi chi può, vacillan le sfere (S, bc)
1.1–97	Soccorso, olà, Cupido (S, bc)
1.1–98	Soffro misero e taccio (S, bc)
1.1–99	Solca il mar da rie tempeste (S, bc)
1.1–100	Solcava incauto legno (S, bc)
1.1–101	Son gradito, e pur m'affanno (S, bc)
1.1–102	Sono in dubbio d'amar (S, bc)
1.1–103	Son principe, son re (S, bc)
1.1–104	Sopra candido foglio, nuncio delle mie pene (S, bc)
1.1–105	Sopra tutte l'altre belle (S, bc)
1.1–106	Sopra un'eccelsa torre cui le nubi del cielo (B, bc)
1.1–107	Sotto l'aura d'una speme (S, bc)
1.1–108	Sotto vedovo cielo, privo de' rai (S, bc)
1.1–109	Sprezzata mi credei, ma non tradita (S, bc)
1.1–110	Stanco dalla speranza di sognante pensier (S, bc)
1.1–111	Stelle, non mi tradite (S, bc)
1.1–112	Stelle sorde al mio pianto (S, bc)
1.1–113	Tante perle non versa l'Aurora (S, lute?, bc)
1.1–114	Tiranno di mia fe' d'affetto ignudo (S, bc)
1.1–115	Tradito mio core, non pianger (A, bc)
1.1–116	Troppo oppressa dal sonno nel suo letto (B, bc)
1.1–117	Tu partisti, crudel, e mi lasciasti (A, bc)

1.1–118   Udite, amanti, un prodigio novello (S, bc)
1.1–119   Un editto l'altro dì in Parnaso (S, bc)
1.1–120   Un Mongibello ardente di mille fiamme (S, bc)
1.1–121   Vaganti pensieri il volo arrestate (S, bc)
1.1–122   Vaghe calme, io non vi credo (S, bc)
1.1–123   Vincesti, vincesti o ciel (S, bc)
1.1–124   Voi siete sventurate, amorose mie pene (S, bc)
1.1–125   Voi volete il mio cor (S, bc)

Secular Cantatas for Two Voices with Continuo

1.2–1   A dispetto della sorte (S, Bar, bc)
1.2–2   Baldanzosa una bellezza (S, A, bc)
1.2–3   Chi dirà che nel veleno (S, B, bc)
1.2–4   Con mesto ciglio e dolorosi accenti (S, S echo, bc)
1.2–5   Fra quest'ombre io cerco il mio sole (S, A, bc)
1.2–6   In grembo all'oblio sommerger l'ardore (S, S, bc)
1.2–7   Io rimango stordito solo in veder (S, B, bc)
1.2–8   Piangete, occhi dolenti, piangete (S, Bar, bc)
1.2–9   Quel tuo petto di diamante (S, B, bc)
1.2–10   Son pur dolci le ferite (S, S, bc)

Secular Contatas for Three Voices with Continuo

1.3–1   Che speranza aver si può (S, S, B, bc)
1.3–2   Di tal tempra è la ferita (A, T, B, bc)
1.3–3   L'avviso al Tebro giunto (S, S, B, bc)
1.3–4   Lilla mia, su queste sponde (S, S, B, bc)

Secular Cantatas with Instrumental Accompaniment

1.4–1   Arsi già d'una fiamma (S, S, S, 2 vn, bc)
1.4–2   Chi resiste al dio bendato (S, S, B, con: bc; cg: vn, va-Mez, va-A, bc)
1.4–3   Ecco Amore ch'altero risplende (S, A, B, 2 vn, bc)
1.4–4   Furie del nero Tartaro (B, 2 vn, bc)
1.4–5   Il barcheggio (S, A, B, tpt/cornetto, 2 vn, bc incl. tbn)
1.4–6   Il Damone (S, S, S, S, A, T, B; 2 con: 2 vn, bc; cg: 2 vn, va-A, bc)
1.4–7   Il Damone (S, S, A, T, B; con: 2 vn, bc; cg: 2 vn, va-A, bc; 'lira' in bc)
1.4–8   Infinite son le pene (S, T, B, 2 vn, bc)
1.4–9   L'accademia d'Amore (S, S, A, T, B, con: 2 vn, bc; cg: vn, va-Mez, va-A, bc)
1.4–10   La Circe (S, S, B, 2 vn, bc)
1.4–11   La Circe (S, S, B, 2 vn, bc)

1.4–12   Lasciate ch'io respiri (S, B, 2 vn, bc)
1.4–13   Lo schiavo liberato (S, A, T, B, con: 2 vn, bc; cg: vn, va-A, va-T, bc)
1.4–14   Misero amante, a che mi vale (S, S, 2 vn, bc)
1.4–15   Or ch'alla dea notturna (S, T, or S, 2 vn, bc)
1.4–16   Per tua vaga beltade (S, S, 2 vn, bc)
1.4–17   Qual prodigio è ch'io miri? (S, S, B, con 1: 2 vn incl. lute and violone; con 2: 2 vn, bc incl. lute; cg: vn, va-A, va-T, bc incl. lute and violone?)
1.4–18   Qui dove fa soggiorno (S, B, 2 vn, bc)
1.4–19   Sciogliete in dolci nodi (S, S, vn, va-A, va-T, bc incl. va da gamba/cb)
1.4–20   Se del pianeta ardente (S, vn, va-A, va-T, bc)
1.4–21   Solitudine amata della pace (Mez, T, 2 vn, bc)
1.4–22   Vola, vola in altri petti (S, S, A, B, con: 2 vn, bc; cg: vn, va-Mez, va-A, bc)

Sacred and Moral Cantatas

1.5–1   Ah! troppo è ver [Sacred] (S, S, S, A, T, B; con: 2 vn, bc; cg: vn, va-A, va-T, bc incl. lute, harpsichord, harp)
1.5–2   Alle selve, agli studi [Moral] (S, S, A, A, bc)
1.5–3   Apre l'uomo infelice [Moral] (S, bc)
1.5–4   Crudo mar di fiamme orribili [Sacred] (B, 2 vn, bc)
1.5–5   Da cuspide ferrate [Sacred] (A, 2 vn, bc)
1.5–6   Dalla Tessala sponda scese d'Argo la prora [Moral] (A, bc)
1.5–7   Esule dalle sfere [Sacred] (S, B, SATB, 2 vn, bc)
1.5–8   Mortali, che sarà [Moral] (B, bc)
1.5–9   Quando sembra che nuoti [Moral] (S, bc)
1.5–10   Si apre al riso ogni labbro [Sacred] (S, A, B, 2 vn, bc)
1.5–11   Spuntava il dì quando la rosa [Moral] (S, S, B, bc)
1.5–12   Voi ch'avaro desio nel sen nudrite [Moral] (S, bc)

THEATRE MUSIC

Operas

2.1–1   Il Corispero (S, S, Mez, Mez, A, T, T, B, B, B; SATB, SATB, 2 vn, bc)
2.1–2   Il Trespolo tutore (S, S, S, A, T, B, 2 vn, bc)
2.1–3   La forza dell'amor paterno (S, S, S, S, S, A, A, T, B, B, 2 vn, bc)
2.1–4   Le gare dell'amor eroico (S, S, S, S, S, S, A, A, T, B, B, B, 2 vn, bc)
2.1–5   Moro per amore (S, S, S, A, A, T, B, 2 vn, bc)

Prologues

2.2–1	Aita, numi, aita (S, A, T, Bar, B, tpt, 2 vn, va-A, va-T, bc)
2.2–2	Che nuove? Oh, ragionevoli (S, T, T, 2 vn, bc)
2.2–3	Con meste luci (S, bc)
2.2–4	Dal luminoso impero (S, bc)
2.2–5	Dormi, Titone, addio (S, S, T, 2 vn, bc)
2.2–6	E dovrò dunque in solitaria stanza (T, 2 vn, bc)
2.2–7	Fermate, omai, fermate (S, S, T, 2 vn, bc)
2.2–8	Lasciai di Cipro il soglio (S, SATB, 2 vn, bc)
2.2–9	O di Cocito oscure deità (S, S, T, B, 2 vn, bc)
2.2–10	Questo è il giorno prefisso (S, S, S, Mez, T, bc)
2.2–11	Reggetemi, non posso più (S, [S,] T, 2 vn, bc)

Intermezzos

2.3–1	Amanti, che credete? (S, S, A, T, bc)
2.3–2	Che fai, Dorilla mia? (S, S, 2 vn, bc)
2.3–3	Chi me l'avesse detto (A, T, T, B, bc)
2.3–4	Chi mi conoscerà (S, S, B, bc)
2.3–5	La ruina del mondo (S, B, bc)
2.3–6	Oh, ve' che figuracce! (A, B, bc)
2.3–7	Soccorso, aita, ohimè (S, S, 2 vn, bc)
2.3–8	Su, miei fiati canori (S, bc)
2.3–9	Su, su, si stampino (S, A, T, Bar, B, 2 vn, bc)

Incidental Music

2.4–1	Il Biante (S, S, A, A, B, B, 2 vn, tpt, bc)

ORATORIOS

3–1	Ester, liberatrice del popolo ebreo (S, S, A, Bar, B, bc)
3–2	La Susanna (S, S, A, T, B, 2 vn, bc incl. theorbo)
3–3	San Giovanni Battista (S, S, A, T, B; con: 2 vn, bc incl. harpsichord and lute; cg: 1 vn, va-Mez, va-A, bc)
3–4	San Giovanni Chrisostomo (S, S, A, T, B, bc)
3–5	Santa Editta, vergine e monaca, regina d'Inghilterra (S, S, A, T, B, bc)
3–6	Santa Pelagia (S, A, T, B, 2 vn, va-A, bc incl. harpsichord and violone)

ARIAS, DUETS, TRIO

Arias

4.1–1	Adorata libertà, dal mio core non partir (S, bc)
4.1–2	Al rigor di due tiranni (S, bc)
4.1–3	Avete torto, occhi miei cari (S, bc)
4.1–4	Avrò pur d'aspettar più? (S, bc)
4.1–5	Begl'occhi, il vostro piangere (S, bc)
4.1–6	Bel tempo, addio, son fatto amante (S, bc)
4.1–7	Cara e dolce libertà (S, bc)
4.1–8	Che mi giovan le vittorie (Bar, 2 vn, bc)
4.1–9	Chi avesse visto un core (S, bc)
4.1–10	Chi mi disse che amor dà tormento (Mez, bc)
4.1–11	Chi non porta amor nel petto (S, bc)
4.1–12	Chi vuol libero il suo pie' (S, bc)
4.1–13	Da Filinda aver chi può (S, bc)
4.1–14	Deh, frenate i furori (B, bc)
4.1–15	Deh, vola, o desio (S, bc)
4.1–16	Delizie, contenti (Bar, 2 vn, bc)
4.1–17	Dell'ardore ch'il core distempra (S, bc)
4.1–18	Destatevi, o sensi, risvegliati, onore (S, 2 vn, bc)
4.1–19	Dormite, occhi, dormite (Bar, vn, bc)
4.1–20	È pazzia innamorarsi (S, bc)
4.1–21	Fedeltà sinché spirto in petto avrò (S, bc)
4.1–22	Il mio cor ch'è infelicissimo (S, bc)
4.1–23	Il mio core per voi, luci belle (S, bc)
4.1–24	Le luci vezzose volgetemi, o Clori (S, bc)
4.1–25	Mio cor, che si fa? (S, bc)
4.1–26	Non fia mai, ah no, ch'io speri (S, bc)
4.1–27	Ogni sguardo che tu scocchi (S, bc)
4.1–28	Parti, fuggi dal mio seno (S, bc)
4.1–29	Pensier ostinato (S, bc)
4.1–30	Pria di scior quel dolce nodo (A, bc)
4.1–31	Quanto è bella la mia stella (S, bc)
4.1–32	S'Amor m'annoda il piede (S, bc)
4.1–33	Se di gioie m'alletta il sereno (S, bc)
4.1–34	Speranze smarrite (A, 2 vn, bc)
4.1–35	Ti lascierò e a poco a poco (S, bc)
4.1–36	Torna, Amor, dammi il mio bene (S, bc)

Duets

4.2–1	Ahi, che posar non puote (S, Bar, bc)
4.2–2	Ardo, sospiro e piango (S, Bar, bc)

4.2–3	Aure fresche, aure volanti (Mez, Bar, vn, bc)
4.2–4	Care labbra che d'amore (S, B, bc)
4.2–5	Dietro l'orme del desio (S, A, bc)
4.2–6	Fulmini quanto sa quel sembiante severo/lusinghiero (S, B, bc)
4.2–7	La bellissima/dolcissima speranza che nutrisce (S, B, bc)
4.2–8	Me ne farete tanto che più non soffrirò (S, B, bc)
4.2–9	Non si muove onda in fiume (S, B, bc)
4.2–10	Occhi belli, e che sarà (S, S, bc)
4.2–11	Pazienza, finirà l'influenza (T, B, bc)
4.2–12	Sarà ver ch'io mai disciolga (S, B, bc)
4.2–13	Sì/No, quella tu sei che il mio cor sempre adora (S, B, bc)

Trio

| 4.3–1 | Trionfate, invitti colli (S, S, B, 2 vn, bc) |

MADRIGALS

5–1	Clori, son fido amante (S, S, A, T, B, bc ad lib)
5–2	Colpo de' bei vostr'occhi (S, A, B, bc)
5–3	È pur giunta, mia vita (S, A, T, bc)
5–4	Feritevi, ferite, viperette mordaci (S, S, B, bc)
5–5	Piangete, occhi dolenti (S, S, A, T, B, bc)
5–6	Pupillette amorose (S, S, Mez, A, T)
5–7	Sperai nella partita (S, S, B, bc)
5–8	Tirsi un giorno piangea (S, S, Mez, A, T, bc ad lib?)

SACRED MUSIC WITH LATIN TEXTS

Liturgical Settings

6.1–1	Ave regina coelorum (S, A, bc)
6.1–2	Benedictus dominus Deus (S, A, bc)
6.1–3	Tantum ergo sacramentum (S, A, bc)
6.1–4	Vau: Et egressus est a filia Sion (A, bc)

Non-Liturgical Settings (Motets)

6.2–1	Care Jesu suavissime (S, A, 2 vn, bc)
6.2–2	Convocamini, congregamini (S, S, S 'ripieno', A, T, B, 2 vn, bc)
6.2–3	Dixit angelis suis iratus Deus (S, bc)
6.2–4	Exultate in Deo, fideles (B, 2 vn, bc)
6.2–5	In tribulationibus, in angustiis (S, S, A, T, B, 2 vn, bc)
6.2–6	Locutus est Dominus de nube ignis (S, 2 vn, bc)
6.2–7	Nascere virgo potens (S, S, B, bc)
6.2–8	Oh maiestas aeterna (S, S, bc)

6.2–9	O vos omnes, qui transitis (A, 2 vn, bc)
6.2–10	Plaudite vocibus (S, bc)
6.2–11	Pugna, certamen, militia est vita (S, A, T, B, con: 2 vn, bc; cg: vn, va-A, va-T, bc)
6.2–12	Sinite lacrimari, sinite lamentari (S, S, B, 2 vn, bc)
6.2–13	Sistite sidera, coeli motus otiamini (S, 2 vn, bc)
6.2–14	Surge, cor meum (S, bc)

INSTRUMENTAL MUSIC

Solo Sonatas

7.1–1	Sinfonia [D major] (vn, bc)
7.1–2	Sinfonia [D major] (vn, bc)
7.1–3	Sinfonia [D minor] (vn, bc)
7.1–4	Sinfonia [D minor] (vn, bc)
7.1–5	Sinfonia [E minor] (vn, bc)
7.1–6	Sinfonia [F major] (vn, bc)
7.1–7	Sinfonia [F major] (vn, bc)
7.1–8	Sinfonia [F major] (vn, bc)
7.1–9	Sinfonia [G major] (vn, bc)
7.1–10	Sinfonia [A minor] (vn, bc)
7.1–11	Sinfonia [A minor] (vn, bc)
7.1–12	Sinfonia [A minor] (vn, bc)

Duo-Sonatas

7.2–1	Sinfonia [D minor] (vn, lute/vc?, bc)
7.2–2	Sinfonia [B♭ major] (vn, lute/vc?, bc)

Trio-Sonatas

7.3–1	Sinfonia [C major] (2 vn, bc)
7.3–2	Sinfonia [D major] (2 vn, bc)
7.3–3	Sinfonia [D major] (2 vn, bc)
7.3–4	Sinfonia [D major] (2 vn, bc)
7.3–5	Sinfonia [F major] (2 vn, bc)
7.3–6	Sinfonia [F major] (2 vn, bc)
7.3–7	Sinfonia [G major] (2 vn, bc)
7.3–8	Sinfonia [A minor] (2 vn, bc)
7.3-9	Sinfonia [A minor] (2 vn, bc)

Sonatas for Large Ensembles

7.4–1	Sonata [D major] (coro 1: 2 vn, bc; coro 2: 2 cornetti, bc)
7.4–2	Sonata di viole [D major] (con: 2 vn, bc incl. lute; cg: vn, va-A, va-T, bc)

7.4–3   Sonata a otto viole con una tromba [D major] (tpt; coro 1: vn, va-Mez, va-A, bc; coro 2: vn, va-Mez, va-A, bc; bc 'si placet')

Keyboard Music

7.5–1   Toccata [A minor]

Pedagogical Work

8–1   Libro de Primi Elimenti [*sic*]

Lost Works

9–1   Ad arma volate (Motet)
9–2   Doriclea (Opera)
9–3   Ecco il petto (Aria or Cantata)
9–4   Expugnate, debellate (Motet)
9–5   Mentre in un dolce (Aria or Cantata)
9–6   Messa a 8
9–7   Non ci pensate mai (Cantata)
9–8   Non è al certo vanità (Aria or Cantata)
9–9   Oratorio (Latin)
9–10   Riderete in verità (Aria or Cantata)
9–11   Santa Caterina (Oratorio)
9–12   Sinfonie a 5 (a collection)
9–13   Sinfonie for strings and lute (a collection)
9–14   Sonate da Cimbalo, et organo (a collection)
9–15   Tantum ergo a 4
9–16   Toccate da Cimbalo (a collection)

For a list of doubtful works and misattributions, see Gianturco–McCrickard, *Stradella Catalogue*.

Appendix 2:
Stradella's Extant Writings

Stradella's extant writings are presented here in the following order: his letters, opera dedications, and motet texts. In each case the original language is given first, and then an English translation. In the transcription of the letters and dedications, the spellings of the words are reported as they appear in the original but capitalization has been made to conform to present Italian usage, antiquated accents have been eliminated, and abbreviated words have been written in full. For easier comprehension punctuation has been altered and capitalization has been modernized in the English translation. As the titles *Signor* and *Signora* are quite familiar, they have sometimes been left untranslated. Stradella's Latin motet texts have been modernized and provided with punctuation.

(*a*): LETTERS

Twenty-four of Stradella's autograph letters are extant. Twenty are addressed to Polo Michiel of Venice, and two to Girolamo Michiel, Polo's brother. They are in the Biblioteca del Museo Civico Correr of Venice (I-Vmc), catalogued under 'Provenienze Diverse' (PD). The existence of Stradella letters here was known to someone who apparently copied all but three of them (numbered here 2, 3, and 14) in the period July–August 1943. He signed and dated each letter, and although his signature is illegible, it might read 'Mario Brunetti', the Director of the library at that time, who died some ten years later without publishing his transcriptions. In 1976 Giovanni Morelli realized that there was correspondence by Stradella in the Correr and communicated his find to Lorenzo Bianconi, who examined some of the letters for their information related to opera; he decided to reveal their existence at the Convegno internazionale di studi 'Alessandro Stradella e il suo tempo', which I organized at the Accademia Chigiana in Siena, 8–12 September 1982. I then made a search of the library files and transcribed all the letters by Stradella (as well as all correspondence relating to him). Another extant Stradella letter is addressed to Flavio Orsini, Duke of Bracciano, and is now in the Archivio Storico Capitolino of Rome, catalogued under 'Archivio Orsini'; a letter addressed to Cardinal Flavio Chigi is in the Chigi family archives in the Biblioteca Vaticana. Full bibliographical details will be given with each letter. The correspondence is presented here in chronological order, a successive number having been assigned to each letter. Although Stradella wrote the place and date in various positions after the body of his letters, they will always be given at the very end of the letter.

1. Stradella to Cardinal Flavio Chigi: Rome, 27 November 1670
I-Rvat, Archivio Chigi, 57, fos. 470^r–471^v

Eminentissimo e Reverentissimo Signor Padrone Colendissimo

Nell'essere introdotto avanti Vostra Eccellenza, restai confuso alla maestà della presenza, e perdei nel medesimo tempo l'ardire di chiedere la gratia maggiore, che desideravo; che aspetto d'un prencipe così grande risveglia sovente, e un gran timore, e un gran riverenza. Onde già che a voce non son'io capace d'esprimere a Vostra Eccellenza quanto mi accade, eccomi in questo foglio prostrato alli piedi di Vostra Eccellenza, eccomi inginocchiato alla Sua Clemenza per supplicar d'aiuto per impetrar dalla Sua benignità di sollevarmi da una disgratia, che mi sovrasta, nella quale se non ho protettore, posso esser soggetto a pregiuditio di robba, di riputatione, e forse anco di libertà. Ben so, che non posso, ne devo ricorrere ad altri, mentre nella mia congiontura v'ed'uopo un signore grande, generoso, benigno, ed a mezzo a far gratie si che da chi meglio potev'io andare, che da Vostra Eccellenza; che ha tutte queste qualità identificate con la Sua propria persona. Sappia dunque Vostra Eccellenza che son già due anni, che io giro in piazza negotiando qualche denaro, e sin'ora con qualche buona sorte; ma perché chi naviga in questo mare, se non ha chi lo difenda dall'ingiurie della fortuna, gli conviene soggiacere a molti incontri di quella; così appunto se io non trovo chi mi dia la mano resterò bersaglio di fierissima tempesta. Dirò per tanto, che essendo tardati molti assegnamenti di riscossione, che dovevano venirmi, e trovando qualche durezza in riscuotere qua, dove speravo ogni puntualità, fra le piazze di fuori, e di qua, mi hanno reso con scarsezza di denaro; et essendo impegnato in questa settimana a pagare sette mila scudi in circa, fra lettere di cambio accettate, e pagarò che son fuori, sono in gran cimento di poter riuscire, a tutti; onde per sodisfare a quello che di necessità mi conviene, sarebbero bastanti due mila scudi, che gl'altri ho già messo insieme; di questi vorrei supplicare Vostra Eccellenza; il tempo che ho da rimediare a questo accidente è solo tutto sabbato presente, che ancora la brevità di questo mi conduce ad incommodare Vostra Eccellenza; se per sorte gli cedesse in pensiero di sovvenirmi, il Suo denaro è sicuro, ne altra sicurtà posso proferirli in questo punto, che la mia persona, il mio sangue, ed il mio pugno, quale obbligandosi, può bene obbligare a Suo favore S.10000–, et entrando questi S.2000– pur restano per assicuratione di Vostra Eccellenza facendomi questo favore Vostra Eccellenza mi mette in maggior credito; io sto in piede, e Vostra Eccellenza è sodisfatto. Il tempo che ho bisogno sono sei mesi, in capo dei quali restituirò a Vostra Eccellenza tutto il denaro con quel tutto, che commanderà. E ben può credere, ch'io non sarei sì privo di cervello, che mi volessi impegnare a un interesse di questa sorte con Vostra Eccellenza, se non sapessi d'esser ben sicuro di poterli corrispondere a suo tempo. Per haver questa gratia tre sarebbero le cose necessarie; una la sicurezza di Vostra Eccellenza; e questa può credere, che v'è. L'altra la generosità di chi la deve fare, e questa non manca. L'ultima è merito di chi la deve conseguire, e questa manca, ma per lo più sogliono i maggiori supplire co l' loro merito, e co l' loro vantaggio sopra gl'altri al defetto degl'inferiori. Torno di nuovo con suppliche, e non vorrei che Vostra Eccellenza abbandonaste un Suo servitore, che non ha altro ramarico, che il non haver occasione di mostrare quanto sia grande in Sua devotione verso Vostra Eccellenza; e perfino senz'altro intercessore che la solita gentilezza, e bontà di Vostra Eccellenza ne spero ogni buon fine. E prostrandomi, e baciando riverentemente la Eccellenza Vostra, resto inchinandomeli humilmente

Di Vostra Eccellenza
humilissimo devotissimo obligatissimo servitore
Alessandro Stradella
Casa Li 27 9bre 1670
[*the following is inserted as a postscript:*]
Prego Vostra Eccellenza questa povera lettera resti sepolta e se non è troppo ardire; un sì, o un no sigillato che per più facilità può farlo lasciare al Signor Apolloni. E mentre non mi resta altra speranza che l'aiuto di Vostra Eccellenza, sto aspettando la sentenza che mi può ritornare in vita, o pure in qualunque modo sia, sempre viverò infinitemente obbligato a Vostra Eccellenza.

Most Eminent and Most Revered Sir, Most Honourable Master,

When I was brought before Your Excellency, I was confused by the majesty of [your] presence, and at the same time lost courage to ask for the most important favour that I desired. The appearance of such a prince often causes great fear and great respect. Therefore, since I am not capable of expressing verbally to Your Excellency what is happening to me, I am here with this sheet of paper, prostrate at Your Excellency's feet, kneeling before Your Clemency to beg for help, and to request your magnanimity to free me from a disgrace which is hovering above me, [a situation] in which, if I have no protector, I could be deprived of my belongings, reputation, and perhaps also freedom. I know very well that I cannot, nor ought I to appeal to others, since in my situation it is necessary to have a great signore, generous, kind, and accustomed to bestow favours. Hence, to whom better could I have gone than Your Excellency, who has all these qualities identified with his very person. Your

Excellency should therefore know that it is already two years that I am free-lancing to earn some money, and that so far I have had reasonable good luck; but, whoever navigates this particular sea, and does not have someone to protect him from the abuses of fortune, must succumb to several encounters with the same. As a consequence of this, if I do not find one who will give me a hand, I will remain the target of a most fierce tempest. I will therefore say that, since many payments of money that were due me were late, and finding some difficulty in collecting [them] here where I expected every punctuality, between the places outside [Rome] and here, they have left me in need of money. And being obligated this week to pay about seven thousand scudi, between letters of credit which have been honoured and promises of payment which are still unfulfilled, I am in great difficulty of being able to manage with all of them. Whereby, in order to satisfy my needs, it would be sufficient to have two thousand scudi since I have already put together the rest. For these, I would like to beg Your Excellency. The time left to remedy this misfortune is only until the coming Saturday; it is therefore the shortness of the [time] that leads me to disturb Your Excellency. If by any chance you would agree to help me, your money is safe, though I cannot provide you at this moment with any other insurance than my own person, my blood, and my strength. As interest you can request in your favour 10,000 scudi, so that when the 2,000 scudi return, there will be others as insurance for Your Excellency. Doing me this favour, Your Excellency puts me in even greater debt. I am saved, and Your Excellency is satisfied. The time I need for this is six months, at the end of which I will give back to Your Excellency all the money, together with all that you will request; and you can well believe that I would not be so empty-headed as to involve myself with an interest of this sort with Your Excellency, if I could not be very sure to be able to give it back on time. In order to have this favour, three things would be necessary: one is the dependability of Your Excellency, and you can believe that this is there; the other [second] is the generosity of the one who does it, and this is not lacking. The last is the merit of the one who is to receive it, and this is missing; but usually the more important persons are used to making up with their merit and with their advantages over others for the faults of their inferiors. I repeat again [my] requests; and I would not like Your Excellency to abandon one of his servants, who has no other regret than not to have any occasion to show how great is his devotion towards Your Excellency. And even without any other intercessor than the usual kindness and goodness of Your Excellency, I hope for a good outcome. And prostrating myself and reverently kissing Your Excellency, I remain humbly bowing

Your Excellency's

most humble, most devoted, most obliged servant,

Alessandro Stradella.

Home, 27 November 1670

[*the following is inserted as a postscript:*]

I beg Your Excellency to be silent about this poor letter, if it is not asking too much; a Yes or a No with your seal, to make things easier, could be left with Signor Apolloni. And while I am not left with any other hope than the help of Your Excellency, I await the verdict that can bring me back to life; but whatever the outcome, I will always live infinitely obliged to Your Excellency.

2. Stradella to Polo Michiel: Rome, 10 October 1676
I-Vmc, PD C. 1063, no. 389

Illustrissimo et Eccellentissimo Signore Padrone Mio Colendissimo

Sono con questa per ratificare a Vostra Eccellenza la mia osservanza, e per renderLa certa che vivo ansioso de suoi commandi; e nel medesimo sentendo qua in Roma, che da Venetia si cercano virtuose per li teatri, e vedendo che se diligenze che si fanno qua in Roma cadono sopra persone, dalle quali non posso credere che ne possino havere honore per tanto mosso dalla giustitia sono a supplicar Vostra Eccellenza che voglia di portare in questa congiontura la Signora Caterina Saminiati, e la quale infallibilmente e superiore in ogni conto a tutte queste, sopra le quali ho visto fare assegnamento qua in Roma dopo però le buone già determinate. Vostra Eccellenza non deve haver repugnanza alcuna in protegger questa virtuosa dalla quale ne può sperare buona riuscita, ed io ne conservarò eterne obligationi, mentre nel medesimo tempo favorirà l'una e l'altra parte, che è quanto e facendogli humilissima reverenza resto per sempre

Di Vostra Eccellenza

humilissimo devotissimo obligatissimo servitore

Alessandro Stradella.

Roma Li 10 8bre 1676

Most Illustrious and Most Excellent Sir, My Most Honourable Master,

With this [letter] I affirm my devotion to Your Excellency, and assure you that I live anxious for your commands. And at the same time hearing here in Rome that singers are sought for the theatres of Venice, and seeing the zeal with which they give [positions] here in Rome to persons whom I cannot believe should have such honour, and therefore moved by justice I supplicate Your Excellency to give this opportunity to Signora Caterina Saminiati,—who is without doubt superior on all counts to all of these [women singers] whom I saw given posts here in Rome—however, after the good ones have already been decided upon Your Excellency need not be at all reluctant to patronize this singer from whom one can expect good results, and I will be eternally grateful; while at the same time you will favour one [her] and the other party [me]. With which, giving you most humble reverence, I remain forever

Your Excellency's
most humble, most devoted, most obliged servant,
Alessandro Stradella.
Rome, 10 October 1676

3. Stradella to Polo Michiel: Rome, 20 October 1676
I-Vmc, PD C. 1063, no. 350

Illustrissimo et Eccellentissimo Signore Signore Padrone Mio Colendissimo
Sempre Vostra Eccellenza vuol confondere con le Sue gratie i Suoi servitori, e vuole esercitare i soliti atti della Sua benignissima generosità; sono dunque con questa per rendergli infinite gratie del bellissimo collaro, e manichetti trasmessomi per le mani del Signore Abbate Olgiati, il quale ancora ho pregato anco meglio di me esprima i miei sentimenti a Vostra Eccellenza che non sono se non che di servir Vostra Eccellenza sinche haverò vita, non con altro fine che per acquistar la gratia, e la buona protettione di Vostra Eccellenza, soggiungo che si potrebbe dare il caso ch'io potessi essere in persona ad'offerirLa me stesso, sendomi successa una certa disgratia qua in Roma, che non me permette per adesso il dimorare; onde in questo caso tanto più havrò bisogno delli favori di Vostra Eccellenza; e si può, e si potrà sempre assicurare d'havere un vero servitore, con che Gli faccio humilissima riverenza mentre resto

Di Vostra Eccellenza
humilissimo devotissimo obligatissimo servitore
Alessandro Stradella.
Roma li 20 8bre 1676

Most Illustrious and Most Excellent Sir, My Lord and Most Honourable Master,
Your Excellency always wants to embarrass his servants with his kindnesses, and wants to practise the usual acts of his most benign generosity. With this [letter] do I then give you infinite thanks for the most beautiful collar and cuffs passed on to me by the hands of Signor Abate Olgiati, whom I also begged to express my sentiments better than I can to Your Excellency, as I wish nothing but to serve Your Excellency as long as I live, with no other motive than to acquire the favour and the protection of Your Excellency. I add that it could be that I will be able to offer it in person, a certain misfortune having happened to me here in Rome, which does not permit me to live here at the moment; whereby in the event I will have even more need of the favours of Your Excellency. And you are,

and always will be assured of having a true servant, whereby I pay most humble reverence while I remain

Your Excellency's

most humble, most devoted, most obliged servant,

Alessandro Stradella.

Rome, 20 October 1676

4. Stradella to Polo Michiel: Turin, 21 August 1677
I-Vmc, PD C. 1064, no. 263

Illustrissimo et Eccellentissimo Signore Signore e Padrone Mio Colendissimo

Non ho ardito sin' hora con mie portare a Vostra Eccellenza quei tributi d'ossequio che si contengono dalla mia partialissima servitù al sommo merito di Vostra Eccellenza, essendo incerto che Vostra Eccellenza havesse accetato con buon cuore le mie espressioni, ma non per questo pretendo haver perduto il nome di Suo vero, ed inalterabile servitore, e mi assicuro tanto nella somma Sua benignità che so molto bene che saprà compatire l'accidente occorsomi, mentre il desiderio di vendicarsi, e l'amore sono due passioni che meritono ogni scusa; onde quando in ciò havess'io male incontrato il genio di Vostra Eccellenza Gle ne chiedo humilissimo perdono sicuro d'ottenerlo dalla solita, e generosa clemenza dell'Eccellenza Vostra. In oltre vengo con le più vive suppliche a pregar la bontà di Vostra Eccellenza a volermi far tanto honore di mandarmi qualche lettera in mia raccommandatione a questa vita. Io sono molto bene informato del concetto grande, e della potenza che Vostra Eccellenza ha in questo luogo tanto appresso Madama Reale, appresso Madama La Principessa, e tutti i principali cavalieri di qua, onde so quanto può giovarmi una Sua calda raccommandatina. La causa per la quale io supplico Vostra Eccellenza di questo favore, è perché essendosi aiutato qua il Signore Aluigi Contarini non con altro che con il dire che io sono un ladro, che gl'ho rubbato denari, con mille altre bugie, le quali veramente meritarebbero un contracambio diverso in quello ch'io vado pregando, ho bisogno di lettere a questa corte che testifichino le mie attioni con tutto quello che può credere Vostra Eccellenza esser bisogno in questo caso. Il medesimo Signore Aluigi non è stato per questo creduto, ed hanno scusato la sua maledicenza con crederlo molto appassionato, ed innamorato, ma con tutto ciò, io mi son sempre dichiarato con questa corte, ed'ho fatto intendere a Madama Reale che son sempre pronto di ricevere ogni castigo, ogni volta che io habbi in alcuna mia attione commesso errore positivo. Per quello che aspetta alla donna, Madama Reale se ne ride con ogn'uno, tanto più che sono arrivati a sapere che io non l'ho condotta via per levarla al Signore Aluigi, ma per la compassione ch'havevo alle disgratie della medema, per i pericoli nelli quali io la vedevo, e per le continue, e infinite suppliche che ella me n'ha fatte. Se mai da Vostra Eccellenza potrò attendere favore in questo mondo che per me sia grandissimo, questo è apunto che concerne alla mia reputatione; non mancano per mia fortuna amici che si adoprano a viva forza per favorirmi con speranza di riuscir di tutto, ma il so molto bene che non posso haver la maggiore, ne la più potenta assistenza di Vostra Eccellenza; di questa gratia supplico Vostra Eccellenza particolarmente per parte della Signora Agnesa, la quale in virtù della gentilezza che Vostra Eccellenza ha con le bellezze humane, si compromette di tutto; e forse nel seguente ordinario Gle v'inviarò le preghiere di sua propria mano, mentr'io faccio sapere a Vostra Eccellenza che non chiedo questa gratia, ne per altro m'affatigo, e cerco buone protettioni se non per poter ben servire la Signora Agnesa, quale io giamai abbandonerò, ne lascerò dal canto mio di far tutto per ben servirla; onde Vostra Eccellenza fa una gratia speciale a lei, e a me, e poi Gl'assicuro che fa un'opera di carità, che tale la conoscerà, quando saperà il tutto, il che hora devo tacere. Per me io servo per levare affatto qualche ombra di malconcetto che ha potuto spargere la passione del Signore Aluigi, del resto Iddio mi dia per la sanità che non mancherà chi mi guarderà con buon'occhio. Torno di nuovo a supplicar Vostra Eccellenza come anco faccio nel medesimo ordinario all'Eccellentissimo Signore Girolamo Suo fratello; e mentre Le faccio humilissimo devotissima riverenza resto per sempre

Di Vostra Eccellenza
humilissimo devotissimo obligatissimo servitore
Alessandro Stradella.
Torino Li 21 Agosto 1677

Most Illustrious and Most Excellent Sir, My Lord and Most Honourable Master,

Until now I did not dare with my [letters] to bring to Your Excellency those tributes of respect which my most favoured servitude owes to the great merit of Your Excellency, being uncertain whether Your Excellency would have accepted my declarations with good heart. But despite this I have not abandoned the title of being your true and constant servant. And I believe so much in your great kindness that I know very well that you will know how to understand the misfortune which has occurred to me, since desire for revenge and love are two passions which merit every excuse. Whereby if in this I have misunderstood the attitude of Your Excellency, I ask most humble pardon, assured of obtaining it from the usual and generous clemency of Your Excellency. In addition I come with the most lively supplications to beg the goodness of Your Excellency to wish me such honour as to send me some letters recommending me in this life. I am very well informed of the great consideration, and of the influence that Your Excellency has in this place with Her Ladyship, with the Princess, and all the leading gentlemen here; whereby I know how much I could be helped by one of your warm little recommendations. The reason why I ask Your Excellency this favour is because Signor Aluigi Contarini having advanced his cause here just by saying that I am a thief, that I robbed him of money, with a thousand other lies, which truly would merit a response of another sort than that which I am asking, I need letters to this court which testify to my actions with all that Your Excellency may think necessary in this case. The same Signor Aluigi was nevertheless not believed, and they excused his slander by believing him to be very passionate and in love; but with all that, I have always been open with the court, and I have informed Her Ladyship that I am always ready to receive every reprimand whenever I have committed by my actions a positive error. As far as the woman is concerned, Her Ladyship makes light of it with everyone, even more so since they have learned that I did not take her away to remove her from Signor Aluigi, but because of the compassion that I had for the misfortunes of the same, for the dangers in which I saw her, and because of the continuous and innumerable supplications she made me. If ever I may expect a worldly favour which I consider very great from Your Excellency, it is exactly that which concerns my reputation. To my fortune, friends are not lacking who energetically favour me with hope to succeed in everything, but I know very well that I cannot have greater, nor more powerful assistance than Your Excellency. For this favour I beg Your Excellency especially on behalf of Signora Agnesa, who in virtue of the kindness that Your Excellency has with human beauties, risks all, and perhaps in the next mail will send you requests in her own hand. While I say to Your Excellency that I do not ask this favour, nor for any other reason do I exert myself and seek your good assurances, but only in order to serve well Signora Agnesa, whom I will never abandon, nor will I ever stop doing everything to serve her well. Whereby Your Excellency does a special favour to her, and to me, and then I assure you that you do a work of charity, which you will realize when you know everything about which I must now be silent. For my part, I work to remove completely any shadow of a bad name which the passion of Signor Aluigi has been able to spread; for the rest, God give me health, because someone who will look after me favourably will not be lacking. I return again to beg Your Excellency as I do in the same post to the most excellent Signor Girolamo your brother. And while I make most humble, most devout reverence, I remain forever

Your Excellency's
most humble, most devoted, most obliged servant,
Alessandro Stradella.
Turin, 21 August 1677

5. Stradella to Polo Michiel: Turin, 24 August 1677
I-Vmc, PD C. 1064, no. 262

Illustrissimo et Eccellentissimo Signore Signore Padrone Mio Colendissimo
    Invio a Vostra Eccellenza due lettere della Signora Agnesa una per
Vostra Eccellenza l'altra per l'Eccellentissimo Signore Girolamo Suo
fratello accio scrivano di qualche calore perché io possa ricevere i favori
delle lettere che nell'ordinario passato ad ambedue supplico onde
reiterando le mie suppliche unite con l'annesso sperarò dalla Loro somma
generosità questa gratia per me molto singolare, e tutta intesa posso dirGli
altro come farò a miglior tempo. Qua io godo bellissime conversationi di
dame intanto, e spero con l'aiuto di Vostra Eccellenza buon esito a tutte le
mie cose. E' stato scritto di qua per l'aggiustamento mio con
l'Eccellentissimo Signore Aluigi, soprache porgendosi l'occasione a Vostra
Eccellenza La supplico d'una buona parola, che potrà operare più
d'ogn'altro mezzo, e l'aggiungeranno queste alle mie infinite obligationi
che tengo con Vostra Eccellenza e mentre con ardentissimo desiderio sto
aspettando i Suoi desideratissimi commandi resto con farLe devotissima et
humilissima riverenza
    Di Vostra Eccellenza
    humilissimo devotissimo obligatissimo servitore
    Alessandro Stradella.
    Torino Li 24 Agosto 1677

Most Illustrious and Most Excellent Sir, My Lord and Most Honourable
Master,
    I send two letters from Signora Agnesa to Your Excellency, one for
Your Excellency, the other for the most excellent Signor Girolamo, your
brother, which urge in writing that I might receive the favours of the letters which in the last post I asked of you both; whereby repeating my
supplications together with the enclosed [ones], I shall hope [to have]
from your great generosity this very singular grace for myself, the full
meaning of which I will tell you at a more opportune time. Here in the
mean time I enjoy a most beautiful social intercourse with the ladies, and
I hope with the help of Your Excellency for a good outcome to all my
affairs. [They have] written from here in order to smooth things out with
the most excellent Signor Aluigi, to whom I beg a good word from Your
Excellency when the occasion offers, which would work better than anything else; and these will be added to my infinite obligations which bind
me to Your Excellency. And while with most ardent desire I await your
most desired commands, I remain, giving most devout and most humble
reverence,

Your Excellency's
most humble, most devoted, most obliged servant,
Alessandro Stradella.
Turin, 24 August 1677

6. Stradella to Girolamo Michiel: Turin, 4 September 1677
I-Vmc, PD C. 1064, no. 429

Illustrissimo et Eccellentissimo Signore e Padrone Mio Colendissimo
Ricevo due benignissime di Vostra Eccellenza una di 22; e l'altra di 28
Agosto passato; in risposta dico che in questo medesimo ordinario mando
al Signore Poleni la lettera, quale desidera sia lasciata in sue mani, onde
mi farà singolarissimo favore consegnare le robbe mie, come quel poco che
vi è rimasto della Signora Agnesa; tanto più che comincio ad'havere
bisogno de miei istromenti; e de miei libri in Torino, dove il tutto mi si
rivolta in favore, si che spero buon'esito a tutti i fatti miei, ne mancarò di
dar parte a Vostra Eccellenza come mio principal padrone di ciò che mi
succederà non volendo io mai lasciare, quando Vostra Eccellenza si compiaccia, il titolo di Suo vero servitore. Non ho cosa precisa di neuno a
porre le Sue potentissime intercessioni con Eccellentissimo Signore Paolo
Micheli [*sic*] per le gratie desiderate resto con pregar Vostra Eccellenza
riverire in mio nome la Signora Maria Felice, e faccio humilissima riverenza a Vostra Eccellenza restando [*The following sentence is inserted here:*]
Adesso appunto ho havuto ordine dalla Signora Agnesa riverire profondamente Vostra Eccellenza.
Di Vostra Eccellenza
humilissimo devotissimo obligatissimo servitore
Alessandro Stradella.
Torino Li 4 7bre 1677

Most Illustrious and Most Excellent Sir, and My Most Honourable
Master,
I received two most kind [letters] from Your Excellency, one of the
22nd, and the other of 28 August just passed. In reply I say that in this
same post I am sending to Signor Poleni the letter which you desire to be
left in his hands, whereby you will do me a very singular favour to give
[him] my things, as well as the little which is left of those of Signora
Agnesa, since I am beginning to need my instruments and my books in
Turin, where everything is favourable to me, so that I hope for a good
outcome in everything. Neither will I fail to inform Your Excellency as
my principal master of what happens to me, not wishing ever to give up,
as long as it pleases Your Excellency, the title of your true servant. I have

no one else who could intercede with the most excellent Signor Paolo Micheli [Polo Michiel] for the favours I desire. I still beg Your Excellency to give my respects to Signora Maria Felice, and I most humbly bow to Your Excellency remaining [*the following sentence is inserted here:*] Now in fact I have received a request from Signora Agnesa to pay respects profoundly to Your Excellency.

Your Excellency's
most humble, most devoted, most obliged servant,
Alessandro Stradella.
Turin, 4 September 1677

7. Stradella to Polo Michiel: Turin, 11 September 1677
I-Vmc, PD C. 1064, no. 288

Illustrissimo et Eccellentissimo Signore Signore e Padrone Mio Colendissimo

Mi trovo favorito d'una benignissima di Vostra Eccellenza con l'incluso in mio favoure al Signore Marchese Parella, della quale mi servirò a suo tempo in mio vantaggio, ed ho ricapitato subito la lettera alla Signora Agnesa; non posso se non che render infinite gratie a Vostra Eccellenza dell'honor che mi ha fatto, aspettando che venga il tempo che Vostra Eccellenza m'impieghi con i Suoi stimatissimi commandi, con l'esecutione prontissima de quali cercarò far conoscere a Vostra Eccellenza quanto sia grande la devotione, e l'osservanza che Le professo unite con una immensità d'obligationi. La signora intanto, la quale sta benissimo, mi ha imposto che ancora per lei renda grate a Vostra Eccellenza dell'incommodo che ad'istanza sua ancora si è compiaciuta prendersi, e si professa humilissima serva di Vostra Eccellenza. Intanto, benché molti personaggi riguardevoli habbino l'incombenza di dar fine aggiustato a miei interessi, per quello che importa l'accidente occorsami e con tutto che i medesimi signori siano inteso grandemente a favorirmi, voglio ricorrere alle gratie di Vostra Eccellenza con supplicarLa, havendo apertura a disporre le Sue potentissime intercessioni con il Signore Aluigi Contarini e sapendo quanto sia grande l'autorità di Vostra Eccellenza, confido più ne Suoi patrocinij, che in qualsivoglia altro favore ch'io possa ottenere. Supplico di nuovo la bontà di Vostra Eccellenza de Suoi da me desideratissimi cenni, e mentre Le faccio humilissima e devotissima riverenza resto per sempre

Di Vostra Eccellenza
humilissimo devotissimo obligatissimo servitore
Alessandro Stradella.
Torino Li ij 7bre 1677

Most Illustrious and Most Excellent Sir, My Lord and Most Honourable Master,

I find myself favoured by a most kind [letter] from Your Excellency with an enclosure in my favour to My Lord Marquis Parella, which I shall use at the right time to my advantage; and I immediately brought the other letter to Signora Agnesa. I can do naught but give infinite thanks to Your Excellency for the honour you have done me, waiting for the time when Your Excellency will employ me with your most esteemed commands; with the very swift execution of which I will try to show Your Excellency how great is the devotion and the respect that I profess together with a great quantity of obligations. The signora, in the meantime, who is very well, has demanded that thanks be given also for her to Your Excellency for the trouble which you have been pleased to take for her, and she proclaims herself the most humble servant of Your Excellency. In the mean time, although many important people have the task of bringing my interests to a proper conclusion, as far as the misfortune which happened to me is concerned and although the same gentlemen agree in favouring me greatly, I turn again to the favour of Your Excellency, supplicating you. Since you have the opportunity of using your very powerful contacts with Signor Aluigi Contarini, and knowing how great is the authority of Your Excellency, I trust more in your support than in any other favour which I might be able to obtain. I supplicate again the goodness of Your Excellency, of your noticing me which I so desire, and while I make most humble and most devout reverence, I remain forever

Your Excellency's
most humble, most devoted, most obliged servant,
Alessandro Stradella.
Turin, 11 September 1677

8. Stradella to Polo Michiel: Turin, 26 November 1677
I-Vmc, PD C. 1064, no. 364

Illustrissimo et Eccellentissimo Signore Signore e Padrone Colendissimo

Sono con questa per dar parte a Vostra Eccellenza come ogni differenza che l'Eccellentissimo Signor Aluigi Contarini havea con me resta totalmente aggiustata non con poca mia sodisfatione anco circa il modo, e ciò tutto ho ricevuto dalla gran protettione di Madama Reale, la quale non ha mai lasciato, né lascia di compartirmi infiniti favori, sì che non havrei assolutamente saputo desiderare d'avantaggio; così anco Madama la Principessa, la quale ha una bontà troppo grande per me, come anco i principali ministri di tutta questa corte che mi hanno portato, e mi portano a viva forza al cielo delle gratie di Madama Reale, e per mia fortuna con il mio poco talento ho incontrato affatto il genio di Madama Reale, e di tutta la corte. Potrei raccontarLe cose di molto gran consideratione sopra i miei accidenti, ma non compete a il parlarne, né devo per molti rispetti. Io per gratia d'Iddio godo la miglior sanità che mai habbia havuto in tempo di vita mia, e sempre al servitio et alli stimatissimi commandi di Vostra Eccellenza.

Prendo al solito l'ardire d'inviarLe una lettera quale supplico Vostra Eccellenza farmi la gratia di farla recapitare in proprie mani del Signore Iacomo Poleni che sta a S. Vitale. E' lettera che mi preme infinitamente; e perciò prendo la strada di Vostra Eccellenza che so che non posso trovare, ne la migliore, ne la più sicura.

Supplico Vostra Eccellenza perdonarmi se così spesso Le apporto questi incommodi, e ne dia colpa alla Sua immensa benignità.

Il Signor Conte d'Aliberti qua metterà in scena il Zappado alli cinque di Dicembre, quale dovevo io porre in musica, ma l'accidente occorsomi me ne levò la congiontura con gran disgusto di Madama Reale per tutte le cause immaginabili. L'ha però composto un tal Signore Giovanni Cieco, il quale si porta molto bene; che è quanto posso dirLe di nuovo.

Potrà Vostra Eccellenza se mi favorisce mai con Sue rispondermi a dirittura, mentre son fuori d'ogni dubbio per le mie lettere, e tanto più che il Signor Marchesa S. Tomasso si trova gravemente ammalato, e Dio sa che cosa sarà della sua vita, che è in vero gran disgratia mia, mentre mi proteggeva con un modo molto grande, e si era molto fieramente impegnato per me, e quello che era il meglio, è l'unico arbitro di questa corte. Porgo dunque a Vostra Eccellenza vive suppliche a volermi mantenere sotto la Sua da me tanto desiderata, e stimata protettione, e La supplico fare humilissima riverenza all'Eccellentissimo Signor Girolamo Suo fratello, e mentre mi rassegno tutto a' suoi cenni, resto con farLe humilissima, e profondissima riverenza.

Di Vostra Eccellenza
humilissimo devotissimo obligatissimo servitore
Alessandro Stradella.
Torino Li 26 9bre 1677

Most Illustrious and Most Excellent Sir, My Lord and Most Honourable Master,

With this [letter] I inform Your Excellency that every difference that the most excellent Signor Aluigi Contarini had with me is completely settled to my great satisfaction, as well as the way [it was done]. And it was all received through the great protection of Her Ladyship, who never stopped, or stops, bestowing on me infinite favours, so that I absolutely could not have wanted anything else. The same with the Princess, whose kindness towards me is too great; and also the principal ministers of this whole court who brought me, and who bring me in spite of everything, the kindnesses of Her Ladyship. And to my fortune, with my inadequate talent I was able to satisfy Her Ladyship and the whole court. I could recount you things of very great importance about my misfortunes, but this is not the moment to speak of them, neither should I out of respect. Thank God I enjoy the best health that I have ever had in my life, and [am] always at the service and at the most esteemed commands of Your Excellency.

As usual I dare to send you a letter which I beg Your Excellency to be so kind as to have put in the hands of Signor Iacomo Poleni, who lives in San Vitale. It is a letter which concerns me greatly, and therefore I send it via Your Excellency, since I know I can find neither a better nor a more secure way.

I beg Your Excellency to forgive me if so often I cause you these inconveniences, and to blame your immense kindness for it.

Signor Count d'Aliberti will stage here the *Zappado* [*Zapato*] on the fifth of December, which I should have set to music, but the misfortune which happened to me deprived me of the opportunity, to the great annoyance of Her Ladyship for all the imaginable reasons. However, a certain Signor Giovanni Cieco [Carisio] composed it, and very well; which is all the news I can tell you.

Your Excellency, if you so favour me, should not reply to me directly, since I am no longer in doubt about my letters [being intercepted]; more so since My Lord Marquis S. Tomasso [Tommaso] is gravely ill, and God knows what will become of his life, which is in truth a great problem for me, since he protected me in a very great way and was very warmly concerned for me; and moreover, he is my only advocate in this court. I extend then to Your Excellency lively supplications to keep me under your so desired and esteemed protection; and I beg you to pay my most humble respects to the most excellent Signor Girolamo, your brother. And while I resign myself completely to your wishes, I remain, making most humble and most profound reverence to you,

Your Excellency's
most humble, most devoted, most obliged servant,
Alessandro Stradella.
Turin, 26 November 1677

9. Stradella to Polo Michiel: Turin, 16 December 1677
I-Vmc, PD C. 1064, no. 317

Illustrissimo et Eccellentissimo Signore Signore Padrone Mio Collendissimo

Ricevo l'honore della benignissima lettera di Vostra Eccellenza, della quale prenderò i consigli e dalla quale conosco sempre più la generosa bontà che Vostra Eccellenza ha per me, onde l'accrescono ogni giorno le mie obligationi. Rendo infinite gratie al Vostra Eccellenza del recapito della lettera per il Signore Poleni e supplico Vostra Eccellenza a scusarmi, se in cui prendo soverchio ardire, mentre la benignità di Vostra Eccellenza mi dà campo di commettere questi mancamenti. Qua si è recitata una miscellanea di scene italiane, francesi, e spagnuole, quale Madama Reale ha gradito, ma il popolo dura fatica a spendere, onde il Signore Conte d'Aliberti può incontrare facilmente qualche difficoltà a ritrarne quel frutto che forse s'imagginava. Do parte a Vostra Eccellenza che nella presente settimana io mi porto in Genova desiderato da alcuni cavalieri di quella città, dove passerò il carnevale, e dove starò attendendo i desideratissimi cenni di Vostra Eccellenza; intanto prego dal cielo al Vostra Eccellenza tutte quelle felicità che potrebbe contentare la mia volontà, la quale ha per oggetto un perpetuo bene nella persona, e nella casa tutta di Vostra Eccellenza; già Vostra Eccellenza è ben informato della mia quiete nella materie appartenenti al Eccellentissimo Signor Contarini, con che facendo a Vostra Eccellenza humilissimo e devotissima riverenza resto

Di Vostra Eccellenza
humilissimo devotissimo obligatissimo servitore
Alessandro Stradella.
Torino Li 16 Xbre 1677

Most Illustrious and Most Excellent Sir, My Lord and Most Honourable Master,

I received the honour of Your Excellency's most kind letter, whose advice I will follow and from which I learn still more of the generous goodness that Your Excellency has towards me, whereby each day my obligations increase. I give infinite thanks to Your Excellency for delivering the letter for Signor Poleni and I beg Your Excellency to forgive me if in doing so I dared too much, but the kindness of Your Excellency encourages me to commit these lapses. Here were performed a mixture of Italian, French, and Spanish scenes, which Her Ladyship enjoyed; but people find it difficult to pay, whereby Signor Count d'Aliberti could easily encounter some difficulty in reaping whatever fruit he perhaps hoped for. I inform Your Excellency that this week I go to Genoa, invited by some gentlemen of that city, where I will spend carnival, and where I will await the most desired requests of Your Excellency. In the mean time, I beg for Your Excellency all the happiness from heaven that could fulfil my wish, which is a perpetual well-being for the person and for the family of Your Excellency. Your Excellency is already well informed of my peace of mind with regard to the most excellent Signor Contarini. With which, making to Your Excellency most humble and most devoted reverence, I remain

Your Excellency's
most humble, most devoted, most obliged servant,
Alessandro Stradella.
Turin, 16 December 1677

10. Stradella to Polo Michiel: Genoa, 8 January 1678
I-Vmc, PD C. 1065, no. 348

Illustrissimo et Eccellentissimo Signore Signore Padrone Collendissimo

Giunto in Genova già nella settimana passata sano, e salvo, dove subito
restai favorito da molti cavalieri quali a gara mi volevano in casa, final-
mente il Signor Franco Imperiali Lercaro principalissimo signore di qua
mi volse assolutamente in sua casa, e dal punto che sono arrivato sin hora
mi è bisognato sempre spendere il tempo con dame, e cavalieri, tutti
curiosi grandemente di me, ed in effetto con tante gratie, con tanti
applausi mi favoriscono, ch'io non saprei, che più desiderare, e mostrano
in tutte le forme un grandissimo gradimento del mio debole talento. Qui
si è recitata l'Alcasta opera già fatta in Roma, qual'è piaciuta, e solo ha
havuto qualche eccetione per essere un poco malinconica. Per Li 9 di
questo va in scena la seconda opera, che è l'Antioco già fatto in Venetia,
ma con la musica tutta ricomposta dal Gobbo del Violino, il quale si è
portato benissimo; ed io non ho potuto far a meno di non intricarmi
almeno a reggere l'orchestra, e dar qualche aiuto a queste donne che
recitano, così commandato da due principalissime dame di qua. Qui son
tre donne, la Centoventi, la Riminese, e l'Antonia, ma la Centoventi si è
guadagnata l'applauso sopra tutti, ed è molto gradita. Supplico Vostra
Eccellenza volermi far tanta gratia d'un sicuro recapito dell'incluso al
Signor Felice Pietogalli al rio di S. Felice, e mi perdoni se troppo spesso
ardito in ciò intendendone Vostra Eccellenza, che premendomi siano stato
questo che meglio non le posso appoggiare che alle gratie del Vostra
Eccellenza; vivo sempre ansioso de Suoi pregiatissimi commandi da quali
vivo sevoso per mio demerito, ma mi fa Le [?] desiderevoli stante la generosa bontà di Vostra Eccellenza alla quale facendo humilissima e devotissima riverenza resto

Di Vostra Eccellenza
humilissimo devotissimo obligatissimo servitore
Alessandro Stradella.
Genova Li 8 Gennaro 1678

Most Illustrious and Most Excellent Sir, My Lord and Most Honourable
Master,

I arrived in Genoa safe and sound already last week, where I was
immediately favoured by many gentlemen who vied to have me in their

homes. Finally, Signor Franco Imperiali Lercaro, the most leading gentleman here, insisted on having me in his home. And from the moment of
my arrival till now, I have always had to spend my time with ladies and
gentlemen, all greatly interested in me, and actually they favour me with
so many kindnesses and so much applause that I do not know what more
I could desire, and in every way they show very great pleasure in my
inadequate talent. Here they performed *Alcasta*, an opera already done in
Rome, which was liked, and had only some dissenters since it was a bit
sad. For the ninth of this [month] the second opera goes on stage, which
is *Antioco*, already done in Venice, but with the music all newly composed
by the Hunchback of the Violin [Carlo Ambrogio Lonati], who did it very
well. And I could not keep from involving myself at least in directing the
orchestra [*from the harpsichord?*], and giving some help to these women
who perform, commanded to do so by two of the very first ladies here.
Here are three women, Centoventi, the Riminese, and Antonia; but
Centoventi earned herself more applause than the others and is greatly
liked. I beg Your Excellency to do me the great favour of finding a sure
way of delivering the enclosed [letter] for Signor Felice Pietogalli in Rio
S. Felice, and I beg your forgiveness if I dare too often to impose on
Your Excellency, which impresses on me that I could not do better than
depend on the kindnesses of Your Excellency. I live always anxious for
your most precious commands, of which I am unworthy, but which I
desire [?] because of the generous goodness of Your Excellency. To
whom, making most humble and most devout reverence, I remain
  Your Excellency's
  most humble, most devoted, most obliged servant,
  Alessandro Stradella.
Genoa, 8 January 1678

11. Stradella to Polo Michiel: Genoa, 30 April 1678
I-Vmc, PD. C. 1065, no. 218

Illustrissimo et Eccellentissimo Signore e Signore e Padrone Colendissimo
  Per seguitare la mia professione di vero servitore di Vostra Eccellenza mi
pare d'essere in obligo di darLe parte d'ogni mio avanzamento, e d'ogni
mio successo, onde sono con questa per farLe sapere che mi ritrovo in
Genova, dove gradito a un segno notabile da questa nobiltà, doppo haver
fatto varie demostrationi del mio debole talento, hanno voluto farmi distinto
da ogn'altro, e fermarmi in questa città motu proprio, con una forma molto
obligante, onde molti cavalieri uniti m'hanno fatto un foglio con l'obliga-
tione di darmi cento doble l'anno di Spagna, pur ch'io mi trattenga qua
almeno per due o tre anni, e queste cento doble non mi obligano né anco a
conoscere chi me le dà, solo che un cavaliere ha la cura di riscuoterle, e di

darmele, del resto per questo denaro io non sono obligato a cosa alcuna in questo mondo solo che di stare in Genova, oltre a questo casa, tavola, servitore pagato. In'oltre mi trovo sei lettioni di sei dame principali, quali si portano ben generosamente; dopoi molti incerti vi sono, e nella cammera, e nella chiesa; dopoi mi hanno messo in mano il teatro dell'anno venturo per l'opere; ma la maggior fortuna ch'io habbia trovato è l'haver qua la Signora Principessa, e Signore Principe Doria, quali mi fanno tanti favori, tante gratie, e poi tante, che mi si rende impossibile e scriverle, e dirle; questi insomma non mancano e con i favori di trattamento, e con procurarmi tutti i vantaggi, e con grossi regali di mostrarmi un'affetto molto grande. Questo è quanto posso dirLe sopra questo particolare.

Sono ancora con questa mia per supplicare Vostra Eccellenza di molte gratie; la prima si è che dovendosi fare qua un'opera vecchia, e un'opera nuova, si vorrebbe fare il Seleuco, opera del signor Minati, e credo io la musica del Signore Sartorio, onde vorrei ardire di supplicare Vostra Eccellenza che prendesse fedele informatione da qualche virtuoso di cotesta città, per sapere se quest'opera ha colpito in Venetia, se veramente è buona di musica, e che cosa è; e se non fosse il mio troppo ardire vorrei Vostra Eccellenza si facesse fare da un virtuoso una nota di tutte le parti come sono poste, cioè qual parte è in soprano, quale in contralto, quale in tenore, quale in basso, che dicendone una parola Vostra Eccellenza ad un virtuoso, subito l'intenderà, e ricorro da Vostra Eccellenza perché so il buon gusto che ha e in questa, e in tutte le cose, e perché mi pare haver bisogno di un signore d'autorità per ricavare ben la pura verità di quanto occorre sopra questo particolare.

La seconda gratia che chiedo a Vostra Eccellenza si è che havendo io lasciato nel mio partir da Venetia in mani alla Signora Maria Felice un libro mio d'ariette legato in carta pecora con un sonetto in altra carta che dice 'Apre l'huomo infelice allhor che nasce' desidererei che Vostra Eccellenza mi facesse tanta gratia di supplicarne l'Eccellentissimo Signore Girolamo suo fratello acciò mi facesse il favore di mandarmi l'uno, e l'altro per il corriero, o altra meglio congiuntura.

Ma sopra ogn'altra cosa supplico la bontà di Vostra Eccellenza condonarmi l'ardire che prendo di chiederLe tante gratie, e v'incolpi la sua solita benignità, che mi dà l'adito di haver tanto ardimento. Raccordo a Vostra Eccellenza ch'io son vissuto, vivo, e viverò sempre, vero, ed humilissimo servitore di Vostra Eccellenza, e che sospiro più un Suo cenno che tutti i beni di questo mondo; e mentre Le faccio humilissima e devotissima riverenza resto per sempre

Di Vostra Eccellenza
humilissimo devotissimo obligatissimo servitore
Alessandro Stradella.
Genova Li 30 Aprile 1678

Most Illustrious and Most Excellent Sir, My Lord and Most Honourable
Master,

In order to maintain my promise to be a true servant to Your
Excellency, I believe I am obliged to give you news of my every advance-
ment and of my every success. Whereby with this [letter] I inform you
that I find myself in Genoa where, greatly pleasing this nobility, having
given various demonstrations of my inadequate talent, they wished to honour me more than any other and keep me, of their own initiative [and]
with a very binding formula, in this city. Whereby many gentlemen
together signed a piece of paper agreeing to give me each year one hundred Spanish doubloons, for which I should stay here at least two or three
years. And for these hundred doubloons I am not at all obliged, not
even to know who has given them to me, only that one of the gentlemen
is in charge of getting them and giving them to me. For the rest, for this
money I am not obliged to [do] anything in this world except stay in
Genoa; in addition to this, [I get] a house, food, [and a] paid servant. In
addition, I find myself [giving] six lessons to six leading ladies [of the
nobility], who behave very generously. After which there are many possibilities, both in the chamber and in the church. After which, for the coming year they put the theatre into my hands for the opera. But the
greatest fortune that I have found is to have here Signora Princess, and
Signor Prince Doria, who do me many favours, many kindnesses, and still
others, so that it is impossible to write them and to relate them; in short,
they never fail to show me very great affection with favourable treatment,
and with obtaining for me all advantages, and with large gifts. This is as
much as I can tell you on this point.

With this [letter] I am still begging Your Excellency for many favours.
The first is that, having to do here an old opera, and a new opera, one
would like to do *Seleuco*, an opera by Signor Minati, and I believe that
the music is by Signor Sartorio. Whereby I should like to dare to ask
Your Excellency to get some reliable information from some singer from
that city, in order to learn if this opera was a hit in Venice, if the music is
truly good, and what it is like. And if it is not too much to ask, I should
like if Your Excellency could get from a singer a word on how all the
parts are disposed: that is, which part is soprano, which is contralto,
which is tenor, which is bass; if Your Excellency mentions this to a
singer, he will understand immediately. And I ask Your Excellency
because I know the good taste that you have in this and in all things, and
because I believe I need someone of authority in order to get the pure
truth about this point.

The second favour that I ask Your Excellency is that, when I departed
from Venice having left in the hands of Signora Maria Felice a book of
mine bound in sheepskin, of ariettas, with a sonnet [bound] in other paper

that goes 'Apre l'huomo infelice allhor che nasce', I should desire that Your Excellency do me the great kindness of asking the most excellent Signor Girolamo, your brother, to do me the favour of sending me the one and the other by courier or some other better means.

But above everything, I beg the goodness of Your Excellency to allow me to dare to ask so many favours, and to accuse your usual kindness, that gives me the opportunity to have so much courage. I remind Your Excellency that I have lived, I live, and I shall always live the true and most humble servant of Your Excellency, and that I sigh for one of your nods more than for all the good things of this world. And while I make most humble and most devout reverence, I remain forever

Your Excellency's
most humble, most devoted, most obliged servant,
Alessandro Stradella.
Genoa, 30 April 1678

12. Stradella to Polo Michiel: Genoa, 11 June 1678
I-Vmc, PD C. 1065, no. 260

Illustrissimo, et Eccellentissimo Signore Signore Padrone Collendissimo

E' tanta l'allegrezza ch'io sento in ricevere la gentilissima di Vostra Eccellenza, dove vedo un'ombra di piccolo commando di Vostra Eccellenza da me tanto desiderato, che non so trovare parole al proposito per renderGlene gratie. In quest'ordinario dunque non mi è possibile il poter servire Vostra Eccellenza di ciò che desidera, perché il tempo è troppo breve, ma per l'ordinario venturo Vostra Eccellenza faccia pur capitale dell'esecutione de' suoi cenni. Devo dirLe però che, in quanto alle canzoni di mio servirò Vostra Eccellenza quanto mai sa desiderare; in quanto a canzoni d'altri compositori, qua non vi è se non il Signore Carlo Ambrogio che faccia qualche cosa, del quale gli trasmetterò pure qualche compositione; del resto qua non vi sono altri compositori, che il paese non produce grand'huomini, ne vi sono altri forastieri. Se Vostra Eccellenza non ha assai fretta, farò venire da Roma d'amici miei, e servirò Vostra Eccellenza. Intanto si compiacerà prender quelle Gli inviarò per il seguente ordinario, e nel medemo tempo farò pratica per servir più a modo mio Vostra Eccellenza. Gli mandarò anco sonate, ed in questo ancora non so come poter bene, e intieramente servirLa bene, mentre havrei bisogno che Vostra Eccellenza m'esprimesse meglio se vuol sonate di cimbalo, d'organo, di liuto, d'arpa, di violini o a due, o a tre, o concerti grossi di viole, o pure ciò che vuole, che in ogni genere che Vostra Eccellenza mi commanderà, io adoprerò tutta quella poca abilità che mi trovo per ben servirLa. Si che io intanto così allo scuro La servirò più al proposito che saprò, dopoi starò aspettando gli avvisi di Vostra Eccellenza più precisi, e non mancarò di compire al debito mio; così ancora nelle canzoni, se vuole ariette, o cantate da cammera, longhe, bizzarre, o pur malinconiche, se chi le deve cantare ha dispositione, se va in alto, che corde ha, in che voce, e tutto ciò domando perché mi sento struggere che vorrei sodisfare in tutto, e per tutto a Vostra Eccellenza.

Del resto so molto bene che Vostra Eccellenza ha gusto d'ogni mio vantaggio, e so che sarà sempre per farmi mille gratie, come ha fatto sempre, ed io non posso far altro che renderGlene altre tante gratie, e supplicarLa che mi confermi la Sua stimatissima, e potentissima protettione. Supplico Vostra Eccellenza a portare una profondissima riverenza da mia parte all'Eccellentissimo Signor Girolamo Suo fratello, ed ogni volta che riceverò il favore del mio libro, mi sarà una gran gratia, e ne resterò infinitamente obligato; e facendo a Vostra Eccellenza humilissimo ed ossequiosissimo inchino resto per sempre

Di Vostra Eccellenza
humilissimo devotissimo obligatissimo servitore
Alessandro Stradella.
Genova, Li ij Giugno 1678

Most Illustrious, and Most Excellent Sir, My Lord and Most Honourable Master,

The happiness is great that I feel in receiving the very kind [letter] from Your Excellency, where I see a shadow of a small command from Your Excellency, so desired by me that I cannot find words sufficient to give you thanks. In this post then it is not possible to be able to serve Your Excellency in what you desire, because the time is too short, but for the next post Your Excellency should count on the execution of your wishes. I must tell you, however, that as far as the canzonas by me are concerned, I will serve Your Excellency as much as you wish; as far as the canzonas by other composers are concerned, here there is no one who does anything except Signor Carlo Ambrogio [Lonati], some of whose compositions I will also send you. Besides, here there are no other composers, the place does not produce great men, neither are there other outsiders. If Your Excellency is not in much hurry, I will have [some] sent from Rome, from my friends, and I will [thus] serve Your Excellency. In the mean time, be pleased to take those I will send you in the next post, and at the same time I will gain experience in serving Your Excellency as I think best. I will also send you sonatas, and in this I am not certain how to serve you well and completely, since I would need Your Excellency to explain better to me if you want sonatas for harpsichord, organ, lute, harp, violins in two or three parts, or string concerti grossi, or whatever you wish; because in everything that Your Excellency will command me, I will use all that little ability which I have to serve you well. Therefore, being so in the dark, in the mean time I will serve you as best as I know how; after which I will await more precise information from Your Excellency, and I will not fail to pay my debt. Again in the canzonas, if you want ariettas, or chamber cantatas, long, bizarre, or even sad, if whoever is to sing them has talent, if he/she can go up high, what [kind of] voice he/she has, in what range, and I ask all of this because I feel myself struggling, because I want to satisfy Your Excellency in everything and for everything.

Besides, I know very well that Your Excellency likes me to do well, and I know that you will always do me a thousand favours, as you have always done, and I cannot do otherwise than give as many favours in return, and beg you to confer on me your most esteemed and most powerful protection. I supplicate Your Excellency to give my profound respects to the most excellent Signor Girolamo, your brother; and any time that I receive the favour of my book, it will be a great kindness to me and I will remain infinitely obliged. And making to Your Excellency a most humble and most obsequious bow, I remain forever

Your Excellency's
most humble, most devoted, most obliged servant,
Alessandro Stradella.
Genoa, 11 June 1678

13. Stradella to Polo Michiel: Genoa, 18 June 1678
I-Vmc, PD C. 1065, no. 260 *bis*

Illustrissimo et Eccellentissimo Signore Signore Padrone Collendissimo

Ecco a Vostra Eccellenza qua incluse tre canzoni, tutte tre di diversa sfera, chi più longa e chi più corta. Intanto sto facendo dilegenza per haver qualchecosa di nuovo dal Signore Carlo Ambrogio, dal quale non ho havuto fin hora, perché nel principio di questa settimana parte per Milano ma al suo ritorno che lo vedrò presto servirò certissimo Vostra Eccellenza. Nel seguente ordinario manderò a Vostra Eccellenza altre mie composition e anderò scrivendole finche ricevo avviso da Vostra Eccellenza che si pare d'esser restato sodisfatto; io per me durerei sempre perché mi sarebbe una gran consolatione haver la fortuna di scrivere continuatamente Vostra Eccellenza; io non posso se non haverne il desiderio tocca a Vostra Eccellenza darmene la continua occasione. Anche faccendo Le humilissima devotissima riverenza resto

Di Vostra Eccellenza
humilissimo devotissimo obligatissimo servitore
Alessandro Stradella.
Genova Li 18 Giugno 1678

Most Illustrious and Most Excellent Sir, My Lord and Most Honourable Master,

Here enclosed for Your Excellency [are] three canzonas, all three of different types, some longer and some shorter. In the mean time, I am trying to have something new from Signor Carlo Ambrogio [Lonati], from whom as yet I have had nothing, because at the beginning of this week he leaves for Milan; but on his return, which I expect to be soon, I will most certainly serve Your Excellency. In the following post I will send Your Excellency [some] other of my compositions, and I will continue writing them until I receive notice from Your Excellency that you seem to be satisfied. As far as I am concerned, I would continue forever because it seems a great consolation to me to have the fortune of writing continually for Your Excellency; I can only have the desire, while it is up to Your Excellency to give me continued opportunity. Also, making most humble [and] most devoted reverence to you, I remain

Your Excellency's
most humble, most devoted, most obliged servant,
Alessandro Stradella.
Genoa, 18 June 1678

14. Stradella to Polo Michiel: Genoa, 2 July 1678
I-Vmc, PD C. 1065, no. 143

Illustrissimo et Eccellentissimo Signore Signore Padrone Mio Colendissimo

Mi giunge una benignissima di Vostra Eccellenza dalla quale sento Vostra Eccellenza haver ricevuto le tre canzoni; nel seguente ordinario ne doverà haver ricevute altre cinque, e in quest'ordinario ancora havrei proseguito a mandare secondo gl'ordini riveriti di Vostra Eccellenza; ma perché la Sua lettera mi sospende l'esecuzione di quello io pensavo di fare, aspettarò i commandi più specifici di Vostra Eccellenza per farLe vedere sempre più la mia osservanza in servirLa. E mentre ho impaziente attendo i cenni di Vostra Eccellenza; La supplico portare una humilissima riverenza dall'Eccellentissimo Signore Girolamo Suo fratello ed a Vostra Eccellenza faccio devotissimo, ed ossequissimo inchino restando per sempre

Di Vostra Eccellenza
humilissimo devotissimo obligatissimo servitore
Alessandro Stradella.
Genova Li 2 lug:o 1679

Most Illustrious and Most Excellent Sir, My Lord and Most Honourable Master,

A most kind [letter] from Your Excellency reaches me, from which I hear that Your Excellency has received the three canzonas; in the subsequent post you should have received another five, and in this post I will again have continued to send [something] according to the respected orders of Your Excellency. But because your letter stops me from doing that which I thought to do, I will await more specific commands from your Excellency, in order to show you still more my devotion in serving you. And while I impatiently await the wishes of Your Excellency, I beg you to convey most humble reverence to the most excellent Signor Girolamo, your brother; and to Your Excellency I make a most devoted and most obsequious bow, remaining forever

Your Excellency's
most humble, most devoted, most obliged servant,
Alessandro Stradella.
Genoa, 2 July 1679

15. Stradella to Polo Michiel: Genoa, 27 January 1679
I-Vmc, PD C. 1066, no. 577

Illustrissimo   et   Eccellentissimo   Signore   Signore   Padrone   Mio
Collendissimo
Le infinite occupationi che mi ha dato il servitio di questi signori per l'opere, insieme con le quali non sono stato senza altri impegni, e l'esser stato nelle feste di Natale un poco indisposto mi ha impedito di compire alle mie obligationi come dovevo. So però che Vostra Eccellenza ha tanto affetto per me, che con la Sua generosa benignità saprà compatirmi, né voglio mancare di dar parte a Vostra Eccellenza di tutto il seguito come mio principalissimo padrone.
Alli 10 di 9bre passato io messi in palco la prima opera mia in questo teatro di Genova, nominata La forza dell'amor paterno, la quale si è recitata con esquisita fortuna quindici volte, e con tanta sodisfatione di questi cavalieri, che seguì il seguente caso.
Il lunedì di Natale alli 26 di Xbre passato, si recitò per la penultima volta la sudetta opera, e finito il primo atto furno gettati da palchetti, e sparsi per tutto il teatro infinità di sonetti, de' quali prendo ardire mandarGlene qui inclusi due, e nel medemo tempo un cammeriere di questi cavalieri mi presentò publicamente molti de' medemi sonetti in taffettano ben guerniti sopra una guantiera d'oro massiccio di molta valuta, e terminò poi questa funtione con un applauso commune. E questo regalo è di soprapiù del denaro che mi devono già accordato fra noi per le fatighe del carnevale; ma l'hanno fatto solo per dare un segno publico della stima, o sodisfatione che hanno havuto di me.
La prima domenica dell'anno novo del 1679 presente messi in palco la seconda opera, nominata Le gare dell'amore eroico, pure opera mia, la

quale ha cominciato con fortuna indicibile, e segue meglio che mai anco con più concorso, perché dentro il carnevale vengono più gente all'opera, né si può alle volte recitare per lo strepito dell'applauso.

Lunedì, o martedì metterò in palco la terza opera pur mia, quale si fa questa per un capriccio, perché è un'opera ridicola, ma bellissima, ed è nominata, Il Trespolo; e perché qua hanno molto genio alle cose ridicole, credo che farà scoppio infallibilmente.

Hora veda Vostra Eccellenza se ho avuto da fare a fare in un carnevale tre opere nove, con l'impegni di dame, e cavalieri scolari, e feste di chiese, e altri imbrogli.

La compagnia de' musici è esquisita. La prima donna è la Signora Caterina Angela Botteghi, cioè la Centoventi; la quale per verità è la dea delle scene, e fa impazzir tutti. La seconda donna, è la Signora Annuccia, la figlia del coco del Signore Contestabile, la quale ha migliorato notabilmente, e recita con applauso buono. Il primo soprano è il Signor Marcantonio Orrigoni che sta al servitio del Signore Duca di Modena, il quale canta benissimo, non è felicissimo nella voce, ma piace però assai, e quel che si stima di più ha recitato, e recita come un'angelo del paradiso. Il secondo soprano è il Signore Francesco Rossi di Roma, quale non è stato gradito, e per questo l'habbiamo fatto cantar poco, onde poco importava. Il contralto è il Signor Francesco Vallerini che stava al servitio del Gran Duca di Fiorenza, fiorentino, recita mediocremente, ma canta incomparabilmente bene. Il tenore è il Signore Francesco Guerra che sta al servitio del Signore Duca di Massa di Carrara, che recita, e canta bene, e ha dato molto gusto. Il basso è un tal Gabella sudito di questa Repubblica Serenissima, il quale ha bella presenza, et ha una voce di baritono la più bella forse ch'io habbia inteso a miei dì. Il buffone è un tal Petriccioli di Roma che da un gusto grandissimo a tutti. La peggior parte che habbiamo havuto è la parte della vecchia, che la fa un tal Federico Generoli di Roma, il quale in questa parte si è reso sino odioso. Si sono fatte scene belle assai: mi ero scordato di dire che la prima opera s'è sostenuta con tutte le fortune raccontateGli, benché si sia messa in palco è recitata sempre con una donna sola, perché una napolitana che aspettavamo che fosse esquisita, ci è riuscita tale, che questi signori non hanno voluto che reciti, onde si fece far quella parte all'infretta ad un castrato di qua molto ordinario chiamato Granarino, e poi si è fatto subito venire la sudetta figlia del coco del Signor Contestabile. Questo è quanto posso dirLe. Io non posso desiderar né più honori, né più utili di quelli che ho in questa città da tutta la nobiltà, con di più la Signora Principessa, e Signor Principe Doria, quali mi piovono addosso diluvij di gratie. So che Vostra Eccellenza mi vuol bene, e sarà buon publicatore delle mie fortune. Supplico Vostra Eccellenza a portare una humilissima riverenza all'Eccellentissimo Signore Girolamo Suo fratello, e parteciparlo del tutto, e mentre humilmente e profondamente m'inchino a Vostra Eccellenza resto per sempre

Di Vostra Eccellenza
humilissimo devotissimo obligatissimo servitore
Alessandro Stradella.
Genova li 27 Gennaro 1679

Most Illustrious and Most Excellent Sir, My Lord and Most Honourable Master,

The endless tasks for the operas which the service of these gentlemen has given me, together with which I have not been without other duties, and having been during the Christmas holidays a little indisposed, has hindered me fulfilling my obligations as I should have. I know, however, that Your Excellency has so much affection for me, that with your generous kindness you will understand me; neither do I wish to omit to inform Your Excellency, as my most principal patron, of all the following.

On 10 November last I put on stage my first opera in this theatre in Genoa, called *La forza dell'amor paterno*, which was performed with exquisite fortune fifteen times, and so much to the satisfaction of these gentlemen, that the following occurred.

On Christmas Monday, 26 December last, the above opera was performed for the penultimate time. And when the first act was finished there were thrown down from the boxes and distributed throughout the whole theatre an infinity of sonnets, of which I make bold to send you two here included [*NB these are now missing*]; and at the same time a servant of these gentlemen publicly presented me with many of the same sonnets wrapped beautifully in taffeta on a tray of solid gold of great value, and this ceremony ended with general applause. And this gift is worth more than the money that they are to give me, agreed upon between us, for the work for carnival; but they did it only to give public acknowledgement of the esteem or satisfaction that they have with me.

The first Sunday of the current new year of 1679, I put on stage the second opera, entitled *Le gare dell'amore eroico*, also my work, which began with indescribable fortune, and continues better than ever with even greater audiences, because during carnival more people come to the opera; at times one cannot perform due to the noise of the applause.

Monday or Tuesday I will put on stage the third opera, also mine, which is for amusement, because it is a comic opera but most beautiful, and is called *Il Trespolo*; and because here they delight in comic things, I believe it will be an infallible hit.

Now Your Excellency knows how busy I have been doing three new operas in one carnival, together with the duties to lady and gentleman pupils, and church feasts, and other chores.

The company of singers is exquisite. The prima donna is Signora Caterina Angela Botteghi, that is Centoventi; who in truth is the goddess of the stage, and makes everyone go wild. The seconda donna is Signora Annuccia, the daughter of Signor Contestabile's cook, who has notably improved and acts to good applause. The primo soprano is Signor Marcantonio Orrigoni, who is in the service of Signor Duke of Modena, who sings most well, is not too favored in voice, but is nevertheless quite liked; and what is admired more, acted and acts like an angel of paradise. The secondo soprano is Signor Francesco Rossi of Rome, who was not liked, and because of this we made him sing little, so that it didn't matter much. The contralto is Signor Francesco Vallerini, who was in the service of the Grand Duke of Florence, a Florentine, acts moderately well, but sings incomparably well. The tenor is Signor Francesco Guerra, who is in the service of Signor Duke of Massa di Carrara, who acts and sings well, and gave much pleasure. The bass is a certain Gabella, from this Most Serene Republic, who has a beautiful presence and has the voice of a baritone, perhaps the most beautiful that I have ever heard. The *buffo* is a certain Petriccioli of Rome, who gave much pleasure to all. The worst part that we had is the part of the old lady, done by a certain Federico Generoli of Rome, who in this part made himself actually odious. They made rather beautiful sets. I forgot to say that the first opera was done with all the fortune told you, even though put on with only one woman, because a Neapolitan we were expecting to be exquisite, turned out to be such that these gentlemen did not want her to perform, whereby a castrato from here, very ordinary, called Granarino, was hurriedly made to do the part; and then the above-mentioned daughter of Signor Contestabile's cook was summoned immediately. This is all that I can say. I cannot desire more honours, nor more profits than those that I have [received] in this city from all the nobles, with even more from Signora Princess and Signor Prince Doria, who shower me with kindnesses. I know that Your Excellency cares for me, and that you will be a good publicizer of my fortune. I beg Your Excellency to give [my] most humble respects to the most excellent Signor Girolamo, your brother, and to inform him of all. And while humbly and profoundly I bow before Your Excellency, I remain forever

Your Excellency's
most humble, most devoted, most obliged servant,
Alessandro Stradella.
Genoa, 27 January 1679

16. Stradella to Polo Michiel: Genoa, 25 March 1679
I-Vmc, PD C. 1066, no. 205

Illustrissimo   et   Eccellentissimo   Signore   Signore   Padrone   Mio
Collendissimo

Il martedì dopo ricevuto il Suo commando mi toccò sopportare qualche
parte della cattiva influenza che corre in questa città, però perla Dio gratia
non ho havuto che pochi giorni di leggiera febre quale mi ha impedito il
servire Vostra Eccellenza et hora son quasi rihavuto e per il seguente ordinario assicuro Vostra Eccellenza che resterà servito nel meglior modo che
saprò. Intanto Vostra Eccellenza compatisca la tardanza la quale ha havuto
una causa troppo legittima e mentre Le faccio humilissima riverenza resto
sempre
Di Vostra Eccellenza
humilissimo devotissimo obligato servitore
Alessandro Stradella.
Genova Li 25 Marzo 1679

Most Illustrious and Most Excellent Sir, My Lord and Most Honourable
Master,
On Tuesday, after receiving your command, I had to put up with some
of the bad influenza which is going around in this city; however, by the
grace of God, I had only a few days of slight fever which stopped me
from serving Your Excellency, and now I am almost recovered; and in the
next post I assure Your Excellency that you will be served in the best way
that I know. In the mean time, Your Excellency should pardon the tardi-
ness which had an all too legitimate cause, and while I make most humble
reverence, I remain forever
Your Excellency's
most humble, most devoted, obliged servant,
Alessandro Stradella.
Genoa, 25 March 1679

17. Stradella to Polo Michiel: Genoa, 2 May 1679
I-Vmc, PD C. 1066, no. 252

Illustrissimo et Eccellentissimo Signore Signore Padrone Collendissimo
Resto honorato doppiamente de favori di Vostra Eccellenza e da un signore così gentile, e generoso come Vostra Eccellenza non si poteva
aspettare se non un eccesso di gratie. Rendo dunque infinite gratie a
Vostra Eccellenza dell'informatione del Seleuco, quale non potea essere
più esatta ne più ben fatta, e per questo io prendei l'ardire di ricorrere a
favori di Vostra Eccellenza. Mi resta solo di supplicarLa con il più vivo

dell'ardire cio che mai l'Eccellentissimo Signore Girolamo Suo fratello rihavesse nelle mani proprie il libro mio ne supplico per poterlo rihavere, che non potrei mai esprimere a Vostra Eccellenza quanto sia grande la premura ch'io habbia; mi consola che l'autorità grande dell'Eccellentissimo Signore Girolamo sarà più che bastante per ricuperare il tutto come Vostra Eccellenza me ne da buona speranza e così vivo quasi certo di dover restar contento anco in questa parte. Qua si seguita a far diligenze grandi per unire una buona compagnia per il venturo carnevale, e già siamo a buon segno; io cercherò dal mio canto servir questi signori quanto mai meglio sarà possibile, e per l'infinite gratie che mi fanno, e perché non possino frenarsi a fare dell'elettione che hanno fatto di me.

Di qua non vi è nuova nessuna se non che parte molta gente per Messina, e pochi giorni sono partite alcune galere, per detto luogo piene di mercantie e dinari per riportare in qua sete, o negotiare a loro vantaggio e si dice che i signori genovesi faranno bene i fatti loro in questa congiontura: giunsero qui poco fa ventidue vascelli olandesi la maggior parte carichi di grano, e gli altri di droghe. Queste è quanto posso dirLa, e mentre sempre più che mai vado sosperando il modo di far conoscere a Vostra Eccellenza la mia osservatissima devotione, supplicando Vostra Eccellenza a portare una humilissima riverenza all'Eccellentissimo Signore Girolamo Suo fratello, resto con inchinandomi humilissimamente e profondissimamente

Di Vostra Eccellenza
humilissimo devotissimo obligatissimo servitore
Alessandro Stradella.
Genova Li 2 Maggio 1679

Most Illustrious and Most Excellent Sir, My Lord and Most Honourable Master,

I am doubly honoured by Your Excellency's favours, and from a gentleman so kind and generous as Your Excellency one cannot expect other than an excess of kindnesses. I render, then, infinite thanks to Your Excellency for the information about *Seleuco*, which could not be more exact, nor better formulated; and for this I take courage to ask Your Excellency again for favours. It remains for me only to beg you as urgently as I dare that in case the most excellent Signor Girolamo, your brother, should have my book in his possession, I beg to have it back, because I would never be able to express to Your Excellency how great my need is. It consoles me that the great authority of the most excellent Signor Girolamo will be more than sufficient to recover everything, as Your Excellency gives me good hope [to believe]; and so I live almost certain of being satisfied even in this. Here one continues to work hard to put together a good company for the coming carnival, and already we are near the mark; for my part, I will try to serve these gentlemen as well as possible, because of the infinite kindnesses they do me, and so that they will not stop favouring me as they have.

There is nothing new here except that many people are leaving for Messina, and a few days ago some galleys left for that place full of goods and money to bring back silk or to trade to their advantage, and it is said that the Genoese gentlemen are good at this business. A short time ago 22 Dutch ships arrived here, most of them full of grain and the others of spices. This is all I can say, and while more than ever I hope to make Your Excellency know of my most respectful devotion, I beg Your Excellency to convey a most humble reverence to the most excellent Signor Girolamo, your brother. I remain, bowing most humbly and most deeply,

Your Excellency's
most humble, most devoted, most obliged servant,
Alessandro Stradella.
Genoa, 2 May 1679

18. Stradella to Polo Michiel: Genoa, 12 May 1679
I-Vmc, PD C. 1066, no. 207

Illustrissimo et Eccellentissimo Signore Signore e Padrone Collendissimo

Maggior consolatione non ho io in questo mondo che quando mi vedo honorato di qualche commando di Vostra Eccellenza, onde mi credo confirmato nella Sua gratia troppo da me dissorbitantemente stimata. Servirò dunque Vostra Eccellenza del mottetto, e se mi havesse mandato la nota delle corde, dove arriva alto, e basso questa virtuosa, havrei più aggiustatamente potuto servirLa, ma io m'anderò in questo contenendo nel miglior modo che mi parerà, come anco nella dispositione, cose necessarie da sapersi per poter ben servire chi si deve; in oltre il mottetto resterà sepolto, né si sentirà più né in Venetia, né in altro luogo, e non lasciarò ogni studio per farlo di Sua sodisfatione; resta solo che Vostra Eccellenza compatisca le mie debolezze, e si condanni da se medemo se ha fatta poco buona l'elettione; supplico dunque Vostra Eccellenza in tanto prepararmi qualche commando di più consideratione, che lo desidero per mercede di questa bagatella, assicurandoLa che altro motivo non ho in tutto ciò che farò commandato da Vostra Eccellenza, che servire Vostra Eccellenza che i motivi della gloria, a quest'hora o ne ho acquistata qualche parte, o non sono più in tempo. E supplicandoLa portar le mie humilissime riverenze all'Eccellentissimo Signor Girolamo Micheli Suo fratello, resto riverentissimamente inchinandomeLe

Di Vostra Eccellenza
humilissimo devotissimo obligatissimo servitore
Alessandro Stradella.
Genova Li 12 Maggio 1679

Most Illustrious and Most Excellent Sir, My Lord and Most Honourable Master,

I have no greater consolation in this world than seeing myself honoured by some command of Your Excellency's, whereby I believe myself secured in your grace, which is inordinately esteemed by me. I will oblige Your Excellency then with the motet, and if you had sent me word of the voice, what the highest and lowest [notes] of this singer are, I would have been able to serve you more exactly; but I will act in the best way I know; also the ability [of the singer], [all] necessary things to know in order to serve as one ought. In addition, the motet will remain secret, neither will one hear it in Venice or elsewhere, and I will not leave off every effort to do it to your satisfaction. It remains only for Your Excellency to pardon my weaknesses, and to blame yourself if you selected badly. I beg Your Excellency then, in the mean time, to prepare for me some more important command that I desire as compensation for this bagatelle, assuring you that I have no other motive in all that I am commanded to do by Your Excellency, but to serve Your Excellency; as for fame, either I have already acquired some or I am no longer in time [to do so]. And supplicating you to give my most humble respects to the most excellent Signor Girolamo Micheli [Michiel], your brother, I remain respectfully bowing before you,

Your Excellency's

most humble, most devoted, most obliged servant,

Alessandro Stradella.

Genoa, 12 May 1679

19. Stradella to Polo Michiel: Genoa, 2 June 1679
I-Vmc, PD C. 1066, no. 201

Illustrissimo et Eccellentissimo Signore Signore Padrone Collendissimo

Dal letto scrivo queste due righe dove sto ancora con un dolore di testa molto fiero, però senza febre ne ho dubbio poter servire Vostra Eccellenza per il seguente ordinario, e intanto Le supplico per l'amor di Dio a perdonarmi; che ancora non mi è bastato l'animo applicarmi come farò con ogni puntualità che è quanto, e Le faccio humilissima riverenza

Di Vostra Eccellenza

humilissimo devotissimo obligato servitore

Alessandro Stradella.

Genova Li 2 Giugno 1679

Most Illustrious and Most Excellent Sir, My Lord and Most Honourable Master,

I write these two lines from bed, where I still am with a very strong headache, however without fever; neither do I doubt to be able to serve

Your Excellency by the next post. And in the mean time I beg you, for the love of God, to forgive me because I have not yet felt able to apply myself, as I will do with every required punctuality. And I make most humble reverence.

Your Excellency's
most humble, most devoted, obliged servant,
Alessandro Stradella.
Genoa, 2 June 1679

20. Stradella to Polo Michiel: Genoa, 10 June 1679
I-Vmc, PD C. 1066, no. 190

Illustrissimo et Eccellentissimo Signore Signore Padrone Collendissimo

Mando a Vostra Eccellenza il mottetto, quale ho fatto a dispetto della mia testa, che ancora non posso reggere bene; per tanto Vostra Eccellenza gradisca il buon'arrivo che ho havuto in servirLo, e mi prepari nuovi commandi quali spero che potrò eseguire con maggior puntualità e meglio in tutto, e mentre Le faccio humilissima riverenza resto per sempre

Di Vostra Eccellenza
devotissimo obligatissimo servitore
Alessandro Stradella.
Genova Li X Giugno 1679

Most Illustrious and Most Excellent Sir, My Lord and Most Honourable Master,

I send the motet to Your Excellency, which I did in spite of my head which I still cannot hold properly; therefore may Your Excellency be pleased with the rapidity that I have had in serving you, and prepare new commands for me which I hope I shall be able to execute with greater punctuality and better in every aspect. And while I make most humble reverence, I remain forever

Your Excellency's
most devoted, most obliged servant,
Alessandro Stradella.
Genoa, 10 June 1679

21. Stradella to Polo Michiel: Genoa, 26 June 1679
I-Vmc, PD C. 1066, no. 251

Illustrissimo et Eccellentissimo Signore Signore Padrone Mio Collendissimo

Ecco qui incluse cinque altre compositioni pur varie di mio, quali presento a Vostra Eccellenza con tutta l'anima; nel seguente ordinario trasmetterò similmente una sonata come Vostra Eccellenza m'accennò; e sto aspettando che torni il Signore Carlo Ambrogio da Milano, che subito mi farò dar qualche cosa di suo e Gle l'invierò: aspettavo che Vostra Eccellenza mi commandasse più precisamente le gratie che voleva mentre si possono [?] di varie sorti; pure manderò [?] se non sarà questa che [? *several lines illegible*]; ma mi sarà possibile incontrare il gusto di Vostra Eccellenza tutto farò, e facendoLe humilissima e devotissima riverenza resto per sempre

Di Vostra Eccellenza
humilissimo devotissimo obligatissimo servitore
Alessandro Stradella.
Genova Li 26 Giugno 1679

Most Illustrious and Most Excellent Sir, My Lord and Most Honourable Master,

Here enclosed [are] five other various compositions of mine, which I present to Your Excellency with all my heart. In the next post I will similarly send a sonata, as Your Excellency mentioned; and I am waiting for Signor Carlo Ambrogio [Lonati] to return from Milan, so that I may have him give me something of his immediately and send it to you. I expected that Your Excellency would have commanded more precisely the favours that you require of me, while one can [write?] various kinds; I will also send [?] if it will not be [? *several lines illegible*]; but I will do everything to satisfy the taste of Your Excellency. And making most humble and most devout reverence, I remain forever

Your Excellency's
most humble, most devoted, most obliged servant,
Alessandro Stradella.
Genoa, 26 June 1679

22. Stradella to Girolamo Michiel: Genoa, 16 December 1679
I-Vmc, PD C. 1066, no. 153

Illustrissimo et Eccellentissimo Signore Signore Padrone Mio Collendissimo

In trovarmi scarso de commandi di Vostra Eccellenza mi hanno reso timoroso in essercitare con Vostra Eccellenza quegl'atti d'ossequio che da ne Gl'erano dovuti; ma hora che mi si porge l'occasione delle sante feste del Natale di Nostro Signore prendo l'ardire di ravvicar nella memoria di Vostra Eccellenza la mia vera servitù, pregandole dal cielo tutte quelle felicità che possono intieramente compiere il Suo desiderio: eccomi dunque tutto supplicante a Vostra Eccellenza acciò mi permetta la gratia di darmi contrasegno della Sua prottetione capitale per me inestimabile, e supplicando Vostra Eccellenza a farmi il favore di passar con l'Eccellentissimo Signore Paolino Suo fratello quegli sfitij, che me le possino costituire devoto servitore e obligato resto facendoLe humilissima devotissima riverenza

Di Vostra Illustrissima et Eccellentissima
humilissimo devotissimo obligatissimo servitore
Alessandro Stradella.
Genova Li 16 Xbre 1679

Most Illustrious and Most Excellent Sir, My Lord and Most Honourable Master,

Finding myself short of commands from Your Excellency has made me afraid of exercising with Your Excellency those acts of respect that are due to you. But now that the Holy Feast of the Birth of Our Lord gives me the opportunity, I take courage to revive Your Excellency's memory of my faithful servitude, praying Heaven for all those happinesses which might completely fulfil your desire. Behold me then all supplicating before Your Excellency; allow me the grace to give recognition of your protection, of inestimable value to me. And begging Your Excellency to do me the favour to engage, with the most excellent Signor Paolino, your brother, in those pastimes which might prove me to be a devoted and obliged servant, I remain, making most humble, most devout reverence,

Your Most Illustrious and Most Excellent [Lord's]
most humble, most devoted, most obliged servant,
Alessandro Stradella.
Genoa, 16 December 1679

23. Stradella to Flavio Orsini, Duke of Bracciano: 24 May 1681 I-Rasc, Arch. Orsini, I. 279, no. 487

Altezza Serenissima

Invio a Vostra Altezza l'opera finita, e consegnata in questo medemo ordinario al corriere acciò sicuramente la recapiti, si che potrà subito far diligenza che Le sarà consegnata. Io non voglio estendermi per renderLa persuasa dell'affetto, e l'attentione con la quale l'ho fatta, perché sapendo Vostra Altezza già quante sono grandi le mie obligazioni suppongo le possa considerare da sé. Vi ho composto con estraordinaria sodisfatione, e per essere commando di Vostra Altezza, e per esser in sé bella l'opera. La troverà copiata di poco buon carattere, perché qua in Genova non vi è copista preciso ma qualche musico va copiando, e un prete che vi era che scriveva bene, è partito di qua appunto in questi giorni; le note però son buone, le parole son scritte di mano poco buona, ma il tutto intelligibilissimo, e stimo che non vi è errore alcuno che è molto bene da me rivista; e si come io l'ho fatta a pezzi, non ne ho altro originale che questo che mando a Vostra Altezza, con che La supplico a farla trascrivere al solito da bella mano acciò possa esser cantata con facilità; anzi desidero che prima di sentirne cosa alcuna la faccia ben copiare, acciò chi canta, e chi suona non habbia da stentare, onde Vostra Altezza ne possa veramente godere; e dopoi può dare quest'originale al Signor Giovanni Battista Vulpio, ch'egli sa come farmelo recapitare con occasione che vi sarà fra poco tempo di Roma in qua. Più presto non l'ho finita, perché Vostra Altezza ha havuto la bontà di non mostrarne fretta et io havendo havuto molto da fare, e per qua e per altre bande, mi son servito dell'autorità che m'ha concessa; ma ho tardato ancora perché l'ho voluta fare senza scrivere necessitato, e per farla a modo mio ben considerata, e nel miglior modo che ho saputo; Vostra Altezza però sa che quando volesse esser servita velocemente, saprei metter l'ali alla penna, e compire ai suoi commandi; ma quando vi è tempo, stimo si possino far sempre le compositioni con più giuditio, e più considerate. Basta, Vostra Altezza deve riconoscere in quest'opera la mia attentione, e la mia osservanza, non la virtù, che non ne ho da poterneLa servire, so che ha tanta bontà che gradirà questo mio povero parto, come ha saputo far tant'altre volte, e così vivo consolato.

Qua si va preparando per questa estate un'operetta di spada, e cappa di sei personaggi da fare in villa, e in mare; questo sì che la vogliono fare di tutta perfettione, e si cercano le parti migliori che si possino havere in Italia, e fuori ancora. Sin'hora è fermata una tal Signora Margherita di Bologna, che ha un'applauso formidabile da tutti, et una sua sorella giovinetta, che dicesi riesce di gran spirito. Si negotia per haver Cortoncino castrato da Vienna, il quale già passa in Italia, o vero si prenderà Gioseppino di Baviera. Il buffo è Petriccioli di Roma, che per la parte che vogliamo non ha eguale, haveremo una vecchia da Milano stimata assai buona, e per tenore si prenderà il Canavese, già che non sappiamo dove trovar cosa rara. Volevano far venire Pietro Santi da Vienna, ma l'Imperatore non vuol dar licenza a nessuno de' suoi musici, e questo Cortoncino la potrà havere perché serve l'Imperatrice. Il più debole sarà la musica come mia, ma l'accompagnaremo con altre cose ben fatte, onde comparirà ancor essa. Nell'entrante settimana faccio in mare un barcheggio di fontione grossa in mare per due sposi ch'hora vi sono qua; li Signori che fanno l'opera questa estate sono il Signor Duca Spinola di S. Pietro, il Signor Duca Doria, il Signor Goffredo de Marini, Signor Francesco Maria Spinola, e il Signor Don Francesco Serra. Con che facendo humilissima e profondissima riverenza resto

Di Vostra Altezza
humilissimo devotissimo obligatissimo servitore
Alessandro Stradella.
Genova 24 Maggio 1681

Most Serene Highness,

I am sending Your Highness the finished opera, and have given [it] in this same post to the courier so that he will certainly deliver it [and] take immediate care that it be given to you. I do not want to exaggerate to persuade you of the care and attention with which I did it, because I assume Your Highness, already knowing how great my obligations are, can appreciate it for yourself. I composed it with extraordinary satisfaction, since it was a command of Your Highness, and since it is in itself a beautiful opera. You will find it copied in rather poor writing, because here in Genoa there is no careful copyist but some singers who copy; and a priest who was here who wrote well has in fact recently left here. The notes, however, are clear; the words are written in a rather poor hand; but all is most intelligible, and I judge that there is no error since it was carefully checked by me. And since I did it in sections, I have no other score than this that I send to Your Highness. Whereby I beg you to have it transcribed as usual in a beautiful hand, so that it may be sung with ease; even more, I desire that before hearing anything you have it well copied, so that who sings and who plays does not have difficulty, whereby Your Highness may truly enjoy it. And afterwards you can give this score to Signor Giovanni Battista Vulpio, because he knows how to get it to me since he comes here soon from Rome. I did not finish it more quickly, because Your Highness had the goodness not to express any haste; and having had much to do, both for here and elsewhere, I took advantage of the authority that you gave me. But I delayed still more, because I wanted to do it without writing in a forced way, and to do it in my well-considered way, and in the best way that I knew. Your Highness knows, however, that when he wants to be served quickly, I would know how to put wings on the pen, and satisfy his commands; but when there is time, I deem that one can always do the compositions with more judgement, and more thoughtfully. Enough: Your Highness should recognize in this opera my attention and my care, not the talent which I don't have but should to serve you. I know that you have much goodness, that you will be pleased by this, my poor offspring, as you have known how to be many other times, and thus I live consoled.

Here they are preparing for this summer a cloak-and-dagger operetta for six characters to do in a villa and on the sea. This they really want to do in all perfection, and they are looking for the best voices that one can have in Italy and also outside. Up to now, a certain Signora Margherita of Bologna has been engaged, who has the outstanding applause of all, and her young sister, who it is said acquits herself with great spirit. They are negotiating to have Cortoncino, a castrato from Vienna, who is already in Italy, or instead they will take Gioseppino of Bavaria. The *buffo* is Petriccioli of Rome, who for the part we want has no equal; we will have [one who does the role of] an old lady from Milan, considered rather good; and for [the] tenor they will take Canavese, since we do not know where to find something special. They wanted to have Pietro Santi come from Vienna, but the Emperor will not give permission [to leave] to any of his singers, and this Cortoncino is able to have it because he serves the Empress. The weakest [part] will be the music such as mine, but we will accompany it with other well-done things, whereby it [the music] will also seem so. Next week I am doing a [composition for a] boating, for a big function on the sea for two betrothed who are now here. The gentlemen who are doing the opera this summer are Signor Duke Spinola of San Pietro, Signor Duke Doria, Signor Goffredo de Marini, Signor Franco Maria Spinola, and Signor Don Francesco Serra. Making most humble and most profound reverence, I remain

Your Highness's
most humble, most devoted, most obliged servant,
Alessandro Stradella.
Genoa, 24 May 1681

24. Stradella to Polo Michiel: Genoa, 21 December 1681
I-Vmc, PD C. 1067, no. 359

Illustrissimo   et   Eccellentissimo   Signore   Signore   Padrone   Mio Collendissimo

Ben mi giunge cara questa congiontura delle sante feste del Natale di Nostro Signore per haver campo di ravvivar nella memoria di Vostra Eccellenza la mia servitù e per farLe sapere che sin dal giorno che habbi l'honore di esserLe servitore Gli desidero [?] quelle felicità che [?] tali compiti e sodisfatti tutti i Suoi desiderij: scrivo dunque questa per ratificare questi miei sentimenti e non per significarli adesso.

Qua si è fatta per la prima opera del Vespasiano che fu recitata in Venetia, ma con poca fortuna. Si attende la seconda opera il medemo l'esito. Del resto Vostra Eccellenza non mi lasci così otioso, e si compiaccia di farmi cognoscere che sono in Sua gratia col favorirmi di qualche Suo commando con che faccendoLe humilissima riverenza

Di Vostra Eccellenza
humilissimo obligatissimo servitore
Alessandro Stradella.
Genova li 21 Xbre 1681

Most Illustrious and Most Excellent Sir, My Lord and Most Honourable Master,

This opportunity of the Holy Feast of the Birth of Our Lord is dear to me for permitting me to revive Your Excellency's memory of my servitude, and for letting you know that since the day that I had the honour of being your servant, I desire for you [?] those happinesses [?] such tasks and to [have] satisfied all your desires. I write this then to reaffirm my sentiments and not to spell them out now.

Here for the first opera they did *Vespasiano*, which was performed in Venice but with little success. One expects the same results for the second opera. For the rest, Your Excellency should not leave me so idle, and should be pleased to let me know that I am in your grace by favouring me with some command. Whereby, making you most humble reverence, [I am]

Your Excellency's
most humble, most obliged servant,
Alessandro Stradella.
Genoa, 21 December 1681

(*b*): Opera Dedications

In two of his operas for the Teatro Falcone in Genoa, Stradella wrote the dedications included in the printed librettos. They appear here in chronological order.

1. Stradella's dedication of *La forza dell'amor paterno* to Teresa Raggi Saoli (Genoa, 1678)

Illustrissima Signora, e Padrona Colendissima,

Un[o] de' più splendidi fregi del sole è diffondere la miniera de suoi dorati splendori non solo sopra i più vicini paesi, ma anco nelle più rimote contrade. Non si meravigli per tanto Vostra Signoria Illustrissima, che io senz'alcuna vicinanza di servitù seco Essa venghi ad implorar la beneficenza di quei raggi, che si come in Lei vantano un sole di vaghezza, così nella nobilissima sua famiglia sempre più illustre per le toghe senatorie del padre riconoscono una sfera di gloria. Se la prima comparsa della luce solare nell'orizonte vien corteggiata dalla melodia de più canori augelli; qual vanto più proprio potevo io rifondere a cigni armonioso delle ligustiche scene, che acquistarmi nella musical tessitura di questo dramma il patrocinio di raggi così propitij? Ne mai più saranno acclamati d'ora ch'escono dalla casa paterna luminosissima alla patria con le nozze d'un de più degni suoi figli: non potendo Imeneo illustrar più nobilmente la sua face, che con sì bei raggi. Son certo, che posti in fronte di quest'opera daranno una gratiosa smentita alla canora bugia de' poeti nelle favole de' Prometei, e de Memnoni: facendo in bocca de recitanti ravvivar la musica, e su la lingua de maldicenti ammutolire l'invidia. A me in tanto sarà di gloria aver somministrato se non consonanza perfetta, almeno luce preziosa al dramma col solo nome di Vostra Signoria Illustrissima, cui consacro la mia divotissima osservanza.

Di Vostra Illustrissima,
humilissimo divotissimo servitore,
Alessandro Stradella.

Most Illustrious Lady and Most Honourable Mistress,

One of the most beautiful distinctions of the sun is to disburse the mine of its golden splendours not only over the nearest countries but also in the most remote lands. Do not wonder, therefore, Most Illustrious Lady, that I, without any attachment of servitude to you, come to seek the beneficent rays which, as they proclaim you to be a sun of beauty, so in your most noble family, made still more illustrious by the senatorial togas of your father, they recognize a sphere of glory. If the first appearance of the solar light on the horizon is courted by the melody of the most harmonious birds, with what better boast can I respond to the harmonious swans of the Ligurian scenes than by procuring, through the musical weaving of this drama, the patronage of rays so propitious? Never more acclaimed will they be than now, emanating from the most refulgent paternal house to the country [Italy] with the marriage of one of your most worthy sons; Imeneo cannot render his own splendour more nobly than with such beautiful rays. I am certain that, placed on the title-page of this opera, they will be a lovely contradiction to the mellifluous lie of the poets in the tales of Prometheus and Memnon: by reviving music in the mouths of performers and silencing envy on the tongues of slanderers. To me it will give so much glory to have provided, if not perfect agreement, at least precious light to the drama with only the name of Your Most Illustrious Ladyship, to whom I consecrate my most devoted respect.

Your Most Illustrious Ladyship's
most humble, most devoted servant,
Alessandro Stradella.

2. Stradella's dedication of *Le gare dell'amor eroico* to Bianca Maria Spinola Fieschi (Genoa, 1679)

Illustrissima Signora Mia Patrona Colendissima:

Se più illustri potessero rendersi le fiamme di quel Mutio che fe' ardere di vergognoso rossore la porpora di un Porsenna, con altra luce al certo più gloriosa non haverebbero da coronarsi, che con la face di quel fresco Imeno, che così degnamente nobiltà le illustri fascie della nobilissima Casa Fiesca. Io che ho meritato l'honore di render sonore quelle fiamme su le scene della Liguria, non so acquistar loro fiati più propitij per farle più gloriosamente avvampare, che quell'aura di applausi, con cui viene da

tutta la città corteggiato il merito di dama si qualificata. Son certo, che a tal rogo di gloria non mancheranno l'arie più vaghe, quando Vostra Signoria Illustrissima compensi le mancanze del mio plettro, con l'armonia di quelle doti, che sì preziosamente si ammirano risplendere nelle sue singolari prerogative. Resterà in tanto la fama di sì rinomata opera distintamente tenuta al suo patrocinio, che può renderla una fenice de teatri rinata tra quelle vampe. Et io segnalando con tale ombra le consonanze della mia tesitura armoniosa resto
    Di Vostra Signoria Illustrissima,
    humilissimo devotissimo servitore,
    Alessandro Stradella.

Most Illustrious Lady, My Most Honourable Mistress,
    If the flames of that Mucius, who made burn with shameful red the purple of a Porsenna, could be made more illustrious with another light, it could certainly not be crowned more gloriously than with the torch of that recent wedding, that so worthily ennobles the illustrious stripes [of the coat of arms] of the noble house of Fiesca. I who have merited the honour of rendering those flames sonorous on the stage of Liguria, do not know how to achieve a more fitting draught with which to fan them more gloriously, than that breeze of applause which from the whole city courts the merit of a lady so qualified. I am certain that such a bonfire of glory will not lack the most lovely currents of air, when Your Most Illustrious Ladyship compensates for the inadequacy of my plectrum, with the harmony of those wise men who are seen to shine so preciously in their singular privileges. In the mean time, the fame of such a renowned opera will remain unmistakably associated with your patronage which can make it a theatrical Phoenix, reborn in those flames. And I, entrusting to its spirit the consonances of my harmonious interweaving, remain
    Your Most Illustrious Ladyship's
    most humble, most devoted servant,
    Alessandro Stradella.

(c): Motet Texts

Stradella's name appears on four of his extant motets as the author of their Latin texts. The works are without proper titles and therefore they are presented here in alphabetical order of their incipits.

1. Care Jesu suavissime

'Care Jesu suavissime,
nil desidero nisi te;

caeli pignus iucundissime,
cibo dulci nutris me.
Care Jesu suavissime,
nil desidero nisi te.
Sic dapes amoris
in panem latentis
laetificant me,
sic unda cruoris
in vino manentis
inebriat me.
Care Jesu suavissime,
nil desidero nisi te.'

Quis est hic qui tam dulciter alloquitur Deum?
Vide Philippum, qui totus in charitatis amore conversus
ad altissimum prorsus extollitur:
ergo, in hoc die tanto heroi dicato
cantemus, celebremus eum.

Canite superi, gaudete mortales
et omnes plaudite.
Caelum radiis, terra gaudiis refulgeat
et tanti diei gloriae
caelitum cantibus, hominum plausibus celebrentur.

In flammis amoris nunc vere iucundus
ardescat liquescat laetissimus mundus
et musicis choris dum iuste laetantur
terrae gaudia caeli sequantur.
Expellat iam fletus serenus hic dies
dum venit, dum redit dulcissima quies
et superum coetus dum iuste laetantur
terrae gaudia caeli sequantur.

Admirabile laetitiae signum,
o gaudium vere dignum,
dum superi et mortales concordi plausu
citharas tangunt laudes pangentes et dulciter exhilarant.

Ergo cantibus aether exultet
tellus resultet
et digno concentu,
in tanto contentu
dum resonet melos,
terrae plausus ascendat ad caelos.
Alleluia.

'Dear, most sweet Jesus, | I desire none but you, | most happy promise of heaven, | with sweet sustenance you nourish me. | Dear, most sweet Jesus, | I desire none but you. | Thus the banquets of love | concealed in the bread | make me happy, | thus the wave of blood | that remains in the wine | inebriates me. | Dear, most sweet Jesus, | I desire none but you.'

Who is it who now so sweetly addresses God? | Behold Filippo who, entirely devoted to the love of charity, | rises up straightway to the highest: | hence, in this day dedicated to so great a hero, | let us sing and celebrate him. |

Sing, heavenly beings; rejoice, mortals; | and all give praise. | Let heaven glow with rays, and earth with rejoicing, | and the glories of such a day | be celebrated by the singing of heaven and the praise of men.

Truly happy in the flames of this love, | let the most joyful world burn and melt. | And as they rightly celebrate with choirs of musicians, let the heavens accompany the joys of the earth. | Let this serene day drive out all weeping as the sweetest calm comes and returns; | and while the heavenly hosts most aptly rejoice, | let the heavens accompany the joys of earth.

O admirable sign of happiness, | O truly worthy of rejoicing, | for which heaven and mortals, with united praise, | play their harps, sing their praises, and sweetly exult.

Hence, let heaven rejoice with singing, | earth reverberate, | and with worthy harmony, | in so much happiness | while the singing resounds, | let the applause of earth rise to heaven. |

Alleluia.

2. Dixit angelis suis iratus Deus

Dixit angelis suis iratus Deus:
'Vindicate scelera hominum,
interficite principes,
implete domus et civitates
confusione gemitu et lamentis.'
Ecce per auras,
ecce iam toto caelo
sonant ferales tubae,
ecce descendunt super terram belli metus
discordiae pestilentia et fames.

Ah, miseri mortales
nunc lacrimatis
nunc suspiratis
sed tardi sunt fletus,

sunt lacrimae inanes.
Non antra, non valles,
non mare profundum abscondent vos
de manu Domini viventis;
non specus inferni,
non lacus abissi eripient vos
de manu Domini viventis.

Ecce erexit brachium suum
contra nos Deus similis fulminanti
sed ad pedes irati genuflexa Maria,
Maria cara mater
et lacrimantium consolatrix,
'Parce miseris,' dixit, 'o fili mi, parce Salvator mundi.'
'Non parcam, vindicabo.'
'Misere, Jesu pie
lacrimantium cara spes,
noli mundum condemnare
Jesu dulcis, Jesu care.'
His vocibus placatus Deus
deposuit gladium furoris sui;
et ecce de caeli nubibus
mille angeli in veste candida citharizantes
in citharis suis annunciabant pacem;
per littora, per valles
Maria dulce nomen resonabat.

Tibi lilia, tibi rosae
tibi gemmae, tibi flores
tibi crines bella aurora
stellato diademate coronent.
Cara Virgo, cara Mater,
tibi fremitu sonoro
mille tubae triumphales
sonent strepitu canoro.
Alleluia.

God said in wrath to his angels: | 'Take revenge for the crimes of men, | slay the princes, | fill the houses and cities | with confusion, lamentations, and cries.' Lo! in the air, | lo! already throughout heaven | resound the trumpets of gloom, | thus descend on earth the terrors of war, | the plague and famine of discord.

Oh, wretched mortals, | now you cry, | now you sigh, | but too late is your crying, | useless are your tears. | Neither caves, nor valleys, | nor

the deep sea will hide you | from the hand of the living God. | Neither
the caverns of hell, | nor the depth of the abyss will snatch you | from
the hand of the living God.

Behold, God has raised His arm | against us like one that casteth a
thunderbolt, | but at the feet of the Enraged One kneels Mary, | Mary,
dear Mother, | who consoles those in tears. | 'Have pity on those in mis-
ery', she said, 'my Son, have pity, Saviour of the world'. | 'I will not for-
give, I will revenge'. | 'Have pity, holy Jesus, | dear hope of those in
tears; | do not condemn the world, | sweet Jesus, dear Jesus.' | God,
placated by her words, | put down the sword of His fury; | and behold,
from the clouds of heaven, | a thousand angels in white garments, playing
harps, | announced with their harps the peace; | along coasts, along val-
leys, | the sweet name of Mary resounded.

Let lilies and roses, | gems and flowers, | crown your hair, beautiful
dawn, | with a starry diadem. | Dear Virgin, dear Mother, | for you
with a vibrant sound | let a thousand triumphant trumpets | sound a
loud song.

Alleluia.

3. Exultate in Deo, fideles

Exultate in Deo, fideles:
somnus odia comprimit altus,
cessant irae in mundo crudeles.
Eia ergo connectite saltus.

Haec sunt munera divinae
bonitatis in terra,
sunt prodigia charitatis
amantis redemptoris.
In lacrimis in fletu
triumphavit saeva mors:
angustias durissimas
caelestis flectit sors.
Iungat nostros affectus
catena charitatis stringat affectus.

Exaudi supplices
praecantes servulos,
O Jesu mi,
et nostris lacrimis,
amaris vocibus
benignus sis.
Bellicosas horribiles furias

rumpe, scinde, frange, repelle;
strages barbaras abige numine.
Radianti concordiae lumine
dies reddant auricomae stellae.
Veni, o Jesu benigne,
dulcis pacis nos rore asperge
et pugnaci ferventes in igne
Stygis aquis infunde submerge.

Rejoice in God, ye faithful; | deep sleep extinguishes hate, | the cruel wrath in the world comes to a halt. | Therefore, join in the dance!

These are the gifts of divine | goodness on earth, | the prodigies of love | from our loving Redeemer. | In tears, in cries, | evil death exulted; | [now] great sufferings | are averted by heavenly destiny. | May our love be united, | bound together by the chain of His love.

Hear the supplicants, | praying servants, | O my Jesus, | and because of our tears, | our sad words, | be kind to us. | The terrible furies of war | break up, tear apart, divide, repel; | with Your will dispel the barbarous slaughter. | With the brightness of harmony, | let the days of the comet return. | Come, O kindly Jesus, | sprinkle us with the dew of sweet peace. | And those roused by the fire of battle, | plunge and drown in the waters of the Styx.

4. O vos omnes, qui transitis per viam

O vos omnes, qui transitis per viam
fulcite me floribus,
stipate me malis
quia amore langueo.
O amor tonantis
quam fervidus es,
tu cordis amantis
et salus et spes.
O quam suavis est spiritus tuus,
dulcissime Jesu,
amandissime Christe,
diligentibus te.

Sordet tellus tua flagranti
charitate; o mi dilecte
inter mille praeelecte,
da quietem laboranti.
Properanti ad superna
vites huius mundi fructus,

cinosura sis et ductus,
care Jesu, suspiranti.

Valete mundi gaudia:
solus amor Jesu me delectat,
illi vivam, in hoc moriar
et requiescam.
Alleluia.

O all you who go by on the road, | support me with flowers, | fill me up with apples, | because I suffer from love. | O vibrant love, how intense you are, | you are to the loving heart | both health and hope. | How sweet is Your spirit, | most sweet Jesus, | Christ most worthy of love, | for those who follow You.

The world is a mean thing [compared] to your burning | love; O my Beloved, | chosen among a thousand, | give peace to the sufferer. | To him who strives toward heavenly things, | vine and the fruit of this world, | be polar star and guide, | dear Jesus, to him who sighs.

Farewell, joys of the world; | only the love of Jesus gives me pleasure, | of it I will live, in it I will die | and will rest.
Alleluia.

Bibliography

This bibliography lists all books, articles (with the exception of some encyclopaedia articles), and theses referred to in the book, as well as those not referred to specifically but which may be useful to the reader. Manuscript sources are fully identified in footnotes. For sources of Stradella's music, as well as editions of his music other than those mentioned here, see Carolyn Gianturco and Eleanor McCrickard (compilers), *Alessandro Stradella (1639–1682): A Thematic Catalogue of his Compositions* (Styvesant, NY, 1991).

ADAMI, IGNAZIO, *I secoli delle principesse di bellezza impareggiabile o vero i periodi delle influenze celesti* (Amsterdam, 1692).

ADEMOLLO, ALESSANDRO, *Il matrimonio di Suor Maria Pulcheria al secolo Livia Cesarini* (Rome, 1883; repr. 1967).

—— *I teatri di Roma nel secolo decimosettimo* (Rome, 1888; repr. with new pagination, 1969).

ALALEONA, DOMENICO, *Storia dell'oratorio musicale in Italia* (Milan, 1945; previously pub. (with different pagination) as *Studi su la storia dell'oratorio musicale in Italia* (Turin, 1908)).

'Alessandro Stradella' (trans. from the Leipzig *Signale*), *Monthly Musical Record*, 3 (1873), 116–17.

Alessandro Stradella e Modena: Musica, Documenti, Immagini. Catalogo della Mostra (Modena, 1983).

ALFONSO, LUIGI, 'Terzo centenario dell'assassinio di Alessandro Stradella', *La Berio*, 3 (1982), 48–56.

ALLACCI, LIONE, *Drammaturgia di Lione Allacci, accresciuta e continuata fino all'anno MDCCLV* (Venice, 1755; repr. Turin, 1966).

ALLAM, EDWARD, 'Alessandro Stradella', *Proceedings of the Royal Musical Association*, 80 (1953–4), 29–42.

ALLEN, DAVID, 'The "Lost" Stradella Manuscripts and their Relationship to the Estense Holdings of his Music in Modena', in Carolyn Gianturco (ed.), *Alessandro Stradella e Modena, Atti del Convegno internazionale di studi, Modena, 15–17 dicembre 1983* (Modena, 1985), 125–35.

—— 'The Five-Part Madrigals of Stradella', in Carolyn Gianturco and Giancarlo Rostirolla (eds.), *Atti del Convegno di studi 'Alessandro Stradella e il suo tempo', Siena, 8–12 settembre 1982, Chigiana*, 39, NS 19 (1988), 155–89.

—— (ed.), *Alessandro Stradella: Four Madrigals for Five Voices* (London, 1981).

ALLORTO, RICCARDO, 'Alessandro Stradella e la cantata a 3 per il SS. Natale', *Musicisti della Scuola Emiliana, Chigiana*, 13 (1956), 91–6.

ALLSOP, PETER, *Italian Seventeenth Century Instrumental Music*, ser. I: *Rome*, nos. 1 and 3: Carlo Ambrogio Lonati, *Sinfonie a 3* (Crediton, Devon, 1990 and 1988 resp.).

ALLSOP, PETER, *The Italian 'Trio' Sonata* (Oxford, 1992).

AMEYDEN (also AMAYDEN), TEODORO [Dirk Van], *Storia delle famiglie romane*, ed. Carlo Augusto Bertini (2 vols.; Rome, n.d. [1914?]; repr. 1987).

ANNIBALDI, CLAUDIO, 'L'Archivio musicale Doria Pamphili: Saggio sulla cultura aristocratica a Roma fra 16° e 18° secolo', *Studi musicali*, 11 (1982), 91–120, 277–344.

ANTONIBON, FRANCESCA, *Le relazioni a stampa di ambasciatori veneti* (*Collana di bibliografie minori*, i; Padua, 1939).

APEL, WILLI, *The History of Keyboard Music to 1700* (Bloomington, Ind., 1972).

ARNOLD, DENIS, 'Stradella's Motets at the Biblioteca Estense', in Carolyn Gianturco (ed.), *Alessandro Stradella e Modena, Atti del Convegno internazionale di studi, Modena, 15–17 dicembre 1983* (Modena, 1985), 99–103.

BACCINI, GIUSEPPE, 'Il Maestro Stradella', *Giornale di erudizione*, 3 (1890–1), 277–9.

BAIRD, JULIANNE, 'The Vocal Serenata of the 17th and 18th Centuries' (MA thesis, Rochester University, 1976).

BARGELLINI, PIERO, *Nuovi Santi del Giorno* (Florence, 1960).

BAROZZI, NICCOLÒ, and BERCHET, GUGLIELMO (eds.), *Le relazioni della Corte di Roma lette al Senato dagli Ambasciatori Veneti nel secolo decimosettimo*, ii (Venice, 1879).

BELGRANO, LUIGI T., 'Delle feste e dei giuochi dei Genovesi', *Archivio storico italiano*, 3rd ser. (1871): 13: 39–71, 190–221; 14: 64–118; 15: 417–77.

BERNSTEIN, HARRY M., 'Alessandro Stradella's Serenata 'Il barcheggio' (Genoa, 1681): A Modern Edition and Commentary with Emphasis on the Use of the Cornetto (2 vols., DMA diss., Stanford University, 1979).

—— , BIAGI-RAVENNI, GABRIELLA, GIANTURCO, CAROLYN, and ZOLESI, ILARIA (eds.), *Alessandro Stradella*: *Tre grandi cantate* (*Concentus Musicus*; Rome, forthcoming).

BIAGI-RAVENNI, GABRIELLA, 'Le due *Circe* dello Stradella ovvero notizie circa l'esecuzione di una *Circe* di Alessandro Stradella', in Carolyn Gianturco (ed.), *Alessandro Stradella e Modena, Atti del Convegno internazionale di studi, Modena, 15–17 dicembre 1983* (Modena, 1985), 31–43.

BIANCHI, LINO, *Carissimi, Stradella, Scarlatti e l'oratorio musicale* (Rome, 1969).

—— 'Gli oratori di Alessandro Stradella', in Carolyn Gianturco and Giancarlo Rostirolla (eds.), *Atti del Convegno di studi 'Alessandro Stradella e il suo tempo', Siena, 8–12 settembre 1982*, Chigiana, 39, NS 19 (1988), 265–76.

BIANCONI, LORENZO, and WALKER, THOMAS, 'Production, Consumption and Political Function of Seventeenth-Century Italian Opera', *Early Music History*, 4 (1984), 209–96.

BIGNAMI ODIER, JEANNE, and MORELLI, GIORGIO (eds.), *Anonimo del Seicento: Istoria degli intrighi galanti della regina di Svezia e della sua corte durante il di lei soggiorno a Roma* (Rome, 1979): critical annotated edn. in Italian of: Anon., *Histoire des intrigues galantes de la reine Christine de Suède* (Amsterdam, 1679).

BJURSTRÖM, PER, *Feast and Theatre in Queen Christina's Rome* (Stockholm, 1966).

BONAVENTURA, ARNALDO, *Teatro Musicale* (Livorno, 1913).

—— [signed A. R. NALDO], 'Un trattato inedito e ignoto di Veracini', *Rivista musicale italiana*, 42 (1938), 617–35.

BONTA, STEPHEN, 'Terminology for the Bass Violin in Seventeenth-Century Italy', *Journal of the American Musical Instrument Society*, 4 (1978), 5–42.

—— 'Corelli's Heritage: The Early Bass Violin in Italy', in Pierluigi Petrobelli and Gloria Staffieri (eds.), *Studi Corelliani IV: Atti del Quarto Congresso Internazionale (Fusignano, 4–7 settembre 1986)* (Florence, 1990), 217–31.

BORDAS, CRISTINA, 'The Double Harp in Spain from the 16th to the 18th Centuries', *Early Music*, 15 (1987), 148–63.

BOURDELOT, PIERRE, and BONNET, PIERRE, *Histoire de la musique et des ses effets* (Paris, 1715).

BOXICH, E., 'Ansaldo Ansaldi', in Emilio De Tipaldo (ed.), *Biografia degli Italiani illustri nelle scienze, lettere ed arti del secolo XVIII, e de' contemporanei*, i (Venice, 1834), 479–82.

BRAGAGLIA, ANTONIO GIULIO, *Storia del Teatro Popolare* (Rome, 1958).

BRIDGES, DAVID MERRELL, 'The Social Setting of "Musica da Camera" in Rome: 1667–1700', (Ph.D. diss., George Peabody College for Teachers, 1976).

BROSSARD, SÉBASTIAN DE, *Dictionaire de musique* (Paris, 1703; repr. Amsterdam, 1964).

BROWN, HOWARD M. (ed.), *Italian Opera 1640–1770* (60 vols. of facsimiles; New York, 1977–83).

—— (ed.), *Italian Opera Librettos 1640–1770* [81 librettos in facsimile] (New York, 1977–84).

BRUZZI, MANUELA, '*Lo schiavo liberato* di Alessandro Stradella', in Carolyn Gianturco (ed.), *Alessandro Stradella e Modena, Atti del Convegno internazionale di studi, Modena, 15–17 dicembre 1983* (Modena, 1985), 44–50.

BUKOFZER, MANFRED F., *Music in the Baroque Era* (New York, 1947).

BURKE, JOHN, *Musicians of S. Maria Maggiore, Rome, 1600–1700, Note d'archivio*, NS 2, supplement (1984).

BURNEY, CHARLES, *A General History of Music*, ed. Frank Mercer (2 vols.; London, 1935).

CAMETTI, ALBERTO, 'Giacomo d'Alibert costruttore del primo teatro pubblico di musica in Roma', *Nuova antologia*, 66 (1930–1), 340–60.

—— *Il teatro di Tordinona poi di Apollo* (2 vols.; Tivoli, 1938).

CAPPELLETTI, GIUSEPPE, *Le chiese d'Italia* (Venice, 1847).

CARUTTI [DI CANTOGNO], DOMENICO, *Storia della diplomazia della corte di Savoia dal 1494 al 1773* (4 vols.; Rome, 1875–80).

CASIMIRI, RAFFAELE, 'Oratorii del Masini, Bernabei, Melani, Di Pio, Pasquini e Stradella, in Roma nell'Anno Santo 1675', *Note d'archivio*, 13 (1936), 157–69.

—— 'Musicisti dell'ordine francescano dei Minori Conventuali dei sec. XVI–XVII', *Note d'archivio*, 16 (1939), 186–99, 238–50, 274–5.

CASOLINI, FAUSTA, 'Caterina di Genova', in Pio Paschini (ed.), *Enciclopedia Cattolica*, iii (Città del Vaticano, 1949), 1145–8.

CATELANI, ANGELO, 'Dell'archivio musicale della biblioteca palatina di Modena, e particolarmente di Alessandro Stradella', *Effemeride della pubblica istruzione*, 2, no. 24 (4 Mar. 1861), 404–5.

—— *Delle opere di Alessandro Stradella esistenti nell'Archivio Musicale della R. Biblioteca Palatina di Modena*, (Modena, 1866; previously pub. in *Atti e Memorie delle RR. Deputazioni di Storia Patria per le provincie modenesi e parmensi*, 3 (1865), 319–52.

CAVALLINI, IVANO, 'Stradella e la musica per tromba', in Carolyn Gianturco (ed.), *Alessandro Stradella e Modena, Atti del Convegno internazionale di studi, Modena, 15–17 dicembre 1983* (Modena, 1985), 77–98.

Cavicchi, Adriano, 'Una sinfonia inedita di Arcangelo Corelli nello stile del concerto grosso venticinque anni prima dell'opera VI', *Chigiana*, 20 (1963), 43–55.

Chaikin, Kathleen Ann, 'The Solo Soprano Cantatas of Alessandro Stradella' (Ph.D. diss., Stanford University, 1975).

Chiarelli, Alessandra, 'La collezione estense di musica stradelliana: Per un'indagine sulla sua formazione', in Carolyn Gianturco (ed.), *Alessandro Stradella e Modena, Atti del Convegno internazionale di studi, Modena, 15–17 dicembre 1983* (Modena, 1985), 116–24.

Chrysander, Friedrich (ed.), *Serenata a 3 con strumenti di Alessandro Stradella (Qual prodigio)*. Supplement, vol. iii to *G. F. Händel's Werke*. (Leipzig, 1888).

Cicogna, Emmanuele Antonio, *Delle inscrizioni veneziane* (6 vols.; Venice, 1824–53).

Claretta, Gaudenzio, 'I reali di Savoia munifici fautori delle arti', *Miscellanea di storia italiana*, 30 (1893), 23–7.

—— *I Reali di Savoia munifici fautori delle arti, contributo alla storia artistica del Piemonte del secolo XVIII* (Turin, 1893).

Clementi, Filippo, *Il Carnevale romano nelle cronache contemporanee* (Rome, 1899; 2nd edn., 2 vols., Città di Castello, 1939).

Cloche, Antonio, *Regola, e costituzioni delle Suore di S. Domenico* (Rome, 1709).

Costantini, Nazareno, *Memorie storiche di Acquapendente* (Rome, 1903).

Crescimbeni, Giovan Mario, *L'istoria della volgar poesia* (Rome, 1698; 2nd edn., Rome, 1714; 3rd edn., 6 vols.; Venice, 1730–1).

—— *La bellezza della volgar poesia spiegata in otto dialoghi* (Rome, 1700).

—— *Comentarij intorno alla storia della volgar poesia* (5 vols.; Rome, 1702–11).

—— *Notizie istoriche degli arcadi morti* (3 vols.; Rome, 1720–1).

Crespellani, Arsenio, *Memorie Storiche Vignolesi* (Modena, 1872).

Crowther, Victor, 'Alessandro Stradella and the Oratorio Tradition in Modena', in Carolyn Gianturco (ed.), *Alessandro Stradella e Modena, Atti del Convegno internazionale di studi, Modena, 15–17 dicembre 1983* (Modena, 1985), 51–64.

—— 'The Characterization of Women in Stradella's Oratorios', in Carolyn Gianturco and Giancarlo Rostirolla (eds.), *Atti del Convegno di studi 'Alessandro Stradella e il suo tempo', Siena, 8–12 settembre 1982, Chigiana*, 39, NS 19 (1988), 277–85.

—— *The Oratorio in Modena* (Oxford, 1992).

Culley, Thomas D., *Jesuits and Music*, i: *A Study of the Musicians connected with the German College in Rome during the 17th Century and of their Activities in Northern Europe* (Rome, 1970).

Cummings, Anthony M., 'Towards an Interpretation of the Sixteenth-Century Motet', *Journal of the American Musicological Society*, 34 (1981), 43–59.

Daniels, David W., 'Alessandro Stradella's Oratorio *San Giovanni Battista*: A Modern Edition and Commentary' (2 vols.; Ph.D. diss., State University of Iowa, 1963).

Data Fragalà, Isabella, and Colturato, Annarita (compilers), *Biblioteca Nazionale Università di Torino, La raccolta Mauro Foà—La raccolta Renzo Giordano* (Cataloghi di fondi musicali italiani, 7; Rome, 1987), with an 'Introduzione' by Alberto Basso, pp. ix–lxxxvi.

de Angelis, Enrico, 'L'idea di potere nell'opera lirica del seicento', in Carolyn

Gianturco and Giancarlo Rostirolla (eds.), *Atti del Convegno di studi 'Alessandro Stradella e il suo tempo'*, Siena, *8–12 settembre 1982, Chigiana*, 39, NS 19 (1988), 109–24.

DE DOMINICIS, ROMOLO, 'Nota sulla casata Altemps', *Strenna dei Romanisti*, 26 (1965), 126–32.

DE FERRARI, GIROLAMO F., 'Storia della nobiltà di Genoa', *Giornale araldico, genealogico, diplomatico*, 25 (1897), 25–42, 57–83, 101–24, 129–53.

DELLA CORTE, ANDREA, '*La forza d'amor paterno* di Alessandro Stradella', *Musica d'oggi*, 13 (1931), 389–96.

DENT, EDWARD J., 'Italian Chamber Cantatas', *Musical Antiquary*, 2 (1911), 142–53, 185–99.

DE RINALDIS, ALDO, *Lettere inedite di Salvator Rosa a G. B. Ricciardi* (Rome, 1939).

DIETZ, HANNS-BERTOLD, 'Musikalische Struktur und Architektur im Werke Alessandro Stradellas', *Analecta Musicologica*, 9 (1970), 78–93.

Dizionario biografico degli Italiani (Rome, 1960–).

D'ONOFRIO, CESARE, *La Villa Aldobrandini di Frascati* (Rome, 1963).

DUFFLOCQ, ENRICO MAGNI, 'Alessandro Stradella', *Bollettino bibliografico musicale*, 4 (1929), 1–13.

DURANTE, SERGIO, 'Note su un manoscritto "martiniano"', in Angelo Pompilio (ed.), *Padre Martini: Musica e cultura nel settecento europeo* (Florence, 1987), 123–33.

DURANTI, ELISABETTA, 'Giovanni Lotti (1604–1686): Biografia, trascrizione ed analisi del codice barberiniano Latino 4220, catalogo delle sue poesie per musica' (*laurea* thesis, University of Pisa, 1985–6).

EINSTEIN, ALFRED, 'Ein Bericht über den Turiner Mordanfall auf Alessandro Stradella', *Festschrift zum 50. Geburtstag Adolf Sandberger* (Munich, 1918), 135–7.

ELWERT, W. THEODOR, *La poesia lirica italiana del seicento: Studio sullo stile barocco* (Florence, 1968).

—— *Versificazione italiana dalle origini ai giorni nostri* (Florence, 1976).

Enciclopedia Cattolica, ed. Pio Paschini (12 vols.; Città del Vaticano, 1948–54).

EVELYN, JOHN, *The Diary of John Evelyn*, ed. John Bowle (Oxford, 1983).

FABBRI, PAOLO, 'Questioni drammaturgiche del teatro di Stradella', in Carolyn Gianturco and Giancarlo Rostirolla (eds.), *Atti del Convegno di studi 'Alessandro Stradella e il suo tempo'*, Siena, *8–12 settembre 1982, Chigiana*, 39, NS 19 (1988), 79–108.

FABRONI, ANGELO, *Historiae Academiae Pisanae* (3 vols.; Pisa, 1791–5).

FAGIOLI, ROBERTO, 'La famiglia Stradella di Nepi', in Carolyn Gianturco (ed.), *Alessandro Stradella e Modena, Atti del Convegno internazionale di studi, Modena, 15–17 dicembre 1983* (Modena, 1985), 17–28.

FELICI, LUCIO (ed.), *Poesia italiana del seicento* (Milan, 1978).

FILIPPI, FILIPPO, 'Alessandro Stradella e l'archivio musicale dei Contarini alla Biblioteca di S. Marco in Venezia', *Il politecnico*, parte letterario–scientifica, 4th ser., 2/4 (Oct. 1866), 433–51.

FRUTAZ, A. PIETRO, and CORANDENTE, GIOVANNI, 'Caterina d'Alessandria', in Pio Paschini (ed.), *Enciclopedia Cattolica*, iii (Città del Vaticano, 1949), 1137–42.

FUÀ, FRANCO, *L'opera di Filippo Acciajuoli* (Fossombrone, 1921).

FUMI, LUIGI, *Il Duomo di Orvieto e i sui restauri* (Rome, 1891).

GALLICO, CLAUDIO, 'Un laboratorio linguistico di Alessandro Stradella: I mottetti', in Carolyn Gianturco and Giancarlo Rostirolla (eds.), *Atti del Convegno di studi 'Alessandro Stradella e il suo tempo'*, Siena, 8–12 settembre 1982, Chigiana, 39, NS 19 (1988), 371–85.

GALVANI, LIVIO N., *I teatri musicali di Venezia nel sec. XVII* (Milan, 1879).

GANDINI, ALESSANDRO, *Cronistoria dei teatri di Modena dal 1539 al 1871* (Modena, 1873; repr. Bologna, 1969).

GAUTHIER, MARTIN-PIERRE, *Les Plus beaux édifices de la ville de Gênes* (Paris, 1818–32).

GENTILI, ALBERTO, 'Un'opera di Alessandro Stradella ritrovata recentemente', *Il pianoforte*, 8 (1927), 210–13.

—— 'La raccolta Mauro Foà nella Biblioteca Nazionale di Torino', *Rivista musicale italiana*, 34 (1927), 356–68.

—— 'La raccolta di antiche musiche Renzo Giordano alla Biblioteca Nazionale di Torino', *Accademie e biblioteche d'Italia*, 4 (1930), 117–25.

—— 'Alessandro Stradella', *Miscellanea della Facoltà di Lettere e Filosofia* [University of Turin], ser. 1 (1936), 157–76.

—— (ed.), *Alessandro Stradella: Forza d'amor paterno. Opera in 3 atti per canto e pianoforte* (Milan, 1930).

GENTILI VERONA, GABRIELLA, 'Le collezioni Foà e Giordano della Biblioteca Nazionale di Torino', *Accademie e biblioteche d'Italia*, 32/6 (1964), 405–30.

GERINI, EMANUELE, *Memorie storiche di illustri scrittori e di uomini insigni dell'antica e moderna Lunigiana* (Massa, 1839).

GIANTURCO, CAROLYN, 'The Operas of Alessandro Stradella (1644–1682)' (2 vols.; D.Phil. thesis, Oxford University, 1970).

—— 'Caratteri stilistici delle opere teatrali di Stradella', *Rivista italiana di musicologia*, 6 (1971), 211–45.

—— 'Sources for Stradella's *Moro per Amore*', in *Memorie e contributi alla musica dal medioevo all'età moderna offerti a F. Ghisi nel settantesimo compleanno (1901–1971)* (Bologna, 1971), ii. 129–40.

—— 'The Revisions of Alessandro Stradella's *Forza dell'amor paterno*', *Journal of the American Musicological Society*, 25 (1972), 407–27.

—— 'A Possible Date for Stradella's *Il Trespolo tutore*', *Music and Letters*, 54 (1973), 25–37.

—— 'The Oratorios of Alessandro Stradella', *Proceedings of the Royal Musical Association*, 101 (1974–5), 45–57.

—— 'Evidence for a Late Roman School of Opera', *Music and Letters*, 56 (1975), 4–17.

—— 'Corelli e Alessandro Stradella', in Giulia Giachin (ed.), *Nuovi studi corelliani, Atti del Secondo congresso internazionale, 1974* (Florence, 1978), 55–62.

—— '*Il Trespolo tutore* di Stradella e di Pasquini: Due diverse concezioni dell'opera comica', in Maria Teresa Muraro (ed.), *Venezia e il melodramma nel settecento* (Florence, 1978), 185–98.

—— 'Alessandro Stradella', *The New Grove Dictionary of Music and Musicians*, (ed.) Stanley Sadie (London, 1980).

—— 'Alessandro Stradella: A True Biography', *The Musical Times*, 123 (1982), 756–8.

—— 'La famiglia Stradella: Nuovi documenti biografici', *Nuova rivista musicale italiana*, 3 (1982), 456–66.

—— 'Music for a Genoese Wedding of 1681', *Music and Letters*, 63 (1982), 31–43; corrective note in 64 (1983), 321.

—— 'Catelani rivisitato', in Carolyn Gianturco (ed.), *Alessandro Stradella e Modena, Atti del Convegno internazionale di studi, Modena, 15–17 dicembre 1983* (Modena, 1985), 11–16.

—— 'Cantate dello Stradella in possesso di Andrea Adami', in Carolyn Gianturco and Giancarlo Rostirolla (eds.), *Atti del Convegno di studi 'Alessandro Stradella e il suo tempo', 8–12 settembre 1982, Chigiana*, 39, NS 19 (1988), 125–54.

—— 'Evidence of Lay Patronage in Sacred Music in a Recently Discovered Document of 1631', *Journal of the Royal Musical Association* (vol. dedicated to Denis Arnold), 133 (1988), 306–13.

—— 'The Italian Seventeenth-Century Cantata: A Textual Approach', in John Caldwell, Edward Olleson, and Susan Wollenberg (eds.), *The Well Enchanting Skill: Music, Poetry, and Drama in the Culture of the Renaissance. Essays in Honour of F. W. Sternfeld* (Oxford, 1990), 41–51.

—— '*Cantate spirituali e morali*, with a Description of the Papal Sacred Cantata Tradition for Christmas 1676–1740', *Music and Letters*, 73 (1992), 1–31.

—— (ed.), *Alessandro Stradella e Modena, Atti del Convegno internazionale di studi, Modena, 15–17 dicembre 1983* (Modena, 1985).

—— (ed.), *Cantatas by Alessandro Stradella, The Italian Cantata in the Seventeenth Century*, (Carolyn Gianturco gen. ed.), ix (New York, 1987).

—— (gen. ed.), *The Italian Cantata in the Seventeenth Century* (16 vols.; New York, 1985–7).

—— 'Flavio Orsini', *The New Grove Dictionary of Opera*, ed. Stanley Sadie (London, 1992).

—— 'Alessandro Stradella', *The New Grove Dictionary of Opera*, ed. Stanley Sadie (London, 1992).

——, and McCRICKARD, ELEANOR (compilers), *Alessandro Stradella (1639–1682): A Thematic Catalogue of his Compositions* (Styvesant, NY, 1991).

——, and PIRROTTA, NINO, 'Alessandro Stradella', in Alberto Basso (ed.), *Dizionario Enciclopedico Universale della Musica e dei Musicisti* (2nd edn., Turin, 1988); with a catalogue of music compiled by Carolyn Gianturco and Eleanor McCrickard.

——, and ROSTIROLLA, GIANCARLO (eds.), *Atti del Convegno di studi 'Alessandro Stradella e il suo tempo', Siena, 8–12 settembre 1982, Chigiana*, 39, NS 19 (1988).

GIAZOTTO, REMO, *La musica a Genova* (Genoa, 1951).

—— *Vita di Alessandro Stradella* (2 vols.; Milan, 1962).

GINGERY, GAIL ALVAH, 'Alessandro Stradella: Solo Cantatas of MS 32 E-11 of the Fitzwilliam Museum (DMA diss., Boston University, 1965).

GIORGETTI VICHI, ANNA MARIA, *Gli Arcadi dal 1690 al 1800: Onomasticon* (Rome, 1977).

GOLDSCHMIDT, HUGO, *Studien zur Geschichte der italienischen Oper im 17. Jahrhundert* (2 vols.; Leipzig, 1901–4).

GOLZIO, VINCENZO, *Documenti artistici sul seicento nell'Archivio Chigi* (Rome, 1939).

GRIFFEN, THOMAS E., 'The Late Baroque Serenata in Rome and Naples: A Documentary Study with Emphasis on Alessandro Scarlatti', (Ph.D. diss., University of California at Los Angeles, 1983).

GRIFFITHS, ANN, and RIMMER, JOAN, 'Harp: Double Strung Harps', *The New Grove Dictionary of Music and Musicians*, ed. Stanley Sadie (London, 1980).

GRILLO, LUIGI, *Elogi di Liguri illustri* (4 vols., Genoa, 1846).

GROPPO, ANTONIO, *Catalogo di tutti i drammi per musica recitata nei Teatri di Venezia dal 1627 al 1745* (Venice, 1745).

GROUT, DONALD J., *A Short History of Opera* (2nd edn.; New York, 1965).

GUALDO PRIORATO, GALEAZZO, *Relazione della città di Genova, e suo dominio* (Cologne, 1668).

GUARNIERI, GINO, *I Cavalieri di S. Stefano* (Pisa, 1960).

—— *L'ordine di S. Stefano nei suoi aspetti organizzativi interni sotto il Gran Magistero Mediceo* (Pisa, 1966).

—— *L'ordine di S. Stefano nella sua organizzazione interna* (Pisa, 1966).

GUASCONI, PAOLO, 'L'Oratorio musicale a Firenze dalle origini al 1785' (*laurea* thesis, University of Florence, 1978–9).

Guide di Genova, new series (Genoa, 1986).

HALL, FREDERICK ALBERT, 'The Polyphonic Italian Madrigal: 1638 to 1745' (Ph.D. diss., University of Toronto, 1978).

HAMMOND, FREDERICK, 'Musicians at the Medici Court in the Mid-Seventeenth Century', *Analecta Musicologica*, 14 (1974), 151–69.

HAWKINS, SIR JOHN, *A General History of the Science and Practice of Music* (London, 1776).

HESS, HEINZ, *Die Opern Alessandro Stradella's* (Publikationen der Internationalen Musikgesellschaft, ser. 2, no. 3; Leipzig, 1906; repr. Walluf bei Wiesbaden, 1973).

HILL, JOHN WALTER, 'Oratory Music in Florence, iii: The Confraternities from 1655 to 1785', *Acta Musicologica*, 53 (1986), 129–79.

HUTCHINGS, ARTHUR, *The Baroque Concerto* (New York, 1965).

HYATT KING, ALEC (ed.), *Auction Catalogues of Music, ii: Charles Burney, Catalogue of the Valuable Collection of Music, London, 1844* (Amsterdam, 1973).

IVALDI, ARMANDO FABIO, 'Gli Adorno e l'hostaria–teatro del Falcone di Genova (1600–1680)', *Rivista italiana di musicologia*, 15 (1980), 87–152.

—— 'Teatro e società genovese al tempo di Alessandro Stradella', in Carolyn Gianturco and Giancarlo Rostirolla (eds.), *Atti del Convegno di studi 'Alessandro Stradella e il suo tempo', Siena, 8–12 settembre 1982*, Chigiana, 39, NS 19 (1988), 447–574.

JANDER, OWEN, 'The Works of Alessandro Stradella Related to the Cantata and the Opera' (Ph.D. diss., Harvard University, 1962).

—— *A Catalogue of the Manuscripts of Compositions by Alessandro Stradella found in European and American Libraries* (rev. edn.; Wellesley, Mass., 1962).

—— 'Concerto Grosso Instrumentation in Rome in the 1660's and 1670's', *Journal of the American Musicological Society*, 21 (1968), 168–80.

—— 'The Prologues and Intermezzos of Alessandro Stradella', *Analecta Musicologica*, 7 (1969), 87–111.

—— 'The Cantata in Accademia: Music for the Accademia de' Dissonanti and their Duke, Francesco II d'Este', *Rivista italiana di musicologia*, 10 (1975), 519–44.

—— (compiler), *Alessandro Stradella: The Wellesley Edition Cantata Index Series (WECIS)*: fasc. 4*a*: reliable attributions, fasc. 4*b*: unreliable attributions (Wellesley, Mass., 1969).

KIRCHER, ATHANASIUS, *Misurgia universalis: Sive ars magna consoni ei dissoni in X. libros digesta* (2 vols.; Rome, 1650).

KOLNEDER, WALTER, 'Motivische Arbeit bei Stradella', in Carolyn Gianturco and Giancarlo Rostirolla (eds.), *Atti del Convegno di studi 'Alessandro Stradella e il suo tempo', Siena, 8–12 settembre 1982, Chigiana*, 39, NS 19 (1988), 425–36.

KRETZSCHMAR, HERMANN, *Geschichte der Oper* (Leipzig, 1919; repr. Wiesbaden, 1970).

KROHN, ERNST, 'Some Solo Cantatas of Alessandro Stradella', *Manuscripta*, 2 (1958), 3–15.

LAUB, THOMAS, 'Den falske og den aegte Stradella', *Aarbog for Musik, Udgivet af Dansk Musikselskab 1924* (Copenhagen, 1926), 7–34.

LA VIA, STEFANO, '"Violone" e "Violoncello" a Roma al tempo di Corelli', in Pierluigi Petrobelli and Gloria Staffieri (eds.), *Studi Corelliani IV: Atti del Quarto Congresso Internazionale (Fusignano, 4–7 settembre 1986)* (Florence, 1990), 165–91.

Il libro d'oro della Nobiltà veneziana. Nomi, cognomi, età, e blasoni, araldicamente descritti e delineati de' Veneti patrizi (Venice, 1714).

LIESS, ANDREAS, 'Materialien zur römischen Musikgeschichte des Seicento: Musikerliste des Oratorio San Marcello 1664–1725', *Acta Musicologica*, 31 (1957), 137–71.

LIONNET, JEAN, 'Les Activités musicales de Flavio Chigi, Cardinal neveu d'Alexandre VII', *Studi musicali*, 9 (1980), 287–302.

—— 'Una svolta nella storia del Collegio dei cantori pontifici: Il Decreto del 22 giugno 1665 contro Orazio Benevolo; origine e conseguenze', *Nuova rivista musicale italiana*, 17 (1983), 72–103.

—— 'André Maugars, Risposta data a un curioso sul sentimento della musica d'Italia', *Nuova rivista musicale italiana*, 4 (1985), 681–707.

—— *La Musique à Saint-Louis des Français de Rome au XVIIe siècle, Note d'archivio*, NS 3, supplement (1985), and NS 4, supplement (1986).

—— 'Performance Practice in the Papal Chapel during the 17th Century', *Early Music*, 15 (1987), 3–15.

LITTA, POMPEO, *Famiglie celebri d'Italia* (10 vols.; Milan, 1819–83).

LOEWENBERG, ALFRED (compiler), *The Annals of Opera, 1597–1940* (Geneva, [1955]).

LUCCHI, MARTA, 'Stradella e i duchi d'Este: Note in margine a documenti d'archivio e agli inventari estensi', in Carolyn Gianturco (ed.), *Alessandro Stradella e Modena, Atti del Convegno internazionale di studi, Modena, 15–17 dicembre 1983* (Modena, 1985), 107–15.

LUIN, ELISABETTA J., 'Repertorio dei libri musicali di S.A.S. Francesco II d'Este, nell'Archivio di Stato di Modena', *La bibliofilia*, 38 (1936), 418–45.

MABBETT, MARGARET, 'The Italian Madrigal 1620–1655' (Ph.D. thesis, King's College, London, 1989).

MAFFEI, RAFFAELLO, *Tre volterrani: Enrico Ormanni, Giovan. Cosimo Villifranchi, Mario Guarnacci* (Pisa, 1881).

[MANCINI, MARIA], *Les Memoires de M[adame]. L[a]. P[rincesse]. M[aria]. M[ancini]. Colonne G[ran]. Connetable de Royaume de Naples* (Cologne, 1676).

MANDOSI, PROSPERIO, *Biblioteca Romana, seu Romanorum Scriptorum Centuriae* (Rome, 1682).

MANGSEN, SANDRA, 'The Trio Sonata in Pre-Corellian Prints: When does 3 = 4?', *Performance Practice Review*, 3 (Fall, 1990), 138–64.

MARINO, GIOVAN BATTISTA, *Le Rime* (1 vol. in 2 pts.; Venice, 1602); incorporated in *La Lira* (beginning Venice, 1614).

MARTINELLI BRAGLIA, GRAZIELLA, 'Il Teatro Fontanelli: Note su impresari e artisti nella Modena di Francesco II e Rinaldi I', in Carolyn Gianturco (ed.), *Alessandro Stradella e Modena, Atti del Convegno internazionale di studi, Modena, 15–17 dicembre 1983* (Modena, 1985), 139–59.

MARTINI, GIAMBATTISTA, *Esemplare o sia saggio fondamentale pratico di contrappunto sopra il canto fermo* (2 vols.; Bologna, 1774; repr. Ridgewood, NJ, 1965).

MARX, HANS JOACHIM, 'Die Musik am Hofe Pietro Kardinal Ottobonis', *Analecta Musicologica*, 5 (1968), 104–77.

MAZZUCCHELLI, GIAMMARIA, *Scrittori d'Italia* (2 vols.; Brescia, 1753–63).

MCCRICKARD, ELEANOR F., 'Alessandro Stradella's Instrumental Music: A Critical Edition with Historical and Analytical Commentary' (2 vols.; Ph.D. diss., University of North Carolina at Chapel Hill, 1971).

—— 'Temporal and Tonal Aspects of Alessandro Stradella's Instrumental Music', *Analecta Musicologica*, 19 (1979), 186–243.

—— 'Stradella's *Esule dalle sfere*: A Structural Masterpiece', in Carolyn Gianturco and Giancarlo Rostirolla (eds.), *Atti del Convegno di studi 'Alessandro Stradella e il suo tempo', Siena, 8–12 settembre 1982, Chigiana*, 39, NS 19 (1988), 347–69.

—— 'Stradella Never Dies: The Composer as Hero in Literature and Song', *Yearbook of Interdisciplinary Studies in the Fine Arts*, 2 (1990), pp. 209–33.

—— (ed.), *Alessandro Stradella: Instrumental Music* (Concentus Musicus, 5; Cologne, 1980).

—— (ed.), *Alessandro Stradella, 'Esule dalle sfere'; A Cantata for the Souls of Purgatory* (Early Musical Masterworks; Chapel Hill, NC, 1983).

MINARDI, GIAN PAOLO, 'G. B. Marino e il madrigale *Feritevi, ferite viperette* di Stradella', in Carolyn Gianturco and Giancarlo Rostirolla (eds.), *Atti del Convegno di studi 'Alessandro Stradella e il suo tempo', Siena, 8–12 settembre 1982, Chigiana*, 39, NS 19 (1988), 191–200.

MIOLI, PIERO, 'Per uno studio sulla cantata italiana del '600: L'opera di Cesti e di Stradella', in Carolyn Gianturco (ed.), *Alessandro Stradella e Modena, Atti del Convegno internazionale di studi, Modena, 15–17 dicembre 1983* (Modena, 1985), 65–76.

MISSON, FRANÇOIS MAXIMILIEN, *A New Voyage to Italy* (London, 1714).

MONTALTO, LINA, *Un mecenate in Roma barocca: Il cardinale Benedetto Pamphilj (1653–1730)* (Florence, 1955).

MORELLI, ARNALDO, 'La tastiera concertante all'epoca di Corelli', in Pierluigi Petrobelli and Gloria Staffieri (eds.), *Studi Corelliani IV: Atti del Quarto Congresso Internazionale (Fusignano, 4–7 settembre 1986)* (Florence, 1990), 193–214.

MORELLI, GIORGIO, 'Giovanni Andrea Lorenzani: Artista e letterato romano del seicento', *Studi secenteschi*, 13 (1972), 194–251.

—— 'Di Giuseppe Berneri e delle sue poesie dialettale inedite', *Strenna dei romanisti*, 38 (1977), 245–54.

—— 'Sebastiano Baldini (1615–1685)', *Strenna dei romanisti*, 39 (1978), 262–9.

—— 'L'Apolloni librettista di Cesti, Stradella e Pasquini', in Carolyn Gianturco and Giancarlo Rostirolla (eds.), *Atti del Convegno di studi 'Alessandro Stradella e il suo tempo', Siena, 8–12 settembre 1982, Chigiana*, 39, NS 19 (1988), 211–64.

MORRIS, ROBERT BOWER, 'A Study of the Italian Solo Cantata before 1750' (DME diss., Indiana University, 1955).

NEGRI, PADRE GIULIO, *Storia degli scrittori fiorentini* (Ferrara, 1722).

NERI, ACHILLE, 'Scrittori di Lunigiana', *Giornale storico della Lunigiana*, 1 (1912), 22–30.

The New Grove Dictionary of Music and Musicians, ed. Stanley Sadie (20 vols.; London, 1980).

NEWMAN, WILLIAM S., *The Sonata in the Baroque Era* (New York, 1972).

ORSINI, FLAVIO [FILOSINAVORO], *Moro per Amore* (Rome, 1679; facsimile edn., vol. 1 in *Italian Opera Librettos: 1640–1770*, ed. Howard M. Brown (New York, 1979).

PAJERSKI, FRED M., 'Background to the String Music of Alessandro Stradella', in Carolyn Gianturco and Giancarlo Rostirolla (eds.), *Atti del Convegno di studi 'Alessandro Stradella e il suo tempo', Siena, 8–12 settembre 1982, Chigiana*, 39, NS 19 (1988), 387–97.

PALAZZI, OSVALDO, *Indagine socio-economica sulla diocesi faleritane Civita Castellana, Orte, Gallese, Sutri, Nepi* (Rome, 1980).

PALISCA, CLAUDE, *Baroque Music* (Englewood Cliffs, NJ, 1968).

PASTOR, LUDWIG VON, *Storia dei Papi dalla fine del medioevo*, Italian trans. Angelo Mercati (vols. i–viii), Pio Cenci (vols. ix–xvi) (Rome, 1942–55); index, vol. xvii (1963). First pub. as *Geschichte der Päpste seit dem Ausgang des Mittelalters* (16 vols.; Freiburg im Breisgau, 1886–1932).

PIGNANI, GIROLAMO (ed.), *Scelta di canzonette italiane de più autori* (London, 1679).

PIPERNO, FRANCO, 'Le viole divise in due chori: Policoralità e "concerto" nella musica di Alessandro Stradella', in Carolyn Gianturco and Giancarlo Rostirolla (eds.), *Atti del Convegno di studi 'Alessandro Stradella e il suo tempo', Siena, 8–12 settembre 1982, Chigiana*, 39, NS 19 (1988), 399–423.

PITONI, GIUSEPPE OTTAVIO, 'Alessandro Stradella', in *Notitia de' contrapuntisti e compositori di musica* [compiled *c.*1695–*c.*1730], ed. Cesarino Ruini (Florence, 1988), 324.

PLANK, STEVEN, 'Of Sinners and Suns: Some Cantatas for the Roman Oratory', *Music and Letters*, 66 (1985), 344–53.

POWERS, HAROLD S., 'Il *Mutio* tramutato, i: Sources and Libretto', in Maria Teresa Muraro (ed.), *Venezia e il melodramma nel seicento*, (Florence, 1976), 227–58.

PROTA-GIURLEO, ULISSE, 'Notizie inedite intorno a Gio. Bonaventura Viviani', *Archivi d'Italia e Rassegna*, 2nd ser., 25 (1958), 225–38.

PROUT, EBENEZER, 'Handel's Obligations to Stradella', *Monthly Musical Record*, 1 (1871), 154–6.

PRUNIÈRES, HENRY, *L'Opéra italien en France avant Lully* (Paris, 1913; repr. New York and London, 1971).

QUADRIO, FRANCESCO SAVERIO, *Della Storia, e della Ragione d'ogni poesia* (5 vols.; Milan, 1739–52).

RADICCHI, PATRIZIA, 'La famiglia Stradella e i suoi rapporti con la Toscana', in Carolyn Gianturco and Giancarlo Rostirolla (eds.), *Atti del Convegno di studi 'Alessandro Stradella e il suo tempo'*, Siena, 8–12 settembre 1982, Chigiana, 39, NS 19 (1988), 17–33.

RICHARD, PAOLINO, 'Stradella et les Contarini, Episode des mœurs vénitiennes au XVIIᵉ siècle', *Le Ménestrel*, 32, no. 51 (19 Nov. 1865), 401–3; 32, no. 52 (26 Nov. 1865), 409–11; 33, no. 1 (3 Dec. 1865), 9–10; 33, no. 2 (10 Dec. 1865), 1–3; 33, no. 3 (17 Dec. 1865), 17–18; 33, no. 4 (24 Dec. 1865), 25–6; 33, no. 5 (31 Dec. 1865), 33–4; 33, no. 6 (7 Jan. 1866), 41; 33, no. 12 (18 Feb. 1866), 89–90; 33, no. 13 (25 Feb. 1866), 97–9; 33, no. 14 (4 Mar. 1866), 105–6; 33, no. 15 (11 Mar. 1866), 113–15; 33, no. 16 (18 Mar. 1866), 121–3; 33, no. 17 (25 Mar. 1866), 129–30; 33, no. 18 (1 Apr. 1866), 137–9.

ROBINSON, PERCY, 'Handel, Erba, Urio, and Stradella', *Sammelbände der Internationalen Musikgesellschaft*, 8 (1906–7), 566–81.

ROCHE, JEROME, 'Alessandro Grandi: A Case Study in the Choice of Texts for Motets', *Journal of the Royal Musical Association*, 113 (1988), 274–305.

ROLANDI, ULDERICO, *Il libretto per musica attraverso i tempi* (Rome, 1951).

ROMANIN, SAMUELE, *Storia documentata di Venezia* (10 vols.; Venice, 1853–61).

RONCAGLIA, GINO, 'La *Cantata per il SS. Natale* di Alessandro Stradella', *Rivista nazionale di musica*, 21 (1940), 4395–6.

—— 'Le composizioni strumentali di Alessandro Stradella esistenti presso la R. Biblioteca Estense di Modena', *Rivista musicale italiana*, 44 (1940), 81–105, 337–50; 45 (1941), 1–15.

—— *Il genio novatore di Alessandro Stradella* (Modena, 1941).

—— 'Le composizioni vocali di Alessandro Stradella [in the Biblioteca Estense, Modena]', *Rivista musicale italiana*, 45 (1941), 133–49; 46 (1942), 1–16.

—— 'Il *Trespolo tutore* di Alessandro Stradella: "La prima opera buffa"', *Rivista musicale italiana*, 56 (1954), 326–32.

RONGA, LUIGI, 'Il *San Giovanni Battista* di Alessandro Stradella', *Bolletino degli amici del Pontificio Istituto di Musica Sacra*, 7 (1955), 8–10.

ROSE, GLORIA, 'Polyphonic Italian Madrigals of the Seventeenth Century', *Music and Letters*, 47 (1966), 153–9.

ROSSINI, GIOACCHINO, *Lettere inedite e rare di G. Rossini*, ed. Giuseppe Mazzatinti (Imola, 1892).

ROSTIROLLA, GIANCARLO, 'La musica nelle istituzioni religiose romane al tempo di Stradella', in Carolyn Gianturco and Giancarlo Rostirolla (eds.), *Atti del Convegno di studi 'Alessandro Stradella e il suo tempo'*, Siena, 8–12 settembre 1982, Chigiana, 39, NS 19 (1988), 575–831.

ROTONDI, JOSEPH EMILIO, 'Literary and Musical Aspects of Roman Opera, 1600–1650' (Ph.D. diss., University of Pennsylvania, 1959).

ROUSSET, JEAN, *La Littérature de l'âge baroque en France: Circe et le Paon* (Paris, 1968).

RUBENS, PETER PAUL, *Palazzi di Genova* (Antwerp, 1622).

SALVETTI, GUIDO, 'La verità di una falsificazione', in Carolyn Gianturco and Giancarlo Rostirolla (eds.), *Atti del Convegno di studi 'Alessandro Stradella e il suo tempo'*, Siena, *8–12 settembre 1982*, *Chigiana*, 39, NS 19 (1988), 201–10.

SCHERING, ARNOLD, 'Neue Beiträge zur Geschichte des italienischen Oratoriums im 17. Jahrhundert', *Sammelbände der Internationalen Musikgesellschaft*, 8 (1906–7), 43–70.

—— (ed.), *Geschichte der Musik in Beispielen* (Leipzig, 1931).

SCHMITZ, EUGEN, *Geschichte der Kantate und des geistlichen Konzerts*, i: *Geschichte der weltlichen Solokantate* (2nd edn.; Leipzig, 1955).

SELFRIDGE-FIELD, ELEANOR, *Venetian Instrumental Music from Gabrieli to Vivaldi* (New York, 1975).

—— 'Music at the Pietà before Vivaldi', *Early Music*, 14 (1986), 373–86.

SFORZA, GIOVANNI, *Saggio d'una bibliografia storica della Lunigiana* (2 vols.; Modena, 1874; repr. Bologna, 1982).

SHEDLOCK, JOHN SOUTH, 'Handel's Borrowings', *Musical Times*, 42 (1901), 450–2, 526–8, 596–600, 756. (Stradella is referred to on pp. 451, 526, 596.)

SILVANI, MARINO, *Scielta delle suonate* (Bologna, 1680).

SIMI BONINI, ELEANOR, 'Stradella negli archivi di Roma', in Carolyn Gianturco and Giancarlo Rostirolla (eds.), *Atti del Convegno di studi 'Alessandro Stradella e il suo tempo'*, Siena, *8–12 settembre 1982*, *Chigiana*, 39, NS 19 (1988), 69–78; 'Addenda', 833–4.

SIMON, ROGER, and GIDROL, D., 'Appunti sulla relazione tra l'opera poetica di G. B. Marino e la musica del suo tempo', *Studi seicenteschi*, 14 (1973), 81–7.

SMITHER, HOWARD E., 'What is an Oratorio in Mid-Seventeenth Century Italy?', *International Musicological Society, Report of the Eleventh Congress, Copenhagen 1972* (Copenhagen, 1974), ii. 657–63.

—— *A History of the Oratorio*, i: *The Oratorio in the Baroque Era: Italy, Vienna, Paris* (Chapel Hill, NC, 1977).

—— 'Musical Interpretation of the Text in Stradella's Oratorios', in Carolyn Gianturco and Giancarlo Rostirolla (eds.), *Atti del Convegno di studi 'Alessandro Stradella e il suo tempo'*, Siena, *8–12 settembre 1982*, *Chigiana*, 39, NS 19 (1988), 287–316.

SPAGNA, ARCHANGELO, 'Discorso intorno a gl'oratori', introduction to *Oratorii overo melodrammi sacri* (2 vols.; Rome, 1706).

SPRETI, VITTORIO, *Enciclopedia storico-nobiliare italiana* (6 vols., 2 app.; Milan, 1929).

STAGLIENO, MARCELLO, 'Aneddoti sopra diversi artisti del secolo XVII', *Giornale Ligustico*, 1 (1874), 363–85.

TALBOT, MICHAEL, 'Vivaldi's Serenatas: Long Cantatas or Short Operas', in Lorenzo Bianconi and Giovanni Morelli (eds.), *Antonio Vivaldi: Teatro musicale. Cultura e Società* (Florence, 1982), i. 67–96.

TAMBURINI, ELENA, 'Filippo Acciaoli: Un "avventuriere" e il teatro', in A. Ottai (ed.), *Teatro Oriente/Occidente* (Rome, 1986), 449–76.

TARGIONI TOZZETTI, GIOVANNI, *Relazioni d'alcuni viaggi fatti in diverse parti della Toscana per osservare le produzioni naturali e gli antichi monumenti di essa*, xi (Bologna, 1777; repr. 1972).

TASSO, TORQUATO, *Tutte le poesie di Torquato Tasso*, ed. Lanfranco Caretti (Verona, 1957).

TAURISANO, INNOCENZO, and CARLI, ENZO, 'Caterina da Siena', in Pio Paschini (ed.), *Enciclopedia Cattolica*, iii (Città del Vaticano, 1949), 1151–8.

TAYLOR, SEDLEY, *The Indebtedness of Handel to Works by Other Composers: A Presentation of Evidence* (Cambridge, 1906).

TIBERTI, MARIO, 'Un importante rinvenimento musicale, la *Doriclea*, opera di Alessandro Stradella', *Musica d'oggi*, 20 (1938), 85–8.

TIMMS, COLIN, 'The Cavata at the Time of Vivaldi', in Antonio Fanna and Giovanni Morelli (eds.), *Nuovi studi Vivaldi* (Florence, 1988), 451–77.

TIRABOSCHI, GIROLAMO, *Biblioteca Modenese* (6 vols.; Modena, 1781–6).

TORCHI, LUIGI, 'Canzoni ed arie italiane ad una voce nel secolo XVII', *Rivista musicale italiana*, 1 (1894), 581–656.

UGURGIERI DELLA BERARDENGA, CURZIO, *Gli Acciaioli di Firenze nella luce dei loro tempi (1160–1834)* (Florence, 1962).

VIALE FERRERO, MERCEDES, *Feste delle Madame Reali di Savoia* (Turin, 1965).

—— 'Alessandro Stradella a Torino (1677): Nuovi documenti', in G. Ioli (ed.), *Atti del Convegno nazionale 'Da Carlo Emanuele I a Vittorio Amadeo II', San Salvatore Monferrato, 20–21–22 settembre 1985* (San Salvatore Monferrato, 1987), 167–79.

—— 'Alessandro Stradella a Torino', in Carolyn Gianturco and Giancarlo Rostirolla (eds.), *Atti del Convegno di studi 'Alessandro Stradella e il suo tempo', Siena, 8–12 settembre 1982, Chigiana*, 39, NS 19 (1988), 35–68.

VOGEL, EMIL, *Bibliothek der gedruckten weltlichen Vocalmusik Italiens* (2 vols.; Berlin, 1892).

WALKER, THOMAS, 'Filippo Acciaiuoli', *The New Grove Dictionary of Music and Musicians*, ed. Stanley Sadie (London, 1980).

WEAVER, ROBERT L., '*Il Girello*, a 17th-Century Burlesque Opera', *Memorie e contributi alla musica dal medioevo all'età moderna offerti a F. Ghisi nel settantesimo compleanno (1901–1971)* (Bologna, 1971), ii. 141–63.

WESSELY-KROPIK, HELENE, *Lelio Colista, ein römischer Meister vor Corelli: Leben und Umwelt* (Graz, Vienna, Cologne, 1961).

WESTRUP, JACK A., 'Stradella's *Forza d'amor paterno*', *Monthly Musical Record*, 71 (1941), 52–9.

WIEL, TADDEO, *I codici musicali contariniani del secolo XVII nella R. biblioteca di San Marco in Venezia* (Venice, 1888).

WITZENMANN, WOLFGANG, 'Domenico del Pane', *The New Grove Dictionary of Music and Musicians*, ed. Stanley Sadie (London, 1980).

—— 'Prime considerazioni sullo stile da chiesa in Carissimi e Stradella', in Carolyn Gianturco and Giancarlo Rostirolla (eds.), *Atti del Convegno di studi 'Alessandro Stradella e il suo tempo', Siena, 8–12 settembre 1982, Chigiana*, 39, NS 19 (1988), 317–46.

ZIINO, AGOSTINO, 'Osservazioni sulla struttura de *L'Accademia d'Amore* di Alessandro Stradella', *Chigiana*, 26–7 (1969–70), 137–69.

Index